# A QUESTIO

"You said you weren't a Puritan," Gideon teased.

"I'm not!" Mary said at once. "Why is it everyone must be a Puritan or a courtesan with you? Don't you know there are many of us who aren't either, and don't like either forbidding all pleasure, or giving in to all pleasure? If you can call what goes on at court 'pleasure,' " she said with a sniff.

"But this isn't court, Mary," he said gently, his lips near to her ear, his arm around her waist. "This is you and me, alone together. I don't ask you to be anything else but yourself. Is what we do pleasure?"

"Oh, Gideon," she said, leaning toward him. "Yes, it is." And she brought her lips to his, giving herself to the magic of his kisses, the rapture of his impassioned lovemaking . . . and allowed the greatest joy she'd ever felt flood though her.

Ah yes, she thought, lying still in his arms. What we do is definitely pleasure. . . .

---

# THE FIRE-FLOWER

## EDITH LAYTON

AN ONYX BOOK

**NEW AMERICAN LIBRARY**

A DIVISION OF PENGUIN BOOKS USA INC.

## PUBLISHER'S NOTE

This book is a work of fiction. Names, characters, places, and incidents either are the product of the author's imagination or are used fictitiously, and any resemblance to actual persons, living or dead, events, or locales is entirely coincidental.

Copyright © 1989 by Edith Felber

SIGNET, SIGNET CLASSIC, MENTOR, ONYX, PLUME, MERIDIAN and NAL BOOKS are published by New American Library, a division of Penguin Books USA Inc., 1633 Broadway, New York, New York 10019

First Printing, July, 1989

1  2  3  4  5  6  7  8  9

PRINTED IN THE UNITED STATES OF AMERICA

*Fireflower:* Any one of a number of strong, common annual plants that flourish where the land is burned over. They spring from the ashes to cover over the scorched earth.

While alone with myself I repeat all her charms,
She I love may be locked in another man's arms,
She may laugh at my cares, and so false she
  may be,
To say all the kind things she before said to me!
  Oh, then 'tis I think there's no hell
  Like loving too well.

But when I consider the truth of her heart,
Such an innocent passion, so kind without art,
I fear I have wronged her, and hope she may be
So full of true love to be jealous of me.
  Oh, then 'tis I think that no joys are above
  The pleasures of love.
                          —Charles II, King of England,
                              Scotland, and Ireland (1662)

# FOREWORD

Britain once had a Civil War—a Revolution ending in the overthrow and beheading of a king. That king's son, Charles II, was restored to his throne in 1660, and proceeded to lead his people a merry dance, instituting a reign filled with excess, lewdness, and license, tolerated by his people perhaps because of their joy at having a monarch again or perhaps because of their pleasure at being freed from the restraints of Puritanism, which they'd thought they'd wanted . . . until they had it.

As passionate as he was compassionate, as tolerant as he was indolent, "The Merry Monarch" Charles Stuart, "The Father of his Country"—who sired so many bastards he was given the name in jest—never forgot the days when he was a king without a country, or the day his father was murdered. But he'd no time for revenge as he had a divided country to heal, for there were also many who never forgot they'd once driven the devils out of Britain and secured a Puritan regime. Nature, too, conspired with politics to occupy the young king. In 1665 plague decimated London and in 1666 a great fire destroyed a third of it. And the mass of common people cared nothing for politics; they cared only to live.

Withal of Charles' wrongs, he must have done something right. Today, decades after most of Europe has shed its kings, Britain still has a monarchy. The fire was put out.

# 1

The sun never set. It was as if the sun had touched the margins of the world as it descended, setting them on fire, because all the west was ablaze. They stood on the deck by day and by night and watched London burning down. And it seemed that it wouldn't stop until there was nothing left for the fire to feed on but the river the ship rocked upon.

The passengers aboard the *Nomad Prince* had stopped exclaiming and commenting to each other, since when the impossible goes on long enough it becomes entirely possible, if no less frightening. They couldn't dock. The captain wouldn't. He'd hauled out a stout cudgel and summoned his men to his side when one passenger had insisted on going into port to help the "poor wretches" that could be seen in the distance, like long lines of ants struggling to flee their overturned hill. Nor would the captain or any of the passengers hear of leaving the vicinity, for no matter how terrifying, what man could leave off viewing Judgment Day?

The fire grew through the day into a night that looked like an eerie orange day. If the flames ever went out, the passengers would disembark in London, if there was still a London then. Because it was disappearing before their eyes, as all their other senses verified. The cinders rained down upon them, blown by the same easterly wind that fanned the flames. When the wind veered, they sometimes smelled the city sour, as though it were a burnt-out fireplace. Other times the scent came to their noses woodsy, as if it were a homey kitchen fire. And there were times that the odor was bitterly acrid as hell itself at high noon.

They saw the city drifting away above them in a mist of black char, and felt it settling on their shoulders in sheets that looked as soft as gossamer but tasted coarse as charcoal when they opened their lips to speak of it. Then they shivered, the bravest of them, realizing that all of it had once been houses and shops and things they dared not even think upon.

No sense was spared, far away as they were, out on the Thames; they could hear the crunching sound of the fire feeding, and now and again a rumbling blast as a house was blown up in an attempt to make a firebreak. And sometimes they heard a terrible high keening on the wind they hoped was only the wind, or the fire singing.

The city burned on into another day, as though it were the judgment some had prophesied God would visit upon it. And for all they knew, those who stood on the Thames and watched, it could have been. But since no man on the deck of the *Nomad Prince* could claim to be in perfect charity with his Creator, no one of them dared say.

Certainly Gideon Hawkes wouldn't. He stood at the rail and watched the fire, his eyes narrowed against the smoke, his face without expression. For if his face showed what his heart demanded, he'd have looked like one of the gargoyles gaping in horror that sat on the ledges of the great cathedrals in the cities he'd lately left. Because it was his homeland that was burning. He'd dreamed of his England for fifteen years, and like the sailor returned from the sea only in time to attend his mother's deathbed, it seemed he was only in time for the end, although he'd done little but dream of new beginnings for the past years.

He was a tall man, seeming taller because of his leanness, with hard wide shoulders that winged out over a long hard body that all his finery couldn't soften the look of. He'd never be a handsome Cavalier, for all he was dressed as the finest of them in the requisite clothes, with his soft high leather boots pulled on over rich wool breeches, and shirt with flounces fine as any in King Charles's own wardrobe, with a soft velvet cape thrown over his silken doublet. Yet still, silk and velvet or even lushest fur couldn't blur the edges of him, for he'd too many, and no grace about him except when he moved—then he flowed like shadows. But standing still he was like a standing stone, and all that might have been beauty in a gentler setting was cast too coldly in him for that.

He was a relatively young man, not above thirty years. And for all he was in fashion, beneath his wide velvet hat he wore his own hair. It was red and gold as the fire on the horizon, and just as harsh, for there were no fashionable soft curls or waves to moderate it. It spread like long tongues of flame alongside his strong neck, and fell blunt to his shoulders. His face was tight and closed, but that may have been because his thoughts were of hell. His eyes were too blue to be merely striking; a glance from them was as painfully blue as a plunge into icy waters, and they stared down at the world from above a high narrow wedge of a straight nose and high slashes of cheekbones cut into that crag of a face. The only emotion he showed wasn't a thing of his dark eyebrows or wide lips or any mobile thing of his own conscious making, but only now and again, unbidden, a tiny twitch convulsed the left side of his face. Strangely, it wasn't unattractive after the shock of seeing it had passed, because at least it showed that cheek was flesh, and that the man beneath that face knew more pain than he'd allow to show.

It gave the man next to him the courage to speak up.

"It's the Apocalypse—do you really think it is?" he asked, as he'd asked himself so many times in the past hours.

"It's London," the deep, soft voice answered, "which is just as bad, and good enough for me." And then his smile came, a small and quirked play of lips, half-merry, half-mockery, but it lent softness and grace to that hard countenance at last. Then it could be seen that he was as accustomed to laughter as he was to pain.

"Do you think it will end?" the man next to him asked, for an odd religious fervor had begun to grip all the passengers.

"All things end," Gideon Hawkes answered, and then, musing, smiling again, he added, "except for my impatience."

But even that was relieved a little, for after another day they docked. They put down anchor at a slip on the Thames above Whitehall, even though the fire, which had subsided by then, had never reached so high. Still, the captain of the *Nomad Prince* took no chances; his whole fortune, as he'd said, was in his ship, and it was clear his whole heart was in his purse.

The passengers flowed off the ship, parting from each other without a backward glance. Those who'd homes in London were themselves on fire to see what had happened to their families, friends, houses, and businesses. Those who were visiting London had just as burning a morbid curiosity to feed. Gideon Hawkes was in as much of a hurry, but he was bound in the opposite direction. He, who had no family, who'd seen enough of death and the aftermath of disaster to last him all his life, and whose fortune lay in his own hands, gave up his plans to visit with friends in London as he stepped down the wood plank that led to shore. The fire had discomfited him. He knew he wouldn't rest easy until he rested his eyes on his one love, his home, once more. Although it was in Kent, far from the fire, now he felt compelled to assure himself of its safety.

He should've gone straight to Dover, he thought as he strode to a dockside inn to command paper and a pen to let his man, following with his belongings, know the change in plans when he arrived. Ivyclose Manor was only an easy ride from the white chalk cliffs of the eastern coast, and now he'd many more weary miles ahead of him. But those weeks ago when he'd envisioned this day, he'd thought to dally in London, celebrating his return with friends. He'd planned to laze about with them, renew old acquaintances, catch up on the news, drink the day and play the night away before he settled down to the work of putting Ivyclose back together and himself comfortably within it again. That was before he'd seen the fire, before this sudden wild unease began to burn in his heart.

Fire, plague—it only lacked flood and locusts. Gideon thought of the condemnation of London and Israel as he wrote to tell his man to wait for him at the Peacock, an inn he remembered being high above the fire line in London, while he satisfied himself that all was well in Kent. He hadn't been in touch with anyone in Britain in long months, and now he fretted about every natural calamity that could befall a house— from lightning to deathwatch beetle—as he blotted the hastily scrawled instructions. Because Ivyclose was what had lured him home again, even as the thought of it was what had kept him going in the years of his exile. It was all he had left in England and the world. And was, as always, sufficient for him.

The landlord took his message and promised its

certain delivery, and smiled his most beguiling smile, and bowed and actually tugged at his graying forelock, for this Cavalier gentleman looked as rich as dangerous. But he wrung his hands as he denied him his second request.

"Not a horse in the kingdom, sir, not a one in the city for hire or sale today, my lord, believe me, your grace, I'd carry you on my own back faster than I could get you a horse. Half of London's on the road out, don't you see? and horses are made of gold these days, believe me, I'm sorry, sir, I am," the innkeeper said in an increasingly anxious voice as he looked into cold eyes the color of his certain death at the hard blue steel by the Cavalier's side.

"I don't believe you heard me correctly. I want a horse," Gideon said simply and implacably as fate as he put gold pieces in the innkeeper's hand, and his hand back on his sword's hilt.

"Well, at least it has a leg at every corner," Gideon sighed hours later as the innkeeper proudly presented him with his mount.

"And two eyes, if no teeth, but then he's got to see the road, not eat it, I suppose," he murmured as he stroked a sagging dun back broad as a couch, before cinching a saddle around a belly round as a drum.

As the innkeeper thanked God the widow Grey had owed him a favor and lent him her horse so as to save his life, Gideon added, "But does it move more than its tail?"

"He'll be full of spirit once he gets going," the innkeeper lied. "The widow kept him on to remember her man with, and he hasn't done more than eat his head off since the funeral. He's likely longing to go."

"I only hope he restrains himself, and lives until I can find a mount a century younger," Gideon said as he swung up into the saddle. Then, looking down at the innkeeper, he relented, for he'd passed the last hours searching for a horse himself, finally seeking even so little as a seat on a stagecoach, to no avail. It had been this nervous fellow he'd terrified who'd got him a horse, no matter how decrepit, so he added gently, "And don't worry, I'll send him back live, if God wills it, and dead with a handsome fee if his heart gives out before my patience does. Assure your widow woman I'll be kind enough to him. After all," he said on a smile, "I was taught to respect my elders."

And such was the power of that rare and transforming smile that as he rode away the innkeeper forgot the terror that made him shiver as he begged the horse from the widow, and remember only the handsome profit he'd seen from this lucky day.

The weather, at least, was with the traveler. Clear and warm, with only a freshening breeze, nothing like the hot west wind that had borne the fire forward on its breath. Gideon rode on toward Kent at a broken-backed, crippled pace. But he left off cursing the old horse when he saw how many silent men, women, and children he passed, bowed under the weight of their household goods, plodding along the road on their own feet as he rode onward. They'd set up tent cities in the fields around London, but the further away he rode, the fewer refugees he met. He was glad of it, because it felt wrong for him to be riding, even on such an antique nag, when old men and childbearing women trudged in his dust.

His horse's exhaustion didn't take geography into account, so he halted by moonlight and slept beneath the sky, like any of the other fugitive from the disaster. He passed his first night wrapped in his cloak in a field, close by his precious, ancient, hobbled horse. He washed his face in dew and breakfasted on memories of fatter mornings when he woke, but felt lucky enough to be able to mount up again.

His next bit of luck came near Rochester, where he bought a decent breakfast and enough ale to put heart in him. When he'd gone on long enough for the fire to have become only a wild rumor where he stopped again, he was able to buy a horse young enough to spur without guilt and send his elderly steed limping back to the widow. Then he rode on briskly, and only then allowed himself to remember. For the landscape around him was familiar, and at last he could believe, after fifteen years of disbelief that this day would ever come, that he was coming home again.

He wasn't the only wanderer returning now that the Protector had gone, although he might be one of the last. The king himself had fled for his life and lived in exile for a decade. Indeed, he'd first met his king on the last leg of that wild flight, fifteen years before, when he himself had been too young to have had fifteen years together on the earth. But even then, he'd been making his own escape. It hadn't been execution he'd fled, it had been the slow grinding down of his soul. He'd been at war with his father, not his countrymen, but his end would have been just as certain. Because he was imprisoned by the old man's miserliness, lashed by his indifference, and fettered by his expectations, and weary unto death with it, even then.

Not that it mattered to his family. He was only a fourth son, of no account, and too willful to even be a prop for his father in his old age. Then too, there was the contempt in his eyes to be reckoned with. Because when the old man threw himself into a Puritan fervor when his neighbors did, so as to save his property and his neck, it was this red-headed whelp's wolf eyes that mocked his piety, scorning it for the expediency it was. The other boys, all older, all as anxious to get along with their father as they were to get ahead, changed their politics with the battle reports too. Gideon, the youngest, stubbornest of them, tenacious enough to finish the last of his mother's milk before she died bearing another, dead son, wasn't any more political than they were. It was only that he refused to be as hypocritical. He didn't care for their new religion, and wouldn't pretend to it.

Even as a child, he refused to pray in public what he never prayed in private, and laughed when his father's live-in whore suddenly became a "housekeeper." And he couldn't like being renamed a good biblical name when all his brothers were rechristened, so that the beautiful pagan "Gifford" he remembered his mother whispering lovingly to him was gone forever, as she was.

Since he wouldn't act the model Puritan, he was a danger. And as a danger, he was shunned and shamed, then starved and beaten—until the look in his wolf's eyes stayed their hands. He'd never lifted his to them, but still they left off, one by one, both his father and his brothers, when they saw his eyes.

When Squire Hawkes's fourth son finally took to his heels in the night and then to the sea, that newly staunch Puritan said a prayer for his wayward boy's disobedience in church. And then sighed his relief as he drank to good riddance alone in his study.

But even the stern God of Puritans had his little jests. For in no time at all, the eldest, most obliging son disobliged his father by breaking his neck at a hedge his skittish horse took for a phantom in the night. The second son, stunned by his sudden succession, scarcely had time to appreciate it before a winter's chill became an ague that took him, still wondering, to his grave. And the third and last obedient son, soldiering abroad when he heard the news of his elevation on the eve of a battle, drank so much to his good fortune that he lost his heavy head to the enemy the next day, before he could sell out and sail home again. Which left only the red-headed wretch who wanted nothing of home to take it as his inheritance. When his father had him tracked down, after ten long years, long after Squire Hawkes was trying to look the best royalist in the land, he discovered the boy to have become a man richer than any he'd ever known, and harder even than that.

Gideon Hawkes had taken to the sea, and found it a more cruel and miserly master than his father. But from it he learned how to read the stars to find his way, climb and tie ropes, brawl, whore, and take the lash without screaming. Escaped to dry land, he became a soldier. Like his father, he fought for whoever paid him the best, but unlike him, disliked it intensely. Still, from his service in several armies, he learned to read maps, live sparingly, gamble, and use a staggering assortment of weapons to kill and maim. And then, weary of this, he learned how to use his head to outmaneuver the officers and move up in the ranks.

Once he'd begun thinking instead of just fleeing, he finally learned to live without using the muscle he'd earned, using instead all the experience he'd learned. He discovered how to use the sea for profit: to use maps to find new ports of trade, develop new markets by gambling with ideas, and secure them with every last bit of cleverness he'd gained. He'd traveled the Continent in the bellies of armies; now a trader, he rested in foreign bazaars. A gentleman and a friend to the king without a country, he visited the English court in exile wherever it happened to be. A merchant prince himself now, he graced foreign courts as a guest—and sometimes, because at heart he was a patriot, as a spy.

He dined with kings, drank with their entourages, quipped with their keenest wits, and whored with all the great and infamous. He did all of that, of course, with the lowest as well, because there came a time when he could scarcely tell the difference. And then he knew it was time to come home. Now he was almost there. Now, as he began to anticipate each turn of the road ahead, he knew he never wanted to leave it again.

Old Squire Hawkes was dead and long buried, to no

one's unhappiness but the vicar's—who hadn't known what sort of epitaph to put on his tombstone, since he'd been everything and nothing in life. New Squire Hawkes hadn't helped, because he'd refused to come home while the old man lived, in fact had waited three years to be sure he was gone. Still, his presence was all he'd refused him, because he'd sent huge sums of money to keep the estate in good heart. His presence— and the chance for his father to make peace with the newly restored king. Because for all the pleading letters, there Gideon never swerved: old Squire Hawkes never got the chance to press his lips to the young king's ring and swear he'd been as loyal as he'd never been.

The gates to Ivyclose lay just ahead, round a turn in the road and to the right. But on a whim, Gideon turned his horse off the road and into the trees. Ivyclose was meant to be seen as it came into view down a long avenue of linden trees. But he preferred seeing it again as he'd loved it most as a boy, riding in after a day of truancy, with the great old house welcoming him in by secret pathways.

He rode high up a grassy highway so that he could look down at Ivyclose, viewing it in miniature as it lay cupped in the gently swelling hills surrounding it. Long and E-shaped, made of white stone quarried, he'd thought as a boy, in heaven, with a dozen, dozen staggering chimneys as its crown. From this height he could see a square of blue that was the pond before it, smaller patches that were neat kitchen gardens behind, and little white shapes that were statues in the midst of the symmetrical flower gardens placed in front, for pure pride's sake.

But what had his father been up to? he wondered as he stood in the saddle and looked down, frowning. There were several front gardens now, and what looked like a regiment of rosebushes forming a great arbored maze to the side. He wondered if all his money had gone to the old man's head as he rode down to investigate, giving up his plan to come in by way of the deep side woods, because he discovered they were no longer there. They'd been leveled, except for a few ancient trees, to make room for the rose garden. That, he thought, as he urged his horse down the slope and it stepped with muffled hooves over the grass between the remaining trees, was a waste and a vanity. He supposed his father had been playing the Cavalier to the hilt, to have put up what he could soon see was a labryinth of bowers and benches and buckets filled with rosebushes all along the white-shelled paths of the ornate garden.

He was frowning at the thought of good money continuing to go for such excess here where no one could see it except for the staff he'd kept on to watch over the place until his return, and was storing up a bitter dressing-down to give to them for it, when he heard a muted clattering and faint murmurous voices. He looked again to see a flash of color that was never roses through the latticework of bushes beneath him.

He grew still as the couple strolled into view. But then, he couldn't have moved when he first saw them. They were so unexpected, so out of place and perfectly fitting, that for a moment he believed he imagined them because the setting called for them to be there. He passed a hand across his eyes and looked again. And still they astonished him. And for all she was so far away, and he up the slope and in the dappled shade, still she blinded him.

The man was a Cavalier, there was no mistaking that. From the long light curls that spilled onto his brightly colored silken-clad shoulders from beneath the wide slouch hat with its brave plume, to the buckled high-heeled shoes that set the gravel path to crunching, the fellow was a complete picture of fashion. But for all his splendor, she outshone him. Her hat perched atop a small head covered with light brown silken curls, and her face was an oval of alabaster, her neck and shoulders milk above a graceful curved figure clad in embroidered silk of blue and yellow and the warm pink of roses. The tips of her little slippers grazed over the paths so smoothly he thought she might not actually have touched down at all, and was only a phantom come from the future. For such a lady was the image of what he planned to bring here one day to share his home with him.

Murmuring, they moved on, turning a corner, threatening to disappear from his view. Then he recalled himself and kicked his horse to set it after them, to treat his eyes again with what he dreamed he saw, before he challenged the illusion. As he bent to avoid a branch and follow, intent on what was ahead, he never knew what had happened until it all happened at once.

Because his boot, swinging inward, never met the horse, but was caught in a hard hand instead. As his gloved hand automatically went to his sword's hilt, another hand captured it, and another his sword, as someone else caught his horse's reins. And too late alarmed, overwhelmed, he was dragged from the saddle.

He was wrenched from his horse as a fool, but landed on the ground as a soldier, and came fighting up, using elbows and fists and feet to advantage in that one moment of surprise. In the next, he was borne down again by the sheer number of his attackers. Although he'd heard cries of pain and alarm at first, as he struggled helplessly he heard only the grunted and muttered advice and cautions of his captors to each other as they worked to subdue him.

"Whoreson! Kick me, will you? Here's a kick then. Damn you! Hold his leg! Damn you. There!"

"Ah, wretch, there, for payment! Ah, have a care with his shirt, loose it, loose it, 'tis lace, fool, don't tear it none."

"Aye, and that silken . . . God's wounds! Joseph, you dolt, you've torn it, damn you for an idiot!"

"And you, you've got blood on his collar!"

"Me? 'Tis 'is lips," a voice next to his ear complained bitterly. " 'E's bleeding like a pig!"

"Then hit him aside the head, fool, where it can't stain, finish him neat, for sweet Jesus' sake. And mind the hat!"

He was, in all the fury and confusion, as they slammed his head on the ground and buried fists and boots in his stomach and sides, stubbornly aware that his clothes were far more valuable than his life, and so struggled to keep his bleeding face from being pushed into the dirt, his last aim to deal them a grim sort of spite by fouling his clothes with his lifeblood. If he were to die now, he'd be damned if he'd let them profit from it.

There was blood in his mouth and such pain in his head he could scarcely hear above the ringing in it, when he managed to jerk his head free of the hand that held it ground into the earth, as the owner of that hand loosed him for a minute to swear at the bite he'd given it, and then:

"God's blood! Stop! Oh, for the love of God, stop! 'Tis Master Gideon! 'Tis Master Gideon returned," the voice shouted, as silence fell, and he felt his limbs loosed at last. But by then it didn't matter.

When he awoke, he wasn't sure if it was day or night, if he were indoors or out, but hearing nothing for a long while before he ventured to open his eyes, he was sure he'd been left alone, wherever he was. He was startled, then, to immediately see a pair of worried eyes gazing at him. And then another, and another, until he realized he lay on a rude bed, ringed round with a circle of drawn and anxious faces.

"Blow out the candle at my head," he said in a voice that sounded strangely cracked even to his own ears, "and take away the one at my toes. Don't bury me yet, friends, I live . . . though, mind you, I don't celebrate it," he added, wincing as he tried to sit up, and several hands reached out to help him.

"Joseph Palmer!" he said then, as his wits returned and the nearest, saddest face registered in his memory. "Joseph," he said as he gingerly felt the growing swelling at the side of his head, and eyed the old gatekeeper that had lived on the estate in his youth, "my thanks for saving me. Who tried to murder me, Joseph?"

"I did, Master Gideon," the old man said softly, "and my son, his son, and four more of our friends."

"Why?" was all that he could ask, as his smile slipped and, unconsciously, his hand groped at his side, where his sword no longer was.

"Because we didn't recognize you, Master Gideon," Joseph answered slowly, "because you were trespassing."

"But I never ordered such," Gideon said, amazed. "Are times that hard, then?"

"No," Joseph said quietly, "but it don't matter no more. For you don't have the ordering here anymore, Master Gideon. You're not master here no more, sir."

It was very simple. Tragedy, he'd discovered, was always simple. Fire, flood, death, and taxes, all easy enough to understand, however mortal a blow they struck. The king had taken his home and given it away to a favorite. Well, and why not? As the Bible his own father had pretended to read had said: you reap what you sow. He'd withheld charity; charity had been withheld from him. He hadn't let his father pretend to love the new king, and so when his father had died, the king had seen only that another Puritan had quit the world—and with no heir apparently taking over, he'd given the land, the house, and all that Gideon had ever loved, away. Three years past, the new owner had ridden in even as his father went feet-first out. Sir

Philip Southern was pleased to be master of Ivyclose now, and there it was.

They wondered, all those hard-handed men who'd felled the Cavalier trespasser with such care to the clothes they'd hoped to sell for profit, if they'd scrambled his brains for him, poor fellow, as well as giving him so many bruises. For he didn't rage or swear when he heard the whole of it. He only gave the crookedest smile his swollen lip could permit. Because it all seemed clear when he remembered the vision he'd seen in the garden, and he recalled his king's favorite sport.

"Ah, the lovely wench, I see," he said with that painful wry grin. "Sooth, I understand, but it's hard to provide a mistress's bed and not be allowed to share it."

They looked scandalized, every one of them.

"Oh, no, Master Gideon, never say so. Mistress Southern is virtuous," Joseph protested.

"Her husband doesn't dance her before the king?" Gideon asked, incredulous, for preference to gentlemen often came from this king's preferring their wives.

"She got no husband, Sir Philip's her brother, 'tis he who's friend to the king. He's a good and fair gentleman, Master Gideon, none gainsay that," Joseph explained.

Then Gideon stopped smiling, for the irony of this betrayal was too rich for laughter. The king had been his own friend, or so he'd thought. So much for the friendship of Kings. He'd seen a play in his youth, before they'd shut the playhouses up, where a young king had renounced the jolly fellow he'd drunk and wenched with in his youth. What had happened to that fat fellow? he wondered now—not that it mattered: that was a play, his was a life. And a life he'd have to get on with.

They brushed off his clothing and mended what they could as best they could. They dressed his wounds and gave him apologies with their thanks for not committing them to the justice of the peace, to hang for attacking a gentleman, and they saw him off with sorrow and shame. He left with sorrow, and no shame, for he refused to meet with Sir Philip and his lady. Where was the sense in it?

*That was my bed. . . . Oh, yes—there's the chair my mother embroidered that cushion for, oh, you use it for your lap dogs now, lady? Very good. . . .*

Oh, yes, he thought as he headed back to London and never looked behind him, much purpose there'd be in visiting with the new master of Ivyclose. He didn't need the fellow's charity, nor the lovely lady's pity. He'd money enough to build another Ivyclose somewhere. He'd everything he needed, he decided— except, of course, for his home, his heritage, and his plans for a future life.

It took twice as long to return to London as it had to get to Ivyclose, because he was in no hurry now. He supposed he could meet with Charles and have it out; but then he supposed not. Enormous as his loss was, his pride was too big for him to swallow. He could pick up with old friends, or make new ones. He could do anything he wished in the wide world, for he was just thirty years old, a gentleman, and a wealthy one too. But he didn't want friendship or any reasonable thing, not just yet. He wanted oblivion, he needed a dark place in which to hide and tend to his wounds. He decided, as he rode in through the east gate to the city, to try to forget for now. He'd get himself as drunk as a man could without dying, find an obliging whore, and seek a dozen little deaths with her. Then, if he found he still lived in the morning, he'd get on with living.

London stank, it always did, but now old smoke and the bitter taste of aftermath lay heavy in the air. Thousands still lived in makeshift ways in the fields surrounding the city; he'd seen such privation before— that wasn't what moved him to hurry past them as though embarrassed at his own health and fortune. It was only that he'd never seen such disorder in England. Yet when he rode on past their encampments, he found that thousands more had got on with their lives within the walls of the city.

Half a million souls lived in London. A great city didn't die after it was wounded; if it was sound, it healed. Drays, carts and horses, sedan chairs, and coaches clogged the narrow streets. The vendors were in full cry; busy people went on with their lives. If it weren't for the reek of dead ashes in the air, he'd have wondered if he dreamed that great fire, and the sea of displaced persons he'd passed. But he didn't ride on to see the site of the fire to verify it. He'd had enough of loss for now.

The Old Swan, near the Embankment, close enough to St. Paul's to be sootier than it had been before the fire, ought to have been called The Old Phoenix, Gideon thought as he gave his horse to a stableboy and hefted his bag from the saddle, for its enclosed courtyard was as lively as a country fair, or the street outside. It was even merrier, because musicians played and it was sweet—if you could hear them over all the talk and laughter. Clearly a man didn't have to dwell on disaster if he didn't want to. If he'd a full purse, he could buy a room and some pleasure for himself on the day of the Apocalypse. This was still London, however scorched.

The room he took was fair enough, for all its bed sagged as much as the crooked floor did. The place had been too old for fashion even fifteen years before, and so suited him perfectly now. Tonight he wasn't looking for recognition. Tomorrow he'd be off to a better inn. He'd arrive at the Peacock with the afternoon and await his man there. Tonight he'd go belowstairs and wait to find the right wench.

Too weary in spirit, if not in body, to change his garments, he went down to the common room to dine and drink, and discovered that in all his hastily mended finery, and with all his purpling bruises, he was the object of curious stares. Not because of his disarray, but for the reverse. Because his clothing, although mended, was finer, and his demeanor, although weary, was more mannerly, than any other man's there. It was a place for the common man. Which was why he, erstwhile master of Ivyclose, felt entirely comfortable, in a bitter sort of way, there among the mercers and carters, minor artisans and apprentices, petty merchants and small men of business. And women of business, of course, he thought as he looked over the crowded room.

It should have been the work of a moment to find a suitable one for the night. He was a man who enjoyed using his body for his pleasure, and considered himself, as so many of his friends did, to be a connoisseur in matters of the flesh. Not a gourmet certainly, but rather a man with a good appetite. For there were times when he sought only the daintiest tidbits for his bed, and times, like tonight, when he'd be happy with good, hearty peasant fare. Lust was an ever-present hunger in him, and he satisfied it according to his mood and the variety available. He seldom bought pleasure just for a night; clever as he was fastidious, he both dreaded pox and liked steady relationships, and was attractive enough to have a choice. Married women at court, courtesans in fashion, and playful ladies of all classes were his usual fare. But he wasn't unyielding in his tastes, and so, was resourceful when the need was upon him.

Yet the evening came, and night followed, and he found himself unable to choose. The whores were there, of course, in great numbers, as they always were at night in such places in any city, but none pleased him, although many sought to. There was one tall wench with a bright smile and fine breasts and a merry laugh, and masses of curling light hair fair as that lady in the garden at Ivyclose had had. But though his eye had gone to her first, it was just that small memory that killed his desire. Another had a rough mane of Gypsy hair and the sort of exotic looks he sometimes fancied, but she laughed once too often and smiled incessantly and it put him off, because tonight it was deep dark and healing silence he wanted to bury himself in.

He let them go to other men, and drank more than he ate, and drank more than he thought he could, and returned the stares of all the women who tried to catch his eye. And it seemed he grew more sober with every mouthful, and sadder as they grew merrier, trying to tempt him with their shows of gaiety, and his lust was as distant and cold, although present, as he himself was in that crowded, noisy, close-smelling room.

And then he saw her, as if the force of her sad, staring eyes had tugged at him. When he focused on her, she looked away sharply, as though embarrassed by her own bold stare, as though ashamed and uncomfortable with it. And that drew his attention more. She stood by the door, apart from the others, or he wouldn't have seen her at all, she was that small and unexceptional. But she'd been staring at him. Little and dark, a scrap of a girl in a blue gown that had a neckline low enough to show she was adult enough for him, and yet high enough to make a man who hadn't spied her where she was doubt her profession. Unremarkable-looking, really, with small even features, except for her tumble of dark curls and those remarkably great sad eyes that looked at him, and looked away, and back to him again. A sad little shy whore, as odd and secret as this night, seeming half-willing; a wench with whom a man could be pleasured without being subjected to laughter and conversation or excuses. He was instantly caught.

It took several moments, and more encouraging smiles and nods of his head until he could hold her eye long enough to gesture to her, to convince her he really summoned her. Then she came, making her way to his table slowly and with uncertainty, until she stood there before him, head down, awaiting his judgment.

"What you are selling, mistress," he said simply, "I find I'm interested in buying."

When she didn't answer, or look up, he was as pleased as he was surprised; courting a whore was a novelty, and if she weren't simple or mute, she'd do nicely.

"Is this enough for our treat?" he asked, putting down far too many coins.

She looked up at that, and her olive skin became rosy with her blush and he was enchanted. He never sought the semblance of innocence in his wenches as some men did, but tonight it seemed fitting. Tonight he'd rejected the merrymakers, the ones who'd be, or pretend to be, his equals in striving for delight. This night he felt a victim; perhaps he needed a partner in sorrow, or to feel a victimizer himself. Whatever the reason, now at last he felt the stirring of true desire, and wouldn't question it further. But though her eyes widened at the coins, it seemed to him that they were fixed more on his plate.

"Come," he said, generous in his relief, "dine with me. Pleasure before pleasure. And then we'll go upstairs together, shall we?"

"You've a room here?" she asked in a small worried voice, and he was pleased to find she spoke, and rationally, as he signaled to the serving wench and ordered himself more ale, and a plate and a mug for his wench now too.

She said nothing else but her name, a blunt "Mary" when he asked it of her, and ate with neatness and great energy when her plate came. But she lost interest soon after, stopping after only a few bites, and pushed the dish away, as though she remembered she was not there to eat with him, after all. And he gazed at her smooth neck and toyed with the strands of hair that lay there, and when she flinched at his first touch, he laughed.

"These bruises are from a misunderstanding," he said, wondering if she worried about his nature once he'd got her alone in his bed, "as are the rents in my clothing. Don't worry, sweeting, love is only love to me, I don't give or wish to receive pain. Would you like to see what I do love? Ah, but it grows late," he said softly as she stared down at her plate again, "and the table's far too small for what I seek," he added as her head came up and her great dark eyes widened in comprehension. A most uncommon whore, he thought with pleasure, but not so much as she pretended, he noted, for she made sure to drain her mug to the dregs before she rose with him.

When he stood, he understood how much he'd had to drink, because his head reeled, but he'd been far drunker in his time. He had only to put his arm around her shoulders to steady himself as they went to the door. Then he wondered what she'd look like in the morning, and was chuckling at the thought that he might find himself bedded with a gargoyle, until she looked up at his small sound of merriment and he stared down into a pair of dark eyes filled with such mystery that it near sobered him.

That was when he noted that the bones in her shoulders were small and light as a bird's beneath his hand, and, unwilling to think of her fragility as they neared the narrow stairway, he removed his arm from around her. And staggered, of course. She took his hand to steady him, and he found it such an odd, childish gesture, especially since that cold little hand fit so confidentially into his, that he laughed again, and shook it off, and held on to the stair rail instead, so that he could sweep her a true courtier's bow without falling on his face. And he said, with a smile that caused her to halt in her tracks and gaze up at him with the nearest thing to happiness he'd seen in her grave little face, "No, after you, sweeting."

As she went up the stair, he could focus on her neat waist, and watch the swing of her hips and the curve of her bottom before him, and he relaxed again, even as desire tightened his smiling lips. Now it seemed to him that he'd been moving all night in a numbness that had nothing to do with the drink. It seemed to him that he remembered losing something too enormous for mere sadness. And so he cherished the flash of desire he felt, because he felt it. It was a small flame that threatened to burn through dull sorrow to make him feel alive again.

Because at long last, with the help of all the ale and the night and the sight before him, he could think, as he followed his quaint little whore, of pleasure, of nothing but pleasure.

# 2

She'd passed the greater part of the last three nights at the Old Swan. Another one spent only standing and watching all that was happening around her, and she was sure the landlord would have her out on the street. He encouraged trade, and whores helped that. Girls in from the street to keep warm and safe took up room, and room, these days in London, was money. Which she had none of. Tonight, then, Mary Monk had made up her mind to make herself a whore, so that she might live. She doubted that she could come back to the Old Swan if she didn't, and if she couldn't, she reasoned, then surely it wouldn't be long until she would be made a whore anyway, by force and without recompence, in the streets she sought to escape from.

But then, she'd been just as resolved for the past two nights, and it had come to nothing. She'd had to leave each night when the merriment died and the common room emptied, and those, the hours before dawn, were the worst. That was when she sought dark doorways and hidden crannies in which to wait for the light. That was when she was in the most danger, although, the Lord knew, she wasn't safe in the light either these days.

Small, dark, and without vanity, she'd never guessed she could be an object of such desire. And from the lack of ardent and intense pursuit of her these past nights at the Swan, she knew full well it wasn't her face or her form, but only her sex, apparent health, and helplessness that made her so desirable in the streets—if the wish to force a chance-met female could be called desire. It wasn't that she couldn't sell herself, for she'd offers enough; it was that she saw how many more offers other, more dashing females got. But she was in far greater demand in the streets. Little, female, homeless, and friendless, she knew herself to be perfect prey now, in a city she had lived in the whole of her life and had never known.

She was Mary Monk, daughter to a respectable shoe-maker. A trained craftsman, with enough regular customers to require an apprentice, aside from his own sons, to pass his wisdom along to. If he wasn't a cobbler of fame, he'd almost been one in his youth. Drink and trouble had robbed him of his creativity and ambition, but his hands hadn't lost their skill. And so he had a shop in an alley near to Friday Street, and three rooms above it, and a son named Martin, and another named William. His youngest was a daughter named Mary, who wore ribbons in her hair and would one day marry John Ashton, the son of a friend, a more prosperous maker of boots.

Or so, at least, all this she had been.

Because it seemed it was true that everything Martin Monk turned his hands to lost luster, just as he'd wept now and then, when deep in his cups. For his good wife had given him three more sons and another daughter who'd gone straight from their swaddling clothes to shrouds, and she herself, poor creature, had sickened on a Monday and died on a Thursday, from bad fish or that rotten tooth she'd feared to have pulled. That had been his grief. Mary had been too young to share it.

Hers had begun a year ago June, when she'd been in her sixteenth summer. That was when the first red crosses had appeared on doors in London, and by July the plague had set in firmly with the summer. And that was when her father had his one good thought, and knowing it for such, clung to it. He sent his daughter away when his elder son sickened, and though she wept and pleaded with him, he could not be moved. She stayed with his ancient deaf aunt in the village of Hampstead until September, when Samuel, his apprentice, summoned her home to nurse her father, the last of the family she had left by then.

By November the plague eased, but what did that matter? Everything was gone—father, brothers, good John Ashton and his family, even the deaf aunt. Mary alone had survived after only a little sickness, soon past, nothing to compare to the pain of surviving. Then she'd only the rooms and tools of her father's trade left to her, and the unsought attentions of the apprentice Samuel to distract her from her bottomless grief.

Even lifelong friends had gone to the Reaper; the plague had been remorseless. They said it had felled one out of five in her section of the city, yet for her it had been more like four out of five, and though she was very good with sums, she still couldn't understand it. If the last of John Ashton's cousins hadn't asked her to move in with his family, she wouldn't have known what to do. Just as she didn't know what to do now that they'd been burnt out of their house, and, homeless themselves, hadn't needed another body to house, another mouth to feed. And too, there was the possibility that she was now considered to be a bird of ill omen; she'd seen the speculation and the fear of it in old Mistress Ashton's eyes that night they'd stood and watched their home blazing, and the next day she'd been asked to make her good-byes. Well, she might be a Jonah, she thought, but she had this stubborn desire to continue living, despite it. She could no more give up than fly away over the rooftops to escape all her sorrow. Determination to live was bred into her and in her very marrow, and even ill omens had to eat.

And so now, fed up with two weeks of living on the dodge in the streets, looking for a home in a city of the homeless, still virtuous through cunning and luck, and starving because of it, she walked up the stair of the Old Swan, light-headed from the ale she'd had without food to anchor it. And it seemed, and it was all the more incredible for the reality of it, that she was about to lie with this huge, battered red-headed Cavalier for a handful of his silver.

But he'd looked as out-of-place as she'd felt. And for all his injuries—and she couldn't help but wince at the sight of those discolored bruises on his high cheek-bones and the puffiness that ruined the mannered line of his lip—he was a handsome man. It was more than that. Hadn't that tanner last night been comely with his midnight-black curls and red cheeks? And hadn't the butcher the night before that, the young one who had chucked her under the chin as he offered her his coin, hadn't he been a pleasure to look at, with his yellow hair and laughing eyes? For that matter, Samuel the apprentice wasn't an ugly fellow, for all he'd spots, and yet she'd sooner have given herself to the hogs than to him. No, it wasn't just his looks, because she'd never known a man, nor felt real lust for one in that fashion, and there was nothing of any desire but to live in this transaction.

She hadn't the words for all the things this big red-haired Cavalier had seemed to her as he'd sat there in that boisterous crowd, neat in all his shabbiness, elegant despite his bruises, mannerly even in his cups. Because most of all, he seemed alone and apart from everyone else she saw, and smiles notwithstanding, it seemed to her he was touched with a deeper sadness than even her own. Then too, for all he was the most alien, he'd seemed more human than the rest because of the tic—or had it been a passing shadow? —that she'd seen shiver across that clenched jaw once, like a stab of remembered pain. She'd watched him that closely. Still, there were things she hadn't seen.

She'd known he was big, but in truth she hadn't realized how he'd tower over her until he stood, for all the size of those hands she'd seen wrapped around his cup. And so she didn't know why she felt so safe with him. Especially in light of what she'd agreed to let him do to her. As she walked down the hall with him and he led her to a door, she realized with a sudden lurching of her heart that for all the talk and for all she'd heard, she wasn't entirely sure of what she was supposed to do with him, for all she knew fairly well the incredible thing he was supposed to do to her.

But this was entirely a terrible thing she was embarked upon, it came to her clear as he opened the door. She must have been mad; sleeplessness and hunger had turned her wits. She was Mary Monk, the respectable daughter of a decent artisan, a man of property and place in this world. She'd been brought up to know that a girl who took a man to her bed was expected to take him to her wedding bed soon after. Or else be called "whore"—and "whore" was the worst word her family knew. She couldn't do this, no, she could not, she realized as she swung around to see him closing the door behind them. He smiled at her.

And then she knew why she'd chosen him of all the men she'd seen and evaluated in these last hungry, fearful days. Now, as he looked at her, his poor swollen lip tilted in a boozy sort of smile, even now she hoped she might hear the magical words from him that surely she'd expected in some corner of her mind from the moment she'd first seen him. For he looked so like the savior of her imaginings—like one of the fine gentlemen she'd so often seen riding by her street on a horse, or in a coach, or borne in a sedan chair as he traveled to some unimaginably wonderful place near to the King. As alien to her as a man from the moon, which she also so often saw and dreamed upon from her window, he was one of the Cavaliers her family so admired and tried to ape, a born gentleman.

"How now, child? Why so frightened?" he'd say, as the phantom man she'd thought about always said after noticing her plight, as she'd imagined him saying while she tried to stay awake these last fearful nights as she huddled in doorways to escape the notice of roaming footpads.

"Don't be afraid. Tell me what it is. Why . . . not so! Oh, no! Why, 'tis a shame and a crime. You're only a child, and of respectable family, and an orphan with it. Here, take my hand and come with me. I've a cousin, I've a friend, I've an aunt or a mother or a sister who needs such a decent sweet maid as you, as companion, or maidservant, or friend, so come along with me . . ."

. . . or so she'd had that phantom gallant rescuer say in her mind.

Now, alone with this real man in his rented room, she saw he looked down at her quizzically, and cocked an eyebrow, just as that miraculous man of her imaginings had done, and smiled gently at her as she shrank back against the door.

"How now?" he asked.

She grew still and held her breath at how her fantasy was becoming truth.

"Come, sweeting," he said then, gently, as a tremulous wondering smile began to grow upon her lips, "take off everything. And be quick about it, please. I need a woman of flesh, not cloth, tonight."

What good would it do her to run? In that moment she knew she could run—he was too drunken to chase her, even if he'd have thought to—but where would she run, after all? And to whom? The other men in the inn? The men in the streets? The whores who'd laughed at her and counseled her:

"It only takes a minute if you're sprightly, dear. Lie like a log and he'll be all night about it. Shake a hip and you'll be down for another soon after, and make your fortune."

Or so they'd mocked her, or honestly advised her—how should she know? Or maybe she should run to the fields outside of London, to sleep in a ditch at the side of whoever would take pity on her? No dowry to be a wife now, no other talent to sell; even a kitchen wench needed a reference these days. She knew it all too well, because she'd tried to become one. That was how she'd found the Old Swan. And found they'd sooner let her in to service the customers than to scour the pots. She'd asked. There were too many homeless for one homeless girl to find refuge. There were even too many bondswomen now, and that was a truly unthinkable thing, for that had to be endured for years, not moments, and to be such would be to become an indentured whore. She knew enough to know that that was for badly born girls, not just bad-luck ones. Better to be a whore. And besides, she was weary, and the ale had begun to close her eyes, and she doubted she could stand awake to guard herself all night one more night.

She avoided his eye and began to take off her gown.

Gideon took off his clothes and folded them neatly. It was dark in the room and he didn't bother to light a candle when he'd done; it was warmth and dark he was after, and he was surprised when he reached for her and found her skin so cold. She gasped something when he embraced her, but he didn't catch it, or care to. He hoped she'd take his lead and be silent with him, quiet as the grave, still as a mouse, warm and full and deep and dark and still, he thought as he pressed her against himself and sighed at the wonderful feeling of full breasts and smooth thighs against his body, before he pulled her down to the bed with him.

It was balm to him, better, the excitement started an exquisite aching that transcended the nagging ones that had been troubling his mending body. Wonderful, he thought as his lips touched soft skin and his hands roved over breasts and belly and bottom in the dark, before, eventually, even in his befogged state, he thought: Wonderful, she's died and I'm bedding a corpse. Because he turned her and cupped her and tweaked her and traced her curves with his hands and lips and she lay still as a stone. He'd wanted quiet, but not death, in his arms.

"Where are you, sweeting?" he asked with some impatience as he lay against her. "Open your lips," he muttered, his lips against hers, and she did, but that was scarcely better, for her lips were cold.

"Put your arms about me," he commanded, and then at least he could attend to her body and prepare his own without wondering if she'd roll off the bed away from him, but, he thought as his body cooperated with his will even as she did not, his luck held in everything, didn't it? For it seemed he'd carefully chosen the most inept whore in Christendom for his pleasure tonight.

Too late to dismiss her, too late to choose another, too late to turn back now, with the drink and his body clamoring for an end to it. "Open your legs," he demanded, and she did.

And then, finally, he understood, when it was too late to matter. For by then, he'd broken through, and his body, attuned to certain stimuli that needed no cooperation, had begun its final flurry. At least it was done in a moment. With any other female he would have been ashamed. Now he was wholeheartedly grateful. There hadn't been any pleasure in it, and he was astonished as well, for there hadn't been any pleasure in it for the first time in

his life. Only a spasm of relief as response after he'd
gained his difficult entry, and a cessation of pressure.
Count three and it was done, and he lay breathless
and angry on her bosom.

She'd tried to ignore him, but that had failed, for it
was simply not possible to leave her body alone to
him on the bed while she went elsewhere in her head,
not when he kept touching things she had herself
never seen, not when opening her eyes would show
her glimpses, even in the dark, of things she'd not
imagined. She tried to bear him. But then, even
the shame was driven out by the pain, and when he
stopped at last, she lay spread beneath him, ready to
die, at last.

But he wasn't done with her.

When he got back his breath, he went back up on
his elbows and cursed. And then looked into her face
and demanded, "Why?"

And when she didn't answer at once, he shook her
shoulders and asked again, this time frightening her,
"Why?"

There was no sense pretending she didn't know
what he meant. No point in lying, now that nothing
mattered anymore.

"I was hungry," she said.

"Oh, thank you," he said, and rolled up his eyes,
and rolled away from her, breathing hard and gazing
up at the dark ceiling. "Yes. It lacked only that. Now
my cup runneth over," he muttered, and then fell
silent.

"Why me?" he finally said, when she thought he'd
been sleeping.

"Because," she said tonelessly, "I thought you'd be
kind."

After another long silence, she stirred.

"Am I supposed to leave now?" she asked cautiously,
for she really didn't know.

"Oh, God," he sighed.

"No," he said then, "stay. I won't need you again, but stay, and sleep, or what you will, it's all the same to me," and sighing, rolled on his side to sleep.

But for all the drink he'd taken on, and all the weariness he felt, he couldn't sleep. His lip hurt like fire now; when he touched it gingerly he could feel it had opened a slit again, and though it didn't bleed, it tasted salty and stung at the slightest touch of his tongue. His side, where an enthusiastic boot had caught him, ached slow and steady as a sore tooth. So he felt her slightest movement, even if he didn't hear anything. He thought she might be breathing hard; then he wondered sourly if she were having some sort of seizure. Tonight no sort of bad luck seemed impossible to him. When he turned over and held himself up on an elbow, he saw her outline, and saw she'd curled herself into a tight knot and her breast was heaving, even as her arms were up over her ears and her head as though to protect herself from blows, as though someone, unseen, was kicking her.

"Ah, lass," he said as he tried to stroke her back, as he attempted to unknot her, "ah, sweeting, I'm sorry for it, I am."

She came undone then, and let him hold her, and she wept until he feared she'd break with it, great gulping sobs, until his own eyes were wet with both of their sorrows. She lay still at last, pulsing with the echoes of her wild grief, warm and trembling and drained, in his arms. And then he kissed the top of her head and whispered, "Done. All done. Stay with me, you're safe now," and, exhausted, fell to sleep, even as she did, deep in his sheltering arms.

She'd never had to share a bed. Not when her father was a skilled craftsman and she'd no sisters. The serving wench had slept on a pallet on the floor, but she'd always had her own cot. But then, she'd never been so exhausted in all her life as she'd been, either, so no matter whom she shared her bed with, she'd slept without moving anything but her eyes behind their closed lids, as she followed mad dreams down through the night. And woke to find one had been true, after all.

She wondered at her daring now, now that it was done, and she'd a whole night of sleep behind her. She gazed at him in the morning light as he lay sleeping beside her, and her first waking thought was to marvel that she'd so much as ventured to speak with such a man, much less let him take her to his bed.

Sleep robbed men of their guile and showed the world the faces nature had given them, without their plans and plots to shade and shape them. As did death, for her father had looked, for all his disfiguring lesions, younger, more innocent in death, and her older brothers had looked like boys before she woke them in the mornings, when they lived. But this man, with his fine, chiseled features in his rock-hard face, seemed forbidding even in sleep, although dark lashes shaded those most dangerous eyes. Still, he looked like a stern knight she'd seen carved on a coffin in church. There was nothing young or innocent about him at all as he slept, although, she noted, he was undeniably youthful, and after all, in her disgrace, at least, he had no guilt, not really.

He'd only bought what she'd sold. Seeing his broad bare chest above the blanket, she remembered the night. And even with all the shame that came flooding back to her, she had to admit he'd not got a very good bargain for his money, either. What he had got was apparent as she sat up and edged off the bed, for her thighs ached and there was another pain that insisted she not forget that desperate bargain. Looking down, she saw a dark stain. Then, although even in her own confused state she realized it was absurd after all that had happened, she flushed, wondering if she'd got her courses in the night—embarrassed and worried that this stranger would know of it, and be disgusted with her for it.

"There's water, and a basin, behind the curtain, there in the corner," he said as she swung her head to meet his bright gaze, before she looked away, wildly shamed by his lazy unconcern with his nudity, as he lay with his arms behind his head, watching her. "And I'm sorry for that," he added, nodding to the stains on her thighs that she tried to cover with her hands. "I'm not accustomed to maidens and didn't expect one, and so took no care to spare you anything."

She gazed at him in utter incomprehension.

He closed his eyes, putting out the piercing blue light of them. "It happens the first time," he said in a weary monotone, "and happens the more, I hear, the more force used."

She nodded abruptly, remembering tales she'd heard, both relieved and newly shamed, and, scurrying off the bed, snatched up her gown and retreated into the curtained corner of the room.

He missed nothing of her reaction or about her person in that brief glance at her in the light. She was small and dark, of course—that much remained true of what he'd remembered. He might drink enough to commit folly, but that folly was always cut short by the rueful knowledge that he never got so drunk that he forgot anything he did, drunk or sober. But he was gratified to verify what only his hands had told him before. Small as she was, she was fortunately formed, not little because of a lack in either leg or trunk, but merely made to a smaller pattern, all in dainty proportion. And all those proportions were shapely and stirred him. He admired her high hard breasts, neat waist, rounded hips, and curving legs. Her face was winsome, at most, her dark eyes the best of it, her curly dark hair an advantage—never a beauty, but pretty enough in her fashion. So what if he'd lately been

struck to the heart by a milk-white maiden? This was
reality, and a nut-brown girl was very sweet, he thought.
And could look even more so with careful dressing.
He was pleased at that notion. But then, hearing the
water in the basin splashing, he remembered the stains
on her body and frowned, and, remembering others on
her neck, he looked sterner, and since he was stern-
looking enough without grimacing, when she emerged
at last, dressed, and looked to him, she shuddered.

She'd have left the room at once if she could. But
she remembered the coins he'd promised her. And,
practical, bred to be practical down through all the
generations of careful tradespeople that had produced
her, she might hate everything about her situation,
regret her actions and despise herself for them, but
pride or no pride, she could never pass up good money
owed to her.

She glanced at him, and away, for his nakedness
reminded her too much of the night, and now she
struggled to pretend it had never happened. She was
unused to nudity, anyway. She came from a decent
family. Some things were unavoidable, so she knew
something of male bodies. Men relieved themselves in
the open air; London stank of it. She'd grown up with
two brothers and a father who worked indoors, so that
when the weather grew too warm for comfort, they'd
think nothing of stripping to the waist. But men reliev-
ing themselves showed not very much of themselves,
and a bare-chested brother was no more naked than
the cat that sat on the sill and cleaned itself in the
sunlight. This stranger who'd shared her body was
nakeder than any man she'd ever known. Or would
again, she vowed as she looked down to her toes and
stubbornly dared to ask for her payment.

"I saw the coins you were going to give me on the
table last night," she said in a small voice that he was
pleased to hear was carefully soft, and only slightly

edged with London stresses, "but I never took them," she explained.

"Oh, too bad," he said with what might have been sympathy.

She looked straight at him, at that.

"Now what will you do?" he asked good-naturedly.

He lay back and watched her face, seeing the struggle to come up with an answer as clear as if she'd spoken.

"Whom to complain to?" he mused. "The landlord? My better nature? Ah, there's a possibility," he said in livelier tones, "but what if I haven't one? Or if I think I didn't get value for my money and decide to take you again, and now, before I give you so much as a good morrow? Or if I decide even then that I've been cheated and give you only blows instead? Yes, it's a bad business you embarked upon last night, isn't it?" he asked as he saw her dark face grow sallow with shock.

"Sit down," he said then, and motioned to the one chair in the room. As it was far enough from the bed, and because she was as frightened now as she was literally sick to the stomach, for his words had been like the blows he'd threatened, she sat.

"I remember, because I make it a point never to forget what I hear, however hard I drink, that you said you came with me because you were hungry," he said, all seriousness now, "and as you were a maid, and as I find myself curious, I'd like to know why. Have you no family? No man? No home?"

"No, none," she said quietly, taking on his cadence with his scorn, but then, because she was the daughter of a respectable family, or had been, some pride surfaced, bubbling up like the last air escaping from a drowning woman's lungs, and she said, raising her head, "But I had all of those things once."

"Tell me then," he commanded, lying back, pleased at the way her chin lifted, though it trembled.

It was simple enough and soon told, for all it had been hard enough and recent enough so that her eyes glittered when she'd done.

"Oh, aye, 'tis a shame and a pity," he said, as she'd prayed he might have last night, but he said it thoughtlessly and his expression didn't soften as he asked, "No other family?" before the look in her eye answered him well enough.

"And this apprentice, Samuel?" he continued, "So loathsome then that you'd rather go to a stranger's bed?"

"Oh, Samuel. He'd enjoy seeing me at his feet," she explained, growing animated with the thought of her dislike. "Trust me on that. But once there, there I'd have stayed forever. No, it's far worse to shame yourself with someone you know is beneath you than with a stranger. I thought selling myself for a night would be better, but I never realized . . . I'll never do it again," she swore, as much to herself as to him.

"Thank you," he said. "It was delightful for me too."

Before she could decide whether she'd wanted to insult him or not, or had, he asked mildly, "And where will you go now?"

And waited, with a look of polite interest, for her answer. When none came, he went on, "Of course, now that I've obliged you, when they pull you down in the streets and have your skirts over your head, and take you one after the other, it won't hurt as much," and as she gazed at him with sick horror, he added, "There's always Samuel. Better the devil you know than ones you don't . . ." he mused, before he looked at her keenly and said seriously, "and then, of course, there's always me, too.

"I've need of a woman," he said bluntly, "and for more than a night. I've only recently returned to London, last night, in fact. I'd thought to live in Kent, but my plans have gone . . . awry," he said with a twist to his mouth, "and now it looks like a stay in London Town for me. I'm weary of wandering the earth and mean to get myself set up in rooms, comfortable ones, and eventually a house somewhere, for I don't love London so well . . ." He shook his head, and went on, "But I'll need a woman to see to my other comforts.

"In return, my mistress will have clothes and food enough, and money for trinkets as well. And my protection, of course," he said, "and it is considerable. And goes across the board, for I'll never shame her by offering to share her with anyone, nor will I desert her without providing for her first, and if there is issue, I'd see to the keep of it until its majority—I'm a wealthy enough fellow, whatever you may have guessed from my garb. Nor would I shame her by flaunting another before her eyes—she'd never have to witness it.

"All I'll ask of her in return," he said, watching her closely, for a look of animation had come into her great dark eyes and it suited her very well, "is obedience, but a woman's and not a dog's, and fidelity, absolute fidelity, for I'll not suffer an unfaithful wench, not for a second, and cleanliness . . ." He paused. "I've lived in the East and the Northlands, and have got used to cleanly woman. Other men may write sonnets to their ladies' fleas, but I'll not. I like to please my nose as well as my eyes. Bathing, at least once a month," he specified, "overall, and in all weathers," and as she widened her eyes, he added lackadaisically, "Your neck is dirty."

And that, more than anything, made her snap, even as her hand went to her neck defensively, "Why me?"

"A very good question," he answered approvingly. "You're not at all good at the work you've undertaken in bed, as you well know, and though you're comely enough, I've seen prettier wenches. It isn't guilt that prompts me either. You'd have taken someone last night—it just happened to be me," he added reasonably, "but as I was the first, at least I know you'll never give me the pox, and that is no little consideration. Second, I believe you don't lack wit. I don't bed just bodies. So far as that goes, yours has great possibilities. You've pleased my eye, if nothing else yet. I think you could learn . . .

"But be sure," he cautioned suddenly, his blue eyes sharply intent upon her to note her every reaction, "that is *very* important. Such play is of profound importance to me. I enjoy it mightily. And often. And love to love a woman well. It can be very well, believe me. Last night was as poor, if less painful, an experience for me as it was for you. If you think you can never bring yourself to it with enthusiasm and without disgust . . . why, I'll give you good-day right now," he said, and rose from the bed in one fluid motion, strode to his discarded clothes, extracted a purse from beneath them, and in another step had come to her and dropped a handful of coins in her lap where she sat.

She looked at them and then up at him. But as he was entirely naked, she found herself staring instead at that shockingly different hard white frame with its patterning of auburn hair that focused her attention on exactly what she didn't wish to be seen gaping at. And so looked down to her lap again in a hurry. However brave she chose to be, it was no easy thing to look at him directly as he stood so close in front of her, just as God had made him. He seemed to understand that, at least, and turned from her so that she might catch her breath as he went behind the curtain at the corner of the room.

She heard the several sounds of his morning toilette as she thought furiously. After a space, his voice came to her ears again.

"Still there? Ah well, then I'll add that this body of mine is a thing you'll have to get used to, so think long and well. I hate deception of any kind and will discover you if you try to cheat me by offering me false smiles or moans. I'll grant you don't know enough about the matter to judge, but I promise, whatever my demands, they'd be considered wholesome enough by most men, and have been by every woman I've ever taken to my breast. Still, I'm prepared to be patient. I realize," he said more cheerfully, "that it might take time for the sober daughter of a respectable tradesman to come to terms with what ladies of the court are trained up to enjoy from the cradle onward. Yet, aside from the sport of it, a guild member's daughter is the very one who should see that the position I offer is one in a proper . . . ah . . . let me say instead, a *legitimate* trade," he corrected himself on a chuckle, "and my rules are simplicity itself. Indeed, I wonder why you hesitate, unless it's for dislike of me, in which case I wonder why you've stayed on even so long as to hear me out. Because it's a common enough profession, after all. Perhaps not in shoemaking circles, but I promise you that fully half the ladies of the court, highborn or low, are so employed.

"As to that," he said after a pause, "what are your politics? Because if you're a Puritan, that explains all, and we may as well forget the whole of it here and now. They hold that fornication's a device of the devil, and pleasure in anything but plain copulation's certain damnation, within wedlock or without. I'd not pit even all of my art and persuasion against training like that. . . . Speaking of wedlock, I'll tell you from the start, don't deceive yourself. You may grow to be the best bedmate I've ever known, and be congenial as a saint out of it, but I promise you I've no intentions of wedlock with you, now or ever, and that is the honest truth. But come, how were you raised? What was your father? Puritan or king's man? Come, come, it'll not leave this room."

Distracted, she hesitated, and then, ashamed that she'd no label to offer him, as she thought a fine lady might, she explained grudgingly, "I don't know. We weren't political. The old king had his head off the year I was born, after all, but Father didn't even go to see it, though it was the talk of the town. He said it was a day's work off to no purpose. Samuel likes to go see men topped," she added with disgust, "but I don't, nor did Father."

She thought for a moment and then said carefully, "But he liked to make shoes for Cavaliers, since he said they could be a work of art and cost the earth. And he often said that in the bad days before Charles came back, a shoe was as plain as it was poor to see, only leather with a single buckle that cost as small as it looked. So I think he must have been a royalist. Or at least," she admitted gruffly, " 'a tradesman's politics are always to be found in his purse,' he always said, and so it's all I can say."

There was laughter in his voice as he called out in reply, "Sweetly said. An honest answer, well enough. And well enough for me. I'll be as plainspoken. If you're still there, I imagine you're considering my offer. Well then, I add that if you decide against me after a fair trial, I'll be generous and expect the same generosity of spirit from you in the event that I decide you'll not suit. Whatever—if I take you up, I'll not cast you out penniless," he said, emerging from behind the screen with a bit of toweling in his hands, which helped to distract her from that huge and angular alien body that would be her main concern if she accepted him.

"Well?" he asked, coming to a stand, feet apart, as he awaited her answer. "Staying with me? Or are you off alone to face the world?"

They both knew there was only one sane answer she could give him.

"I will stay," she said as slowly and shyly as if he'd asked her to be his bride, not his mistress. Because for all the fear he caused in her heart, she was more afraid of how she'd get on without him. Whatever else he was, she believed every word he spoke, and he was a strong prop against a hard world. What he asked might be impossible, but what she'd faced alone had been surely so.

He smiled and reached for his clothes to continue dressing. He'd expected her answer, but wasn't prepared for her question.

"But . . ." she said softly, looking at her twisting fingers in her lap as she played absently with the coins he'd given her, "what is your name, sir, please?"

# 3

It was inappropriate, and damnable besides, he knew, and yet his grin was irrepressible. So Gideon was very glad his back was turned to the girl as she'd asked her question, and he kept it that way when he replied as soberly as he was able.

"My name is Gideon Hawkes, sweeting. And what is yours?"

"Mary Monk," she answered politely.

"No relative to the great general?" he asked, turning now, letting his smile show.

"No," she said wistfully, "no relative to the great anyone," and then, remembering her new position, and unsure of how to ask this unpredictable red-headed giant who was so newly important to her of her other duties, she asked hesitantly, "Would you like me to go belowstairs and bring something up for you to break your fast with . . . is it to be 'Gideon' or 'Master Hawkes,' please?"

"Gideon," he said, a strange expression crossing over his hard features before he grinned and added, "No, you're too little to carry so much. Wait half a moment, and I'll come down with you."

He pulled on his clothes as she gazed at the window,

and then ran a brush over his long blazing hair before he placed his slouch hat over it. And turned and smiled and bowed a graceful sweeping bow, making a beautiful leg to her before he straightened and offered her his arm.

She was unsure if she were being mocked, but saw no malice in his bright eyes. He'd changed from his torn waistcoat to a beautifully embroidered green satin doublet that he'd taken from his traveling bag, and now looked, fading bruises or no, so breathtakingly the fine gentleman that she hesitated. But then she realized they were only going down to breakfast, and so, trusting that since her courage had got her this far it would take her those few steps farther, she placed her hand lightly upon his silken sleeve. Then she took in a deep breath, and remembered to hold her head high before she walked out with him.

She got no more notice than an absent approving nod from the innkeeper as he showed them to a private alcove, and then a rueful look from the serving wench, before she found herself seated at a table being set with foods she'd only dreamed about for the past weeks: fresh breads, at least three sorts, an assortment of cold meats, cheeses, and herrings, and a cake filled with plump currants that her eye immediately went to. But her hand did not, for her companion tapped it smartly with his spoon when she reached out for a piece of it.

"No, no, not until you've had something sustaining as well as tasty," he admonished her as he put his mug of ale down. "A wench ought to have a gently swelling belly, like the cheek of a ripe peach, and not one that looks as if it's stuck to her backbone, as if she's holding in her breath all the time," he added, to turn her frown into a blush as she ducked her head down. "Sooth," he went on, charmed by her readily rising color, "I never knew females had so many bones to them. Imagine, two as sharp as knives on either side of that poor hollow belly of yours! To guard your virtue? I'd never seen the like," he mused as he piled ham upon her plate.

"I never had the like before!" she flared, hurt by his criticism of her newly starved state, for it implied she'd been badly reared. "But it's hard to eat ashes. And poor guardsmen those bones proved to be, however sharp you found them," she grumbled, before she recalled herself and gasped, both because she'd been stung into speaking of something she'd rather have ignored, and because he might take it amiss.

But he laughed at her impudence with what seemed to be genuine appreciation of it, his head thrown back, white teeth gleaming. There was a softened look in that eagle's eye when he'd done.

"Yes," he said more soberly, "but then, I'd have gone on last night if you'd more bones than this herring, I think. I was more soused than it too, I believe. Next time will be better for us both in every way, you'll see."

She lost her appetite entirely at the reminder, and it may have been that he knew it, for all that she tried to mask the instant surge of distaste and fear she'd felt at the thought of how she was expected to pay for this meal, and all the ones in the future she could see. For he put his hand over hers gently and said in a softened voice, "But that won't be for a while, for all I regret the delay. I want flesh on those bothersome bones of yours first. Our games were too vigorous for a beginner. I think you need a rest from them for a bit. And too, the more you know me, sweeting, the more natural, if not instantly agreeable, you'll find it, I promise. And then agreeable as well, I'll warrant. Eat slowly, because an empty stomach fills quickly," he advised, to take her mind from her new duties, to take the threat from his promises.

As she ate, he reflected again that it was beyond strange for nature to have made those of his sex so ready and randy so young, while it made maids so fearful, and with good cause. Because though he'd not had many virgins, he'd encountered a few. It was his experience that they felt little but discomfort the first times, however tenderly they were initiated, finding small pleasure until they'd grown well accustomed to what nature had equipped his own sex to instantly enjoy to the fullest. Yet it was said they eventually found even more joy than men did in the act. Or so he'd heard said, so he supposed that was their recompense, although for the life of him, he doubted it. At least, he couldn't imagine anyone enjoying sexual matters more than he did. But then, realizing where his thoughts were leading him, and taking into account the situation, the hour, and his new mistress's condition, he grinned to himself and deferred his favorite pleasure, turning his whole attention to a more readily available one, and set to his breakfast with gusto.

"Now then," he said when he was done, and had served his tablemate her promised bit of currant cake, which she'd nibbled down to crumbs, and was staring wistfully at, unable to finish, "we'll go on to the Peacock, because I've arranged to meet my valet there. It's a better hostelry anyway, near to Whitehall," he explained, "and after we settle in there, I'll look around for more permanent rooms for us."

He'd said "near to Whitehall" but he might as well have said "near to Jerusalem," because she'd never gone far from Friday Street and the alleys and mews surrounding it. She'd only ranged further in these past weeks in search of a haven. Because for all she'd been cosseted in childhood, she'd never traveled unless with her father on some special errand, not until she'd gone to Hampstead to stay with her aunt, and there she had literally "stayed," since the old woman was too feeble to move from her doorstep. And as she'd gone weeping all the way there and back, she scarcely remembered the journey at all. Even with all that she'd done last night, and with all that she'd promised this man in her future, nothing frightened her half so much now as the sudden realization that she'd be leaving everything she'd ever known, burned out of her home and all familiar haunts as well.

But she was made of resilient stuff, or she'd not have gotten this far.

"Yes," she said, "very well," she said, "but please, I must get my things first."

When he looked down at her with inquiry, she straightened her spine.

"I haven't got much," she said simply, "but I've got more than the clothes I stand up in. I can't leave my things behind any more than I could carry them with me all over London, even if I didn't manage to take much. They made me burn most of the things my father touched, after he died," she explained, "and most of what was left got burnt up before I could get it out, along with the rest of the Ashtons' house. But I saved some things from both fires, and I have to have them. Some gowns, my best shoes—you don't have to come with me, I can meet you at the Peacock . . . I will . . . ah, but it would be a terrible waste otherwise," she said a little desperately, for he looked at her with no expression in those bright, cold eyes.

"No, no, we can't have that. We can't have waste," he agreed after a moment.

They'd been told to leave the horse and go on foot, and he understood why after they'd begun to pick their way through the crumbling rubble that was all that was left of the streets that one-third of London had called home. The heat was gone from the ashes they stepped on, but it was treacherous underfoot even for a careful man in soft boots—it would have been certain undoing for the slender legs of a horse, however carefully it was guided over the debris on the cobbles. Still, he was glad he'd accompanied his determined new mistress, for although there were other people everywhere, walking, sifting through the ruins, or merely standing and staring at them, he knew enough of the world to know that disaster always follows ruin. If the fire had roasted all the rats that had thrived here, he'd no doubt their human brothers still flourished in the darkened corners of the shells of houses and churches in the narrow alleys.

At least the air was tainted by nothing but the ever-present smell of ashes and the heavy sour scent of dead debris. It may well have been the one section of the city not reeking of the stenches of industry now. There wasn't a trace in the wind of the soapmakers', brewers', or dyers' trades, or even the light scents of the carts full of vegetables, fishes, and meats that were vended everywhere else in the city. Not to mention, of course, the fact that no sewage flowed down through what had been the streets, there being no one to add to the running cistern that was usually there—or wherever people lived in great numbers in town. So for all it wasn't the sweet fresh air of the country, it smelled like nothing else in London now.

"Not much further," she said, breathlessly, because she found her recent hunger and sleeplessness had sapped her usual vitality, and the walk across the uneven streets tired her more now than when she'd originally passed this way, when the paving beneath her feet had still been warm even through the soles of her shoes. "There," she said, excitement giving her more energy as she hurried on, "there, St. Katherine's was spared, though others were not. And they promised they'd deliver my pack to none but me."

He restrained himself from commenting that none other would have wanted the treasure she unfolded to him moments later, when she emerged triumphantly from the centuries-old stone church. The shoes, at least, he could see were of fine quality, as he'd expected. But the two gowns she so tenderly refolded after she'd inspected them were poor, plain things to his eye; and the bits of linen and pieces of silverware and the few dishes and household oddments she'd rescued seemed scarcely worth the glee she showed as she counted over them before she fastened the bulky package together again. She never saw the bemused and tolerant smile he'd worn as she gloated over her hoard, for it had gone by the time she looked up to him again. By then he'd recalled that, withal, she'd salvaged more from her lost home than he himself had done. All he had were memories of Ivyclose, after all.

He'd certainly no true memory of London, he decided after he'd left her in the rooms he'd hired at the Peacock to stroll through the city alone. He'd left her standing in the center of their new bedchamber, uncertain, the huge canopied bed that dominated the scene a reminder to her of the reason for her hire, and a consolation to him. Because in all her drabbery, and her grime, she'd nevertheless looked very tempting in that last glance he'd had of her as she'd pushed one shoulder of her gown down in preparation for the tub of water he'd ordered up for her. Uncertain, untrained, as mannerless with a man as a wild thing, but with enough hints in her sudden laughter, and now and then in her unguarded eyes and swift rise of color in her cheek at a sudden thought or spoken word, to tell of the fire he believed he could bring forth from her. With patience, he sighed to himself, with control. Because an unwise or unrestrained urge on his part could discourage her forever—or for the next several months, which was all the same to him.

He could have saved himself the trouble and hired on an experienced wench, of course. He'd thought he had, in fact. And so there was that guilt he felt for changing her state, real enough guilt for all that he knew it was really unearned. And there was that matter of her previous innocence ensuring her freedom from the pox, the one thing that had made him hesitate before far more heavenly gates than the one to which she'd sold him entry. He'd seen the toll it had taken on other men all across the world: the disfiguration of body leading to destruction of mind—the pain and indignity of it, as well as the unsuccessful cures for it. No, Venus' tax was too high a price to pay for any hour in sensual heaven. He always looked before he leapt to love, and had been lucky, even so. Too often even that was no guarantee of safety. But he knew she was, by the very nature of what she'd sold him, entirely, blessedly safe.

And too, and not least of all, inexplicably, he desired her far beyond her merits. It might have been that surging spirit that attracted him even as much as her pretty little body did. Whatever it was, he looked forward to teaching her his favorite game. He looked forward to it so eagerly that he took himself out of the room and for a long walk so she could bathe in peace, and not overset his good intentions.

That was how he discovered fifteen years had changed this London almost as much as the plague and fire had done. It was the third change he'd witnessed in it. He'd vague but merry memories of his boyhood visit to a city filled with color, noise, and excitement. He'd been disappointed, returning when Parliament had held sway, to see the cold and closed face the whole city had worn. Or, at least, had worn in the parts of it his newly Puritanical father had permitted him to see.

Now there was life and vibrancy again, all around him. So much now, in fact, in this city that had been pleasure-starved for a decade, that it was obviously still new to the people even after half that much more time had passed, and so, joyously redundant. Street performers, musicians, tumblers, and puppets played for pennies on the very doorsteps of the reopened theaters.

Some other changes relieved his mind, as well. Because he'd begun to be uneasy even as he'd approached London Bridge, long before he could consciously remember the shock he'd got here that first time, when he'd stared up at all the heads on pikes—those disembodied and deserted houses of humanity, proudly displayed there so as to put the fear of tyrants, if not God, in men's minds. Charles had put a stop to that practice only last year, he'd heard; now a man had to walk to Tyburn Hill to see the fun. Not because the king was any more a softhearted man or a coward than he himself was, Gideon thought, as he himself well knew. They both were as well-acquainted with death as with life, and not afraid of either. But perhaps a king whose father had lost his head took pity on others who did—pity, after all, was a royal prerogative. Most likely, Gideon decided, it was because Charles was too genial a man to celebrate death. Or too canny, despite his carelessness, to antagonize anyone overmuch. After all, in such a changing world, could an intelligent man ever sit secure on his restored throne?

An intelligent, if forgetful and fickle, man, Gideon reminded himself with a frown as he walked on.

It was as well that he'd never simply sat and waited for his inheritance as a valued older son might do. Because now, Gideon thought, he still had things no king could take from him unless he took his life. He'd still his business interests—his expertise, here, abroad, independently and with the East India Company. Interests that were so far-reaching they survived the wars and changing alliances in an ever-changing world.

Profit, after all, flew under every flag, and he was always there to march under its banner, because he'd also his sound reputation as a merchant and a gentleman. And he had all his money, of course. All, except for all that he'd already sent home so that Sir Philip Southern and his beautiful sister could live in greatest comfort in Ivyclose for the rest of their favored days.

He was still frowning when he approached the Peacock again, so involved with his brooding that he didn't realize at first that the merry cry he absently heard was directed to him.

"I'faith! Look you, Jamie, is there no end to our misery? First plague, then fire, and now the Viking horde's returned to plague us. Why, see, there's their battle-scarred leader striding toward us! I quake!"

There was laughter, and then the same amused voice continued with much mock horror, "S'wounds! Draw your sword, Jamie, for see—he comes on like a red tide, unswerving, and will crush us underfoot!"

Gideon paused, and focused his eyes, to see two exquisite Cavaliers standing in front of him, blocking his way. One was as tall as he, but slender as a reed, with a cascade of softly waving nut-brown hair framing his fine-boned thin face, and with a long, high-arched nose and a pair of merry but watchful indigo eyes that were surveying him with vast amusement. The other, both younger and smaller, was a lightly built fair-haired fellow, pure-complexioned as a choirboy, but with nothing of a boy's carelessness in his light observant eyes or in the firm, although laughing, mouth beneath his light mustache.

"By all that's unholy!" Gideon whooped, his sudden cry unsettling passersby as he descended on the pair. "Tristram Jones! And Jamie Beauchamp! Joined at the shoulder, as always! Well met!"

They thumped each other soundly, and hugged like schoolboys, so pleased with each other that they caused the previously alerted passersby to relax: this handsome trio of wellborn gentlemen were clearly about to kill each other with the enthusiasm of their greeting, and not with the long swords they all wore at their sides.

"Bruges! It was Bruges last we met," Gideon laughed.

"Monster! You don't remember Brussels?" the thin-faced man he'd called Tristram challenged him.

"It was Paris, my friends," the younger man reminded the other two, "when Tristram and I went to buy silk cheap and sell wool dear. And only last year."

"And next he'll tell us it was a quarter past six in the evening, on a Tuesday in Lent. Plague take the boy, he's always as right as he's exact," Tristram Jones said on a smile, "so there's no sense disputing it another moment. Come, Gideon, you great red rooster, buy us some ale and tell us why the wanderer has returned—and why so battered too."

But at that some of the pleasure left Gideon's face, and though still smiling as his two friends exchanged quick looks, he said more temperately, "Me tell you? But you've obviously survived plague and fire, surely you've better stories. You did survive fire?" he asked quickly, remembering both his friends had rooms in London as well as their estates in the countryside.

"Not so much as a singed whisker," Tristram assured him. "I lodged near Whitehall, and Jamie made a face at the flames and stopped them two streets from his doorstep. No, no, nothing about us has changed but our clothes since we met last . . . and I'm not too sure of Jamie's at that," he said, sniffing, and as they laughed, continued, "The news is that you've returned. Gideon, don't cheat us of it."

Gideon shrugged his wide shoulders. "I've rooms at the Peacock" he said, "just down through this mews. Come along, friends, they've a dark corner and more good fresh ale than any of us deserve. I'll tell my story, if you've a mind to hear a comedy."

But when they'd ordered their ale, and sat round a long oaken table near to a dead fireplace, the tale he'd promised took only a moment to tell, and when he'd done, there was no laughter at all.

"There must be some mistake!" Tristram Jones said with certainty. "Charles is careless, certainly. But faithless? Never!"

"You're his friend, Gideon," James Beauchamp protested. "Tris is right: he never forgets a friend."

"Perhaps not, but then, some friends are more valuable than others. Don't you forget, he's a king, and they've their own notions of friendship. No," Gideon went on carelessly, "let God and kings bestow favors when whim moves them; a mere man must put his faith only in himself. Don't despair. I did put faith in myself. And more. I've gold, a good name, and broad shoulders. I'll do well enough. And, oh yes, I've a charming new mistress and a night ahead for merriment—come, I've been gone a lifetime. This is your city, where shall we go?"

"Ivyclose was your life, Gideon," Tristram persisted, ignoring his question. "As we are your friends, don't deceive us as to your heart. There must be something you can do."

"As you are my friends," Gideon said firmly, "leave off. There's exactly nothing a man can do when fortune trips him up but get up on his feet again, and not snivel. I don't recall your wailing over Greenwood Hall when it went to the Roundheads, Tris."

"Well, but he knew it would go back to him as soon as they turned their backs," Jamie said on a smile.

They all grinned at that, although there'd been a time when they never believed they would. Because Tristram's father had been stripped of his lands for supporting the king, and being as madcap as he was angry at it, had made a game of it, becoming a famous, gracious rogue: "Gentleman Jones," the Cavalier Highwayman, robbing travelers on the high road to London, with elegance and charm. When he was hanged for his sins, his son had nothing but his name to his own name. His name, and a bitter smile which hid the secret of the last words his father had whispered to him. Because months before that May morning Charles returned, long before the king could reward his loyalty, Tristram Jones had himself returned, and got the money from somewhere to buy back every brick and acre that had been his. And no one doubted that his father's best, last jest had been that the gold for it had been his own ill-gotten hoard, never discovered by Cromwell's troops, got back by his son digging on that same land in the dark of the night. Tristram knew all too well what a man's love and longing for his home was like.

James Beauchamp, Lord Claverly, was son of an old and true loyalist who'd got his own back from Charles's own hand. But they'd both passed too many enforced years abroad to quibble about how they'd been restored to their home. Jamie looked at Tristram after Gideon spoke, and neither needed to do more in order to understand what had passed unspoken between them. They'd been friends since the first day of their exile, and, faithful to friendship as they were to their king, they remained so now that they were home again.

Gideon had met both of them on foreign soil, but then, half of his life had been passed there. They'd become friends because they'd in common a sense of humor, a love of pleasure, and a willingness to work for what they desired. And no matter how far they'd roamed, a love of home. All three had been strongly influenced by their fathers. Only Tristram and Jamie had loved, and been loved, by theirs.

"Well then, you stubborn Kentish man, we'll say no more on that head," Tristram sighed. "But tell us, back only a night and you've already got a new mistress in tow? Alas, poor Elizabeth, Katerina, and Lady Hyde. Yesterday's fish, are they? But tell us, is this new one a little Dutch girl? Or Parisian? Or did you take her from the sea as you crossed over it? Are we to be treated to a mermaid?"

"You're to be treated to nothing," Gideon answered with a grin. "I don't share my toothbrush either."

"Selfish swine," Tristram complained. "But don't worry, I don't really care, for I've my own, my dearest, sweetest, my one true love now."

As Gideon raised one russet eyebrow in inquiry, Tristram sighed and went on, "Yes, my own ruby-lipped Cecilia. And if she's busy, of course," he said pleasantly, "there's always Phyllis or Frances or Isobel."

They laughed, and drank and gossiped about friends and lovers and business and politics. And ordered more ale and drank more, and the afternoon seemed to vanish like the clouds that had been pressing on Gideon's brow. As did the sense of time going by. He wasn't aware of the lengthening shadows of this early-autumn evening until a small shadow paused on the doorstep of the common room and he saw Jamie look up and then immediately grow still. For a moment he caught himself looking at the wench with lively speculation himself, until he recognized her and met her frightened eyes with a pleased and growing smile.

He'd never have believed water could be such a wonderful cosmetic. His eyes went to her hair first, for even in the shadowed room it glowed dark and lustrous as a sable pelt and curled about her high forehead, crackling and clinging to her fingers like unruly raw silk as she pushed it back so as to see him better. Her skin was still dark, but glowing camellia, not just dun now, and flushed with dusky rose to match her lips. Cleaned and dressed in her "good" plain gown of a deep saffron shade, she looked delicious to him,

even though he disliked the fear he saw in her wide
dark eyes.

"I wondered where you were," she said softly, as
they all grew still. "I heard your voice . . . I'll go
now," she said, and turned, only to be stopped as he
rose and moved with the sudden unexpected swiftness
that had deceived so many opponents, to put a hand
upon her shoulder.

"Friends," he said, still smiling down at her, "I
make you known to Mistress Mary Monk—no relation
. . . no. And here, sweeting, are two rogues you may
sit with, and drink with, and trust your life—but never
your delicious little person—with, believe me. Tristram
Jones is the fellow with the wondrous nose, and the
innocent-seeming lad is James Beauchamp, Lord
Claverly."

"James, or Jamie, please," the slight young man
said at once, rising and bowing low.

"It would please me if you'd not please him *quite* so
much as he's sure to ask," Gideon said with a sigh,
watching Mary blush as she ducked a curtsy.

She smiled shyly, but with true pleasure, as she rose
and faced the two Cavaliers she'd been introduced
to—a sudden engaging little turning-up of her lips that
showed only a glimpse of her even white teeth, but far
more of her unexpected winsomeness. Gideon was
amused to see how her smile was echoed on his friends'
faces, until he realized he was beginning to grin as
foolishly as they were. Yes, he thought bemusedly,
laughter suited his little mistress every bit as much as
soap and water did.

"Now then, gentlemen," Gideon said when he'd
seated Mary by his side, "my man, who knows everything, is not here yet. So you two, who know nothing
worth knowing, and so know all the latest fads and
fashions, are the very ones to ask. As Mary has need
of them, I need to know the names of some dressmak-

ers who can make her some new gowns worthy of her beauty."

Color rose in Mary's cheeks. She wasn't sure of Gideon's welcome, for all his smiles, because the two gentlemen he sat with were grander than any she'd ever seen so close, and so she wondered if he really wanted her with him. But she'd begun to think he'd left her alone forever, that it all had been some mad jest she'd have to somehow pay for, when he hadn't returned as the hours wore on. When evening fell, her hunger and doubt grew together and she'd ventured belowstairs. Now, at his words, despite the fact that she was still unsure of his pleasure at her entrance, and was thoroughly awed by his fine friends, her pride surfaced again. She'd take the gowns because she had little to wear, not because she was greedy. It was important that his friends, as well as he, know that.

"I lost most of my things in the fire," she explained in a small voice, keeping her gaze on the table.

"Ah, from London then," Jamie said at once. "And where did you live?" he asked with great interest.

"Near to Friday Street," she answered, and as Jamie asked eagerly, "Do you know John Carlyton? He's an excellent wit and a man of rare good humor and had a house with green shutters . . . ?" she said quickly, "No, no. I lived *near* to Friday Street, not on it. My father was a cobbler, we'd a shop in the alley close by. But he went with the plague, with the rest of my family, and the fire took the shop since."

"But I remember it well," Jamie cried with the air of a man who'd made some great discovery, "though I regret now I never stopped in to—" he began, as Tristram interrupted him with a sharp look, and put in smoothly, "He knows all London well, because he never forgets anything he's seen or heard. A human blotting pad, but of use when a shopkeeper accosts me, for he knows to the hour if and when I've paid my bills, or so he's famous for saying, and he's pleased to be as honest as the moment requires, for a friend's sake."

They laughed, and Tristram turned the talk to fashion; they ordered food with their drink, as the talk of fashion soon brought them to dishing up gossip of the court again.

Mary sat quietly within the circle of Gideon's arm, and listened to their deep voices in merry conversation. It was a revelation to her. The tall, stern-faced man she'd met last night and feared all day was gone, even as he sat with one hard hip touching hers, his long arm wrapped around her, one warm hand cupping her shoulder. Because he was witty and easy-spoken now, and although still economical with his speech, he jested often; and although he was so near she could feel the laughter rumbling in his deep chest, he didn't make her feel uneasy now. It helped, of course, that for all his closeness, he was so involved he seemed to have forgotten her. She was even gladder of that when the talk she heard began to stagger her.

The men were obviously familiar with court; the easy way they spoke famous names confirmed that. Somehow she wasn't surprised to discover that Gideon Hawkes was a friend to the king; everything that had happened since the moment she'd summoned up enough courage to walk to his table had become the stuff of fable to her. But she was agog at the things they said. Her family hadn't been Puritans, no. But neither had they been libertines. They'd been good, decent guild members, not so low-minded as those who lived in the gutters—or those who lived in the palaces either, it seemed now. Because the things these elegant men jested about were shocking to her. Although she knew enough and feared ridicule or banishment enough not to show it.

"Rochester runs tame as any of Charles's spaniels?"

Gideon asked, as Mary listened, forgetting to close her mouth after having heard a tale about a lady and a courtier and that courtier's lady all doing things to spite each other—with each other—that she couldn't quite absorb all at once. "Does he still chew on reputations the way his master's favorite curs tear up his slippers, and to his same, indulgent delight?"

"Softly, Gideon," Tristram said, smiling. "Rochester runs tamer now even than that. I agree he's an annoyance and a pest, but he's clever enough, and has spies salted over the palace—male, female, and not-entirely-sure—that provide him with enough material for his satires. And they please the king well enough, so he's still got the royal ear and indulgence. Still, Charles knows him very well, and swats his ears back when he slips his rope. He spent a fortnight in the Tower last year for kidnapping a little heiress in an attempt to win from her by force what all his persuasion couldn't get him. She was saved in time to save her maidenhead, but the rumor is she's lost whatever sense she had in her pretty little head anyway, because they say she found the attempted rape so romantic, they wager she'll wed him by Christmas Day anyway."

"I've some gold on it myself," Jamie explained, as Gideon shook his head and sighed.

"I've nothing against merrymakers, God himself knows," he said. "I like Buckingham well enough, he's a man for all he's a devil-may-care one. Wycherly makes me laugh, and Jermyn's a bad but charming rogue, withal. I even find some of Sedley and Buckhurst's exploits amusing, from what I've heard of them from abroad . . . although making water on the populace of London after treating them to a naked revel isn't my idea of sport."

"But remember, it was all done from the balcony of the Cock tavern," Tristram reminded him with an admirably straight face.

Gideon grinned, but went on without humor, "But Rochester's another matter entirely. Not just a drunken fool, more's the pity. I met him abroad when he was just a precocious schoolboy rake. I disliked him even then. He's dangerous in that he'll sacrifice anything for a pat from his master, and yet is enough of a cur to turn and bite that hand if it gets him approval from someone else. Doesn't Charles see it?"

"Now and then, when it pleases him. Or angers him enough," Tristram reported, and smiled in fond recollection as he continued, "For example, when the haughty Castlemaine won Rochester's displeasure—one of the only good things she's done lately—and he tried to pay her back. He tacked a note up on her door, in Latin, which she had someone translate, so it got wider circulation, and then screeched such a screech that Charles came running out of some other wench's bedchamber into the corridors. He was in such a hurry that he was still dressed in only his royal skin. Rochester got his own ears tacked back, for all he denied being the author. And that, after he'd actually gone and signed up for the Navy to show Charles what a man he was—before he came scurrying back to fight royal mistresses and whores instead. So it was a forced march to the country for our little wit, exile from his audience at court. He came back, belly low and licking the royal fingers for favor—and the royal mistress's arse too, if she asked, I'll wager," Tristram said on a smile.

"Although it was such a terse, precisely witty piece," he said thoughtfully, "I wonder if he did compose it. It was too vicious for Rochester's old friend Saville—a rogue but a decent one—so it may have been by his newest confidant, Sir Roger Mobely. It had all his aim, and nothing of his name in it, as usual. If Rochester's a rat, trust Mobely to be the flea on his back," he said wisely.

"Another fool for me to despise at court? And you

urge me to go there to beg?" Gideon asked in amazement, before he shook his head to stop his friends' protests and asked, "But come, what's the verse so terrible to set Lady Castlemaine ashriek? She's got a hide thick as her bond with Charles."

"And heavier pretensions, that's why it got to her. It was short and sour:

" 'The reason why she is not ducked?
Because by Caesar she is—' "

Over all the men's laughter, Tristram added, with a show of innocence that he knew very well sat amusingly on his long, ironic face, "And yet I can sympathize with Rochester on that, at least. Because Charles never seemed to mind the masterpiece about himself half so much—the one Rochester himself recites when he's not nearby—which says, in part, in nicest meter:

" '. . . Restless he rolls about from whore to whore;
A merry monarch, scandalous and poor.
Nor are his high desires above his strength;
His scepter and his penis are of a length.
And she that plays with one may sway the other . . .' "

This time their laughter was so loud Mary could hear it above the blood that rushed to her head. When Gideon noted that hectic flush, as much from the heat it generated to his arm as from the look that Jamie shot to her, he took pity on her, realizing it might have been the word "whore" as much as the frank language that had upset her. Lady Castlemaine, he thought, mightn't be the only woman who found the blurring of the fine distinction between "mistress" and "whore" to be distressing.

"Do you know," Gideon said casually, stretching, "I believe it's time for my dinner. And as I have to change my finery in order to go out with you gentle-men later and not disgrace you, I believe Mary and I will sup in our room. I'll meet you after—say . . . the stroke of ten. I doubt our planned amusements will entertain Mary, and she ought to be abed by then. At ten, and not upstairs," he added, rising, "because as I haven't so much as a flea bite of royal blood in me, I don't care to parade my mistresses in their natural state before my friends. So at ten, then, and here," he said firmly, "in this very room."

When the rawboned Cavalier and his little dark mistress had left the room, she, head down, still in the circle of his arm, Tristram looked to Jamie, who stood staring after them, wearing a troubled look.

"He's not in the habit of beating his wenches," Tristram said softly, for he knew Jamie and his sudden passions well enough to understand precisely where his impressionable friend's problem lay.

"He didn't have to call her that before us," Jamie said grudgingly, low.

"He wasn't bragging," Tristram said, "he was only stating what is."

"It's not because of us, it's her, can't you see?" Jamie said unhappily. "She isn't accustomed to think-ing of herself as such, for all she is. You could read it in her face. And as to why she is what she is? Huh. That's clear as the nose on your face, Tris."

"Then it must be abundantly clear even to a blind man," Tristram answered languidly, "but I still don't see it."

"She went with him in order to survive. Oh, why did I never stop in at that shop?" he said in chagrin. "Plague, fire, loss of home and family, and she's only a child. So little and brave."

"And Gideon is so big and possessive," Tristram said with a frown. "Look you, Jamie, she's his, and she's a whore, however she came to it, and he is your friend. Or was. Take care—what he has, he keeps.

And for all I know few better men, I know few more
dangerous ones."

"Ah, don't trouble yourself," Jamie said on a long,
drawn-out sigh, which caused his friend to echo it,
since he was being alerted to the fact that he'd now be
subjected to much silent languishing, interspersed with
readings of fervored hastily composed lost-love verses,
for a while. Or at least, if Jamie ran true to his form in
such matters, until some other wench caught his fancy.

"I can do nothing else, can I?" Jamie asked helplessly.

Which would have reassured Tristram if he hadn't
seen how Jamie's clear and candid blue eyes remained
fixed, sadder than usual, and more thoughtful than
commonly in such cases, as he gazed at the empty stair
the oddly matched couple had climbed, long after
they'd gone out of sight.

# 4

"You didn't care for the poetry," Gideon said when they'd got to their bedchamber, and he saw Mary, distracted, walk to the bed, then the window, then stare down, unseeing.

But as he hadn't asked it as a question, he answered it himself.

"It was crude. But funny. Bawdy, nothing more. You said you weren't a Puritan," he reminded her, watching her as she stood and pretended to be engrossed in whatever it was outside that she was supposed to be seeing.

"I'm not. I just realized I'm a whore now," she said.

He was not unprepared. He went to her and stood behind her and held her slight shoulders, finding them not so fragile and childlike now, but delicate and soft beneath his hands.

"Should I rather have said you were my sister?" he asked, and that ridiculous thought caused her to break from her grim reverie and her eyes opened wide, letting in the outside world again, as he'd hoped.

She was his mistress now; nothing he could or would say would change that, nor did he want it to. And if she were to be his mistress, then the sooner she accepted it, the better for both of them. He wouldn't be made to feel like a despoiler or a cruel man, not when all he'd done and planned to do was to accept her on far better terms than she herself had offered him. But not only did he know that cruelty and selfishness were the death knell to affection, he wanted affection from her as well as willingness. Any man could buy a female body; he sought more. He felt that this little brown waif, this oddly spirited girl, was capable of giving more to him. He wouldn't permit this foolish matter of the naming of names to destroy what he sought to build.

"As my physician then, perhaps?" he asked. "Or should I have introduced you as my valet?"

She giggled.

"Better," he said in a low voice, and lowered his head to kiss the side of her neck, noting with pleasure how clean and cool it was now, and faintly scented with the soap he'd given her. He would have to buy her some scent, he decided. She stiffened in his arms as his lips moved to her cheek.

"Ah well," he said, and moved away from her at the sounds of tapping on the door, "another pleasure saves you from my pleasure—dinner," he said, and went to let the servant in with the food he'd spoken for.

"Put it here," he said, motioning to a small table, "for my mother and me," he added as he flipped a coin to the lad. Mary gasped and giggled again as he inspected the dishes and looked to her to ask an innocent, "Better?"

The food was excellent and she made a better meal of it than she had the night before, although for a moment she'd wondered if she'd be able to, remembering his remark about pleasure, with the echoes of last night's "pleasures before pleasures" that he'd promised her, before his pleasure had torn her world apart, still sounding in her head.

"I believe you've deceived me," he said when she'd done, and she realized he'd eaten little, having passed his time watching her. "I believe I've got myself a trenchwoman."

"I told you I wasn't used to showing bones," she said merrily, before she recalled why she'd said it, and grew still, and expectant, worrying about why he was watching her so closely.

"Come here," he said, and gave her no chance to obey, since he came and swung her up in his arms and bore her with him, away from the table, and away, she noted with relief, from the bed, to sit in his lap in a chair by the wall.

"Better and better," he said, and positioned her deep in his arms and held her close to his chest. They sat so, quietly, in the growing dimness of the coming evening, until she began to breathe normally again, and stopped worrying about how she felt to him and waiting for whatever he might do next, and wondering at the strangeness of the hard shape and feel to the body beneath her. He sighed at last, and as she realized he bore the not-unpleasant scent of the red wine he'd drunk on his breath, he lowered his head and brought his lips to hers and kissed her long and deep.

He broke off the kiss only when the touch of his tongue between her lips caused her shoulders to tighten again, just after he'd felt them begin to relax beneath his hands. He left off kissing her mouth then, and attended to her neck and shoulders with his lips. It was a marvel, he thought, how he could play her—feel her clench and soften against him—the pliancy of her body increasing as he stroked and gently kissed her, the tension springing up again whenever he opened his mouth too much or let his fingers become invasive in any way. Interesting, he thought, as he noted that his hand on the curve of her breast brought a rapid increase of her breath, yet all the while, she yielded, but the touch of his finger to the peaked crown of it caused her to stop breathing and her back to grow rigid again. Which was nothing to the way she snapped to attention when his hand strayed beneath her skirt. Sweet, he thought, restraining himself from smiling, forbidding himself to laugh, knowing that while most laughter at such play was balm, it would be slow-working poison now.

Sweet, but early days, he thought regretfully, and stopped his experimenting. Since he was now sure of his method, he continued to only kiss and stroke her and hold her close, so that she'd feel coddled, and so that he'd begin to feel less strange to her. But the best of plans made by the most cautious men go awry, and before long he found himself growing too involved with what he was doing for the sort of distance he needed in order to do it, and recalled himself only when he felt her stiffen again, even as his lips sought to confirm what his hands had been feeling.

"Now then," he said abruptly, drawing away from her and pulling up the top of her gown for her, "I must go. Now, or I'll not be able to give you the respite I wanted to."

He picked her up again, only to set her down in the chair alone, and went to his traveling bag to seek out his last clean shirt.

She watched as he dressed, seeing for the first time that the hard frame she'd just been so close to was a long but well-proportioned and smooth-skinned one. His shoulders winged out wide and she could see the movement of muscle and sinew in them when he moved, just as she'd felt when he'd been close. But for all his leanness, his body was no awkward arrangement of bones, it was a supple thing that seemed to be made all of tightly linked muscle. And for all his strength, his hands had been gentle and his breath sweet and his lips so oddly comforting until they'd begun to remind her of that stranger's lips last night and frightened her again. As she watched him pull the shirt over his head,

she remembered his kindness, how he'd stopped whenever she'd feared he'd start that painful, embarrassing
business of last night again. When his head emerged
from the shirt, his face expressionless, his mind somewhere far away now, a new and newly terrifying thought
occurred to her.

"Ah! Because I was so . . . Do you go to another
woman now?" she blurted.

He gazed at her and grew still.

"That's a question you must never ask me again,"
he admonished her gently, but seeing her bite her lips
and look aside, hurt, he said softly, "But this once, I'll
answer. No. I leave you to go and play other games
with my friends, to forget my desire for you with the
lesser excitement of cockfights and gambling on bear-
baiting and what-you-will. I'll wait for you, sweeting,"
he said as he pulled on his coat again and attended to
his hair in the glass on the wall. "You're wearier than
you know, and still bruised, in many ways, from my
former play."

She sat quietly, knowing it was foolish to regret not
being molested; afraid to offer more, frightened because she'd given less, hoping she'd pleased him every
bit as much as she hoped she'd not displeased him,
confused about all her emotions now, as he'd hoped,
as he'd planned. But he hadn't counted on her forth-
right spirit. She was a product of plain-dealing people.

"Then why did you hold me and touch me so?" she
asked.

He paused at the door. Honesty for honesty then,
he thought, pleased as well as amused with the novelty
of her.

"I just wanted you to know it doesn't always have to
end with me on or within you," he said, and as she
caught her breath at his sort of plain speaking, he
added, "But it's far better if it does, believe me. I've
also been taking your measure. Yes, and you'll soon
believe me, I'll wager, no matter how strange it seems

now. After all," he said, his stern face softening as his smile lightened it, as always, "just think. Only yesterday morning, you and I had never met. We were strangers last night. Yet now I'll think of you all night even when you're not with me. As you'll think of me, I hope—without fear. Because I'll not trouble you with myself anymore now. The most I'll take from you tonight is some warmth, at your back, because it will be cold when I creep into our bed toward dawn. Good night, get good rest."

And smiling, he left her, leaving her to think of him and "our bed" for a long while before she could bring herself to clamber into it, alone at last.

The gowns he insisted on having her fitted with were so elegant she was afraid to move in them, much less wear them for something so simple as walking out on a fine autumn day. She felt the soft long skirts hiss over her toes as she stepped along beside Gideon, and was glad of the lace hood she'd pulled over her hair, for it obscured much of her face if she looked down—as she did, so as to have privacy in order to adjust to her new finery. The long narrow front of her bodice was stiff. But it held her no more stiffly than she carried herself as she trod carefully so as not to see the tops of the mounds of her compressed breasts quiver outrageously as they surged up from the close-fitting bodice. Blue and rose and cream, satin and silk and swags of lace. She held her breath as she shimmered and glistened in the light, all the more at the thought that this was only for today; he'd ordered four more gowns for the future!

But then, he looked very fine in his new long coat, and now she matched him in more than the blue color of it, she thought, and the thought made her lift her head.

"Yes," he said, looking down at her, and only that, but the look in his eyes caused her to color up again.

If this was what it was to be a man's mistress, she thought as they strolled back to the Peacock again, why then, she'd been mistold by her father's jests and her brothers' contempt for the women who worked at nothing but pleasing their gentlemen. But after all, what had they, poor hardworking lads, to do with such ladies, aside from spying them as they passed? They'd never even known such a man as Gideon, a man who might have done her mischief in ignorance, but who'd dealt nothing but kindness to her since.

She remembered this morning, when he had awakened her with gentle kisses, and had only held her close to himself when she'd awoken past murmurous content to sudden panic. And then they'd jested, and they'd eaten, and then he'd taken her by the hand and bought her gowns and ribbons and hose and gloves and a fan. And a bottle of scent that smelled like all summer in a bottle. No, she thought, there'd been things she'd never been told because those who'd told her hadn't known about them. But now she did. And was convinced that she'd been misled, after all. Something so bad could never feel so fine, she thought, and smiled up at Gideon—such a sudden, saucy smile that he checked in his tracks, before he quirked a brow and his face gentled, before he started on again.

She was doubly glad of her new gown, even though she hesitated to eat while wearing it, when their luncheon was interrupted by the arrival of Gideon's valet. He was a shadow of a man, quiet, cool, and dark; as swift to bow as he was to disappear on his master's errands. Only the shadow of distaste in his eyes when he was introduced to her disturbed her, but as it was gone before she could be sure of it, she let it pass, as he did, when, after bowing, he seemed to forget her. But had she been wearing her best gown—the best one she'd known before meeting Gideon, at least—the plain saffron one with the smell of ashes still in it, instead of this perfumed concoction of satin and lace, why then, she'd not have forgotten, she knew.

She wasn't a mercenary creature, but an entirely feminine one, Gideon thought as he watched her from the corner of his eye, enchanted. The gown had more than enhanced her looks, it had refreshed her spirit. He noted how she couldn't seem to get used to it, for all she pretended to. He hadn't missed any of the proprietary pats she'd given the lace at her bodice, on the excuse of smoothing it, or the many times she'd retied the bows at her belled sleeves, or any of the little shiftings and stirrings she made, as though she sat on a prickly seat—all, he knew, so as to watch the folding and creasing of the fine fabrics that adorned her as they moved with her. Watching the sweet trembling of her breasts above her bodice as she moved, he wished he had such excuses in order to touch her now. He restrained himself. Unlike his sovereign, he disliked showing off his ardor in public. But like him, he was a man of endless appreciation of the subtleties of sexual play, and so was content to enjoy her innocent enticement, knowing he'd end it abruptly if he acknowledged it.

He'd bide his time, and it approached. There was the night coming, and he meant to act on it, it was time. Too long playing at being her brother and he'd become so in her eyes, and then in her arms. So none of this was wasted; it was all fuel to make the act even better when it came.

He had to leave her in the afternoon, to see to the new clothes his man, Rountree, had selected and commissioned tailors to fit to him. Continental clothes were very fine, and much admired here, but he was in England now and there were small differences, large to his careful valet's eye, to be restyled, and some new garments to be ordered, as well.

He came back to their room to smile at seeing her resting on their bed, her half-closed eyes still fixed dreamily on the gown she'd so carefully laid on a chair. But he had to leave her once more to have a look at a set of rooms Rountree had discovered for his inspection. Which was as well. Because she'd also looked warm and sleepy and dazed with good food and good fortune as she'd lain there. She'd had on only a plain underdress, and as he knew very well what was under that, he'd been sorely tempted to bring on the night before its time. But as both a canny merchant and a clever man, he knew that unripe moments netted bitter results, and so he went on his way.

She was very good for him, he thought, even as he left her. She diverted him entirely. That was more necessary than he'd imagined. Because he'd discovered that now and again, if he wasn't careful, or was bored—as when the action in the cockfight last night had palled, or when chatter in the coffeehouse had turned inane, and the songs of the players in the tavern they'd frequented later had become repetitious—his thoughts turned, and his mood changed from boredom to disquiet to an odd dread.

He understood why later, when he'd left Tristram to his mistress, and abandoned Jamie to the embrace of an unknown at Mother Bennet's brothel. Then he walked alone along the streets as the stars dimmed above him. He wasn't afraid of the shadows, whatever they held. He was seldom molested in the streets of any city. He was big, and well-armed, and adept at dealing every sort of death, and everything about him spoke of this to those whose business it was to listen to such things. But then, at last, stepping across that bridge between night and the next day, distracted from vigilance by his weariness, he'd remembered that he had lost Ivyclose. And the thought had fallen upon him with all the impact of the sudden death of a beloved friend.

He'd never get over it. He knew that now. But one day, he supposed he'd accept it. He'd have to, and he was a man fate had taught to be excellent at doing what he must. Until then, his new odd little mistress would provide distraction, and finding suitable lodgings in London would make for more diversion. And then, as he'd planned to come home to stay, he supposed he would, even if he'd lost the place where he'd planned to stay the rest of his life.

He decided to make it into a quest. Since distraction banished sorrow, since he was a man who had to have a mission now, he resolved to find himself another home. When he did, he'd make it comfortable, beautiful—a place to take pride in, the best substitute for Ivyclose he could create. Although no intelligent man expected to replace his dream of perfection with any reality, he'd at least have the game of trying to occupy himself with. Then he'd furnish it and live in it, and find a wife to have the sons he'd pass it on to in his own time.

This thought of replacement, of rebuilding and renewal, revitalized him as much as the lavish gown had cheered his little mistress. He found himself striding back to the Peacock with vigor, even though the set of rooms Rountree had found had been wholly inadequate and he'd rejected them immediately. And if in some small part of his mind he knew very well that he was only finding himself work to busy himself with, because no new house would ever replace his home or heal the pain of betrayal and loss he'd endured, no more than any gowns would restore Mary Monk's father or brothers or honor or virginity to her, he was careful to disregard it. He was a man bent on living, after all.

And he got on with it.

"What, dressed? Very good, because it's time for us to see what the landlord serves below. It has to be better than what he sends upstairs, thinking those who won't leave their love bed don't care if their suppers are decent or not," he said as he came into the room to see Mary rise at once to greet him.

She'd been sitting by the window watching the daylight die, and came to him tentatively, all the new joy and liveliness he'd seen in her face gone, as hesitant with him now as she'd been at the start.

"What's this?" he asked, tipping her face up in one hand, looking down at her. "What's happened while I was gone to make you so sad and shy of me?"

"Nothing," she said, and he shook his head and frowned. "No 'nothing' please, Mistress Monk, something's been eating away at your heart, hasn't it?"

"Ah, well," she said, moving a step back and looking at the lace at his throat, not his eyes, "I suppose it was 'nothing' that began it, because I was sitting at the window and thinking about the past . . . evening always makes me do that, you know, or you don't, but it does. . . . But I didn't know what I was supposed to do," she said all at once. "What am I supposed to do when I'm not with you, Gideon?" she asked, gazing up at him helplessly.

"Ah, Mary," he laughed, folding her in his arms. "I'truth I've been too busy thinking of what you're to do with me to have thought of that. Well, mistress," he said, holding her an arm's length away and smiling, for she did amuse him wonderfully, "I suppose I've never thought on it either. My other ladies were either married or settled in their occupations—changing masters was all they did—so they got on with their usual lives, I suppose. But you've no usual life now, have you? We'll have to give it some thought," he promised her. "What would you like to do?"

"I meant," she said softly, "what do you expect of me?"

He grew silent, and looked down at her oddly.

"We'd a wench at home who cleaned and helped me cook," she explained seriously, "but I'm a good plain cook, and Mistress Ashton had me help her every day.

I went to market, oversaw the running of the household as well as the accounts as I did at home—I'm very good with sums," she added, before she went on quickly, "When I was free, I walked out, or visited with friends. But you live at an inn, where they cook and clean for you. And Rountree says he needs no help from me. I think I insulted him by offering it today. After you left, I didn't know if you'd mind if I went out by myself, or what it was you wanted me to do, so I sat and waited. That's why I'm not livelier," she said, her great dark eyes searching his face, looking for understanding.

"You may go out without me," he said gently, "but I think not alone anymore. I'll have a talk with Rountree, we'll see what's to be done," he said, holding up a hand to halt her flurry of protests about not disturbing Rountree, as he said, smiling again, "Sooth child, he's a servant, not a man you must look to please. I'll look into the matter, I promise," he said, touching her cheek gently, "Ah, this getting of a young mistress," he murmured, almost to himself, as he shook his head, "is like taking on a young pup. It's not enough to want the pretty thing, you must kennel it and see to its needs and training until it's old enough to see to itself."

"I'm not a dog!" she cried, startled into raising her voice to him.

"No? Then don't snap my nose off. No, no, you're not," he laughed. "I only meant that you're young, Mistress Monk, and innocent of this wicked world, and make me feel very old. Come, make me feel young again, instead," he said, "and give me the kiss of peace."

She offered him a chaste kiss, and he thought again of the wisdom of waiting for the night to come, deciding that as it was almost time, he could wait awhile longer. A little wine, enough food, and darkness were the best allies any seducer could have. At the thought that he'd be seducing his own mistress, he smiled and shook his head again. But he was a thorough man, and so he took her hand to take her down to dine with him as though she were a gentle young lady, as though he weren't absolutely sure of the outcome of the night.

Their pleasure in the fine dinner the landlord set out was interrupted only by a message being delivered to Gideon. Mary sat still and expectant until he'd read it through. Having a written note delivered was a rare thing in her experience, and receiving one had always been a sure harbinger of some sort of disaster in her family, but she relaxed when he laughed and crumpled it in his hands as though it were of no account.

"Tristram and Jamie beg the pleasure of our company tomorrow," he explained, "and being too lazy to take themselves all the way here on the chance that we'd be out, request we await them after noon. As if I expected them to drag themselves forth before the sun was directly over their heads!" he commented, giving his full attention to his roast meat again.

When they'd done with the meal, and after they'd listened to the musicians playing a few songs for the pleasure of the company, Gideon arose and stretched and held out his hand to Mary.

"Come, love," he said lazily. "Come, sweeting." She rose and walked with him, only losing her smile when he whispered as they came to the stair, " 'Tis time."

He'd poured her three glasses of wine, and she'd felt pleasantly warm and light until that moment, and then it seemed that she froze, and had to drag her feet up the stair. But it was wonderfully warm in his arms, and he took her into them as soon as he'd closed their door. He was in the midst of taking her from her gown, when he paused.

"Come, Mary," he said. "What is this?"

And since she knew what it was, and regretted it, since he'd been so kind to her, and knew the bargain they'd struck, she went back into his arms and tried not to shiver, and when she couldn't help it and did, only murmured. "I'm so cold, Gideon."

"I'll remedy that," he laughed against her neck, but he didn't, for the heat of his skin when he'd pulled off his own garments and joined her on the bed caused her heart to contract and grow icy with fear.

She knew no cruelty at his hands—he handled her with great care, as he'd done in the morning—and yet as she knew his intentions now, she found she could know no comfort in his touch now either. Now that she knew the use of the body pressed to her, she knew that to welcome him as she tried to do would be to also welcome invasion. But she was grateful enough and had grown to know and like him well enough to try to overcome her distaste for what was to come, and if she could offer him nothing else, at least she offered him no resistance. It wasn't enough.

"Come, Mary . . . come, sweeting," he murmured in her ear eventually. "Open your eyes. No, look. This is what a man is, this is what life is, what love is . . . no," he whispered, pulling back, his eyes glinting a fierce blue in the cold light of the moon, "no, it will be much better for you one day soon. But for now . . ." He caught his breath and bent to her again, going on, still speaking on, for he was as free with speech in intimacy as he was spare with words in company. Indeed, it seemed to her he'd no more leave her alone in her mind than he would in her body, and was reaching out to her with both his body and his words. He murmured assurances as she tensed when he grasped her hips to hold her ready.

"I'faith, sweeting," he whispered harshly, angry with his treacherous body for finding stimulation where he knew none was offered, "I cannot deny myself longer, not for all my art, or for all your chances for joy in this. There, Ah, there.

"So," he said on a sharply drawn-in breath then,

willing himself to stop, just for that one moment, "not so terrible this time then, is it? Is it?" he asked, before he sighed and began to move again. "Ah, love, ah, mistress, I do wish you knew the whole of it as I do . . . there, yes, just so, relax and let me . . . just so, yes," he murmured.

She rocked with him, glad there was little pain in it for her this time, sorry she had this office to perform for him, determined to try to perform it to his satisfaction. Because hers, she realized as he groaned and clutched her and caught her up close, before he drove her down into the bed again with the force of his finishing with her, his release a startlingly hot flood in her, was as imaginary as her image of joy or real pleasure in their bargain had been.

"It will be better," he said after he'd gotten his breath back, "it will improve," he said as he rolled up on his elbows to look down at her. "You can get up and wash if you'd like," he suggested when he saw the glint of tear tracks on her cheeks. "It's natural for it to take time. You'll see, it will be better for us," he lied.

Because as she left him in the aftermath of his hard-won meager pleasure, he decided that it was a great pity, and he was sorry for it, but it would never do. He wanted love freely given, with laughter, and had no desire to continue to bed a victim. He often liked to pass the whole of the night in pleasure, but now nothing would induce him to touch more than her shoulder when she eventually crept back to bed. He eyed her high hard breasts and neat bottom with regret. Too bad, he thought sleepily, thinking of ways he could free himself from their bargain at the least cost to her, for he'd hopes . . . But then, all his hopes had come to nothing, hadn't they?

She knew she'd failed him, and was more unhappy about that than worried for her future, because it never occurred to her that he'd be so displeased as to abandon her. He'd had his pleasure, hadn't he? She'd heard, seen, and felt it. What more did a man want than what she'd reluctantly given, after all? It was the reluctance, she decided, as she gave herself over to sleep, that she'd have to correct.

He was kind to her in the morning. Patient and friendly, and distant, and for the second time since she'd first met him, she knew a real fear of him. This newly cool and polite attitude seemed entirely wrong and misplaced now, after he'd been so close as her own skin to her, sharing her breaths, after he'd actually been in her body with her last night. So her hands paused as she did up her new gown, and for the first time she wondered if he'd tell her to leave. As she ate breakfast she began to wonder how he'd say it. When they'd done, and he'd paced about the room and glanced at the watch he held, she wondered how soon it would be.

"Tris and Jamie should be coming any moment now," he commented pleasantly. "I'd best be going down."

She smiled, and instantly turned to close an already closed door to the wardrobe so he'd not see how tremulous her smile had become. Because for all it was a bad profession she'd got herself into, and with all that she was sure it was better to be done with the whole business of caring for the strange pleasures of his hard body, she was now acutely aware that she'd failed. Above and beyond her fear for the future was the realization that she'd failed both him and herself.

"Come along," he said gently, wondering if she were so revolted with him that she could bear his presence no more in the day than she could in the night now. "Or aren't you coming?"

"You want me to come?" she asked in amazement.

"If you'd like," he said, and the sudden light in her dark eyes so enhanced her that he knew regret again for how soon they'd be parting.

But the light in Jamie Beauchamp's eyes when he first saw Mary as they came into the parlor of the

Peacock went a long way to banishing Gideon's sorrow. Even as he saw Jamie struggle to compose his face and conceal his transparent feelings, Gideon was thinking of how well it would do, after all. Jamie was fickle, to be sure, no more constant than could be expected of the youth he resembled, and that youthfulness was as false as his protestations of constancy would prove to be. He fell in love every changing of the moon, and he'd seen his share of them, Gideon thought, for despite what he looked like, Jamie was of an age with himself. Still, he was kind and generous, and Gideon had never heard any of his mistresses speak ill of him—indeed, their only complaints had been that he grew bored with them too quickly. He'd be good for little Mary, and would see her well taken care of when he was done with her, even as Gideon would. Between the two of them, she'd show a handsome profit. So Gideon wore a warm smile when he greeted his two friends, for they'd relieved his mind and lightened his spirits. But not for very long.

"Are you mad?" he thundered as he arose from the table where he'd seated himself, after Tristram finished speaking.

But although Jamie's blue eyes grew as wide as Mary's became at the sight of the huge red-haired man looming over the table, one hand on his sword hilt, Tristram Jones merely sat, tilted his head back, looked down his long nose at his friend, and then waved a languid hand at him.

"Oh, do be seated, Gideon," he said. "Look you, Jamie, at the ingratitude of the man. Ah, but maybe it isn't that at all. Do you think it's because he doesn't think his hair looks well enough? Perhaps he wonders if a week is long enough to have a wig made up to match his royal Highness's? But those jet curls of Charles's are his own! What a quandary. Still, we can but try. Do you think your wigmaker will take him on today, Jamie? Will that do, Gideon?" he asked innocently, as Gideon stood rigid with anger and looked down at him with eyes cold as blue death.

"What do you think ails the fellow, Jamie?" Tristram continued blandly. "Here we come, fresh from an audience with his king, who's panting for his presence—he's got an audience at Whitehall Palace within a week, his sovereign adores him so, it took all my arts of persuasion to make him even wait so long to see his beloved Gideon Hawkes again—and he glowers at us for it! Or is it his doublet he's worried about? Outdated, yes, but Charles will forgive that, or take it for the new style on the Continent, which would be even better," Tristram continued guilelessly. "Although Charles will forgive him anything now . . ." He stopped only as Gideon broke in at last, speaking on a long exhalation, as though he'd taken his temper firmly in check and was letting out his anger even as he slowly sat again and spoke.

"Will Charles forgive me the death of one of his favorites too, do you think?" he asked. "No, I won't challenge you, Tris, although I'd gladly have run you through the heart a moment past. I see you meant it for the best. But I'll never go to beg Charles for what is . . . was mine. You ought to have saved your breath. You almost lost it forever there, at that," he added on a small laugh, as he shook his head ruefully. "I'truth, Tris, you almost did."

"Aye, but you'll lose your head if you don't show up at Whitehall now," Tristram said comfortably, "because you're expected next week, and when a man's summoned by his king, he goes, or pays a handsome, or, as in your case, an unhandsome—excuse me, Mistress Mary, but I don't share your enthusiasm for the fellow's face—price for it. I hear they boil the heads in salt now, to keep the crows at bay, but that won't improve your looks much, I think.

"Seriously, Gideon," he said quietly, "I told him all, and he was all ablaze with anger—at himself. He

never knew the godly Puritan Squire Hawkes to be
your father: 'Never say the Roundheaded rogue was
sire to my red-headed friend Gideon, 'Od's fish!' he
cried. 'What's to do?' And he'll take the week to think
of what's to do, my friend, and do it right, and then he
wants to see you. And what Charles wants, he does
get, whatever your pride wants, Gideon.''

"You may get Ivyclose back again," Jamie said eagerly, as Gideon shrugged, for it was a desire so strong
he dared not speak or even think of it seriously again,
for he didn't believe he could bear to lose his heart's
love twice. Instead, he chose to speak carelessly of it,
to Mary, using the excuse of answering the questions
she didn't dare to put to him that were clear to see in
her eyes.

"My home," he explained, "was given to another
while I was gone abroad. My father was a Puritan—"

"Oh, was he really?" Tristram asked, knowing that
the thing had to be talked out now if his friend were to
come to terms with it well enough to be able to bargain with the king later.

Gideon laughed and began to speak of his father,
and then Tristram joined in, and Jamie as well, and
soon the three men were talking freely about Gideon's
father, Ivyclose, and everything else Gideon had lost.
As they spoke, Mary listened. She learned as much
from Gideon's eyes as she did from his words, for she
began to know him well enough now to know that his
silence was as deceptive as a footpad's in an alley—it
concealed his plans and violence of feelings as well as
his pain.

All men had to love something. She wouldn't believe that a man capable of such tenderness and consideration to a girl he'd found in the street could lack
the ability, and since he'd nothing to love in that terrible family of his, perhaps it all had gone into the
bricks and mortar of the home surrounding him. None
of his gentle words in the night, or his touches, or any

of the presents he'd given her softened her heart so much as the softened look she saw in his eyes when he spoke of Ivyclose. He'd loved this Ivyclose of his every bit as much as she'd loved her home, her father, and all her brothers combined. And he'd lost it. And he still grieved for it.

This, she suddenly saw, made him, who'd seemed so invulnerable, as much a victim of fate as she herself was. She was ashamed as she realized that for all his kindness to her, she'd never offered any to him. Now she remembered that he'd come to her beaten and battered—his bruises were only now healing—and yet she'd only feared for herself. It was hardly fair. For all he was a man, and a strong, wealthy one, he was, it turned out, only another orphan of the world. And she'd never thought to ask, never tried to comfort him.

But she could. There was something he wanted of her; however distasteful she found it, it was a simple thing. Although she'd no experience, she sensed that with another man it mightn't have been. Or if it was, she didn't doubt he'd have already gone on his way, leaving her with only the price of a day's food and the promise of even more degrading nights with other men. Gideon Hawkes had given her more than food, a roof over her head, and new gowns; he'd given her kindness and a position in life, however uncomfortable she found it. She owed him something for that. She owed him more if only for the same sweet charity's sake that he'd shown her. He needed some happiness. She resolved to try to give him some.

At first, she knew, she could only give him the sort he asked from her, but time might bring her other, worthier ways to repay his kindness. She'd try this very night, she resolved, by trying to forget her distaste and remember his need. And she soon became too involved with planning how, to realize that the thought brought no shrinking of her soul now, and no troubling to her spirit.

"Well, then and I'll do it," Gideon said at last, "although if I have to dress up like you two peacocks, I'd just as soon send him a letter. Sooth, Tris, if you'd more lace about you, I'd take you for a bed hanging."

"Thank you," his friend said pleasantly, "I like it too. Are you afraid you won't look fine as Mistress Mary? She'll charm them, especially if she wears something as lovely as that new gown. Passing fair, Mistress Monk," Tristram said, smiling, "you look wonderfully well in it."

"Indeed, you do," Jamie said at once.

"Thank you," she answered, but then added quietly, not laughing at the bitter nonsense of imagining she'd ever be asked to court, "but I'll not be going."

"Indeed?" Gideon asked. "And why not?"

He watched her amazement and then the dawning of her transparent happiness indulgently. He could afford this last little bit of pleasure for her. And too, he thought, a visit to court might win her an even better protector than Jamie.

They dined together, they laughed frequently, drank heartily, and the only diminution of Mary's happiness came when she worried about being so glad. She'd been grieving only lately, then she'd sunk so low and been so dishonored she couldn't understand how she could be so happy now. But she was young, and alive, and safe at last. Even with death all around her, it was behind her, and she'd been taught that life was for the living.

All she told Gideon when they went up the stair was how happy he'd made her by letting her go to court, leaving out the part about how happy he himself had made her, for fear of undoing it by naming it. And he, who'd asked Tristram and Jamie to wait for him until he got her safely to their room, only grinned and thought how young she was, and how drunk he'd gotten her, for all he was pleased to see her merry.

"What, you're going?" she demanded as he turned to the door to their room after he'd taken her there.

"Mistress Mary, you're reeling, my pretty," he laughed, and smiled down at her when she came to him, her chin up and her eyes filled with reproach and something he didn't recognize in their dark shining depths.

"Only with happiness," she said softly, so soberly he knew it for a truth. "Will you leave me now, Gideon?" she asked, stepping closer, her hand on his sleeve, the look in her eyes becoming something he'd seen in other women's, and had given up on finding in hers.

He touched her cheek, her hair. "Sweeting," he said gently, "our lessons haven't gone that well, you needn't thank me in this way, I do understand."

"Indeed, how can you when I do not?" she asked.

He bent to kiss her, just a gentle good night, and found more on her lips than that, and so gave more in return. This time he found her as warm and welcoming as he'd thought she might be, and when he took her to the bed, he discovered her wondering, hesitant touch as enchanting as it was exciting. And she found for the first time that remembering who this man was made it possible for her to forget to be ashamed at what he was doing with her, and thinking only that it was he who was doing it made it better than endurable.

No, it had been more than that, she thought when he was done. It might've been the drink, it might've been his skill, but she'd actually forgotten to think anything for a few minutes there at the end, and in those moments it had been more than gratitude, if less than lust, but very different, very nice, and almost something more.

She fell asleep in his arms, content, although all she'd gained was a loss of fear.

He smiled in the dark and held her close. She'd surprised and delighted him, even if she hadn't entirely satisfied him, for he'd been more considerate than impassioned, more gentle than gratified. But there was time now, and if he wasn't sated, he was at least pleased—with her, as well as with his latest turn of luck. And so he lay awake for hours, his body lulled at last, his mind astir again, thinking, planning, with renewed excitement, what his future might hold.

"I do believe," the beautifully dressed Cavalier said, on a yawn, "that our friend Gideon's found better things to occupy himself with. It's been an hour, and I believe we can find better and similar things, as well."

His friend sat staring into his empty mug of ale, as he'd done for the past hour as they'd waited for Gideon to return.

"Thou shalt not covet thy neighbor's whore," Tristram said merrily, and then, seeing the scowl he'd won for it, and noting how badly it suited that fresh and guileless face, and remembering how that innocent face mirrored his friend's soul, if not his years, he added, "Sooth, Jamie, he did nothing ill. I've known him long enough to know he's no rapist."

"But I'd have sworn he showed no interest at all in her tonight. I thought him distant with her when he wasn't ignoring her."

"Not all men show their hearts on their sleeves," Tristram said lightly. "Have you ever seen me languish half so much as you do, for instance . . . ah, but who could?" he laughed.

"But though you conceal it, you've a heart," his friend said on a scowl.

"So does he," Tristram said.

"Does he, I wonder?" Jamie said softly.

"You wonder too much. Take care you don't wonder once too often," Tristram cautioned, before he relented and said with care, "Ah, Jamie, you know better. His heart wouldn't ache so much if he lacked a full one, and he's shown nothing but kindness to you, even in his sorrow. Don't begrudge him a little pleasure because you've looked enviously at where he's taking it. Yes, you should look abashed. But cheer up, because remember, if he gets his heart's desire, you may well get yours the sooner as well. He only consoles himself now. But can you see him carrying his little brown street sparrow off to ornament his greatest love—Ivyclose? Aye, just so. So just bide your time.

"Now then, as for tonight, there's that new blond at Mother Bennet's they're all talking about, the one with the intriguing mole, isn't there? Shall we see just how intriguing it is?"

His friend looked up, smiling, his candid blue eyes clear and expectant again, but it wasn't all because of the new blond at Mother Bennet's, and they both knew it.

# 5

She hesitated. She stood with her skirt held in her hands so that the hem cleared her toes, and she'd already ducked her head to one side, about to enter the coach, and yet she hesitated.

Gideon sighed. She'd taken great care with her dressing and had taken his compliments with pretty grace. Was her spirit failing her now?

"You look very fine, Mistress Monk," he whispered as he bent to her ear, for he didn't want her publicly disgraced, and the coachman was staring down at her, even as the footman was as he held the door open and his arm out so she could hold it as she climbed the short stair to the coach.

"Oh, thank you," she said distractedly as she took in such a deep breath he could see her bosom swell with it, and held it as she held her head high and went up the steps. It wasn't until she was seated, and he'd swung into the coach to sit beside her, that he noticed she still looked white-faced. The pallor ill-suited her dark complexion, and detracted from her new splendor.

"The gown is a rich dusky rose, just as the clothier said," he said casually, "But I don't think you really need to have a green face to do it justice."

"I'm sorry," she said at once, looking at him as though she'd just seen him. "It's only that it's hard for me."

"I understand." He smiled at her. "It can be impressive. But only in looks. Remember, the people at court aren't half so fine as they look. And they don't act even half so fine as that. That's the point. Child, if they see you're frightened, some of them will be unkind. Come, more spirit, you're a brave little person, aren't you?"

"Oh, but it's not the court," she said, turning to him, "Of course, I expect to be impressed by everything there—but I'm not very frightened, because I think they won't notice me much at all. It's the coach, Gideon," she said in a low voice, biting her lip as she felt the carriage swaying as the coachman clambered up to his seat, and the footman stepped up behind. "I haven't ridden in many. And I've never liked to . . . it's like getting into an eggshell, isn't it, and hoping the horses won't set it spinning, and won't . . ." She paused and looked into the darkened interior as she held her breath, for the wheels started moving as they began the ride to Whitehall. ". . . shatter us apart," she whispered then, falling still.

Of course, he remembered, while there were many more coaches than had been in town before he'd left, so many that the bargemen were getting angry at the loss of business, a trademan's daughter wouldn't have occasion to travel about in them very much. He gazed at her pinched face and saw how worry leached the soft blush from her cheek, making her look older and plainer, shrunken and ill. So he put his arms around her and pulled her into his lap, and held her there until he could feel her heartbeat slow. He thought she'd pull away when some time had passed, for no woman he knew would suffer such mishandling of her gown on the way to an important social event. But she only sighed and nestled next to his chest, as though he could hold the "eggshell" together if it were threatened, as though his arms around her were all the assurance of safety she needed. And so he smiled, and settled back, and held her that way all the way to the palace at Whitehall.

It was as well that she hadn't watched their passage through London, because riding under the gate, and then seeing the palace in its entirety as they approached it might well have unsettled her, despite her denial. It stretched out, sprawled along the Embankment like an indolent, luxurious thought in the mind of its regal occupant, and there were so many doors and entries, courtyards and pathways to it, she'd have worried that they'd never find the right way. But the coachman Tristram had sent for them knew it perfectly, and too soon Gideon released her, patting her on her bottom with a wicked leer as he did so, before he stepped from the coach and awaited her exit, his usual closed expression in place. Then he offered her his arm and the one word, "Faith," before he led her into the palace at Whitehall, where he would introduce her to his friend, her king.

She'd told him nothing less than the truth as she'd known it. She was plain Mary Monk, despite her new and lavish gown and the patronage of Gideon Hawkes, gentleman. Never a beauty, nor ever familiar with anyone rich and titled, she never expected any of them to pay her any mind, so her only fear had been for the ride to the palace in the terrifying coach. Or so she'd thought. As she walked with Gideon down the corridors of power, she understood that she'd only allowed herself fear of the ride so as to distract her from the true terror she faced now.

She could feel the weight of office, of privilege, of unimaginable power and influence weighing down on her head as she walked under the great hanging chandeliers, beneath the towering and gilded ceilings. All round herself she caught glimpses of people dressed so finely that her new and glorious rose gown seemed as plain as her oldest washday costume, and it took some time for her to realize that half those people who shamed her with their elegance were footmen. She'd never seen such opulence. Although she kept her eyes ahead and caught only glimpses of it, she'd never felt so insignificant and thus conspicuous because of it. She kept close to Gideon, as if she could shelter beneath his magnificence and be absorbed into his aura of confidence.

He walked with his usual long-limbed grace, his movements no less fluid than the fall of the silken folds of his cape as it draped over his shoulder. His clothes were in all the colors of a peacock's today, and yet they were overwhelmed by the blaze of his hair. But every blatant hue was subdued by the keen blue bite of his imperious stare. Truly, she'd never appreciated him, she thought as she stepped silently at his side, until this day when she tried to fade into his shadow so as to escape scrutiny by those of his kind.

At first she didn't recognize the two magnificent Cavaliers who accosted them, and she literally shrank back in alarm until she heard their voices clear, and saw Jamie's clear, honest blue eyes looking down at her with welcome and admiration. He and Tristram were gotten up in raiment so replete with bows and ribbons and swatches of fine lace that she was glad their plumed hats had been set to rakish tilts over their smiling faces, so she could make that her excuse for not recognizing them at once.

"That," Tristram said merrily, "and the fact you're too polite to mention, which is that Jamie, for reasons best known to himself, is wearing a sheepskin on his head today."

"Sheep don't have golden curls, unless they're fresh from Jason's ship," Gideon commented, "S'blood Jamie, what *is* that thing?"

"It's the latest thing," Jamie said unhappily. "You

mean you don't like it?" he asked, but he looked to
Mary as he did, and looked so woeful that she immediately protested how much she admired it. And she
did, although it overwhelmed her almost as much it
did Jamie. Because she'd been so glad to see him
she'd not noticed the huge, long, curling bright blond
wig he wore. Which was, she decided now, a measure
of how amazingly nervous she must have been. But
once she got used to the shock of it, she decided it
made him look young and almost angelic, and so she
told him, to his slight smile and his friends' hoots of
laughter.

Once they'd begun laughing, the world returned to
its proper shape, and no matter where she was, Mary
felt comfortable as she stood looking up at the three
handsome gentlemen.

Then, one by one, ladies and gentlemen of the court
came to greet them, and one by one they eyed Mary,
but with eyes she'd never seen before. She'd seen
women pricing poultry in the market, narrowing their
eyes and poking fingers into feathered breasts to see if
they'd be getting young tender stock and their money's worth per pound. And those eyes had been kinder.
She'd seen men eyeing women in the taverns those
nights she'd waited for enough courage and hunger to
step out of the shadows, seen them as they fingered
their coins and speculated about the women's bodies
and looked into their faces to judge what they seemed
willing to do to earn them. And those eyes had been
less lustful and knowing.

The women of every age, size, and condition smiled,
simpered, jested, or teased, but undeniably, they looked
at Gideon with invitation. And at Mary with appraisal,
and then not at all again. The men never left off
looking at her, as though by staring they could tell
why Gideon had chosen her, and he laid constant
claim to that fact by the fact of his arm about her
waist. She'd passed her seventeen years in the city of

London, one of the largest, she'd been told, on the earth. Almost a half-million people, they said, lived here. But never before had she seen so many people so apparently concerned with her. Nor ever, of course, had she felt that so many wondered at just what she and Gideon did in their bed together. Because she knew that as she was not half so gloriously beautiful as most of the ladies of the court, nor rich, nor famous in any way, and yet he held her with proud possession, as though she were worth much to him, they all must imagine that what she did in the depths of that feather bed must be unique, and so astonishing. She very much wished she hadn't come.

As did Gideon, she knew, for his face was growing more impassive and his answers to questions more curt by the moment. Tristram and Jamie noticed his mood, and glanced to him warily every so often. Indeed, Mary thought, who wouldn't see his displeasure—except for those thick-headed women who were trying to charm him out of his lowering mood and succeeding only in lowering it further.

"At five, you said," Gideon said flatly when they'd been left alone for a moment. He turned his back to the room to signal his inaccessibility and so cornered Jamie and skewered him with his stare. " 'Tis half-past and more now."

"He's late in all things today, Gideon," Jamie exclaimed. "He's had a rigorous day. Up at dawn to walk in the park, then tennis, then riding, then a set-to with Castlemaine, they say, because she saw his new interest, who's years younger than herself. Then a conference with the queen and one with the council and an hour alone with the new interest, and now one with some gentleman he said he must see. But he said to hold you, Gideon, and so I will, if I must, because he charged me with it," Jamie explained staunchly, if nervously, looking young and defenseless as the sheep

Gideon had mentioned, his eyes wide beneath his beautifully curling fair wig.

Gideon said nothing, but Mary could hear his sigh as he turned back to the room again, his face set hard enough to discourage a couple who'd begun to approach him, so that they veered and pretended to be surprised at finding an old acquaintance they'd just left moments before, instead. Mary saw that sudden instant contraction shiver across his tight cheek, and knew he was even more unhappy than he allowed to show now. It was no easy thing for him to come to this meeting; his hopes were very high, and he'd tried to keep them low. He hadn't mentioned the matter to her again since the night it had been brought up. But from his distraction ever since then, she knew that he'd thought of little else.

Then she saw his body stiffen, and his face, as though despite himself, begin to soften into a small smile. She looked to the direction of his stare and saw what must be the king—Charles Stuart, her sovereign lord, ruler of all her known universe—and he looked so exactly as he should that for a second she was too stunned to sink into the curtsy she knew she must.

He was as tall as Gideon, but dark as night to Gideon's glowing sunset. His skin was Gypsy dark, just as they all said, and darker still were his lustrous midnight curls that framed that long, long-nosed sardonic face. His heavy-lidded eyes were darkest yet, and as they settled their gaze upon Gideon, the full dusky red lips beneath his dark mustache curved into a smile of sheerest satisfaction. His smile was that of a man who'd just been deliciously kissed, and Mary realized, as the force of his personality dropped her into a deep curtsy as he approached, that there would probably always be something in his face that spoke of lazy gratification of a sort she'd never have recognized before her recent experiences with Gideon.

"Gideon Hawkes: Rogue, Puppy, Love—Gideon,

my dear fellow," the king said as Gideon swept into an extravagant bow, "you've been too long in coming. Aside from the fact that we've missed you, see the pother you've caused me."

"Majesty," Gideon said as he rose and his eyes were level with his king's, "that's nothing to the one you've caused me."

Mary drew in her breath sharply as the king struck Gideon lightly on the shoulder, and the company around them laughed.

"Aye, 'tis Gideon himself," Charles said on a laugh. "Bold and saucy and courteous with it, be thankful you've a neck too thick for my axmen to try. Welcome home, Gideon," he said more simply. "I've a score to settle with you, my friend, and you've given me sleepless nights deciding how to go about it. But I've wasted my time feeling sorry for you, haven't I? Just look at the pretty way you've passed the time while your king was tossing and turning to far less interesting effect, I'd wager. Lady," the king said, dropping his deep voice to a purr as he smiled down at Mary.

Her heart leapt into her throat as she looked up into those knowing eyes. She looked down at once, and then up—to find him gazing at her with such intent she scarcely knew where to look.

"May I present Mistress Mary Monk, Majesty? No," Gideon said dryly, "no relation to your warrior, General Monck. But a close and peaceful companion of mine."

There was only the slightest stress on the word "mine," and it was acknowledged by only the slightest flicker in the king's slumberous eyes, but then he smiled again, and breathed, "Pity, that. Do let me know if you tire of peace, Gideon. I've always had a partiality to nut-brown maids, you know. Why, they're the only ones who don't make me feel like a Moor," he said lightly. "Not like my pretty Lucinda, here," he said, and gave a nod to a fair-haired girl who'd been standing nearest to him.

She came to the king at the mention of her name, and smiled up at him eagerly. A pretty enough maid, Mary thought critically, but not beautiful, with wan skin and a slender body, yet with full enough breasts that Mary noticed—because, to her astonishment and absolute shock, the king casually slipped one long hand down into Lucinda's bodice to fondle one of them as the girl stood smiling at his side.

Although she wanted to look anywhere else, Mary found she could not, and was beyond mere gladness when that lace-draped dark long-fingered hand gave up toying with the white breast it held and left it, and the king's deep voice, with more than a hint of laughter in it, said, "But you didn't come today to meet Lucinda, any more than I'll warrant you wanted to come to meet with me either, did you, Gideon? Come then, into my chamber, you—and your two companions. 'Od's fish, Gideon, I envy you your friends as much as I do your peaceful dark girl, you know. Come along," he said, laying an arm about Gideon's neck, turning him so that they might walk close and speak together, with no one else in that crowded room the wiser as to what they'd say.

But Gideon paused. He smiled back to Mary and told her to wait for his return. Which caused the king to chuckle, and say, distinct for anyone's ears, "As modest as she's tiny. And still innocent in many ways. Refreshing. Ah, fortunate Gideon, in friends as in lovers, as always, eh?"

"Oh, lucky, indeed, Majesty," Gideon said softly, "as you well know."

Charles stopped in his tracks and frowned before he gave Gideon's shoulder a hard shake and continued walking with him. "Vexatious fellow," he said. "Come along, I've been busy at your work this past week. I'll put things right, see if I don't."

But when they entered the small chamber where Charles led them, it was Gideon who stopped short and stared at the man awaiting them there.

There was no mistaking that even-featured fair face or the long fair hair; even though he'd seen him from afar, Gideon had a sailor's vision, and would have known him anywhere. If the memory of the man who'd usurped his home hadn't printed itself into his mind's eye clear from the moment he'd spied him, the pain he'd suffered a moment after had driven it in deep. But it was a pleased and eager young face that turned to him, and he was given a smile and a bow, and no blows this time.

"Sir Philip Southern, I make you known to my good friend Gideon Hawkes," the king said softly, as Gideon recovered himself and sketched a bow.

Charles walked to his chair and gestured to two others for Tristram and Jamie. But he indicated one chair and motioned both Gideon and Sir Philip toward it.

"Now, what's to do?" the king said whimsically, as both Gideon and Sir Philip hesitated. "One chair, two fine men. 'Od's body, but it's a problem, isn't it? Very like another that's been vexing me. Sir Philip's father was one of my supporters who beggared himself in my cause, whose home was blasted out from under him because of it. A proud house, staved in, like the man who'd built it. So I gave his son a fine estate to replace it when one became available, and there he's lived for three good years.

"And here's Gideon Hawkes, who aided me first when he was only—gad, all those years ago!—a babe, with only fifteen years to his credit. 'Are you a friend to Caesar?' we asked him that dark night, 'Aye, always, I am,' he answered, and I'll swear his voice was still changing as he did. But so he was. Only a boy, and yet he rode on the high road to Brighton before me, searching the shadows for soldiers, prepared to do battle with them for my safe passage to the coast.

" 'Always' it was. Can I forget how he paid for my rooms that embarrassing night in Brussels, when I hadn't the funds to get out—and then again in Bruges, when I hadn't the funds to get into a bed. A king without a country needs generous friends, and Gideon Hawkes never kept accounts, nor ever stinted with his life or his funds in my cause. And yet, how do I repay him?

"Just so," the king sighed, "by giving his home to Sir Philip. But how should I know some plaguey old Puritan who'd turned up his toes was the villainous papa my Gideon was escaping from all those years ago on the Brighton road?"

Charles turned and gestured his helplessness with two hands. Not for the first time, Gideon thought what a loss to the theater the world had suffered when England regained her king.

"What's to do?" Charles sighed. "Shall I have one sit on the other's lap?" and as the men in the room laughed, the king smiled and said, silencing them with his words, "Exactly—or something like. Oh, I've thought long and hard this week, for all I've played hard too. Listen, you two, and hear me out. I think I've a solution with honor and much good in it. But I'll not command you to it, only to listen to it. Now then.

"Sir Philip, did you note the little lady I sat you next to last night?"

"How could I not?" the young man replied, sighing. "I'd been staring at her all day."

"She doesn't speak much," Charles commented idly.

"She doesn't have to," Sir Philip said, the look in his eye reminding Gideon of the one Jamie had whenever he was in the throes of a new infatuation.

"Indeed not," Charles answered, "not with twenty-five hundred a year, a fine estate in the Midlands, a face like an angel, a form to tempt the devil to piety—

and she a lonely widow this twelvemonth. Widow of an old man too," he added, as Sir Philip's eye brightened even further.

"I scoured the land for one such as she," Charles said with a luxurious sigh, "and summoned her to court just this week—as I brought you, Sir Philip.

"Now then, Gideon," the king continued, "when you visited Ivyclose last," he said as Gideon's jaw tightened, "do you recall seeing a lady there?"

Gideon only nodded; he wasn't a man to speak his heart, and so he left unsaid what it said: as if he'd ever forget. Her fair face was firmer in his inner sight now than his own image was in his looking glass.

"She's Sir Philip Southern's sister: Celeste," the king mused, as Gideon tolled the name like a bell in his mind. "Celeste. Unwed at three-and-twenty, beautiful and virtuous, but with an overvigilant, doting brother," he added with a great regretful sigh and the tilt of a brow toward Sir Philip, "and so at Ivyclose, protected and sequestered at Ivyclose, where he, cruel fellow, vows she'll remain until she's wed. . . ." The king looked pointedly at the two men and the empty chair.

He smiled.

"So neatly done it terrifies me, sire," Tristram said with great admiration.

"Just so," the king said, and then, frowning, added, "Sit in each other's laps, you dolts . . . don't you see it? The widow needs a strong young man to take her to the marriage bed, and take her estate as well. It has more acres than Ivyclose—don't be greedy, my lad, no man needs two estates, unless he's your king."

As dawning realization made Sir Philip's face split into a grin, Charles continued, "And have you any objection to taking a beautiful, virtuous maid to wive when you take Ivyclose back, Gideon?"

"I do think we ought to name you Solomon, sire,"

Tristram said with awe when the king had done and only sat watching Gideon's growing perceptible joy.

"Don't overdo," Charles said with laughter. "Such immodesty pains me—it was mostly your idea, you mad rogue, and I bless you for it. Well, what say you, gentlemen?"

Gideon was smiling despite himself, despite the fact that he was afraid to give in to so much glee as he felt rising. To have Ivyclose back, and with it such a wife as he'd dreamed upon?

"I say it's wonderful," Sir Philip cried, and stuck out a hand to Gideon, but even as Gideon, smiling so fully that his two friends grinned to see it, put out his own hand to take it, Sir Philip hesitated and drew back.

"Ah . . . but," he said, as Tristram muttered, "How I hate 'ah, buts.' "

"Only one thing, only one little thing," the young man said tentatively. "I know I'm a fool for it, I know it, but Celeste's younger than I by only a few years, and I have so much fellow feeling for her . . . and the plain fact is, as everyone knows, I dote on her. And s'truth," he blurted, growing red, "I know she'll like Gideon Hawkes, from what you say, why shouldn't she? . . . she's a good gentle girl, not one to go against her brother—or her king, of course—but . . . but . . . ah, sire, I cannot bear to see her weep. Can I say, 'Wonderful, I'll do it . . . if Celeste agrees'?"

"Of course," Charles said, chuckling. "Why should she not? For if the red-headed rogue don't charm her to an inch, she's no mortal maid."

"But if he doesn't?" Sir Philip asked hesitantly, whether for fear for his sister or worry that he'd miss out on the widow, no one could say. "Will she go shamed, forced out of what I promised her was to be her home for so long as she lived as reward for her patience during our long exile?"

"Sooth, I'm no monster," Gideon cried. "Take your

widow and let your sister keep Ivyclose if she hates me."

"She's given her heart to no other, has she?" Tristram asked at once.

"No, she's free," Sir Philip said immediately.

"Then your work's cut out for you, Gideon," Jamie put in happily.

"So it is," Gideon said, smiling at the thought of such joyful occupation, as Sir Philip strode forward and the two men grasped each other's hands firmly.

"Well?" Charles asked, looking offended. "Come now, gentlemen, I see a place for you to sit, get on with it."

And laughing, Gideon sat in the chair and pulled a surprised Sir Philip down into his lap, as all the men in the room began to laugh like boys.

Mary knew a real moment of panic as she stood alone and watched Gideon leave. And so was beyond pleased when a merry-looking older woman who'd been in the king's company smiled at her and beckoned her over to her side. She stood with a group of women, all of them lavishly gowned, immaculately got up, with such an assortment of fanciful beauty patches on their smooth and handsome faces that to Mary it seemed that there'd been some strange pox that had turned them all beautiful even as it had marked them.

The woman introduced herself at once as Mrs. Moll Fletcher and then introduced Mary round to all the others, whose names, some familiar, some not, Mary didn't recollect a moment later. But she'd never forget their talk. Because after they'd asked her some questions to do with where she'd been born and raised, they only wanted to know how long she'd known Gideon. When she answered shyly, honestly, "It's been, best I can estimate, a week and three days," they seemed deflated.

"Oh, early days," one red-haired beauty said angrily.

Even as Mary wondered why that should disturb the lady, another put in, with just as much chagrin, "And he's known to be constant. Look to see him next spring, if you're lucky, Alice—that is, if you're not breeding another for Chartworth by then," she added with a twist to her words that made the other woman look at her sharply and retort, "At least Chartworth breeds. Hawley's pleasures don't bear fruit, as we all know, unless you've taken to carrying babes in your teeth, Henrietta."

It was lucky their laughter covered over Mary's gasp as she finally understood the gist of the comment. But she forgot it when another woman, looking down at her with avid interest, asked quickly, "But who cares for that? Tell me, Mary, is it true about Gideon Hawkes? They say he's got a monstrous big tool—just like Old Rowley's" ("She means the king's," Mrs. Fletcher put in laughingly, seeing Mary's expression and recognizing the incomprehension, if not the disbelief, she saw there), "which is why he admires him so—is't true?" the other woman finished saying.

"Aye," another lady put in eagerly, "I heard from Cat, who had it from Elizabeth Grange, who had Edward Royce, who passed three years there, that the ladies at the French court reckoned it formidable. And he's surpassing good with it too, they say, no here-and-gone fellow, either, but able to stay the course through the night. Is't true, Mary?"

But as she was still off-balance from the first jest, this completely boggled Mary and she could do nothing but gape, hope she'd misheard, and stammer something about how she couldn't say.

"Or won't," Mrs. Fletcher said, nudging Mary in the ribs. "Sly boots. But who can blame her?" she asked merrily. "Only a week in his bed, and not fool enough to brag up a storm of competition for him. We'll ask again in a month. The sweetest cakes, and lovers, grow stale by then," she said to their laughter.

Reprieved, Mary was allowed to remain still and listen to gossip such as she'd never heard before.

It seemed no one who played at love at court—and that seemed to be all that were at this court—minded discussing the finest details of her play at all. In fact, when the heat in her face died down long enough for her to think coolly, Mary began to wonder if they didn't take up lovers only so that they could leap out of bed to report on their experiences the moment they were through there. Because in the course of that hour, she learned far more about the act of love than Gideon had taught her.

She wondered if she'd ever be able to meet a "Lord Devlin" without thinking about his "crooked shaft" that the ladies all giggled about, or curtsy to the "Sir Wills" without wondering about that odd mole on his male part, the one they all said looked like a fish's eye. Or even ever greet the king again with composure now that she'd such a detailed and perfect word picture of his privy member painted for her by several of the women. And when she'd heard about this gentleman's lack of courtesy, and that one's "rabbity" habits, and another's peculiar methods, she found that for all she wished never to clap an eye on a male again, she heartily appreciated Gideon, and longed for him to come and rescue her from this too convivial company. Because not only was she disgusted by their chatter, it frightened her. She worried if she was expected to be like them. And worried far more about whether she might become so someday.

She was genuinely happy when it seemed they'd forgotten about her and moved on to another part of the room without looking back to see if she followed. Until she heard her name said very softly, and looked up to find two gentlemen staring at her with far more pleasure than that simple act should have given them.

One was a young gentleman dressed in wondrous fine fashion: a willowy, too wan youth with a hollow chest all his lace couldn't disguise, shadowed eyes, and fine long curling hair that drifted about his thin, weary face. The other man was older, although not so old as to have had his strongly marked features so heavily bracketed by the deep lines he bore, and with dark thick eyebrows that quirked over deep-set black eyes.

"Pretty, indeed, wouldn't you say, Mobely?" the younger man asked as his overly brilliant eyes roved over Mary.

"Too pretty for Hawkes, by far," the other man agreed.

"Good day to you, sirs," Mary said firmly, backing up a step. Court might be new to her, as were so many experiences she'd had this day. But every market held mashers, and every good woman knew how to deal with them.

"Oh, no, Sweet Mary," the younger man said softly, "say rather: 'I give you good evening, masters.' "

And at that, she was afraid.

"What, speechless, a girl of such apparent spirit? I think that consorting with that brute must have made you forget your tongue, for fear of your teeth. I'd be kinder, and more generous," the younger man said teasingly in his high, light voice, as the older one watched, leering, although Mary thought, darting a look to him, it might have been that he couldn't help that, for he seemed to always look so. "Very generous," the younger man continued. "I could give you far more, and you'd enjoy it far more too . . ."

She might not have had a formal education, but no one would ever say that Mary Monk was slow to learn. Her distaste and coldness didn't bother these men, and she knew that her timidity would only encourage them. Because she'd been so small, her brothers had taught her some means of self-defense that could work with surprise to aid her, but she knew that an attempt at physical violence to them would look badly here, in this glittering court, no matter the provocation. Practical to the core, she knew it would go ill, too, with two of them to her one. She understood that the weapons she must use were ones that women of this world used. And so, remembering the ladies she'd just been speaking with, she looked at the young man with an expression of just such contempt, hauteur, and cruel humor as she'd seen on their faces as they'd told their tales of men's deficiencies in body and soul.

"*You*," she said, as even her voice took on the bitter, bright accents of the fine ladies she'd heard, "you, sir, could scarcely give me half so much as Gideon does . . . of anything."

Her words were greeted with smothered laughter, and she realized there'd been witnesses to their meeting. But though the onlookers were amused at her retort, the thin young man was livid. He'd grown paler and his lips twisted in a sneer. "Oh, you think not, little whore? I think you've much to learn—"

"But never from you, Rochester, didn't you hear her? Now," Gideon said as he came up behind Mary and put one hand on her shoulder and the other lightly at his own hip, on his sword hilt, "if you'd care to take some fencing lessons from me . . . why then, I'd be delighted. Now? Or tomorrow, before breakfast, so you can be buried by noon?"

The young man stepped back, even paler, looking like death himself that Mary had once seen sketched on a tombstone near to her mother's.

"I never . . . I was only toying with the girl, Hawkes," the young man stammered, backing until he heard the king's deep voice say, with a mixture of regret and amusement, "Hold, Gideon. I've not so many friends that I can lose them at such a clip. . . . Rochester—to your sword, you—to exile again for it. Have done with the lad, his tongue is quicker than his wit, betimes."

"As you will, sire," Gideon said, too recently made glad to be angry too long now.

"I won't fight him, then," the young Earl of Rochester promised, as someone in the interested crowd around them tittered at his sudden bravery, and the king himself grinned at his pet, this audacious overbred puppy that amused him so much.

The moment passed, and Mary would have gladly forgotten it if she hadn't heard Tristram comment, low to Gideon, "A bad enemy, Gideon, and now it will be worse."

"A good enemy, Tris," Gideon said with his usual economy, "is a contradiction in terms."

They stayed on at the court until evening came, and when the night's amusements were beginning, Gideon made his good-byes to his king, and then his friends, as Mary waited for him. They all seemed loath to see him go, but she saw one, a fair-haired, even-featured young man, rush to take Gideon's hand.

"I'll leave for home in the morning," he told Gideon earnestly, "and write to you soon after."

"It can never be too soon," Gideon promised with deep conviction as he walked him to a quiet corner to bid him a more private farewell.

They rode back to the Peacock in silence, Mary too busily thinking of her eventful day to worry about the coach, Gideon too busy musing about his tomorrows to notice her silence.

But they chatted at dinner, and when she asked him if he'd had a good audience with the king, venturing nothing more for fear of touching on something she wasn't supposed to ask, but so anxious to know about the outcome of his interview that she had to use every bit of her self-control to deny the questions that sprang to her lips, he smiled. Both at her forbearance and her tact.

"I've great hopes," he admitted. "It may all work out well, little Mary. I've a chance now, at least, to reclaim my home."

She was glad for him, and her face showed it. At that, he reached over the table and touched her cheek.

"Stay away from the Earl of Rochester, sweeting, he's a bad man."

"I didn't know who he was," she said, and then for the first time, as the full significance of it came to her, she grew red with shame, remembering what the ladies had said about the Earl of Rochester, and so suddenly understanding why her words had cut him so.

"Well?" Gideon said. "Out with it! It's no use, you've no face for secrets. What is it that you just tried to swallow that's choking you with laughter . . . and shame, I'll warrant."

There was no help for it. So much as she was embarrassed to speak about it, she wanted very much to share with Gideon, so she began to tell him, in the most roundabout terms she could dredge up, what the conversation of the ladies at court had been like.

"Oh, yes, I know," he said, laughing heartily, but then, she'd noticed he was much freer and easier now since he'd come back from Whitehall. "That's why I have as little to do with them as I can. Some men like having their measure taken," he said on a grin, "but I prefer mine to be a secret."

She couldn't resist that, and they laughed, and then she told him what the women had said about the Earl of Rochester's apparent deficiency, giggling uncontrollably over the term "little man" they'd used in both ways.

"Yes, but with a large store of spite, so beware of him, sweet," Gideon warned before he lost his somber expression, because indeed, he didn't seem able to hold it long tonight. Then he teased and prodded and encouraged her until she began to repeat all she'd heard, exactly, and in the tones she'd heard it, so it wouldn't seem to be herself saying such things. Their laughter grew so loud that other diners turned to stare at them.

"Upstairs," Gideon whispered, "and then tell me all about poor Danvers, 'a spotted dog,' indeed!"

Still laughing, they went up to their room together.

After she'd parroted all she could remember, her face grew still even as he still smiled.

"Gideon," she asked, suddenly shy again, "when men are together, do they speak of such things about their women?"

"Some," he said. "Not I."

Her expression didn't lighten, although his words relieved her. She gazed at him in the soft candlelight. All the things she'd heard today had made her ashamed of herself and Gideon and their pact—embarrassed at all the things that went forth between man and woman, for that matter. But this laughter tonight and the way he'd understood her emotions and shared them had made her curious to know more—if not about men, then about Gideon. She'd lost everything before she'd found him and so he'd become very important to her very quickly, but she still didn't know him well. Yet she'd cause to believe she was becoming important to him too. He'd always treated her with care, he'd saved her from the streets, and today he'd defended her at court and claimed her as his own before his king.

Her heart felt full of new gladness, her body, with new longing, if only for the reassurance of his touch. She'd not been with him for a week, because she'd had her courses, and he'd been either too kind or distracted to care. Now, incredibly boldly for her, she rose from her chair and walked to him, and when he looked up at her, she put her arms about his neck and sat in his lap.

"Gideon," she said, and only that, before she lost confidence and laid her forehead against his shoulder.

"Take care, sweeting," he said in a husky voice, "for what you start, I will finish. It has been a long while."

"I know," she said shyly, "but it was my time of month. But now it's not, and I did take a bath—again."

"Again?" he said with laughter and delight. "Again!

And all for me she braves the waves," he said as his arms tightened around her. "So then how can I do less? Let me show you a few things, Mistress Monk, so that you can have some conversation next time you go to court."

He showed her much, for aside from amusing himself by pointing out aspects of his strong male body and ridiculing it so that she couldn't feel shame for staring at it in the light, he showed her tenderness and patience.

"If it curved—here," he said as she watched with astonished fascination and suppressed excitement, "I suppose it would look like they say old Devlin's does. Here— like poor Howard's . . . and if it looked like this," he said as he hid what she'd been staring at completely between his muscled thighs, "like Rochester's."

She doubled over with laughter, whooping with it, both with appreciation of his jest and the sensation of relief that he could joke about such a thing, make sport of what had terrified her so much.

He grinned at her. He'd all the time in the world now to indulge her, this night and the next one, and all the newly joyful ones until he could return to Ivyclose again. Because if the lovely lady of the garden were half so virtuous as her brother said, it would take time and patience to woo her. He'd be surprised if it didn't. Even if she fell in love with him on sight, as instantly as he'd done with her, he intended to take his time. A man who'd not known much pleasure, he knew how to extend and make the most of it when he found it. So, too, then, he played with Mary tonight, with this newly loving girl, this sweet little brown girl who'd comfort his body until he could take his heart's desire.

As Mary learned more about the body that she'd been told, in all the gossip this day, was so extraordinarily gifted and well-shaped, she also conceded that part of it could be considered attractive—yes, they were right, it could be thought so, she decided, in its own especial and different way. But she discovered another astounding thing, which was that he knew as much about her body as his own, and showed her things she'd never known or understood about herself. Nor was it possible to be skittish now, not after they'd been so candid about his privy parts. So she laughed, then sighed, then, unwary, relaxed, and so found, at last, part of what he'd been seeking for her.

For he turned to her, his mood grave and tender, and embraced her, which she liked very well, because he was both serious and gentle with her. His touch was pleasant, but then, she'd realized how sensitive her breasts were from the time she'd gotten them. Long before Gideon, when the horrible apprentice, Samuel, had touched them, they'd betrayed her. But Gideon had seen that from the first, and now showed that he knew even more startling things. He caressed her, and before she could recoil, had discovered and then revealed to her the tiny secret triangle, the concealed nubbin that shrank, then swelled at his touch just as his larger member—that he swore was its counterpart—did. Then he covered her shocked face with kisses and whispered as his hand reached to that same hidden place again, "Now I'll show you how it's used."

And did.

He showed how his hands could give her ease to equal his own before he brought his body to her. And smiled after she'd recovered from the embarrassment and then the unexpectedly great pleasure of it, and told her it was only the beginning. But she couldn't believe there could be more.

Because despite that thrillingly new sweet sensation, the greatest pleasure was her most secret one. For she began to believe, against all reason, that there might be far more to her pact with Gideon. She was so filled with the comfort of that thought, as well as with her first small successful lesson at love, that she offered him as much encouragement as she could. And for all that she still took little more than the pleasure of knowing she pleased him in the actual act, there was great joy in the fact that he took her offer, and herself, time and again this night.

He lay in her body, at last, exhausted by the demands he couldn't as yet fulfill, for all this sweet child now allowed him anything. But it wasn't in her power to give him what he wanted most. He kissed the top of her head, and gently withdrew from her only so far as to lie by her side. And then gathered her warm, curving, compact form in his arms and fell asleep with a smile, thinking of what it was he yearned for: Ivyclose and the vision he'd take to wive.

They both slept with smiles on their lips then, for all that they neither one of them would have if they'd known, for all their intimacy, why the other one was smiling.

# 6

The young man threw his horse's reins to a waiting stableman, and paused only to knock a great clod of mud from his boot before he went through the front door at almost a full run.

"Celeste!" he cried joyfully. "Celeste," he called as he strode into the morning room, because if she wasn't there, he intended to shout her into his presence, although he could as easily have sent a footman to summon her. But Sir Philip, for all his guileless looks, was no fool at all, and knew the uses of theater in everyday life. Dramatics might carry the day where reason would not; he'd thought about this long and hard on his hard ride back to Ivyclose.

He wanted the Widow Meecham; she fit into his arms as though she'd been tailored to suit him, and it was as though she had been in every other way too. She'd a fortune and an easy disposition, and for a bonus, she was handsome, young, and anxious to please.

He'd not find a better match, with all of Charles's gratitude, because Charles was forgetful, and a wise man snapped up favors before the reason for offering them was forgotten as well. In any event, he knew very well he'd little chance of ever securing another such brilliant match. His father and his inheritance had been lost when Cromwell had usurped; all he had now was what Charles had given him in recompense, and it wasn't very much. Not enough for him, at any rate. He was a courtier to his fingertips—but all he had to recommend him, aside from his wit, his looks, and most of his teeth, was the pittance he could eke from Ivyclose, and the estate itself. It was a handsome holding, true, but he was no estate manager or rustic squire, and however fine it was, it was far from London and the court he adored. Moreover, he'd have to share it with Celeste. Until she wed—which might be never, he mused, losing his joyful expression as he thought on it, unless he could be very clever today, careful tomorrow, and wise every day after—until she was wed to Gideon Hawkes. Then it would be the red-haired Cavalier's concern, and he looked as if he could handle anything.

"Celeste!" he shouted again, and she smiled at him from the chair where she sat, and put down the book she'd been making careful notations in, and rose from the desk to greet him. She was radiant as she glided across the room to him, shaking her head at his unseemly noise, while all the while she smiled with purest pleasure at the sight of him. He put out his arms to greet her more heartily than was his habit, and watched her from a distant place within his head as he did, like a merchant assessing his stock the day before market.

She'd do. Beautiful. She'd been famously beautiful in France and had grown lovelier since she'd come home, because of her content with being home. Her skin was clear and pale as milk, her eyes the most admired shade of blue, her nose straight and thin, her lips palest pink, her hair, light brown shot through with gold from the random fingering of the sun. Her form was slender and yet she was grown woman enough for any man, grown enough so that he quickly put her aside soon after he embraced her. She'd never cared for physical proof of affection, and for the first time he understood why she might not. Not because he'd ever desired her, he'd no such problem, but maybe precisely because he'd never appraised her womanliness before, he was newly uncomfortable holding her close.

Then she tilted her head aside and gave him her cheek to kiss in her usual way, and then, as his lips brushed that smooth and scented surface, he sighed at the coolness of it, for that was the problem exactly. He had to set her on fire.

"You're very merry. What did Charles have to say?" she asked in her melodious, amused voice.

"Say?" he cried. "Say?" he caroled. "Why, he spoke purest poetry into my poor ear!"

Now she looked at him curiously, so he dampened his enthusiasm a little. But not too much. She must know how happy he was, how expectant and eager, before she knew how easily she could dash his spirits down. That was the way he'd decided to play this game. First she'd learn of his great happiness, and only after that he'd let her know of her power to decide if he might keep it. The joy of sacrifice was bred into her; if they'd let her keep little other joy, at least she'd that in full measure. He decided that might succeed where he knew more common ambitions wouldn't.

"I met a lady, Celeste," he said, taking her hands in his gloved ones and staring down into her questioning eyes. "Oh, one such as I'd never met before. Such a little love, she was, Celeste, and wholly virtuous," he added sincerely, repressing a smile at the memory of those wholly virtuous lips hot against his own, and the way he'd had to tear himself from them to keep her virtuous. But he had. Too much given too early might lose him his little widow, for all her ardor. Like a wise virgin, he'd decided to give her only enough to make her yearn passionately for his return—Charles's word or not, she was as rich as she was randy, which was to say extravagantly so, and competition was keen at court. Let her ache for more from him, rather than deciding to settle for less than he'd delivered, from some more available other.

"Charles introduced us—nay, Celeste, don't frown. He's grown a great deal. Even if he hadn't, he's your king. But he wants the best for those he loves, and you know he loves me dearly. So at dinner he sat me next to the widow of Lord Meecham, late of Epping Forest. He put me there because he knows I'm a jolly fellow, and the poor lady was grieving."

That the lady grieved most because he'd escaped her clutching hands was a thing he didn't let show by so much as a twitch to the lips beneath his fair mustache, as he went on, all thriving admiration now, with not a trace of lust in it. "Lord Meecham was more father than husband to her, truly, since her grandfather wed her to one of his own cronies. But still she mourns his passing, and such is her nobility that never a word of her feelings at finding herself in such an uneven match ever 'scaped her lips," he swore, remembering how nicely her tongue, at least, did escape those plump red lips, for it helped him sigh most realistically as he added, "I'truth, Celeste, you'd love her."

She looked up at him, smiling faintly, and said dulcetly, "Not as much as you did, obviously."

"Just so!" he said with great enthusiasm. "Oh, Celeste, if you could see her! She doesn't look at all like you, can't hold a candle to your beauty, but she suits me well. She's a tiny thing, with blond hair and great brown eyes, and she's plump as a partridge, a fussy little robin to your swan, but wholly adorable."

"How many children?" she asked, and such was his concentration on his role that he didn't hear the flattened tone to her voice as she did.

"None," he answered quickly. "Sooth, she was only married two years and he was so much older—only think, she's a year younger than you are, Celeste, and already wed, widowed, and ready to marry again."

But then he caught her expression, and cursing himself for a fool, foundered before he added, "You must meet her."

She sighed. "So it seems I must, and probably shall, shall I not?" she asked.

"I hope so!" he exclaimed, before he paused, and then added with as much sorrow as he really felt at the risk he was taking, so it was considerable unhappiness she heard in his softened voice, "I do hope so, Celeste, but that's all up to you, of course."

She looked at him sharply.

"Invite her here as our guest then," she said, before she caught a glimpse of his woebegone face as he averted it, and her own expression softened. "Oh, Philip," she said gently, "don't take on so. I never expected to queen it here forever, i'truth, I didn't. Of course, I knew you must one day wed. And I know I'll get on with whomever you choose, if you love her. As I love you, I'd have to, wouldn't I? Ivyclose is big enough so that I'd never get in her way, nor would I attempt to. Philip! Now come, if you've fallen in love, if this brief meeting was enough to show you it *is* real love," she added with a hint of rueful laughter, "why then, go to it. I'll welcome her, never fear."

"That's not what I fear," he said, turning to look at her with all the doubt and fear he felt clear in his eyes.

"You see," he said, stumbling for words, because so much real emotion was tripping him up now, "I'd be given my lovely Annabelle's hand, and her home with it. She'd never come to live here, not when she's got her own great estate and a fine house in London as well. Lord Meecham had a fortune great as his count of years. No, there'd be no need for you to share Ivyclose with her," he said, as his sister's eyes grew a light of such joy that it resembled religious fervor. "But you see . . . Ah, sit down, here, Celeste. We must talk this thing out," he said, all his careful phrasings gone from his head now, because it was suddenly too important for him to be able to continue to play at the game. So he always failed at his deep plots in the end, he thought with resignation. Maybe that was why he'd never succeeded at advancing himself very far. Ah, well, it was enough he'd begun it right, he sighed; the rest would have to come as it came.

He sat down with her in the sunniest room of Ivyclose, and keeping his eyes on her face the while, so he could argue with her every unspoken objection, he began to tell her about his interview with his king, leaving out nothing, except for his most secret fears, and all the ribaldry, of course.

"And after I told Charles that the widow pleased me entirely," he said, pausing for a moment to collect his wits and order his thoughts, for one missaying could cost him much, "he bade me wait, and then left me alone, and returned with a gentleman that he introduced to me as Gideon Hawkes."

Her eyes grew wide, it seemed to him that her breathing stopped, so he paused, wondering how to go on.

"Gideon Hawkes," she said softly, as though tasting the name and trying to discover if she liked the flavor.

He hesitated. He didn't know what to tell her about the man for fear of telling the wrong things. He hesitated to praise his looks, for in truth, he thought Gideon Hawkes wasn't handsome, at least, he wasn't to his eyes. He preferred a more elegant, smoothly fashioned breed of man, like all the others at court. Still, women liked Hawkes's looks very well, although he knew that was the last thing he should tell her. But he realized he might give her cause to worry by not describing him. Women, even such as Celeste, set great store by a man's appearance. So he hurried to it, but with care, because if she found he'd lied in anything, whatever he built now could collapse later. He decided to be bluntly honest, the way she liked best.

"I'll not say he's my idea of a Cavalier," he said carefully, "though he was properly dressed. But his is a hard face to forget. He's very tall, and well-built, not at all fat—in fact, he looks half-starved, for all his muscle," he said, admitting what she'd see immediately anyway, if she agreed to see him. "His face is strongly featured, smooth-skinned—he's not marked by pox, never fear—but it's all crags, and, now here's something wonderful," he added, glad at finding something he could honestly praise. "His eyes are clear as blue glass, and as brilliant. He's got hair the color of fire, true, but then, he wears his own," and as she grew thoughtful, he added, almost desperately, "If you didn't like it he could probably be persuaded to wear a periwig, like everyone else has begun to, but he's just come from abroad, you see, and hasn't settled into our ways yet."

"But, Philip," she asked softly, "why should it matter what I think of how he looks? And why should this Gideon Hawkes care if I approve of his hair or not?"

He swallowed hard. The worst would have to come now, he thought, or never.

"Gideon Hawkes," he said, "is . . . was heir to Ivyclose. Don't you remember?"

"Oh," she said, sitting very still, her face now closed to him. "Oh, I remember," she breathed.

"He's been abroad for years," her brother went on hurriedly. "That money that kept being paid into the estate, why, it was his, because he never knew Charles had given Ivyclose to us. Charles owes him a favor, is fond of him, and was appalled when he realized he'd given his home away. Hawkes loves this house very well—the way we loved Rosewell, perhaps more—and . . . and, ah, well, Charles thinks he could mend all by giving me Annabelle's hand and home, and giving Hawkes Ivyclose and . . . you . . . in marriage," he

said in a rush, having said all and wondering what else
there was to do aside from pleading with her, which he
knew would never do any good.

"Gideon Hawkes . . . and I, in marriage?" she asked,
as though to herself, and his heart sank as he saw tears
spring to her eyes, and watched her turn her head
away.

He couldn't know why she almost wept, for no one
knew, she thought as she struggled to regain her air of
tranquillity so that she could continue to talk with
Philip, and he mustn't guess, lest he, the most transparent of men, let Gideon Hawkes know, before time,
how her heart was filled with joy.

Because there was nothing on earth she could have
wanted more than this unexpected, miraculous solution to all her woe. She'd never set eyes on Gideon
Hawkes, and yet she'd never loved any man more.

She'd never known another man so well either. And
since during the three years she'd lived here, she'd
met few others, she'd time and opportunity and incli-
nation to know him even better. She knew his favorite
rooms and places in the garden; where he loved to
fish, and where to hide; she even knew the sort of
sweets he'd preferred, and when she sat in the morning sun, it was under the very apple tree he'd put his
initials on. She'd lived with him intimately for three
years now, because she'd met his unquiet ghost the
day she'd come to Ivyclose.

Then, mixed in with her joy at having a home again,
there'd been a certain sadness knowing that a devout
and godly gentleman had left his worldly home, Ivyclose,
even if it was a godsend to her and her brother. Soon
after, when she'd discovered there was a rightful heir,
she'd begun to pity the man deprived of the home she
was coming to love so much. But after she heard the
tales about him, she came to love him fully as much as
she'd pitied him.

Because every servant remembered him, every tenant had a story about him, and she listened to them all. Soon, although Gideon Hawkes lived in exile somewhere out in the wide world, the lively and companionable ghost of his past walked the halls of Ivyclose with her, an invisible friend to a girl who found his home both a refuge and a cloister. She grew to know in him all his guises: the red-headed boy, the imp who was so good with animals; the gangling youth who was so good with younger children, the youngest son so neglected by his father and yet so full of merry pranks and laughter—she'd heard all about Gideon Hawkes, even to his falling-out with his father. But a godly man forgave everything, and honored his father. So it was with Gideon Hawkes, for his money had continued to keep the old man when all the world had abandoned him, hadn't it?

"Celeste, you can't . . . you oughtn't judge a man without knowing him," Philip said a little desperately when she remained silent.

"Ah, but I know of him," she said softly, her face still averted, her voice stifled by some great repressed emotion.

Her brother felt his stomach grow cold. What in God's holy name had she found out about Gideon Hawkes? he wondered frantically. The man was a famous swordsman, but said to be fair about his fights; he'd made great amounts of money by trade and travel, but never treason, they said; he'd taken a score of mistresses on the Continent, everyone knew that—he'd got himself one here already, in fact, and he was said to be marvelously well-equipped for such sport, and good at it too—but what else he'd done or was, he didn't know. Nor had he the slightest intention of mentioning any of this until he knew just what she was getting at. One wrong word could lose him his widow and his estates.

It wasn't that his sister was overbearing or cruel.

Celeste was everything that he'd told his king: good, obedient, and virtuous. That was exactly the problem.

He'd never been able to bend her to his will, not once since the day she'd joined him in France after their grandmother died. When he thought how wealthily and well she might have wed years ago, if she'd listened to him, he could have wept. When he thought of the preference they could have gotten at Louis's court in France, or Charles's own, here or there, for that matter, if she'd just seen her way clear to be free with her favors, he could have howled with frustration. But by now he had no more hopes or illusions about her ever doing anything she didn't believe in the rightness of doing. She was the sort of woman, he'd often thought, they'd have given to lions in ancient Rome, and she'd have died singing "hallelujah" all the way down their throats too.

He damned himself silently again, as he'd done for these many years, for a wrong decision made early that bore bitter harvest so late. But whatever they'd done to her, or whatever she'd let herself become, and however much it was a damnable pity that he hadn't taken her with him into exile, no matter how young she'd been, instead of leaving her to their addled grandparent to ruin, it was done. Still, whatever else had happened, she loved him. He'd that last card to play at least, he thought as he waited for her next question with dread.

It was so unexpected that it took him a few moments to realize that for once fate had dealt him a caress and not a blow.

"This *is* Gideon Hawkes, the Puritan?" she asked.

He would give money to the church, he decided, as he let out all his breath and said with a hiss of satisfaction, "Oh, yes, yes, that Hawkes, the Puritan."

And bit his tongue so that he wouldn't say another word about it, because what she guessed, he couldn't be faulted for mistakenly telling her. It was so obvious and perfect, he couldn't have invented better. But he'd never have thought of trying to deceive her as she'd just deceived herself, because he'd never have thought of trying to pass off that red-haired devil as a Puritan. But then, Hawkes had a devilish way about him, and if he met Celeste he might very well find a way to mend all, despite her mistaken notion of him. It would do.

Philip thought furiously for a way to firm up his position, and then, like the wind that knocks down one tree that, in the falling, fells another, he thought of a wonderful thing that was true to say to her.

"He was here again, yes, here, less than two weeks past. I found out he came home to Ivyclose. As I said, he never knew Charles had given it away. He came riding in, and only stopped—there, I hear," he said, pointing out the window to the slope beyond the rose garden. "And stared at us—thinking *we* were the intruders. Alas, old Joseph and the other men didn't recognize him—took him for an intruder—and almost killed him before Joseph finally saw who he was. You ought to see his face—oh, better you don't—after all this time, the cut on his forehead isn't healed yet. To say nothing of the bruises on his cheek."

Her eyes grew wide, her breath came quickly; he'd never seen her in such a passion. Oh, if only Hawkes could see her now, he thought with glee, the fellow would carry her off bodily to either a priest or a bed.

"And why didn't we hear of it?" she demanded.

"Ah, well," he said on a diffident shrug that was difficult for a man so elated to pretend to, "he didn't want the men punished for only doing their job," and as her nostrils pinched together, he added, "and he didn't stop to see us—because, Charles said, and said he must never know he said, mind—he didn't want our pity."

But a look at her face showed he'd got that—and far more.

"We must have him here, and at once. Oh, Philip, send for him, please," she begged him.

"Oh, of course," he said, "but I think you should write it out, Celeste, you do it so prettily, and since there are few women who can, we should let him know about it. He's got some say in the matter too—it would be well to show him some of your graces right off, don't you think?"

She cast her gaze down, remembering the true reason for Gideon Hawkes's visit if he came, as her brother smiled and said something about changing his travel-stained clothing, and took himself out of her sight. He'd left her much to chew over, he thought merrily as he left her alone, while at last he himself could almost taste his own wedding toast, as well as the Widow Meecham's warm lips again.

Celeste stood stock-still after he'd gone, and clasped her hands together hard. But for all her quietness, soft color rose in her pale cheeks, and her light blue eyes glistened with tears that started up of themselves. She dashed them away with her hand, and sank to a seat at the desk to think.

She couldn't believe her good fortune, and so wouldn't. It was too much after too little. She'd been trained to temper elation, subdue emotion, and accept what God had given her with a calm and seemly grace, and so she sat and tried to do so. But still, because she was still young and with a willful spirit, excitement rose in her and threatened to overwhelm her. A comely woman who'd begun to fade to a pastel loveliness, now she glowed with an inner joy that made her vividly beautiful, and if she'd caught sight of herself in a glass, for once she'd not have called it vanity to rejoice in her beauty, because for once, she welcomed it. Now it had a purpose for being again.

She hadn't believed she'd get another chance, that fate could be so kind, at last. She loved Ivyclose with the whole of her heart; here she'd found her heart's ease, if not its fulfillment, and now its true master was returning—to ask her to wed him. And the magnificent irony of it was that he, that long-lost sufferer, was, as she was in her secretest heart, a Puritan, a person of principle and godliness.

Celeste Southern had been born to her station and class, and if the world had continued on the way it had begun when she'd been brought into it, she'd have been wed and bedded and delivered of many babies by now. Her husband would have been a carefree gentleman, and she'd have loved him, because she was a good and obedient girl by nature. He'd have been picked by her father and blessed by the church they neither of them would have believed in very much. But by several strokes, of luck and fate and a headsman's ax, she'd been saved from such sinfulness when the kingdom had been delivered of a tyrant and into the hands of godly men. Or so Celeste Southern had been taught by her newly converted grandmother, after she'd been left to her care when her brother had fled for his life to the Continent.

Philip had no way of knowing—he'd been a desperate youth in desperate straits. His father recently parted from his own head for his stubborn support of the king, his mother dead the year before, his home now literally shattered, he'd no thought but flight. And no way to take care of his little sister. But he'd a grandmother, and Cromwell didn't make war against women unless they insisted on it. Grandmama had taken Celeste, and he'd never known that she'd also taken in a new religion with equal devotion. Both had filled the emptiness left by the terrible losses of her husband, son, and grandson.

By the time Grandmother died, Celeste had grown to a loveliness that made her brother gasp when he was reunited with her in France. His happiness had known no bounds until he'd taken her to court with him, to show them all his beautiful sister, to show her

the glories of Louis's magnificent court. She managed
to keep her faith a secret for all of three days, because
she'd been so well-trained to suppression and knew
that her beliefs in France would be as unpopular as
her brother's would be in England.

But training the mind can't always subdue the body,
and on the fourth night he'd discovered her in a darkened corridor retching after fleeing one of the more
intimate and glittering fetes. Then he discovered it
wasn't the rich food but the sight of the exotic way the
guests entertained themselves that had sickened her to
her stomach. And it hadn't even become an orgy yet.

Grandmother had warned her, but there'd always
been a thin streak of rebellion in her that had been
Grandmother's despair and her own cross to bear. She
hadn't entirely believed all royalists were depraved.
Even after she'd seen the court those first days in
France, she'd been so glad to see Philip again, so
sinfully enchanted by all the fine clothes he bought her
that she'd been willing to forget her upbringing and
believe there was good in all men, and that a sober
mien and plain garments did not necessarily mark a
man for heaven. And then she'd seen what marked
them for hell.

As the night had gone on she'd wandered from
Philip's side, a little tired of the constant flattery from
his friends, more enticed by the splendors of the palace they'd been in. She returned to the room to find
Sodom and Gomorrah. The beautifully clad people
embraced in plain sight, their actions more shocking
and lascivious than she'd ever imagined. Such was her
weakness of spirit then, just as Grandmother had
warned, that she'd felt a tinge of secret lust just watching from the shadows, a tremor of excitement to match
her growing horror and disgust. Then she'd seen what
Philip and the half-clad lady were doing, and then
she'd turned to flee, to find herself in some gilded
courtier's arms, attacked by his suffocating mouth,

and only the force of her self-loathing had given her the strength to break free, to seek a quiet corner to be sick in.

Philip found her, and she told him the truth. And just as she'd kept his whereabouts during his long exile secret, despite the risk of the damnation of her soul, so he kept the secret of her true convictions now, to the ruination of all his plans and hopes for advancement at court. She knew that.

As the years went by, it became harder for him, and no less so for her.

He said he was an overly protective brother to account for her spinsterhood; he claimed that no man was good enough for her to explain why he kept her from court. But when he met too many men that he thought were good enough for any woman, and didn't wish to offend them, he began to keep her close at home. She didn't mind. When they came to Ivyclose, she minded less. And he left her more. But oh, she thought again, with a pang that was almost a physical pain, how she minded the barrenness of her body and her heart!

She could have won him his heart's desire many times, for his was a simple heart. All she'd have to do was to wed, or bed, a man of influence and position. Enough had wanted her. But she'd seen how they lived, and what they wanted from her was a thing she couldn't give, not even to save her own life, should it ever come to that. Oh, she could dissemble; it wasn't virtuous behavior, but it was only kind. Poor Philip had suffered enough, surely; he, friend to the king and popular at court, didn't need the further shame of having a Puritan sister. Swordplay might be the rule, but gossip was surely the most killing weapon at Charles's glittering court.

So she wore the garments fashion decreed, and if she felt some furtive pleasure in seeing how well she looked in them, how good the silks and satins felt against her skin, how pleasant it was to see admiration in men's eyes—well, then, she plagued herself enough later for it when she was alone, for penance. Guilt was a constant bedmate, even if no living man was. There'd been no man but ministers in Grandmother's house. Lessons learned young were hard to shake, impossible if they were still believed and needed. She'd seen nothing in Philip's world to turn her from them.

She'd seen more than lechery and sexual license in that time when she'd been forced to grace the French court. She'd noted pox-addled courtiers, child harlots, betrayed wives, cuckolded husbands, bastard children, and brokenhearted discarded lovers enough to see that Philip's way was no eternally pleasant path. If she were ever tempted, and she was still a young and lonely child enough in many ways to be tempted, she'd only to remember her lessons: the flesh was only the house of the soul. Adornment of the flesh was sinful. Pleasures of the flesh were sinful without God's sanction. The soul should surmount the weak and sinful call of the flesh, and if marriage came, demands of the flesh might be met—but only if second to spiritual ones.

But even a deeply religious woman was still a woman, and as she remembered that now, an old grief shadowed her fair face. She was three-and-twenty, and always aware that she was alone. Not always through choice. Because as she'd thwarted Philip by her honest convictions, so he'd banished her one chance of happiness through his own. There had been one man she'd wanted as husband, a man whose principles matched her own. But by the time they'd returned to England, John Wentworth's politics were as dangerous as Sir Philip Southern's had been a decade before. The table had turned, but it was Celeste who was served ill by it. John Wentworth, Puritan, hadn't been welcome as suitor to Lady Southern, for all she yearned for him, and had done from the moment they'd met, at a neighboring home near the one Philip rented on his return.

A man of morals didn't come between a brother and his rules for his sister; no, he obeyed God's command in all things. God set man up to be woman's master in life in preordained order: first father, then brother, and then husband. So because he couldn't be her husband, and was newly impoverished by Charles's return, and was discouraged from practicing the harsh religion he loved, John Wentworth took a bride and went to America, and never returned, except every night in Celeste Southern's dreams.

She'd only those dreams now. And the legacy of both her royalist and Puritan backgrounds. She also had beauty, wit, skill at the needle as well as the guitar, and a light and lovely singing voice to accompany both her strumming and stitching. She'd the ability to both read and write, speak another language and manage a house, and a kind heart—all the things a generous creator had given her, as well as that which her parents and grandparent had thought a woman needed to enchant a man, or praise her Creator. But there'd been no man her brother had known whom she'd have suffered to so much as hold her hand, much less ask for it in marriage, and no way to meet other marriageable men, now that her church was forbidden to her, her friends exiled or wed to men her brother didn't acknowledge. So she'd become an expert dreamer too.

But now she'd something new to dream upon, a man not forbidden, but rather exactly the reverse: someone whose successful wooing would both bring Philip great advancement and meet her own secret and exacting standards. And someone who'd suffered as she had, for his beliefs.

It had been four years since she'd seen John Wentworth, and now she could see him clearly only in her dreams. Even so, to her continual sorrow, she found that the vision of his thin, sad face faded a little more with each new dawn. It was much easier to dream upon Gideon Hawkes, even in the light, because she knew so much more about him.

Celeste sat at her writing desk dreaming with her eyes open as she stared down without seeing the paper she'd soon write upon to summon home the true master of Ivyclose—and perhaps begin to live her favorite dream with. She sighed, and had trouble thinking of the correct and polite words to put to paper to lure him home from his roving, to his destiny, because she was already far beyond that in her thoughts.

She dreamed of coming happiness: of an end to loneliness and abandonment, of craggy-faced, home-sick red-haired Puritans in Cavalier garb, of virtue rewarded, and then of red-headed children and pranks and laughter in the corridors at Ivyclose again.

She was dreaming. At first he'd opened his eyes in alarm, tensed in readiness to leap from bed and defend her from attackers, and then he'd let his muscles loosen as he'd realized that there was nothing in the room with them but moonlight, and that Mary's muted cries were to protect herself against invisible enemies. Gideon was very weary; it was that hour when dawn was as far off as midnight, and he'd occupied himself vigorously that day with his friends, riding and walking, and then again, this very night, by loving exuberantly, with her. He was about to take her shoulder in his hand, to shake her out of her dream and yet not quite into wakefulness, so that she'd fall silent and let him sleep again. But then he made sense of her muffled words, and recognized the note of blind terror in her strangled moans, and knew that to only partly rouse her would be to let her drop back into the claws of the nightmare again when he fell asleep and left her. She deserved better. She deserved comfort, at least.

"Hush, Mary," he murmured, pulling her into his arms. "Hush, 'tis a dream, nothing more."

She opened her eyes to the blind night, and, lost between what was real and where she'd been, cried, "The Death Bird! Oh, God in heaven, it's the Death Bird come for me!"

"No, no, 'tis nothing, a dream, nothing more," he crooned, holding her close, despite the discomfort, for her naked body was slick with a sick night sweat of fear and she slid against his chest, damp and cold and trembling.

She saw him then; perhaps it was his words that caught her as they vibrated in his chest, or it might have been that she felt the night air on her body then. But she was only half-free from her terrible dream, and though she'd never have dared trouble him with such nonsense if she'd been entirely aware, now it was important to tell him the whole of it.

"It was the Death Bird, Gideon," she said in a weak and trembling voice, her forehead resting against his hard shoulder, her hands going round his back as they did when he closed with her in love, although it was a different sort of patience she sought from him now. "He came to my room and poked his head in the door and I saw his eyes shining as he looked for me, and William said, 'She's not here,' and my father said, 'Oh, no, she's not,' and my other brother begged him to leave, but he only kept looking. I was under the bed, and then on the ceiling, and then out the window looking in, and everywhere I looked it was the Death Bird after me."

"Only a dream," he murmured, taking the bed-clothes and wrapping her so the night chill wouldn't dry her to a chill and then a sickness. "Only a dream," he said as he saw sense returning to the eyes he uncovered as he stroked the damp sleep-tangled curls from her face, "because only in a dream could proud Mary be frightened of a bird. A bird! Come, sweet, I see you chirruping to them in their cages at the bird-sellers'. Never say they give you a fright."

"It wasn't a real bird, though in my dreams it is, it's the Death Bird, Gideon," she said softly, weariness winning over numbed terror now. "I've dreamt it since last year. When the plague came, the doctors came all in leather smocks to their toes, with big gloves so as not to touch anything, and with masks over all their faces, with glass eyes and a long cone over their noses to keep sweet herbs in so they wouldn't breathe in the contagions. They wore great hats overall, and as they walked from house to house they looked like nothing so much as big birds, because you couldn't hear their voices, so they only nodded like birds pecking, up and down: yes, plague, yes, dead, and we all feared them . . . oh, Gideon, they still come for me so often in the night."

There was nothing he could say. He'd seen such doctors, and plague, but he'd never lived long where they visited, for they always set him on his way again. She'd lived through certain hell, but she was lucky that she'd lived through it. And knew it. He couldn't blame her for her fear, any more than he could reassure her there'd be no more disease or death in her future; he was only a man, after all. But the night gave his imagination certain powers, and her exhaustion gave him power over her, and so he whispered, rocking her, "Ah, Mary, next time they come, tell them to be gone or Gideon Hawkes will get them. They'll fear a great, cruel, red-headed Hawke, love, just you see if they don't."

He grinned in the dark, charmed by his own invention. Then he looked down, to see her smiling, and felt her body relax against him, and it wasn't long until he laid her down to sleep again, since she was already halfway there.

"Good dreams, safe dreams this time, Mary," he said.

He curled against her, and although he was reluctant to sleep these nights, since his daytime dreams were now so much sweeter than any imaginings he might do in the night, he soon found her warmth and the musky scent of sleep that arose from her seductive. Not for the first time he appreciated the wisdom of having a comfortable maid in his bed, for pursuit of ease of all kinds, and, smiling about that, as well as sighing at the thought of his future bedmate, he soon found complete rest again.

# 7

Gideon stood firm, feet planted apart, hands on his lean hips, jaw tightened, and narrowed his eyes against the light.

"I'm certain, I'm sure," the landlord said anxiously, eyeing the grim-faced Cavalier, "that anything lacking can be made to suit, sir. That I am certain sure of."

"Oh, good," Gideon said. "Then this window can be made to face west so I'm not waked too early in the morning?"

"Oh, but, sir," the landlord began, his round face growing so troubled that Mary took pity on him, and was glad when Gideon left off his teasing and laughed.

"No, no. It will do, as it stands. I'truth, I think the whole place will do," he said musingly, but as the landlord began to grow a smile to shame his former frown by its intensity, Gideon made it vanish immediately by adding, "Ah, but that's only what I think. What think you, Mary? Will it do?"

She almost stopped breathing as she gaped at him. She looked for a teasing smile on his face, saw nothing but curiosity there, and her pride and pleasure knew no limits. She'd never thought she'd have a voice in choosing their new lodgings, and since she hadn't, she'd never looked to see anything but Gideon's reactions. It was a spacious set of rooms, in a pleasant lane, two houses from a bustling street, far from the fire-ravaged sector of the city, and if Gideon thought it suited, it suited her very well. But since her opinion had been asked and the landlord was now watching her keenly, she couldn't let him simply snap Gideon's money up with no advantage taken, no extra effort for it given. That just was not how such matters were arranged.

"It's very fine, Gideon, and pleases me well," she said in statelier accents than she usually used. As Gideon's eyebrows rose, she added with such innocence and yet such transparent intent that he was hard-put to suppress his grin, "But the carpets! They must have been saved from the flood . . . if not the fire," she commented, touching a toe to the well-worn design, "and that table in the other room! Should we cut off a leg on each chair to match the tilt to it so it seems even when we sit at it, do you think?"

"Wretch! Rogue!" Gideon laughed when the landlord had gone, promising a new table, carpets, and even a grudgingly given wardrobe.

Mary found herself swung up in the air, and, lightheaded with happiness at having a home again, she laughed delightedly. She stopped only when she found herself being soundly kissed, right where they stood, in the middle of the sunny room that would be their new front parlor. It was the first time he'd ever kissed with no intent to do more, only for the sheer friendly pleasure of it, and, knowing this, it was sheerest pleasure to her for the first time too. He could feel that in her mouth and her body, and when his lips left hers, there was a moment's regret in his blazing blue eyes because he'd other things to do now, and no time or opportunity to do what he found he most wished.

"Tonight," he breathed against her cheek as he stood close to her, his body telling her more than that.

Then he sighed and stepped away, and touched her nose lightly with one long finger.

"And as to that," he said, recovering his poise, "you might have argued against our bed, and saved your breath about the carpet. I'll oblige you there, if you wish, but I prefer to spend most of our time in our bed—and that heap looks like a nest full of dead birds to me. Never mind," he said, seeing her stricken look, "I only jest. A man is responsible for his own bed. Out it goes."

"Something bigger," she said, stupidly, she knew. But she was so dazzled by his openness, his charm, and his treating her as a friend and more . . . almost as a new bride, that she could only speak from the shallows of her mind, while deep within, she rejoiced at this end to loneliness, at this finding of a friend in what had started as a master, and was surely becoming a lover.

"Bigger, of course," he said, "fuller of feathers, and with more to it than a coverlet. A man is judged by his bed," he said, and she knew this was true; she'd had only a pallet at home, but her father had had a good bed with four posts, until they'd burned it, along with all his other intimate possessions.

"It needn't be kingly," he said, as though to himself, "for I've a fine bed at Ivyclose, with hangings and a carving at every corner, waiting for me . . ." His voice trailed off even as her happiness did, as he grew silent, thinking of what he'd lost and would soon reclaim, and she remembered that everything he did with her was temporary.

But then, she thought, refusing to despair, pleasant habits often became permanent ones. And then too, she decided, squaring her shoulders, changes might mean changes in her own opportunities too, in her ability to change her profession, and she must never forget to look for them. Because present joy was often only a trap to future sorrow, as her mother had always warned her, and she wasn't bred to be any man's body servant—his unwed body servant, at any rate. She couldn't let a few kind words and a good home lull her. Gideon was unique, and so was her situation; that was the reasoning that kept her dignity intact. But if he tired of her and if she took another such master, why then, no amount of reasoning could change the fact that she'd no longer be just a girl forced to fend for herself, she'd be an official whore.

"Rountree will see to the things we need and the move to be made, and I'll choose a bed and send it back. Then I'm to meet with some men of business, and you're to pick out the best of your new gowns, for we're to the Spring Garden at Vauxhall this very evening," he said, ordering her from the room, "and there we're to drink and eat and stroll about, before we're to test out that new bed, this very night, and here," he said, looking down at her and smiling so as to melt her every rational resolve.

Fashionable women had maids to dress their hair, but Mary had a quantity of thick and curling hair that went meekly into the desired fashion—all ringlets about the face, a jumble of curls all about the sides of her head. She wore no beauty patches, for all she'd seen them everywhere at court. Where she'd grown up, a lady with spots was a lady with disease, and she wouldn't hide her best feature. Although she knew she was darker than fashion celebrated, camellia-complexioned at a time when the white lily flourished, she was proud of the overall smoothness of her skin.

She chose a silken gown of deepest rose that opened over a panel of pink, and with a neckline so low she shivered at her bravery in wearing it. Looking down and noting the contrast between her own dusky skin and the gown that was the exact color of the nipples it barely covered, she remembered how much Gideon liked what was displayed, and shivered again, for a very different reason.

He'd taught her her duties patiently, he'd used her well, but for all that, she never felt more than pleased at her effect on him, and even the swift joy he brought her with his hands was tainted with her self-consciousness and a pervasive sense of shame. But since this afternoon when he'd taken her with him to establish their new home, since that one bright moment when he'd kissed her with more comradeship than lust, she discovered herself anxious for the evening to come for more than the promised trip to the pleasure gardens at Vauxhall, and waiting for the night for more than the security of moving into their own rooms.

She applied a dab of scent, smiled at where she'd put it, and walked, with a satisfactory rustling of her silken skirts, to the window that overlooked the street below their room at the Peacock, to seat herself and watch for his return. In the few weeks since she'd come to know him, she'd come to know him more than intimately, and it seemed to her she knew him better than she'd ever known any man. He was gracious and proud, clever and determined, and although impatient with fools, never cruel. The only thing about him that disturbed her was his strong hunger for her body, and the strange and powerful relief he so obviously took from it. But now, and only so lately that she only now could examine it, she began to feel the stirrings of a longing to know what he wanted to teach her, for more than his satisfaction.

And now, as she sat in the growing dimness of coming evening, she found that the sudden impulse she had to touch him as he handled her, to accommodate him without shyness and shame, was a thing that came from within herself alone, and was sprung from more than gratitude or curiosity. She'd known she needed him from the first, realized she liked him soon after, and only now began to wonder if she loved him.

But since she always lost everything she loved, and since she'd never really loved a man before, that thought frightened her as no other had done, and in more ways than she could cope with. So she left off thinking it and instead played a game with herself by wondering where each person on the street below was headed.

The season just past had been a strangely tropical one; the great fire that had eaten her part of London had been able to dig its teeth into sun-baked thatch and wood dried in the kiln of an uncommonly hot summer. Now the autumn was coming in temperate and mild too, and so the passersby below hurried for reasons that had nothing to do with the weather.

A red moon rose over the thatched houses opposite, and it and the dwindling setting sun overcast the street with an odd and crimson glow. There were tradesmen and servants moving in that reddish haze, maidservants hurrying home, linkboys with newly lit torches coming out, gentlemen and ladies being jogged by in sedan chairs run by silent, panting men, an occasional carriage rumbled past, and there were horses everywhere, horses headed home and out. It was a good feeling to sit above it all in silken skirts, touched with scent, awaiting the courtesies of a gallant gentleman. It was a very good feeling until she noticed who else was venturing out-of-doors with the growing night.

There were more after the fire, of course, as there'd been more after the plague. Wherever men lived in great numbers, there were whores, and wherever they'd recently died in great numbers, there seemed to be even more. Someone had to see to feeding the women who survived, after all, and it was usually the women themselves. There was only one talent every woman possessed, and every man had reason to buy. So they came edging out of the shadows now, in all costumes and colors, in every age and condition, and they stood in groups and waited for trade in the kindest light, the darkest light.

As the night grew, so did Mary's concentration on the scene below. The women attracted the passing men, spoke with them briefly, and then went with them—either off and away down the street, or back into the deepest shadows of it. Some called to the men passing, some only let their shawls slip as they were passed by, and some stood hunched and silent as though hesitant and shamed, and those, Mary saw, got as much custom as those who were on display.

So when Gideon finally came into the room, as he always did, bursting into it, bringing light and life and the sound of his voice with him, she saw him through a mist of tears. But he never knew it, for she ran to him at once, into his surprised but welcoming arms, running to what she most feared, for fear he might cast her off if he saw her weeping, yet filled with the fear that she might already be what she most dreaded becoming, with or without him.

"I missed you," she said at once to his wondering gaze, and wordlessly he closed his arms about her, bent his head, and brought his lips to hers.

The kiss was as nothing she'd ever known, for all she'd known far more than his kiss in these past weeks. But the warmth and sweetness of his mouth seemed new to her, and her great eagerness and growing wonder were all new to him.

"Mary, Mary," he sighed, surprise giving way to a more familiar feeling, taking his mouth from her, only to return it to hers again. He ran his hands over her new silken gown, over and then beneath it, and, feeling her breath quicken to match his own, had caught her up to take her to the bed, when a sound at the door made him groan. He put her down carefully and grinned. "I'm in no condition to answer that, sweet, thanks to you," he said, and when she saw, first from his rueful expression, and then from the obvious state of his body, what he meant, she flushed to match her gown.

"Gideon," Jamie called impatiently from outside the door, "come along, man, we've a coach waiting, and you said you wouldn't be a minute."

"I'll only be two more. I must dress," Gideon called, and shooing Mary to the door, opened it enough to prod her out, adding as he shut it again, "Take Mary as surety against my promise to be quick, and entertain her nicely while I try to keep my word."

"Don't hurry," Jamie called back, as Gideon, frowning, stripped off his clothes, and then, glowering, scrambled into his finery for the evening, without so much as calling for Rountree's assistance.

Gideon was dressed in several shades of brown; his soft brown boots with their wide rolled tops were worn over lighter brown stockings, and he wore fawn-brown breeches, with a long doublet of fine rich golden-brown velvet, and a cape of satin so dark green that it shimmered brown, over all. The ribbons tied on his stockings and billowing sleeves were the only other color than the white of his lace and shirt, and they, and the plume on his wide hat, were gold and yellow. Tristram might look fine in his blue-and-gold costume, and Jamie caught the eye at once in his glorious shades of pink and red, but Gideon, Mary thought as she walked the garden paths at his side, was beyond handsome tonight. He was, she thought with smug propriety, elegant, purely elegant.

They'd dined well at the gardens, and the men had talked of court and horses until they'd their fill of that as well as their dinners. Now they walked through the handsomely landscaped gardens in companionable silence, nodding every so often to other strolling well-dressed gentlemen and ladies they met along the way, breathing in the scent of the last roses, until Tristram broke the silence and Mary's mood of pleased content.

"Lobster and nightingales and thou," Tristram said

sweetly, "a heady combination, true, my friends, but now I must leave you to seek a little more . . ."

"Charles is having a masque tonight," Jamie volunteered.

"Thank you, but no," Tristram answered, adding, as Gideon laughed softly, "I did want to dine with Gideon tonight, and you know we'd not find him within a league of court, so much as his king adores him. Not very courteous, Gideon, especially in light of Charles's recent declaration of love of you," he chided.

"Oh, I love our king well, but I don't love his court, and he knows it as well as you do," Gideon replied in a bland voice.

"Perhaps that's why he loves you," Tristram said thoughtfully, "even though you don't flatter or dance to his tunes. Perhaps exactly for that—because you can't be flattered or bartered or bought. But ah, poor Mistress Mary," he said, laughter clear in his voice now, his mood changing suddenly, as it often did. "Is she to be denied the frolics at court too? Beware she doesn't start looking for a livelier fellow, Gideon," he teased.

"Oh, but I don't care for court at all," Mary blurted, forgetting herself in her haste to deny what he'd said, forgetting that she'd not been invited into the conversation.

It was her habit to simply listen to the men when they met; since she didn't know her place, she took none at all. Their voices were a comfort to her too; the only daughter in a household of men, she'd grown up to the soft music of men's low voices in conversation. That might have been why, she thought, she'd been at ease with the three of them from the first. She never tried to jest or call attention to herself when she was with them, although in those vanished days with her family her wisdom and opinions had often been sought. Now she lowered her eyes and kept walking, embarrassed, wondering if Gideon was angry at her interruption.

But he only laughed, and placing a hand on her shoulder, ran his thumb along the back of her neck as he asked her a question she was hard put to answer.

"Come, Mary. Is it true? You don't like court? You don't want to consort with your king?"

She wasn't as deft with words as they were; she knew that. But she wasn't a fool, and if she were plainspoken, at least she knew how to tiptoe around a truth; any good tradesman knew that—as her father used to say: not every shoe was made of Spanish leather, but there was no need to advertise it.

"Oh, it isn't that," she said carefully. "It may be only that I know I don't belong there."

"But you're the equal of any maid there," Jamie said gallantly. "I'm sure you could grow accustomed to court."

"But I don't think I'd want to," she answered. "The life is too high for me, I think."

"Oho," Tristram said with laughter, "a Puritan miss!"

"I have no politics," Mary snapped, forgetting that was just how her brothers would get her to give over her high-and-mighty airs, because she was always susceptible to teasing, "but that doesn't mean I have no morals."

"I see," Tristram said slowly, his voice suffused with merriment. "Perhaps it's only that you're unaccustomed to the ways of men. Gideon, you must have raided a nunnery to win your lady," he said, as Gideon shot him a warning look—too late, because now Mary was upset by the accusation, as well as the reminder of her present position and what she took as scorn for it.

"Why," she declared, in such a passion to be understood that she forgot her tact, "I grew up in a house full of men, and if my brothers had handled a woman so in front of me, as I saw the king do with his woman, my father would have beaten them soundly for it. And if my father, who was king to us, at least, even touched my mother so when he knew we were still awake, we'd have carted him off to Bedlam! He was a respectable tradesman, we were seemly people," she said with dignity, until she stopped, aghast at how she'd forgotten herself. Aghast and sorry, because Gideon's face was grim, and the men were silent. And after all, how was Tristram to know that she wasn't just a common whore? she admitted, now both frightened and shamed by her actions, all of them.

But, "I give you my apologies, Mary," Tristram said in a muted voice, and she looked up to see what seemed to be genuine shame in his sad, dark blue eyes. "I was but teasing you—I've sisters at home too, you see," he said. "Forgive me, please, as they would do—if I asked nicely enough."

She couldn't ask for more than this, his apology and the honor of being compared to his own sisters, so she ducked her head and said softly, "Forgive me, Master Jones, for my ready temper. My brothers always said it was a curse to me."

"It's one of the most delightful parts of you," Gideon said firmly, "and leave off now, or you'll both be begging each other's forgiveness till morning. Charles's openness with his loves isn't why I avoid his court. I wasn't brought up so well as Mary, I think," he added, as they all laughed, "but as to that, why, Mary, he's a king, and never does anything in private. E'en so, he's not so bad as his French cousin. They say Louis even has someone to hold his chamber pot."

"So Charles says," Tristram put in, laughing again.

"And at least Charles has a secret stair he uses for his greater adventures," Jamie added, pleased to turn the subject.

"Adventures, precisely," Tristram said approvingly. "That was my original theme. Because so much as I love you, Gideon, I find some lacks at court too, and not being king, like my privacy for my pleasures very well, and so far as that goes—and I do hope it does—just look there. Yes, there she is, just as I bade her to be at the rise of the moon. Lady and gentlemen, come, I'll make you known to Mistress Charity Combe, late of Wiltshire, and now resident of my heart."

As the buxom, fresh-faced young woman Tristram approached left the side of the older woman she'd accompanied and came out of the shadowy park to take Tristram's hand and then simper and curtsy to them, Mary curtsied back—only to be stopped midway by Gideon's hard hand beneath her arm. When she looked up to him questioningly, she saw his face set in its most implacable expression.

"Then, as you have found her at last, we bid you good evening, Tris," Gideon said coldly, as his friend took the young woman's hand to his lips, causing him to stop to look back in momentary surprise. Then he shrugged, laughed, wished them good night, bowed, and walked off into the shadows with his ladyfriend.

"Buckingham's own latest plaything!" Jamie whistled beneath his breath. "Tris plays with fire."

"Tris can fence as well as Buckingham, and his wit's even sharper than his rapier. He'll get by," Gideon said as he continued to walk down the path.

"But to run such a risk, and for such a slut," Jamie said with wonder, "though it may be that Buckingham's weary of her in his bed," he mused, as Gideon answered dismissively, "Likely. She's nothing out of the common. Still, Tris likes the challenge of robbing other men's beds better than using what he steals from them, I think. And she'll take whatever is paid by anyone and never notice who's changed places in bed."

Both men chuckled, as Mary grew cold in the mild night air.

Late crickets accompanied the sound of the strolling musicians who fiddled and played their Jew's harps, now and again there was the sound of laughter from deeper recesses of the little landscaped wildernesses they walked past, but though Gideon and Jamie chatted in light tones, Mary said nothing as they continued to walk down narrowing garden paths. She was too busily wondering what Gideon would consider "out of the common," as well as wondering if Jamie, gentle and charming Jamie, would call her a "slut" too when she walked away.

The evening had grown from dark gray to deepened dark when their small party diminished once again. Because after a while Jamie, after one last long look down to Mary's downcast head, sighed, and then said brightly that he spied a group of friends he had hoped to meet on the riverbank in the distance, just leaving the barge that had delivered them to the gardens. Although Mary couldn't see how he could make out any faces in the darkness, she mustered a smile that she hoped he'd notice, and dropped to a curtsy for his departure. This time Gideon's hand stayed beneath her arm and upheld her, and then steered her onward into the gardens. He stopped only for a moment, to snap off a velvety rose, dark as a black rose in the shadows of the bower they stood within, and fragrant, warm, and damp from evening dew, but no more sweet or soft and warm than the mouth he then placed over hers. And then she'd no more thoughts of "common" or "uncommon" or good-byes of any sort, not with his arms around her and his mouth so gently insistent and his hands so knowing.

"How you've come around!" he said at last, as he held her close against his long hard frame, so close she could feel his heart's steady beat beneath her flushed cheek. "I think we may begin to see more than I'd bargained for," he said on an oddly broken laugh, before he bent to devour her mouth again.

"But not here," he said after more long moments, pulling up the gown he'd pulled down to give his lips access to the breast that lay over her wildly beating heart. "No, not now," he said emphatically, rearranging his own clothing that he'd begun to drag apart. "Sooth, that would be lovely, to be stumbled over, coupling in the dark," he commented as if to himself. "And I'm no king," he muttered, as she blushed hotly, both at his words and at the incredible fact that she'd forgotten her whereabouts just as completely as she'd criticized her king for doing.

"No," he said, touching her cheek and chuckling at her confusion, "not when we've a new bed waiting for us at home," and she forgot all her shame at his word, the best one she knew: "home."

They laughed over foolish things on the way back to their new rooms. She was so flustered at her boldness with him in the gardens that she couldn't think what she was saying to make him laugh so readily. And that was one of the reasons why he did. He looked down at her as she walked the last steps toward their new home beneath his sheltering arm, holding herself in some sort of readiness, staying with him as lightly and hesitantly as a bird he'd once trapped in his palm had done, as though it needed only a moment's inattention on his part for it to fly away.

He was well pleased with her. Small and dark and charming, pretty enough to interest a king, sweet enough to entice his own best friend—a feminine but spirited little creature with enough wit to amuse him, enough welcome in her shapely body to fire his own, and enough breeding not to make him sorry for this brief infatuation with her. And now, the new passion she began to show traces of intrigued him. There might be even more to his little mistress than he'd hoped to find that night he'd offered her asylum out of guilt and pity and loneliness.

Virtue would seem to be its own reward, he thought, remembering his previous patience with her, and if its rewards were late in coming, at least they were at last in evidence. He smiled at the thought of that evidence, remembering how her mouth had sought his instead of only obeying it this very day—how she'd molded herself to him in this rose-scented night. He took both pride and lively curiosity in this new evidence as he guided her up the stairs to their new rooms and their new bed with growing and, he noted with amusement, evident excitement.

But the sight of a man's shape in his doorway killed all thoughts except those of defense, and he swept Mary to the side of the stair even as he drew out his sword. And replaced it when he heard Rountree's cool voice.

"I awaited your return," Rountree said imperturbably, "to be sure you had this note tonight, as the messenger requested. Shall you need me anymore tonight, sir? Or shall I to bed?" he asked, with a glance up the stair that led to his own small room behind it.

Gideon opened his door all the way and lit a candle and held the note to it. Even in the wavering light Mary could see his stern face grow a look of such delight that she caught in her breath and began to smile for it. She'd never seen him so moved, so youthful-looking, so joyous.

"I need you," he said to Rountree. "Pack, and at once. I'd like to leave when you're done. I could leave at first light," he said, as though to himself, frowning at the thought, "but the roads are clear of traffic at night and there's a moon, and I know the way—and I can hardly wait to start out!

"Mary!" he shouted then, turning to lift her in his hands, swinging her up in the air as she laughed with him, for such joy was contagious, and his face was wonderfully relaxed, free of the constraint he usually wore like a second skin. "Sweeting!" he chortled, celebrating with her because she was there, all real thought of her and what he'd planned to do with her tonight forgotten, since he was in the grip of a greater lust than that for the joining of mere bodies.

"Mary!" He laughed. "I'm off to Ivyclose again! I've been asked to come home!"

They rode through the night under a swelling autumn moon, and if Rountree found it difficult or odd in his master for him to take off for Kent in the night, leaving a warm bed and a warmer mistress behind him in order to do so, he said nothing about it. His curiosity about Ivyclose might have been equal to his love of his master, whom he'd met on foreign shores. Or it just might have been that he'd have followed this master to the ends of the earth if he'd been bidden to, because of the man he'd discovered him to be in those wandering years. For whatever reasons, he traveled at his side wordlessly as they rode the moonlit lanes down to Kent and Ivyclose, the beat of the horses' hooves as steady and hard as the pounding of Gideon's heart.

They stopped at a decent inn on the road at an indecent hour, because for all every instinct urged Gideon onward, he realized his valet and his horses needed rest, even if he felt he'd never rest again until he was beneath his own roof again. He lay on his rented bed and only closed his eyes and thought of Ivyclose, and yet when he opened them again it was full morning and he was still at the inn. Then he had a breakfast he didn't taste, swung up into the saddle, and took to the road again. But he didn't smile again until he came to the rise in the road where he turned to the left, and then, remembering his previous welcome, shook his head and swung his mount toward the entrance to Ivyclose that was there for visitors. Because that was what he was, he reminded himself, his rueful grin slipping, and that was what he'd be forever unless he made this visit a success.

It was full noon when they rode up to the entrance to Ivyclose. And as he sat his horse and stared, it seemed to Gideon that nothing had changed, the white house was bathed in the autumn sun, and he remembered every window, every shutter, every chimney pot on its roof, and every blade of grass between the flags of the court where his horse stood. He was filled with such a feeling of love as he'd not known since he'd left this very courtyard. He was a man come home.

But then the front door swung open and he remembered it was no longer his home. Because Sir Philip Southern walked past the footman and stood in the wide doorway and smiled, and for all it was a welcome, it was the smile of a man who greeted a guest. Then Gideon swung down from his horse and approached Sir Philip Southern's home.

As Sir Philip prepared to come down the steps, Gideon bent his leg and swept him a bow, and if there was a hint of self-mockery in the elaborate sweep of his plumed hat as he made his deepest bow, there was nothing but polite interest in his eyes when he straightened up again. Until he saw the lady who came down the stair on Sir Philip's arm.

Now he saw her close, and so now he could drink in the details of that smooth and faintly smiling face. And he did, like a man who hadn't seen a woman for long, starved years of his life. But then, he'd never seen her like, except in his dreams, except for that once when he'd seen her drifting through his gardens. Her skin was pure and finer-grained than he'd been able to notice then, and white as the lace at the top of her gown; her mouth was small and pink and shaped for whispered confidences and gentle sweet kisses; her hair was a tumble of saffron-and-brown gilded curls. But her soft blue, long-lashed eyes held curiosity, and trepidation, and then, he saw, a hint of fear.

Of course, he thought, cursing himself for an idiot, he was a great rough-looking rack of bones, and here he stood gaping at her like a man released from a dungeon after a decade in the dark without a woman. And however much he felt that was true now, he softened his expression even more than he'd automatically done as he'd recognized her fear. He smiled slightly. He spoke what he hoped were the right words, for first words, like all first experiences, were always remembered.

"Sir Philip," he said in his deep grave voice, "we meet again, and I'm happy for it. Lady," he said, and he meant every word he spoke, "thank you for asking me here. For many reasons. Your words of invitation were sweet, but the sight of you makes me forget all my manners, forgive me. You are balm to my eyes. If anyone but myself had to shelter beneath Ivyclose's roof, believe me, I'm glad it was you."

She bent her head to acknowledge his words. Then she raised it, looked up, and spoke, and as she did, she smiled over the few words with trembling lips.

"Gideon Hawkes," she said softly, "welcome home."

"Well then," Sir Philip said with very great gladness. "Now. If I may introduce you?"

# 8

There was a light rain falling, but Gideon was used to worse weathers and it was a soft misty rain, for all it was so thoroughly soaking the grass. But he worried about the lady at his side, and once again asked if she'd care to go back into the house.

"I'll not melt," she said, laughing up at him, her face glowing as if from the radiance of the sunniest day, or so he thought. Because as she peeped up at him, her fair face shone pure and white, a halo of honeyed curls giving it an aura of light even in the shadows cast by the enveloping folds of her hooded cloak.

"I'm a gardener," she explained as she led him across the long lawn, "and how could a gardener that was fearful of the rain survive in Britain? Or have you forgotten our beautiful weather? Oh, but I believe you've been too long abroad, Master Hawkes," she teased.

He gazed down at her, his blue eyes still sparkling from their recent laughter, and yet suddenly sad and serious. "Oh, that's true. Yes," he said softly, "I have been gone too long—but then, though I was gone fifteen years, I thought it seemed too long after only five days. Yet now," he said, staring at her, "I believe five minutes was too long."

She smiled and looked away as she continued to walk on with him. She didn't duck her head or blush or grow embarrassed, so as to discourage him, nor did she bat her eyelashes and giggle to encourage him. She accepted his flattery as she'd accepted his presence since the moment they'd met the day before—gracefully and with peaceful contentment, as though they were good friends met after an absence, rather than new-met strangers with the question of a union proposed by their king hanging over them. He couldn't have been more pleased, or surprised.

She was everything he could have hoped for. Beyond beautiful, in his eyes, since she was in the exact physical style of women that he preferred: milk-white and light-haired, with a willowy yet shapely figure. She was perfect for him in other ways as well: she was charming and gentle; her education, a rare thing in a woman, showed in her words every bit as much as her attraction did in the lips they issued from. A woman he could speak with, live with, and love with, all in one, and that one beneath the roof of Ivyclose, was almost more than he'd expected.

The most amazing thing to him was that from the moment they'd met—from the conversation during and after dinner last night, to the regretful good night he'd made to her only because he knew he had to for the form of it, to this morning, when he'd bounded from bed near dawn to come downstairs to find her waiting —it was all of it so wondrous as to be almost unbelievable. It was almost as though they were reacquainting themselves, as if they'd known and loved each other well in some previous time or place. He felt as though he could set the wedding date this afternoon. But he dared not push too hard lest he push through the walls of this fragile dream he was somehow living.

"This wasn't here when we came to Ivyclose. I had it made so that I could enjoy my roses fully," she said as she led him into the rose garden. "But it meant taking down part of the wood. Although I disliked felling the trees, this is the sunniest spot near to the house, and they love sun dearly," she explained apologetically. "Do you mind very much? They were ancient trees, you must have known them as a boy."

"Oh, yes, I knew them well," he said, pausing to squint up at the sky to see if the dwindling drizzle foretold a clearing day, before he looked down to her with a grin. "I despair now that they're gone. It's very kind of you to ask, because, yes, thank you, I'd like them put back."

She smiled again, acknowledging and then rightly ignoring his teasing. Then she led him on down the paths of the garden, pointing out the various roses she'd had planted, sighing over the fact that so many were past their bloom and so many more were already showing the browned leaves of exhaustion, even though the weather had been mild enough to spare them a few weeks longer before their winter sleep. He walked by her side and nodded, and somehow managed to comment intelligently, while all the while he marveled only at the fact that he was now walking inside the very picture he'd stood outside gaping in at with wonder and envy, before he'd been pulled down to earth and pain, only a few weeks before.

Except, he thought wryly, more than a light rain changed the picture now. By no stretch of the imagination could he be called a handsome and gallant Cavalier; no, it was a long-legged rough rogue that strolled through the garden with the fair lady this time. Thinking that, he felt outsize and awkward for the first time since he'd got his full growth, and rawboned and unhandsome for the first time since he'd accepted himself as a man. For all the women he'd

loved, and who'd been well-pleased with him in love,
and they were not a few, he felt inadequate now,
unworthy of this beautiful, beautifully bred woman he
dared think to take to wive.

But he did think it, and he did dare it, since that
was how he'd always gotten everything he'd needed.
Much had been withheld from him in his life, and if he
hadn't learned early on to reach out and take what he
could, he wouldn't have survived to this day. He
mightn't be worthy of her, he could think of no man
who was, but he'd claim her and reclaim his home if
he could, and so he did dare. And so he reasoned it
was time to put away his astonishment at his good
fortune and begin his courtship.

Maybe because he'd never had illusions about himself, he'd learned the art of wooing very well, and had
gotten the practice of it to an art. An artist who knew
his craft, he knew that if he wanted a good result he
must take his clue as to how to proceed from the
material he worked with. Celeste wasn't shy, coy, or
distant with him, and she knew of Charles's plans for
them. So he saw he could omit several first steps, and
regretted it only because he enjoyed every step he
took with her. But he knew pacing was of great importance in any form of lovemaking. If she were so be-
forehand with him, he could scarcely hang back without
interrupting the flow of their relationship. They'd moved
on quickly past meeting and being interested in each
other. If they weren't to settle for being friends, it was
time for him to move them on to further intimacy of
all sorts.

"I see what you meant about the rain," he said as
the thin clouds shredded away above them, "or is it
only that spying you in the garden, the sun tore the
clouds from his eyes in order to see you better?"

It was only a little poetic speaking; the men of court
would think it poor stuff—they composed sonnets in

order to get their boots over a lady's doorstep, entire romances to get into their boudoirs. But Celeste showed her first sign of discomfort at it; she lowered her long lashes and hesitated before looking up and smiling at him again.

"It's only that soft rain before dawn often signals a clear morning," she said quietly, before she added, now with a bit of teasing in her voice, "But you know that, Master Hawkes, you grew up here—and you were a sailor too! Everyone knows they have weather eyes even keener than Kentish men do."

"Now, who told you about my freebooting days?" he asked lazily, looking at her with a slight smile, before he lost it and his seductive air as well, when he heard her answer.

"Not Seth Sykes?" he exclaimed. "Why, that old rogue! Sooth, I thought he'd be growing daisies from the inside of the earth out by now. He was old when I was young—when m'father was young—nay, when the world was young!" He laughed. "Never say he's still around?" he asked, so delighted he forgot his immediate aims.

She'd found a nearby stone bench and sank to it, patting the empty space beside her.

"Come sit," she said, "and I'll tell you the whole of it, because he'd some other things to say. What a handful of boy you must have been, Master Hawkes," she said, shaking her head in mock disparagement.

"But it's wet . . ." he said at once, dismayed at seeing her sit on the wet stone bench. "Here, let me—"

"That's why I wear a good wool cloak," she said. "I like it out here in the mornings. Come, sit by me, Master Hawkes, . . . unless"—she managed a realistic gasp, hiding her mouth behind her hand—"you're like all the rest of Philip's friends from court . . . and if so, then I beg pardon for the suggestion, and you've my leave to go back to the house and get a cushion before you join me. Are you afraid of dampening your finery?" she asked, looking up at him with a pretty show of anxiety, although she could only barely control her smiles.

His ringing laughter set a flock of little birds that had been feeding on the lawns to flight, and he sat by her side at once.

She told him about Seth Sykes, and old Joseph, and the other workers and tenants on the estate who'd known him as a boy. They laughed together over the stories Granny Camden spun, and he corrected a tale Tim the smith had got wrong, and added something to the story Jennie Dale had forgotten, and agreed with the incredible account of the dog in the well that she'd heard from Ned Green. They reviewed his years at Ivyclose one by one, yet though they smiled over much, still there were times her face clouded over at other things he could jest at now, but she would not, for he might laugh at forgotten pain, but she could not. By the time they were only half-done, he'd learned how much she'd learned of him, and the sun was out full, the bench was bone dry, and she'd shrugged off her hood and shed her cloak entirely.

"I'd forgotten half myself. I seem to have lost half my history along with Ivyclose," he commented with wonder when they'd done with the story of the long-past day he'd come home late—explaining, as he'd waited for his deserved thrashing, that he'd been waiting to spy out the owls' homes in the oldest oak trees, "and I don't mean just that story about the owls. So many more I'd forgotten, and yet I'd thought I'd only tried to forget the unhappy hours," he mused.

"I thank you," he told her with a warm smile, "for recovering some of my pleasantest ones for me too. But come," he said briskly, shaking off the past, sitting up straight, his attention full upon her now, so bright and piercing a look in his vividly clear eyes that she felt their keen blue regard as intently as she felt the melting warmth of the strengthening sun, "I'm human as any man, and would enjoy hearing about myself until owls come hunting over us tonight. But I begin to feel like a man preening before a looking glass, and you're far too lovely to only reflect my image. What of you, Celeste? Where was your childhood passed? What foolishness did you get up to? What did you do before you came to Ivyclose to become my biographer?

"And as to that," he complained with mock accusal, "three years at Ivyclose must have given you more to speak of than me— out with it!" he commanded. "I'm pleased you know so much of me, but I'd hear about you now. Please, lady," he asked gently.

It was more than flattery to her ears, it was destiny. It was as if she'd waited for this man to ask her this question for the past three empty years. He was here at last, in truth, his long voyages ended, sitting at her side in her favorite garden, wanting to know of her journeys before she came to Ivyclose, and him. It wasn't exactly as she'd dreamed it would be, but near enough. He was bigger than she'd imagined he'd be; wider-shouldered, his shining fiery hair softer-looking, the face harder-looking than she'd envisioned, and the blazing blue eyes were steadier and sharper than any man's she'd ever seen. Strong, colorful, and watchful, he was so vividly alive as to almost frighten her, and he might have, at that, if she'd not known him so well before she'd ever met him, before she'd given her heart to him.

Her grandmother might have taught that it was wrong to love for love's own sake, and she too believed that love should come after marriage, instead of marriage coming because of it, but she couldn't regret her feelings. No, she might worry that her faith had been diluted by all those years without her church, but she couldn't regret this happiness. So she first spoke a silent thanks for joy received, as she was taught to do before she partook of any of the nourishing fruits of the earth. And then she gave him a brief and edited history of her life.

"I was born and raised at Rosewell Manor, in the west," she said softly. "It was a beautiful place—or so I've been told," she added, "because I remember it half with my own eyes and half by what I've heard tell, and the two have become one in my memory. I was six when I was taken from it, and rising eight when the Protector took it from my family. It's rubble now. Not a straight wall remains. When Philip returned to see it, he wept," she said sadly, "not that it was ever such a great fortress or even a grand castle, but my father's will was so strong that his enemies must have thought it equal to him and so overestimated its condition. Nothing of it remains.

"But don't look so solemn, at least not for my sake," she said at once, as she saw Gideon's face grow grim. He looked so stern he almost frightened her, since sometimes, as his jaw clenched, a shiver coursed across it, and that made her shiver too. So she went on truthfully, "Because I didn't suffer—I was far too young. My memories of the manor are not of stone or splendor but of kisses and coddling, because I was much loved, and my mother lived there. When she died, I grieved, it's true, and when my father died, I was sore afraid. And when Philip left me, I was sure the world had ended, but nay, Gideon, don't look so," she said, interrupting herself to comfort him for his apparent distress. "Sadness came to so many of us during those years. But if a thing is to be healed over, so as to be remade better, it first must be wounded. Or so, at least, I was taught," she said with a peaceful smile as he looked at her curiously, "because I was fortunate enough to be put into my grandmother's care then, and she healed me entirely.

"She was a good woman, a godly woman, a person of devout virtue, like . . . like your own father," she said, casting her glance down, and so missing his startled reaction entirely, "And though you didn't get on with your father, for all his virtue, I loved my grandmother as much as honored her. When she died I joined Philip in France, which I didn't like at all, as you may guess," she said pointedly, with a sniff.

"When we returned to England . . ." She hesitated. "We stayed not far from here. But," she said carefully, for the memory of her abortive courtship with John Wentworth still stung, "I didn't find true ease and happiness until I came to Ivyclose. And here I am.

"In less tumultuous times," she added, looking up again, seeing his scowl and misinterpreting it, "there'd have been less for a maid to tell of her life, but I'm lucky for all my troubles, because at least I have my life. And I've learned, as you have, to endure all with patience, and with faith."

"Lady," he said, his dark auburn brows long straight lines over his narrowed icy eyes, "you mistake me. I didn't love my father, nor did I honor him, nor respect him. He wasn't a godly man, nor decent, nor devout in any faith save his own faith in his own virtue—which didn't exist. He became what he needed to be, when he needed to be it. Not to save his soul, but his skin."

She stared at him. He was beyond rage. There was a weary sickness of the soul in his voice to match the sudden pallor of his skin. She understood. His father might or might not have been what he claimed. But a man raised to the faith would be sick at heart if he felt his own father had only pretended to it. It was a heavy burden for such a man to love where love wasn't warranted, however much he knew he must. She could help him reconcile himself to that. Her faith was strong.

It gave her a little thrill of pleasure to know that she could in some way help this man who looked so powerful, so entirely self-contained. Her hand in marriage would give him his home again, but her heart in marriage would help restore his own heart. She was grateful for this unexpected boon; when God gave, he gave with both hands, she thought with gratitude.

"I think," Gideon said then, using all his hard-learned control to shake himself free of the mood her words had forced on him, abandoning the past so that it wouldn't have a chance to mark his future, "I do think we've had enough of the past for now. If things go well for us, we've years ahead to mumble over old bones. Celeste," he said gently, taking up her hand in his, marveling at its softness and long-fingered grace and the purity of the white skin against his own hard browned hand, "I would speak of the future with you. Of our future."

She glanced away at that, and he was enchanted. All this while she'd sat and spoken with him without artifice or coquetry, with simple and perfect clarity. Yet nothing about her straightforward manner was anything like the boldness of the whores he'd met in his travels, either at royal courts or in the streets. Now, at the mention of the union she surely must have held in the back of her mind, even as he had since they'd met, she cast her long lashes down over her mild eyes, and showed him her profile as charmingly as any flirt at court had ever done. In truth, she was a treasure. He'd taken every forward step with care with her, and now in her pretty show of meekness and gentle submission at his words, she showed him how to go on, signaling her readiness for his wooing.

"Celeste," he said softly, putting his other arm lightly around her shoulders, "you know that the king has proposed our mating. But i'truth, I prefer to do my own proposing. I'd want you, lady, if you'd nothing to offer but your own sweet words and lips. That's the miracle of all this for me," he said as he felt her shoulders stiffen at his touch. "When I saw you that day in this garden of yours," he continued in a lower voice, "I realized it *was* yours, and that Ivyclose had a mistress who knew its heart. Now I can only hope there's room in your heart for me. Tell me, have I a hope?"

He'd slowed. Her slight gesture of shock at finding his arm around her warned him, and he'd immediately lifted it a fraction from her shoulders. Her hand had grown rigid in his own; he'd loosed his pressure on it. Now her silence made him sit quietly and wait. His every impulse was to catch her up and kiss her, letting his mouth and hands show her his admiration, his ardor becoming his most flattering tribute, his passion a promise of their future happiness. Most other women would have expected it, desired it. She didn't, all too obviously. At least to a man who could read such subtle signals, she didn't. But he wouldn't judge her, or press her. It may have been that another man had hurt her. That was understandable, if regrettable, because it would make his own wooing more difficult. Still, it explained the one question she hadn't answered, because he'd been too clever to risk asking it. But it accounted for the oddity of her single state at her advanced age and with her extreme beauty.

He slowed to a standstill, awaiting her next move. He didn't remove his arm or release her hand, but sat still as a man watching a doe that happened, all unknowing, to cross his path. He wanted her more at this moment than he'd done since they'd met, but waited for her permission, spoken or unspoken, to continue. He was a practiced hunter; this quarry was too important for him to risk frightening her away.

She drew in a breath. She knew her answer as well as her heart, but it was beating so rapidly she couldn't get breath to reply right away. His touch had done that. His nearness was doing more. She understood he must be an affectionate man, starved for closeness after that sad childhood of his, but still, it was more than unseemly, it was terrifyingly wonderful for him to touch her. She blamed herself for her fright. Faith! she thought, if a brotherly hug from him did this, what would their marriage bring? The thought of that made her smile tremulously as she turned back to him and said in a quavering voice, "Gideon Hawkes, what the king proposes pleases me. What you might propose pleases me more, and what you just said pleases me best."

"Love!" he said, triumphant and delighted. "My lady love," he said tenderly as he gathered her in the crook of his arm. "My lady wife," he breathed as he brought his lips to hers.

At first her lips were warm and quickened just as he'd wished, and he relaxed against her and drew her closer, rejoicing in the perfumed scent of her, the feel of her. But then, too soon, before he could properly deepen the kiss and their embrace, her lips became thin and hard against his, and he felt her trying to pull back. He released her at once.

When she didn't speak, he did.

"How have I offended?" he asked.

He was genuinely puzzled. The more so when she averted her face, not at all charmingly this time, because he thought he saw tears in her eyes and was as confused as he was amazed by them.

"Was it something in my kiss? Or something about my person? Sooth," he tried to jest, as his heart grew cold, "I had no onions when I breakfasted this morning. What is it?" he asked, wondering wildly what he could have done to disgust her.

"Gideon," she said in a low, choked voice, "you must know . . . it's wicked. Sinful. Lust is . . . not what I expected from you." She faltered, having dared a glance at his face.

"Why not?" he asked, astonished. "Do you think I'd offer you a handshake of a marriage because the king recommended it? Did you think I lied about your effect on me? If you weren't to my taste, I'd have ridden away from Ivyclose at once and never looked back, I promise you. I didn't begin by caroling over your beauty, but, lady, that was in itself a compliment. I thought you too clever for that. I thought it would make you doubt my sincerity. I'truth," he admitted ruefully, "compared to my fellows, I'm scarce with words. But not bereft of them. I couldn't want you more. I didn't speak out at first, or attempt you in any way yesterday or today, because I was so stunned by you. I thought you . . shy. But if you wish . . ." he said, and shrugging, smiled as he took her in his arms again.

"Now, shall I begin with your eyes or your lips?" he asked. "Ah, but if I start with your lips, I'll never get to say what I think of your eyes, my own lips will be too well-occupied, so—"

"No!" she cried, struggling to disengage herself, for no reason, since he'd dropped his arms from her. But he seemed more angry than contrite.

"What game is this, lady?" he asked coldly, rising and crossing his arms over his chest and staring down at her.

"Gideon," she began, seeking the right words, "Gideon Hawkes," she said, dropping her voice and stumbling over her words, "are you not . . . are you . . . I thought you were as I am. Gideon," she pleaded as he looked at her without comprehension, "I was raised a Puritan, even as you were. I'm not devout anymore, but I've not given up the faith. Have you?"

"S'wounds! A Puritan? Me?" he asked, astonished, sinking to sit beside her again. "Lady," he said, shaking his head in wonder, "I never was, for all my father's masquerading as such. But you say you are? Sir Philip Southern's sister a . . . Puritan? No, never say so. Come, what sort of jest is this?"

"I am, I was . . . Oh, Gideon," she cried, then looked about the rose garden, and in a low voice, shamed and proud and shaking with emotion, she asked him to keep her secret. "It will be hard for Philip if they hear of this at court. He's not as I am, you see, but our grandmother brought me up, not him, and she was as I am. He knows, he protects me, as I'd protect him now if I could." She spoke quickly, her eyes searching his face as her words raced on. "No, he'll not be shunned, or punished, but I worry that he'll be mocked, and he's a proud man and in no way responsible. I am what I've been trained to be, and for all my faith, I wouldn't wish to bring such a proud spirit down because of my pride. I can, I have lived among other faiths, but they wouldn't understand—can't you see?" she asked, pleading with him now, for she could read nothing in his clear cold eyes, and see nothing in the set to his mouth but wariness.

But he saw a lovely lady, distraught. *His* beautiful lady, in need. He saw her soft lips trembling, and that fair face racked with woe, and nothing would have induced him to betray any of her secrets, and so he told her as soon as she stopped speaking. But it took all his willpower not to try to discover the secrets of that sweet mouth he watched, although he knew enough now not to tell her that.

"Now, trust me," he said when he'd done promising her that her religious beliefs would be his close-kept secret, and she'd calmed herself, "and if you do, then tell me. Does this mean you'll have none of me? For I tell you straightly, lady, I've little religion, and what I have is Church of England. I'm not a Puritan, nor have I love for any of them—but you. I still want you. Will you have me?"

She smiled sadly. "Have I a choice?" she asked.

There wasn't such unhappiness in her heart as in her voice. Because she reasoned that whether he was of her faith or not, it would take a martyr to go against the king's wishes, and she wasn't sure she could be one—and it would take a monster to go against a brother's orders, and she was an obedient woman. She conveniently forgot or didn't wish to consider the fact that if she hadn't wanted Gideon Hawkes, no power on earth could have forced her to take him as husband. Her strength of character would have made martyrdom not only possible but also pleasurable, and her brother never could stand up to her righteousness. But it was simpler to think that if her brother commanded this union, it was her duty to submit. If Gideon were her husband, whether he'd a pilgrim soul like her own or was a decadent Cavalier, it was oddly exciting to realize that in either case submitting to him would only be submission to God's natural order. But his next words tore that excitingly comfortable thought from her.

"A choice?" he hooted with derision. "Sooth, lady, you have that! In plenty! Didn't Philip tell you? He insisted on it. As I did when I heard his reasons—I wanted Ivyclose, but no unwilling bride. Now I've met you, I'd want reluctance even less. No, you've a doting brother. It's singular, but you can refuse me. You've the king's, your brother's, and my permission—but never my wish. I pray you don't. Now, shall I stay? Or go? Again, will you have me?"

She hesitated. She'd a choice? But she'd always had one. Now that she hadn't wanted one, it was official. The irony struck her, only to be hidden away, for such thoughts were dangerous. She knew what she wanted to answer at once, but her conscience forbade it, for Gideon wasn't what she'd originally thought. It went against her teachings to wed an unbeliever. But she'd already learned to love this man. He might try to lead her astray. Still, a good soul could influence a strayed one; there was so much she could teach him. There was an argument on every side. The one that spoke loudest was her own heart's.

Her choice, then, would be to buy herself time, to let Gideon know she was a thoughtful woman, and to rationalize long enough to allow herself to have him.

"Gideon," she said at last, "I'll try. If you'll have patience with me, I'd learn your heart before I give my hand. It's not necessary to love before marriage, I know that. But since neither of us is what we'd thought, I believe it's necessary to know each other first. I'll try—I believe we should try. Give me time, I pray you, will you?"

"You've all my time, lady," he said, and took her hand in his again and brought it to his lips.

She grew rigid, and he sighed.

"Celeste," he said softly, "I put much store in this matter of touching. I won't deceive you as to that. Will that be a bar? For if it is, then we can't go on. So much as I yearn to, I'll not lie about that, it's too important to me."

It was a noble declaration of an ignoble thing and she was lost for a moment because of the complexity of it. But for all that his words struck terror to her heart, the thought of the loss of him forever frightened her more. She learned, as many holy men had before her, that Scripture could be twisted to the immediate need.

"It's not forbidden for a man to take pleasure in his duties with his wife," she said quietly, averting her eyes. "Marriage is for just that, so that a man will not burn for his . . . natural needs."

"I understand. I can wait. My need for you is greater than my 'natural' needs just now," he said as he brushed another light kiss across her hand.

It was true enough. There were other women for

quenching immediate needs. There was adorable Mary, for instance, in London, for slaking his great thirst. He could go slowly with Celeste. To win her, for all that she tempted him . . . to win her and Ivyclose and all his future, he'd slow to a crawl. She was a Puritan, but she was young, and she was a woman, and she wanted him—he was old enough and man enough to know that. Slow water could wear down stone, slow seduction could win this poor frozen heart for him. He'd thaw her, he'd win her, he'd have her and her warm heart here in the heart of Ivyclose one day. He had, after all, all the time in the world, and every advantage and weapon for a sort of warfare she didn't even know about. He smiled.

"Now, then," Gideon asked slowly, grinning devilishly, "my dear Puritan, what of that gown you're wearing? Or do you mean to tempt the devil so you can snare and convert him?"

As she grew flustered and began to explain her need for duplicity for Philip's sake, he blessed Philip, and laughed away her embarrassment. Because it was a beautiful morning, bidding fair to becoming a glorious day, he sat next to a wondrously fair woman and the sun was shining down on him in a garden at Ivyclose, at last.

Mary stood at the door and dithered. Delight and despair warred in her eyes. She was all contradictions today. Her dark curly hair was even more tousled than usual, her cheeks were flushed, one redder than the other, because it had been resting on her arm when she'd fallen asleep in her chair by the window. And so her pretty blue-and-white gown was rumpled too. She'd roused at once when she'd heard the rapping on the door, so surprised that someone had come that she'd forgotten to ask who it was before she flung it open.

Two gorgeously dressed gentlemen stood there, and

such was their finery that for a moment she'd been frightened when she hadn't recognized them. Then she heard the unmistakable note of underlying humor that was always in Tristram Jones's drawling voice as he chided her, "What? A London-bred girl opening the door to danger without one question put to who it might be? Shame, Mistress Monk, for shame."

There was understanding in Jamie's great blue eyes, but even so, Tristram was right and she knew it, so, still dazed with the unreality of waking from unexpected afternoon napping, she blurted, "But, I didn't expect anyone . . . I was sleeping."

"Sleeping on such a glorious afternoon? That's criminal!" Tristram exclaimed, as Jamie said, "He's right, that's why we came to ask you out, Mary. Winter will be on us before you know it—this weather can't last. I'truth, I'm surprised to find you in."

"Oh," she said, "but I'd nowhere to go."

"We do. You might ask us in to discuss it," Tristram pointed out more gently than was his usual manner.

She hesitated.

"Don't you want to see us?" Jamie asked, hurt.

"Oh, yes! It's so good seeing you!" she said immediately, because it was. "And it's a beautiful day, I know, but I don't know if Gideon . . . I can't even ask Rountree, because he's with Gideon, you see . . . Oh, come in, please," she said, remembering her manners, before she put her hand to her mouth and stammered, "Oh, but should you? Oh, s'truth, Master Jones, Lord Claverly," she sighed, defeated, and so, absolutely honest, she admitted, "I don't know what's to do.

"Please . . . can I ask you in?" she asked meekly, so much embarrassment and confusion on her face that she looked wholly adorable to both gentlemen on the doorstep.

"You can, and you should," Tristram said with conviction. "I don't believe even one of us alone would be a problem, but certainly two of us calling on you wouldn't cause Gideon to so much as fondle his sword's hilt," and then he smiled as he saw her woebegone little face grow a broad smile as she stepped back to let them pass into her lodgings.

She was as excited as she was delighted at their company. Gideon had been gone for over a week. In that time she'd seen no one, except from her window or on her walks, and she'd spoken to no one but vendors, merchants, and herself. A woman alone remained aloof from men if she were wise, and remained apart from other women if she were ashamed of why she was alone. Sometimes she'd walk to the edge of the fire-ravaged district that had been her world, and she'd stare at the devastation, wondering who'd survived and where they'd gone, but she never dared to seek them out, because she couldn't forget how she'd survived.

Gideon had been invited back to his heart's home by the people who owned it now; she could scarcely accompany him, and understood that. But it was hard to be alone, for all she couldn't forget how she earned her way when he was with her. She discovered it was no easier to be alone even if she was fed, clothed, and kept in luxury. Now here were his two good friends, and never had visitors been more welcome.

After they'd been seated, she prattled on about how well she was doing, pointing out how fine her lodgings were, assuring them how nicely they suited her. The two men nodded and smiled and noted how her hands twisted in her lap as she spoke, and saw the bright anxiety in her eyes whenever the conversation lapsed, and how quickly she resumed speaking, as though afraid that if she stopped, they'd leave, and they never believed a word she spoke so blithely.

"And whom have you seen?" Tristram asked gently.

Her spate of conversation ended, but as Jamie cast a hard look to his friend, she said on a little sigh, and with a tiny shrug, "Ah, well, Master Jones, you're my first visitors."

The two men exchanged glances.

"But I've seen . . . others," she said hesitantly, and then, giving over all her fears as well as her problem to them, she added, "That's why I don't go out so much, I think. I met . . . I saw some of the people I'd seen at court in the street the other day, but they were . . . rude, so I passed them by. And yet one said he lives nearby. I don't want to meet them again, so I stay here. But the window's open and there's a lovely breeze," she said brightly, because the sorrow in Jamie's eyes almost undid her, and she didn't want them to think Gideon had treated her badly by leaving her. She was a grown woman, after all, even though there were times she almost wished she were a child he could have hired a nursemaid for. Especially those times when she walked past that frightening, languid courtier and his cold-eyed companion.

"Uh! Rochester and Mobely," Tristram said on a strangled grunt, as though he'd tasted something bad when she told him their names. "I don't breathe when the wind is in the east, because the lovely earl dwells on that side of my own house, but I'd forgotten, the wretched Mobely does live nearby. You did right to ignore them. Gideon once thwarted the little earl, some trivial matter years ago, but he's never forgiven him for it—that, and the fact that Gideon never bothers to conceal his dislike, which is exactly why Charles loves him even more than Rochester, to the little weasel's eternal irritation."

"What did they say? Did they give you insult?" Jamie cried, and then sank down in the chair he'd leapt from, after Tristram reminded him gently, "Softly, Jamie, it's not your fight, Mistress Monk is not your boat to paddle."

"I don't know if it was insult," Mary said, refusing to meet Jamie's eyes, or to consider Tristram's words, because she'd been bred to be frugal and knew she hadn't such a store of friends that she could afford to look for insult in these two men's words.

"They asked after Gideon," she said at once, "but I wasn't born the day before yesterday, even if I did open the door without thinking just now. I said he was well, and never mentioned he was gone, and when they started to ask if I'd like their company since he wasn't with me, they asked in a way that made me want to hit them, so I left them standing there instead.

"But I met them again the next day too—that's when I stopped walking out. This time they greeted me and asked me other foolishness, and when I began to walk past without speaking, the dark one—Sir Roger—handed me a note. I took it because it wouldn't have been right to toss it away. It's for Gideon," she explained, motioning to a folded note that lay upon the table near to Tristram.

"And it wouldn't be right for you to deny us your company," Tristram said decisively. "Gideon said we might look in on you, and we're disposed to walk out with you while we look in. Now you've got such fine lodgings, you've probably been eating from cookshops, and I'm surprised you've survived to this day. But Jamie and I know a tavern the King himself slips off to—he likes his dinners as sumptuous as his other pleasures—oh, don't fret," he laughed, "no one from court will be there, there's a play they're all off to see, so they'll dine at the Rose near the theater, or Chatelaines, the French house, where they can swagger and squander their money. We're after good food."

"Even if they were there, we'd be there too, and you'd suffer no insult," Jamie promised.

"Go—wash the sleep from your eyes or whatever it is you do to look so wondrous fair. We'll wait. And don't worry about what that red-headed brute will think, he'll think it fine, my word on it. Go now,"

Tristram said with amusement mixed in with some softer emotion as he saw both her indecision and her eagerness.

She bit her lip, and then, not at all like a pretty young woman ought, but exactly as a street urchin might, she grinned from ear to ear, crinkling up her eyes and fairly glowing with mischievous joy, before she ducked a curtsy and fairly danced into the next room.

Tristram chuckled, as Jamie gazed after her as though he'd seen the sun rise in that other room. Then Tristram stretched his long legs and arms, and rose and roamed around the room, restlessly and idly inspecting the furnishings.

Jamie had just opened his lips to finally venture a whisper about his anger at finding Mary so lost and forlorn, although his friend had it read in his face from the moment they'd arrived, but stopped when he saw Tristram standing absolutely still with the note for Gideon in his hand. He was about to caution him to put it down when Mary appeared in the doorway, her hair pushed into a mass of curls, her gown straightened, her cloak over her arm, and a happy anticipatory smile on her lips.

"What a gem you are, to be sure, Mistress Monk," Tristram said, looking up, unperturbed. "Most ladies would have only got their left cheek painted in such a short time."

"I don't paint," Mary said, her smile fading as she saw Gideon's note in the slender Cavalier's hand.

"Oh," Tristram said, waving the note in the air, "this message—I've my man going to Ivyclose this very evening, to deliver Gideon some papers he asked me to send—to do with proof of property or some such the new owners need. Shall I send it on to him?"

"Ah," she said on a quick breath such as someone

might take at a stitch in her side, "then he's not coming home so soon?"

"I think not, but even if he is, the papers are for the new owners. Shall we send the note, or wait until the rogue returns for him to read it?" he asked casually. "I think," he added lightly, "It would be best to send it on, so long as my man's going."

"Then yes, then fine," she said, distracted, as he slipped the piece of paper into the deep pocket of his thickly embroidered long coat.

They walked the evening streets, one elegant courtier to either side of the pretty little dark-haired woman who was laughing so merrily. She had little to do but laugh as her two escorts argued wittily over which tavern or restaurant to visit now that most of their favorites were ashes. But it seemed they'd known all along, since they walked her straight to the river steps and helped her into a boat that took them down to the Bear, by the bridge side. There they commanded a table by the fireplace, ales and victuals enough for an army of diners, and everyone's attention with their constant laughter.

It was late in the night when they finally saw Mary back to her rooms, and after Jamie prowled them as though hunting rats, they waited until she'd bolted her door behind them before calling their final good night to her.

It wasn't until the two men had walked fully two streets away that Jamie asked what had been burning on his tongue all night.

"You've never got anyone going to Ivyclose!" he said. "Nor would you send Gideon any note from his worst enemies at court. What's happening?"

"It's not for Gideon, so it hardly matters he'll never see it," Tristram said, reaching into his pocket. "I'll say it was some mistaken matter. Here," he said softly. "Best to read it in the night, it's not fit to see the light of day."

They paused near to a brightly burning torch on the outside of a tavern. Jamie picked up the bit of paper and read, with no difficulty, for the few sentences were writ black and bold and sprawled across the page:

Now here's a sad tale of a Hawke gone to earth,
Leaving his whore no loving or mirth,
To pay such high dues
For a bed he don't use!
There could be reason for such tricking,
More than his conscience may be pricking.
And who in the world knows,
better than his lady at Ivyclose?
. . . Only Mary's new friends at court
Who'll be pleased to provide her livelier sport.

Jamie crumpled the note in his fist after he'd scanned the lines, and was about to cast it away, but Tristram plucked it from his hands.

"The fire, not the gutter, for this plaguey thing," he said coldly.

"I don't understand," Jamie sighed after they'd walked on in silence. "Why would she send it on to Gideon? To get him to hurry back, do you suppose?"

"Dear child," Tristram lectured, "she's not such a good actress. She'd have been devastated if she'd read it, she'd have burned it instanter, but we'd have read it in her face. No, here, look again. She wouldn't have recognized it as being for her," and as he held the paper up for Jamie to see the "Mistress Mary Monck, Fine Whore" that was scrawled there, he added, "That's no spelling of her name she'd recognize. Too many words to alert her for one thing. For another, Gideon said it was 'M-o-n-k,' and the other fine embellishments were likely not sensible to her. She can't read, thank God."

"It would've killed her," Jamie swore as Tristram stuffed the note back into his pocket.

"Or Rochester. Gideon's got a temper," Tristram remarked.

"Gideon's got a treasure, he's a fool," Jamie said vehemently.

"Perhaps he's found a better one at Ivyclose," Tristram sighed. "Patience, we'll see. He's not a fool, but it may be that that house of his holds his heart in thrall as no woman can."

"Then he *is* a fool," Jamie spat.

"Then," Tristram agreed softly as they walked on into the night, "then, yes, he would be."

# 9

In eleven days' time Mary grew to recognize every sound in her new lodgings far better than she'd ever been able to identify the noises in her own house in the seventeen years that she'd lived there with her family. But then, the sounds of other voices—of laughter, argument, sneezes—the hundred everyday noises caused by movements of people getting on with their everyday lives had overlaid the simple house sounds. Then too, she'd lived in a busy alley, and even when it was relatively still inside, street cries were heard from dawn to late night, even with the windows closed against the evil vapors of the night. All this, as well as the sound of her own diverting thoughts, had distracted her then.

So it might have been that in those days gone by, if she'd heard an odd high creaking in the night in the corner of her bedchamber, she'd have wondered what it could be. No need now. She knew exactly which floorboard was in the habit of sighing at that hour of the night. As she knew what the rain did to the shutters on the little window on the northern side, and what the wind caused every other window to whine about, and at which hours. These new lodgings were

on a wider, and so quieter, street than the alley she'd
lived in, and moreover, they were higher up, so she
didn't hear so many street noises either. As it was a
well-constructed house, the sounds made by neighboring lodgers were faintly heard. But she loved them
most because they reminded her that she still lived
among people.

Other than that, she heard nothing but the floors
and walls murmuring at changes in temperature and
time, noises made by rooms empty of everything but
herself. Those, and, of course, the interior sounds of
the dreary, repetitive thoughts of a girl left to herself
for eleven days. And as the time went on, those became the loudest sounds, and in time they all began to
say the same word, louder than all else, and that word
was simple enough, since it was always: "Go."

And since she always answered it promptly by asking, "Where?" she didn't find her own company too
diverting.

Tristram and Jamie's visits were her only joy. They
brought her news of the world, and brought her out
into it, and their very presence reminded her of Gideon. Which was as well, because in her isolation she
began to have odd fancies. With Gideon gone for so
long, and herself so new to these lodgings, sometimes
she found herself forgetting her purpose for being
there, as well as her new profession. And when Jamie
and Tris—as they'd insisted she call them now—came
to visit, she sometimes forgot or made herself forget.
Their gallantry made her think of herself as a respectable young woman with gentlemen callers; at other
times their informality made her believe herself to be
a relative of theirs. But then they'd always mention
Gideon and she'd be reminded of what she'd never
really forgotten.

Now there was her newest worry—that he'd never
return. Sometimes the thought caused pure panic: she'd
wonder what she'd do in order to live if he abandoned

her. Other times the pain was even sharper than when
she thought of getting by on her own again: when she
thought of his kindness and laughter and care for her,
and, worse still, when she lay alone in the dark in the
night and remembered his touch.

But today she was thinking of nothing but the folly
of fashion. She was dressing herself, grumbling and
complaining aloud as she'd begun to do in order to
feel less alone. Her petticoat was on, but her corset
was only half-on, and she began to think, or so she
told the listening walls, that she'd never get it all on so
she could finish dressing. The corset was quilted so
that the whalebone wouldn't cut the thin skin that lay
over her ribs, where the bodice pinched in so as to
push her breasts up high. But the corset was only
half-laced after ten minutes of her work at it, because
she'd had her clothes made when she'd first come,
half-starved, to live with Gideon's generosity, and aside
from having to twist herself into a knot to lace it up in
back, she'd gained just enough weight to make the
daily chore a painful one now. If it wasn't done up,
even her naturally high young breasts wouldn't fit into
her fashionable gown as they ought, and she'd look
odd if she buttoned the gown over them—slatternly if
she dared button the gown under them. Her clothes fit
right only if she wore the corset, so she'd been twisting
and fumbling at the strings for several minutes, mut-
tering, her cheeks growing red and her fingers numbed.
Her complaining grew so loud that she had no warning.

Then she heard the door fly open. And before she
could snatch up a robe or gather her wits together,
there was the sound of booted feet and a deep voice
and she looked up and he was there. He dwarfed the
room, his plumed hat scraping the ceiling. He dropped
his traveling bag and looked down at her and smiled
like the sun coming out, and cried, "Mary! Sweeting!
What a wonderful way to greet me!"

Before she could protest, if she'd a thought to, she

was scooped up in his arms and was breathing in the fresh scent of him, a scent of outdoors and sun and horse and soap and leather and Gideon. Then, her nostrils filled with scent of him, her ears ringing with the sound of his deep voice, she felt his warm mouth over hers and she was so completely absorbed in and by him that she forgot there'd been such a thing as loneliness, or a time when she'd been without him. She remembered soon enough.

"Oh, Gideon, no!" she squealed as he laid her down on their bed, and taking off his gloves, began to unlace what she'd so painstakingly done up.

He stopped to look at her, but there was no laughter in his eyes now. That brought her up short, making her remember that she'd gotten above herself in these days by herself, because it wasn't her place to say no without good reason.

"No? Why?" he asked as he lay propped on his elbows over her, waiting. "Is it your time of the month? Are you in pain from it?"

"No," she said breathlessly. "That was last week."

"So I thought I remembered it might be," he said pleasantly, sliding his hand up beneath the corset so as to further loosen its ties, "so I thought you'd have a warm greeting for me too. It was a long ride, and it grows chilly now. I didn't think to find a chill in my own bed," he murmured against her breast, his watchful stillness easing, rapidly fading into something more overwhelming and concentrated. "Come, sweeting, didn't you miss me?"

"I did. Oh, I did," she whispered, relaxing, succumbing, only to struggle again as he finally freed her from her corset and began to pay tribute to what he'd uncovered, all the while sliding her petticoat off as well.

"Gideon," she said into his ear as he bent his head to her, feeling the softness of his long hair against her lips, opening her eyes to see herself surrounded and consumed by the flames of his hair even as she was in his embrace, "Gideon," she said, struggling up from it with growing alarm, "Tristram and Jamie . . . they're coming here, they'll be here soon . . ."

"They are?" he asked lazily, running one hand along her body and beginning to unbutton his coat with the other. "What of it?"

"But they'll be here any minute," she insisted, lifting her head and trying to lift her shoulders so as to look over his wide shoulders to the door. "Oh, and you've left the outer door open! Gideon, please!"

The note of true anguish in her voice reached him.

"Damn the door," he muttered, "I'll shut it," and, rising with a reluctance she could see the reason for, he backed from her, never taking his eyes from her, and then turned and strode to the door. He closed it emphatically and came back into their bedchamber, smiling as he loosed his lacy collar.

"Now, then . . ." he said, before he heard the rapping on the door and an indignant voice calling.

"At dawn, or now, villain? I'll not have a door closed in *my* face as I come to it after climbing all these stairs, without having my revenge. Name the hour, whoreson!" Tristram called.

"Oh, gods," Gideon sighed, stopping in his tracks, "I'll send them away."

"But, Gideon," she protested, "I told them they were welcome today."

"Well, now they're not," he said, advancing to her and resting one knee on the bed as he looked down at her, the blue fire of his eyes intense, "and he's only jesting," he added as he shrugged off his coat. "He'll not be offended, he'll understand."

"But they'll know," she said unhappily, her eyes on the door, ignoring the man before her as she listened to the murmur of voices in the hall. "They'll know what we're doing," she whispered frantically.

"I should hope so," he said against her cheek as he bore her downward. "They're old enough.

"God's blood, woman!" he cursed a moment later, finding her attention still far from his attentions, her lips stiff and cold, her body tensed beneath his, but not with sweet expectation. "So what if they 'know'? They hardly think you're here to merely decorate my house. They don't believe I hired you on as my valet! Of course they'll understand—and good! Because they'll leave when they do. They've mistresses of their own, you know!"

"Oh. Yes. Of course," she said stupidly, realizing her foolishness in thinking for a minute that they'd ever think anything else or expect anything else of her. And realizing that, she subsided: quiet, limp, and ready to accommodate him.

What she thought showed on her face, as always. But he'd already read it in her body and it robbed him of his desire to do anything but comfort her. It was his damnable fate, he thought, rolling over onto his back, to need acceptance before pleasure. It had been that acceptance he'd been seeking as much as anything else in her arms just now.

He'd passed a week being careful, restrained and frustrated with his cool, beautiful shy Puritan lady. He'd gazed on milky smooth skin and the slight arch of a breast and the curve of an arm and the rounded arc of a hip, and all he'd been able to do was to gaze, since the slightest advance had caused his fair lady to retreat. So he'd thought of the warmth awaiting him in London all the way here. And had arrived, to open his door on tousle-haired dark-eyed Mary sitting half-dressed in her petticoats, with her bodice gaping open showing all her ripe flesh, and he'd felt desire flood through him. She was his, they'd a bargain; not only was her purpose for being in his rooms to please him, but her sudden joy welcomed him into her arms—where he'd gone, only to freeze. Both mistresses and true loves seemed fated to thwart him. He sighed, but her sudden intake of breath and her look of guilty alarm made him roll to his feet and arise.

"Don't fret," he said as he walked to the door. "They can come now. It'll be my turn later."

By the time he'd opened the door to greet his friends, the bedchamber door was closed, and half his smile was for his friends and half for the glimpse he'd got of her face before she'd shut the door, since it had been flaming almost as much as his hair.

"Thank you," Tristram said sweetly as Jamie looked anywhere but at Gideon, trying to set his face in lines of unconcern. "I love being locked out, and having to threaten my way into a friend's house. Would you like to strike me a few times before you bow me in and offer me a chair?"

"I'd rather put one over your head than beneath your rump," Gideon said, "but since I have as much trouble as you do telling one from the other, you're safe enough."

"Welcome home," Tristram said, bowing, very pleased with this greeting.

"We thought Mary would be alone, but as she's not, if you'd like, we'll leave now," Jamie said stiffly.

"I might have liked, but she didn't," Gideon remarked as his friends came into the parlor with him and he shut the door behind them. "Have you been giving the girl ideas above her station while I've been gone," he asked pleasantly, "or have you come to some sort of arrangement with her, Jamie?" he asked just as mildly.

Jamie's hand flew to his sword, his face pale and his astonishment clear in his wide blue eyes.

"I would never offer her anything while she was under your protection," Jamie said clearly after a pause, "but if you wish, I'll offer you a chance for satisfaction of your imagined insult."

"That's not the sort of satisfaction I was after," Gideon sighed, leaning back against a table's edge. "Oh, stow your weapon, Jamie. If you've not been employing your other one with my mistress, I don't care to fight you. And I didn't think you were. It's only that I find her more . . . puritanical"—his lips twitched at the word—"than I'd have wished."

"You shouldn't be surprised," Tristram lectured, his tensed muscles easing as he watched his friends both settle down, "as you wouldn't seek an apple in a cherry orchard, Gideon, you shouldn't have picked a mistress from the home of a 'respectable tradesman.' "

All three men laughed at the familiar words, Mary's favorites, as Tristram went on, "Mistresses should be lured from noblemen's beds. Their disgruntled wives and lovers and even their flighty daughters are fine for the work of play. Or they should be culled from the gutters or theaters or farmyards. Anywhere but from a guildsman's house. Although I do see the charm of Mary Monk and see that it lies precisely in the fact that she's uncommon goods.

"Speaking of which . . ." he said too casually, "Gideon, my dear, you're mighty lucky the girl has honor, and your friends almost as much. She was so lonely these past weeks that she'd no one to talk to, much less deceive you with. Shame, Gideon, because she's only a girl, and a bright one at that. Don't bother to rattle your sword," he said, waving a limp hand. "I speak out of concern, not lust, for her. I've got my own beautiful Phyllis to ease me these nights, and she's just my sort of woman, her only sensitivities are external, thank God, and highly visible and entirely at my disposal."

"Until next week," Gideon said, amused, "when you'll be bored with her."

"Exactly," Tristram said gently, examining his fingers, "and then I'll move on, but so will she. Because I remember what my good mother taught me, and I'm not greedy. I take only what I intend to use on my plate, always remembering that children are starving in the East. And while I never understood how eating all my supper helped starveling brats elsewhere, I can see how letting a likely lass free to pursue other interests when my own wanes, frees her.

"The girl," he said, not even blinking as he looked up to see Gideon's cold blue eyes fixed on him with sudden intensity, "was as lonely as any prisoner in a dungeon, for all you've locked her up here in the sky in comfortable rooms. She was talking to walls when we dropped by to pay her a visit, and would have been answering them if we hadn't come back soon again," he added softly, so that his words couldn't be heard beyond the room.

For all that Gideon's face was set in lines of such implacable grimness that many other men would have reached for their cloaks or their swords on seeing such an unblinking gaze fixed on them, Tristram didn't blink an eye. But Gideon's own soon closed, as he let out a long sigh and then opened them again to look at his friend with clearly rueful acceptance of his words, as he said on a small shrug, "I didn't think I'd be gone so long. I was too pleased to be gone to think of settling things here before I left . . ." and as Jamie looked up with a sudden light in his eyes, it went out again as soon as Gideon went on, ". . .I could've seen to her better, s'truth. Because I've no desire to be done with the wench yet."

"Ah," Tristram said wisely, "then the rumors were false? Celeste Southern resembles a fish? Or a fowl? Or has the wit of a swan rather than the looks of one? Still, for Ivyclose and the approval of your king, I'd think you could tolerate much more, or less."

"I've nothing to tolerate but my own impatience," Gideon said. "The lady's beautiful and sweet and wise as any man could wish, Ivyclose or not—i'faith she's too wise to tumble into the marriage bed with me as soon as I'd wish. You'll see—wait until you see her!" he added with a wide, white-toothed smile.

"And you want the cobbler's little daughter too?" Tristram asked.

"It's been done," Gideon said, growing cooler as his thoughts returned from the lady of his dreams to his friend's audacity, "but I doubt I'd do it. For what it's worth, I learned from my mother too—and I don't discard dirty water until I get clean."

Jamie arose from his chair slowly, his face white, his hand on his sword, but without seeing him, Gideon started shaking his head and said on a low laugh, "Oh, but what a bad comparison! I've not got your way with words, Tris. My little Mary's as refreshing as purest spring water. I only meant that although my wedding's a consummation most devoutly to be wished—as they say in your favorite play—it'll be a time until that happy day. But you'll understand soon enough, I hope. Celeste will be coming to London with her brother soon, although not soon enough for me."

"And soon enough for Mary too?" Jamie asked quietly, as Tristram stared at him thoughtfully, for although Jamie abandoned his warlike stance, his voice trembled with suppressed emotion.

"Sooth no!" Gideon said at once in low but strong tones, looking at him in astonishment. "What are you thinking of, lad? Mary's not one of your practiced, experienced women of court! It would distress her, she wouldn't understand. Why should she suffer rejection before it's a fact, or feel she's failed where she'd no hope of winning? No, it's best she knows nothing of this. I've told her nothing of it, at any rate . . . have you?" he asked, suddenly wondering if that was why she'd rejected his amorous greeting.

"Of course not," Tristram said swiftly, before Jamie could speak, "but you might as well know that Rochester and Mobely tried. Mobely lives nearby and dropped her a hint, which she didn't get. But," he said before more questions could be asked, "if your lady's arriving soon, I don't know how you intend to keep it secret long."

"I don't need to keep it secret," Gideon snapped, turning away, annoyed at the question and the answers it demanded. "I just prefer not divulging it before it's time. And that may be a long time, at that," he said, wheeling around and confronting his friends. "They travel in different circles, and I intend to keep it so. But enough of women troubles, don't you agree?"

"Definitely," Tristram said. "Now for some women pleasures. We'd come to take Mary to dine, as promised. Now we can take our own dinner partners as well as you and Mary. Coming?"

Gideon hesitated only so long as to think longingly of what he'd rather do, and wonder how he'd be able to do that pleasurably with Mary, who hadn't learned the full extent of such pleasures— especially after he'd refused her a treat she'd prefer.

"Of course," he said on a sigh, bowing to the inevitable. "Only give me time to get my gloves on."

Jamie's dinner partner was much prettier than Tristram's, Mary thought, but then, Tristram's lady was a lady, and she supposed that was her major charm. Certainly she showed no others. She hadn't even showed her face for the first hour they'd been together. Then after she'd removed her half-mask— after Tristram convinced her that a woman with her face swathed in black feathers would be more remarked on than anonymous—she seemed disappointingly plain by contrast. But since she then proceeded to hide her face very effectively beneath Tristram's for the rest of the coach ride, it hardly mattered—except to Mary, who was so scandalized she scarcely knew whether to watch the carryings-on or to ignore them

altogether, and so passed the time with her eyes on
stalks, or so Gideon was pleased to whisper in her ear,
to her great embarrassment and his greater amusement.

But although Tristram's lady had crept out, hooded
and masked, from a very fine house, Jamie's companion stepped out of a finer one, with more footmen and
torchlights and gold on the door. Even in the leaping
torchlight it could be seen that she was amazingly
lovely. In the greater light in the tavern they finally
arrived at, it could be seen that her loveliness was
underlined by art: her hair a more lightless inkier
black than humanly possible, her eyes and lips outlined in paint, and her maidenly blush a constant pow
dery one. But she spoke in such low accents and the
things she spoke of were so much lower that Mary
soon understood that she was a workingwoman, and
the house she'd been taken from was her house of
employment.

The uncomfortable coach ride was made longer by
constant argument. So many of their favorite taverns
had been lost in the fire, the famous Boar's Head,
Miter, and Pope's Head being just a few, that the men
couldn't agree on where to dine. Mary was subdued
because the Mermaid on Friday Street, near to her
own lost home, had been mentioned, as well as because of the nature of the other women in the coach.
Tristram and his lady seemed to be proceeding to
intimacies she wasn't yet acquainted with, although in
all fairness, she had to admit that Tristram often attempted escape, but his companion was as single-minded
as she seemed many-handed. Jamie mostly ignored his
beautiful companion, but ignoring a woman with such
a loud voice was impossible for anyone within earshot,
which would have been, Mary thought, half of London. So she was more than grateful when The Devil
was chosen and then arrived at.

Her relief was short-lived. She soon found that sitting at a table with a beautiful whore of the lowest

mentality and a great lady of the lowest morality was no treat. And so she was only too pleased, to Gideon's great pleasure, to try to concentrate all her attention on him. That wasn't easy.

"Where do you work, dear?" Jamie's companion asked Mary when there was a lapse in the music being played and Gideon was occupied with attending to his ale. "I disremember seeing you afore," she mused, "neither at court, because I have been to there, nor neither at Mother Bennet's, nor Mother Jane's behind the House of Lords, nor at the house at Dog Lane where I visit my sister where she works, nor neither at the theater where everybody goes, and I never forgets a face, dear."

"Mistress Monk is not in the trade," Jamie said, casting a smile to Mary.

At that, Lady X, as she'd been introduced, left off crawling over Tristram, disengaged her lips from his ear, and left him to his dinner for a moment. She eyed Mary narrowly and asked in a shrill hard voice, "Your name again—Monck 'twas?"

"Mary Monk," Mary said in a low voice, looking down at her plate.

"Ah, the Moncks. General's family, from the country, new to town, are you?" the lady said on a bark of a laugh, "and gobbled up the great red Hawke right off. Lucky girl. Have you had Old Rowley . . . Charles," she explained as Mary stared. "Have you had him yet?" she asked as casually as she'd have asked if Mary had tried the lamb.

Before Gideon could speak, Mary did, after she'd swallowed hard. She spoke up steadily and clearly, though she never raised her eyes. "No, not those Monks. I'm from London. My father was a cobbler, not a general. And I am in the trade now. But I haven't had Old Charles anyone yet."

The lady shrugged and went back to her diversion, this time reaching beneath the table for it. But this time Tristram brought up her two hands in one of his, smiled sweetly, and said distinctly, "Lady, we're not at court now. Contain yourself or you'll find yourself going home to your husband while he's still awake. Now, you wouldn't want that, would you? Behave, you're in the company of a respectable tradesman's daughter."

And though the lady gaped at him, and Mary jerked her gaze upward to stare hard at him, there was no mockery in his voice, and nothing but seriousness in his dark blue eyes.

Jamie smiled as his companion gawked. And Gideon took Mary's hand in his own and brought it to his lips.

"Thank you, Master Jones," he said, though his gentled smile was all for Mary.

The gentlemen's conversation excluded her after that, and, thwarted of her primary aims as well, the petulant lady picked at her food and began to gossip. To Mary's complete surprise, Jamie's companion took up the topic, and soon the two women were chatting merrily, swapping stories about gentlemen at court they both had known, comparing intimate notes on them as freely as the ladies at court had done that day Mary had gone there with Gideon. It was when Lady X began to extol the Earl of Rochester's gift to her that Gideon rose to his feet, cutting her off in midsentence as she was warming to the virtues of the remarkable "Signor Dildo" that the earl had imported from Italy, in bulk, for the pleasure of all the ladies at court.

"I give you good evening, ladies, my friends," Gideon said. "I've only just arrived in town from the country and have slept little. Although I'd give up much to remain in your company, my eyes insist on it, whatever my heart demands."

"Sweetly said." Tristram nodded approvingly. "You're excused then, Master Hawkes . . . but oh, are you

taking Mistress Monk away too?" he asked with great
mock disappointment as the men all laughed, the two
women at the table looked relieved, and Mary sighed
happily.

"Gideon," she asked when they sat in the darkened
interior of the hackney coach again, "what, or who, is
Signor Dildo?"

He told her, briefly, and she was very glad they sat
in a darkened coach.

"Still, I can see why Rochester imported them," he
added musingly. "He'd be the first the ladies would
find lacking in that respect. For all his talk, I believe
he tires even more quickly at the task than we do of
his poetry about the matter. But s'truth," he laughed,
"some of the ladies at court would do well to depend
on an instrument of leather and padding, because they'd
wear mortal men out—just look at Tristram's delight
tonight! Or don't—as you tried not to. At that," he
said more thoughtfully, reaching an arm around her in
the dark to draw her closer to him, "it's likely a favor
to them. At least the little Signor won't give them the
pox, which is more than I can say for Rochester or
most of his friends. What's this?" he asked, diverted
from his thoughts, looking down and trying to make
out her expression. "Are you becoming like the sun,
mistress? So warm in the afternoon, so cold at night?
Have I said aught to offend you, Mary?" he asked
more seriously as he felt her body upheld stiffly alongside his.

"No," she said, and shaking her head, went on
softly, trying to phrase what she barely understood,
"it's just the ladies, the things they spoke about, made
me feel . . . bad about being near any man, and just as
bad about being a woman." She paused to think of a
better way of describing the shame she'd felt.

"You said you weren't a Puritan," he teased.

"I'faith! I'm not!" she said at once, annoyed enough
to forget to try to please him. "Why is it everyone

must be a Puritan or a courtier with you? Don't you know there are many of us who aren't either, and don't like either forbidding all pleasure or giving in to all pleasure? If you can call what goes on at court 'pleasure,' " she said with a sniff.

"But this isn't court, Mary," he said gently, his lips near to her ear, his arm round her waist. "This is you and me, alone together. I don't ask you to be anything else but yourself. Is what we do pleasure?"

"Oh, Gideon," she said, leaning in toward him, "yes, 'tis," and as his lips came to hers, she thought: Ah, yes, I'm sorry to say, it is. Because she knew this wasn't court, he was Gideon, their situation was different, entirely different, or so she told herself again and again as she closed her eyes and tried to forget all of it but his kiss.

After that one kiss, he did no more than hold her close as the coach carried them to their lodgings. He wanted to let time elapse so the lusty conversation she'd found so unsettling would be forgotten. They rode in silence; she was afraid to speak disapproval of the night to him, and he unwilling to bring up anything that might disrupt her softened mood. But his mood was anything but tranquil.

His abstinence and frustration at Ivyclose, the interrupted lovemaking of the day, the talk this evening, and the feeling of her warm body next to him in the coach combined to feed his passion. He could barely wait to close their door against the world and resume what he'd begun hours earlier. But once they'd gotten up to their bedchamber and she turned her head to look everywhere but at him, knowing what he needed, and yet too shy to provide it without being asked, the only thing that surprised him was that he discovered himself equally eager to have her as to have her happy with him as he did.

"What's this?" he asked, coming to her and taking her in his arms. "Shy with me again? Will every time

with us be as the first time?" And then he could have
bitten his tongue, for she looked up at him with real
sorrow and said softly, "There was no shyness the first
time, Gideon, don't you remember?"

"I don't want to," he said, and that was true enough.

He drew her close, fitting her to himself, his chin
resting against her tumble of dark curls. He rubbed
her back with one hand, making wide circles, feeling
the small bones beneath his hand as much as he felt
the womanly body pressed so close to him, the thought
of both her fragility and her femininity producing tenderness and burning need in him.

He wanted her, and wanted her to want him as
much, but wouldn't lie to her any more than he'd
force her. But there were truths and truths, and for all
he always said he wasn't a man of many words, he
knew a great many, and how to avoid saying a great
many more.

"Mary," he whispered, "I have missed you very
much. I've thought of holding you thus very much.
And I've dreamed of holding you even closer even
more in these past weeks." And that was true enough.

She responded to those truths as well as to the
fearful and fascinating obvious need of his body so
close to hers. She'd relaxed in his arms; now she
shivered slightly, and he read it right.

When he'd drawn her clothes from her and shed his
own, when he finally had her close and was at last
close to the beginning of what would be his comple-
tion in their wide bed, he paused again. He had her
body beneath him, he had her acquiescence, but it
wasn't enough after such a drought. He knew that
what he wanted most she couldn't give him yet, not, at
least, until he gave her ultimate pleasure, and he'd no
way of knowing when, if ever, that might be. But even
if he couldn't have her eagerness match his own, he
wanted more.

"Sweeting," he said low against her neck, his damp

forehead resting on her shoulder, his body tensed, awaiting her signal to begin, "sweet," he said, "I've wanted you so. Mary, I need you," he whispered, and thought how God himself knew that was true.

That was what she'd never expected to hear, the other meaning of it never occurred to her, and her heart flew up. She forgot to take note of each and all the mechanics of what he was doing to her, step by step, as she did each time they made love, and instead brought her arms around him for more than the sake of the mechanics of it. She touched his cheek and touched his back and kissed his lips in sudden joy and gratitude, with something very like love. Which was what he'd been waiting for.

So even the last part of it, the part she'd always found too long and a little frightening, when he was so active and she seemed so far away even when he pressed closest as he drove to seek release, became something very different for her. It became almost something that explained what he so obviously found when he stopped and groaned and sank down to her again. And he seemed to know it. Because when he was done, he stroked her as he held her close and said on a shaky laugh, "Almost, Mistress Monk, almost, eh? Perhaps next time, then, we'll see."

Then it was his turn to be surprised, when after a silent time, as he was reluctantly closing his eyes, readying himself for sleep, not wanting to tire her or lose the ground he'd gained, he felt her hand upon his shoulder, then his collarbone, then his chest. It was light as a random thought, tentative as a tactful question. Which he answered, perhaps, he thought later, a bit too completely, because there were things she hadn't meant to ask, perhaps, although she learned them soon enough, and before she slept again those hesitant hands knew the whole shape of him at last. But at least at last she'd touched him intimately of her own accord, and so perhaps next time . . .

There'd be many next times, he thought, and whispered to her as he pulled her near again, to partner her in sleep this time. He was pleased with her, and so he told her, and more so when he heard her sleepy thread of a whisper of, "I too am pleased, Gideon," as she settled against him to sleep.

He was more than pleased in the morning, he was jubilant when a messenger arrived with a note for him. After he'd read it, Mary was so delighted with his merry whistling and broad grin that she came into his arms without his asking when he came back into their bedchamber. And so, all unknowing, she helped him celebrate the news he'd just gotten, the news that made him so exuberant in his lovemaking.

The news, from her own hand, that Celeste Southern had decided Ivyclose was empty without him. Or so at least he was pleased to think, because she'd written that she'd changed her plans, and so was coming to London soon, much sooner than she'd planned.

# 10

"Do I look right? Oh, Gideon, do I look well enough?" Mary asked anxiously, craning her neck backward to see him

He paused to look down at her, with her cape held high in his hands. "Well enough for what?" he asked softly. "For me, certainly. So well, in fact, that I'd as soon take you back to bed as out into the world now. But don't fret," he said, smiling wryly as he saw the consternation on her face, "I won't make you waste an hour's primping just on me."

She lowered her gaze and looked straight ahead. "It wouldn't be wasted time, then," she said quietly, and had she dared to look back into his eyes after her bold confession, she would have been rewarded by seeing the smile he grew soften his hard features into something very much like those of a man in love. She would have been rewarded, but not necessarily surprised. Because the last week together they'd been very much like lovers together.

Since he'd returned from Ivyclose he'd spent every hour of his every day with her, and had made her forget the loneliness and doubt she'd suffered while he'd been gone. He'd treated her like a favored girl-child some days—touring the city with her, showing her that every fine day in London could be like a small Bartholmew Fair for the rich and idle. He shared her laughter when they'd paused to see quack doctors and their zanies entertaining to draw crowds and customers for their pills and elixirs—the laughter they produced the best medicine they sold, Gideon said—or stopped to see street performers, tumblers and acrobats, Raree, and Punch and Judy shows. Better yet, they'd not stopped to see more popular entertainments that made her blanch. Because he only hurried her past the hangings, the displays of heads of traitors, and the remains of gibbeted men, forgoing invitations to bear-baitings and cockfights, as well, for her sake. And further for the sake of her company, he gave up invitations to meet his fellows at coffeehouses and clubs and other places where women weren't welcome.

On other days he was like her older, wiser counselor, talking her out of the sudden bouts of sad memory that overcame her, helping her to resist the urge to revisit what remained of her home, to keep her from further regret. Still other days he was a madcap rogue, lighting all their hours with laughter. And every night he was her ardent lover, teaching her, trying to show her how to take for herself as much as she was giving him.

Day and night for the past week, he'd been not only her closest friend but also her only companion. For all that his friends sought him and left messages for him, for all that they were in the center of the busiest city in their world, still he'd managed to keep her isolated and entirely alone with him. Everything he did was designed to teach her more about himself. And she was careful to find out even more.

She found that asking questions about the sights they saw could encourage stories about other sights he'd seen and places he'd been. Any well-placed question at the right time could end in fascinating reminiscenses. Even a touch in the night could lead to a tale for her to take to sleep with her, since sometimes so much as venturing a question about a scar she traced on his back could take him back in time. A man known for his economy of speech, still he was free with words when they were alone together and was as generous with his past as he was with his purse with her. But she was no spendthrift. All she wanted was more of him.

So all the while Gideon was carefully training his new mistress to suit him in all things, she was tumbling deeply into love with him. Which might not have been precisely what he'd been after, although he soon discovered it suited him very well. He'd had mistresses before, in other lands and times. But they'd been women of experience in such matters. Mary had been untutored in every aspect of her new profession, so he'd taken pains with her as he'd never done with any woman before, and found it a delightful chore, and the results more than entertaining. Now a week had passed, and something in her voice, some little thing in her smile, and some new warm and wonderful thing in her kiss disturbed him as much as it pleased him. So, he decided, now was the time to bring her back and out into the world with him; they weren't newly wedded, after all; it was time to live life as he meant to go on with it.

"No," he said now, sincerely, "I want you to delight the people we'll meet at the playhouse as much as you do me. I'll have my own private play with you after, after all."

He was amused that his newly tutored mistress could still blush even now that she fully understood what he meant by such references. And decided that it flattered her, as everything she wore seemed to do this day.

Her dark hair was parted in the center and allowed to curl, like the petals of an opening flower, all about

the sides of her animated face. She wore a gown of
dull gold embellished with pink roses and ribbons, the
sudden dashes of uplifting color suiting her dusky rose
skin as exactly as they did the heavy hue of the gold.
The cleft between her breasts, the expanse of flesh
above—her neck, her cheek, all of it, he saw, gazing
down as he helped her into her cloak, was the warm
color of dark meadow honey, and remembering how
the pink of the roses echoed other tones on other parts
of her body, there was a moment when he regretted
his plans for the evening.

But then self-congratulation mixed with desire to
end his regrets. He remembered that however they
passed the evening, it would end precisely where he
wanted it to. Subtly shaped and guided by him, she
was now everything he needed in a pleasant little
friend, and if not yet fully learned in getting her own
pleasure in bedwork, still she was as good at her tasks
as any man could ask. Pretty—pretty mannered, obliging, and merry; he was, he knew, a lucky man.

Gideon felt real pride in what he'd produced when
he saw his friends' faces as Mary stepped into the
street with him. But Tristram's look of complete approval and Jamie's of scarcely concealed sick envy
were as nothing compared to the stir she made on his
arm at the theater. No high lady of the court, no low
wench on the hunt in the pit, could really compare to
her this night. There were certainly more beautiful
women present, and many more lavishly dressed. Many
used more attention-getting devices: one lady of court
had fashioned her beauty patches into tiny black birds
that seemed to wheel and flirt over her face and breasts;
another had so many false curls in the latest, most
absurd French style that she gained as much notice
from others in the theater as she did groans from those
seated directly behind her on the low benches; still
another wench wore a gown so low as to make the
Orange girls look like Puritans going to church on a

Sunday morning. But none glowed with as much pure happiness as Mary did; perhaps that was why she took every eye.

She was supremely happy. She sat beside Gideon in a high-backed seat under the first gallery, near to the stage, his hand over hers, his solid, reassuring presence next to her. After a week entirely with him, she felt almost as though she were an appendage of his. Wrapped in his care, her body still warm from his lingering loving in the late afternoon, his scent still on her, his brilliantly bright gaze always upon her, she felt she basked in the radiance of his regard as some flower might have blossomed under the more common sun of heaven.

Tonight he wore his favorite colors and was all in the several shades of brown, except for the white silk of his billowing sleeves and the loose lacy fall of his cravat. But his startling blue eyes and flaming hair made a mockery of the sober Puritan tones; even in their sedate hues he was colorful as the setting sun. They were matched, she thought smugly as she saw people gaping at them, they were a pair tonight, she thought: two golden, gifted people.

Gideon's friends weren't so fortunate. Jamie's companion was a buxom dark-haired wench from the same house his last girl had come from, although this one spoke little and only clung to his side, as close, inevitable, and ignored by him as a bit of lint on his sleeve might have been.

Tristram had a round-faced girl he introduced as Mrs. Cox with him this night. Although much younger, she was just as single-minded as the lady Mary had seen him entertain the time before, in that she seemed more interested in him than in anything around her . . . except for gossip. Because as a lady from court, she wasted no time scanning the audience for faces she recognized so she could attach names and scandal to them for Tristram's entertainment. Whenever that palled, she'd turn to Tristram and try to add some scandal to his name and hers, but that would have been difficult, if not impossible to do, even if Tristram had permitted it—at least from what Mary could see of the rest of the audience's activities.

The play was late in starting, but the audience didn't mind, since it was clearly entertaining itself. Men and women in the pit directly in front of the stage sat on long backless benches shamelessly ogling, flirting, or fondling each other. Cavaliers and ladies, common wenches in uncommonly revealing gowns, ordinary men in extraordinary high spirits: they all chattered, trading easy humorous insults with the Orange girls, who sold their fruits and favors of all kinds with the same sort of loudly theatrical good-naturedness. High in the gallery, where the commonest sat, the footmen and servants awaiting their masters and mistresses created their own fun and frolic to equal, or surpass, their betters below.

The theater filled. The hundreds of candles in the chandeliers above the stage were lit, and after they smoked and spat, each one contributed its small steady flame to make one great blaze of white and yellow light; the babble of voices rose, and Mary sat back, content. The play, written by one of the king's own set, was said to be as wicked and merry as it was improbable, but it didn't matter to her what it was to be. Nothing on the stage tonight could equal the golden fantasy she'd been living since her one brave desperate act had, against all reason and expectations, brought her a happiness to equal the suffering she'd known.

"Etherege wrote it," Tristram commented. "Charles will stay awake through it for his sake, I suppose, so everyone will want to see it."

"And you?" Gideon asked.

"Of course. How can I taunt him about it if I don't? Of course, if you're on your way to the poorhouse after spending all your gold on Mary's finery, I'll understand, and you may leave—we'll meet you later at the Dog. I'll save you some scraps from my plate too, if you'd like," Tristram offered sweetly.

"Very kind. But I'll stay—if it pleases Mary," Gideon remarked.

She nodded, scarcely able to answer, as flattered by his consideration as she was thrilled at the prospect. She'd stay unless they took to crushing kittens on the stage. She'd been to the theater only twice before, and never in such fine seats. If Gideon hadn't liked the play, she'd have left at the end of the first act without a backward glance. But though she'd have known it was a matter of taste with him, she'd have disliked feeling like one of the audience who always left then, pleased with the play or not, in order to avoid paying when the admission was collected. The apprentice, Samuel, had always bragged about all the plays he'd seen, although she'd known very well that like all misers, he'd never seen one beyond the first act. But she was with Gideon now, she reminded herself, and so all her problems with the crass Samuel were only as a troubled dream she'd once had. This was a wonderful dream she was actually living.

"Ah, here he is, and here they are," Mrs. Cox said with great satisfaction, leaving off trying to climb into Tristram's lap for a moment.

But they hardly needed her to tell them that the king had finally arrived. He came in like the first act of a drama, trailing a long string of courtiers, ladies and gentlemen as exquisitely dressed as they were languidly affected. But they could have come in rags or in their velvet gowns, as the mocking rhyme went, because all eyes were on the tall, thin "black boy," Charles, their king. A magnificently gowned but bad-tempered-looking and haughty auburn-haired beauty was with him, very much at his side ("Ah, Castlemaine's dropped another filly for him, that makes it five—though she swears six—and she's come right from childbed to keep him from getting another on some other lucky girl," Mrs. Cox commented wisely), but the king smiled and waved good-natured greetings to everyone in the theater before he took his seat and the play began.

It was an amusing play, or at least so Mary thought once she'd got over her shock at it, and after she'd stopped worrying about anyone else in the audience noticing her reaction to it. It was very naughty, of course, and even though she knew she wouldn't have understood half the jests so much as a month before, she felt very clever and worldly because she did now— even if in a corner of her mind she was uncomfortably aware that the characters were more to be pitied than laughed at, more to be censured than envied, and their situations more to be feared than she wanted to admit. It all had to do with infidelity and the risks associated with it, and the actors and actresses hid under beds and in closets and watched their lovers meeting with other lovers and mistakenly meeting with each other as the audience roared its approval—at least those of the audience who weren't busily furthering their acquaintances with each other in exactly the same way, did.

But Gideon sat close to Mary, and from time to time he glanced down at her, as entertained by her reactions as he was by the play, and so she could have been watching a funeral and she'd have been exalted. Afterward, she'd been told, they'd dine, and after that they might go on to an assembly or even to Whitehall. But now she feared nothing. If Gideon were there with her, there'd be nothing to fear.

When the play ended, the actors came out to get their applause, or abuse, according to how the audience felt about them. Mary was enchanted to see that they gave back as good as they got of both, as both audience and actors called comments to each other. Even the king traded quips with a saucy black-haired wench who'd been wonderfully impudent onstage. Mary stood, charmed and astonished, totally engrossed in this interplay. And Gideon, gazing down at her, was touched by her childlike absorption. His normally stern features softened in that moment, and he ducked his head and let a light kiss graze against her cheek. She started at that, and looked up, bewildered, before she lowered her head, smiling as well as trying to hide her pleased confusion at his simple gesture, because it was his way never to touch her in public, no matter how much and how thoroughly he did in private.

He continued to smile gently, bemused. Until he absently looked up and then out across the theater. Then he started as much as Mary had just done. He narrowed his eyes to be sure it was who he thought it was, and then froze in place as he spied, behind that one, another, more incredibly familiar face. He stiffened; his smile vanished. Then he abruptly turned his back and put a hand on Jamie's shoulder, since Tristram was inaccessible at the moment, having been dragged down into an embrace by his lady's latest attempt at her favorite form of dialogue.

"Jamie," Gideon said quietly, his lips at the fairhaired man's ear, "I need your help, lad. Look—to the right, across the room—softly . . . move only your eyes. . . . Aye, it's Sir Philip, damn his eyes. Here, and with no warning to me, and with my lady on his arm. The Goddess, yes, she. I must go to them, and now. Please, as you love me, take Mary home for me, and now."

Jamie only nodded, though his eyes narrowed.

"Mary," Gideon said pleasantly, "my plans are changed. Go home with Jamie like a good girl, will you? I'll see you later. Good night, Tris, Jamie," he said lightly, and bowing as politely as if they'd all just been introduced, left them and made his way swiftly across the crowded theater.

Mary could only stand and stare after him, and would have stayed to stare as he approached the fine

Cavalier who immediately bent into a bow as he approached them, and would have stayed to gape at the beautiful honey-haired lady who arose from her curtsy with a smile as he took up her hand in his, and would have remained to simply stand and stare at all that passed, forgetting herself entirely, if Jamie hadn't put a hand on her shoulder to turn her bodily at last, since she hadn't heard a word he'd said to her since Gideon had left her side.

"Who's that?" she said stupidly then, slewing around again, forgetting that it wasn't her right to stare, or her place to ask.

Jamie was white-faced, and his companion looked on as dumbly as Mary did. But Mrs. Cox had been disengaged from her kiss, and hearing the question and sensing some gossip, forgot her frustration as she squinted across the room. Then she said, a little breathlessly, after all her exertion, "Oh, the couple with Hawkes now? That's Sir Philip Southern. Yes, definitely. 'tis he. He runs with my husband when he's in town. I don't know her . . . but she must be . . . yes, his sister. Because I've never seen her before. He doesn't have a wife or a mistress at the moment. I know the little widow he's got his eyes on too . . . so it has to be her, his sister, the recluse, the one everyone says is so beautiful. Well, so she is, isn't she, Tristram?" she asked coquettishly, fishing for his denial of anyone's beauty but her own.

"I haven't any idea," Tristram said too casually, but his indigo eyes were suddenly alert, and he placed his arm around Mrs. Cox's plump waist to steer her away.

"It must be his sister . . . Celeste, yes, that's the name." Mrs. Cox shrugged. "We were talking about it just the other day. Everyone was expecting her at court soon. It has to be . . . she looks like Southern, she's the right age too. She's here to make a match with Hawkes. The king's sponsoring it, everyone knows that. Lucky Hawkes, she's a fine-looking creature," she said critically as she stared back over her shoulder despite Tristram's now ungentle prodding, "although she doesn't have to be, not with her being such an heiress."

"Heiress?" Mary asked.

"To some place in Kent," Mrs. Cox answered, digging in her feet, determined to get her gossip spread even as Tristram pushed her onward. "That's the idea, to even the score again—he gets his home back and the heiress both, you see. She's from where Hawkes comes from, a place called . . . yes, Ivyclose. Tristram! Oh, Tristram!" she squealed in delight as he finally found a way to get her to stop talking.

Mary only echoed "Oh!" on an exhalation.

"Oh," she said abruptly, but she said it the way, Jamie thought, she would have if someone had hit her, hard, in the stomach.

"Lady," Gideon said as he bowed over Celeste's hand, "I hadn't looked to see you here in London so soon. I'm both pleased and grieved—it would've been my pleasure to escort you tonight."

"It's never too late," Sir Philip said happily, looking over the heads of the nearby crowd to give his little widow a significant glance, because after his footman had reported no one home at Gideon Hawkes's lodgings, he hadn't hoped to be able to find someone to take Celeste off his hands so he could get his own on his hoped-for bride.

"We sent word," Celeste said softly, watching Gideon's face for reaction to her words, and winning only a look of polite inquiry, "but evidently you'd already gone."

"Yet only here, so we're well-met," he answered, "and as the evening's only just begun, we've lost nothing. But I'll have gained everything if you accompany me now," he said softly.

"Where?" she asked, looking up and then away,

amazed to find he lost none of his vital presence even
when in the presence of dozens of other men in a
crowded theater. He looked at her in such a way as to
make her think they were all alone in the garden at
Ivyclose again. It thrilled and frightened her at once.
Because for all she'd told herself she was coming to
London to judge him more objectively, she knew she'd
also come to meet him in the midst of thousands just
so she wouldn't feel so pressed and vulnerable to him
when he was near. But, she realized with a pinch of
panic, it seemed he brought so much of himself to
every occasion that it hardly mattered where it was
that they met.

His eyes told her he knew this, and he smiled before
he answered her with a question, playful, teasing,
pretending she had some control of the situation.

"Wherever you'd like to go, my lady," he said.

They went to dinner with a mass of people, and with
Charles, their king, at the head of the table, and
roisterous courtiers everywhere else. They couldn't
say a word without its being heard, or make a move
without its being documented. And their every movement was observed, since it appeared that everyone
knew of the proposed arrangement and were all eyes
and ears to find out how it commenced.

When Celeste had met him that very day, the king
himself had inspected her with a look of appraisal that
she would have slapped off any other man's face. The
royal mistress Castlemaine had looked on from his
side, with cautious, crueler assessment, only leaving
off when she rightly read Celeste's lack of reciprocal
interest in the king. Now, at dinner, Celeste could
scarcely eat, as rows of similarly painted royal harlots
observed her narrowly, and their men also watched
her, but with a different sort of greedy curiosity. Now,
too, she had only to lean in Gideon's direction to see
the king's slight uplifted smile and nod of approval.

Yet still she breathed a sigh of relief, because in this

crowd nothing could be done between any but the most abandoned lovers but conversation and flirtation. And, because she had lived so many years with an alien heart hidden from all those around her, those were the skills she was best at. So, unfettered, unwary, and at last unafraid of Gideon again, she unbent and was at her most charming and flirtatious with him. Worldly as he was, sated as he was, still she drove him almost to distraction with it.

Her conversation was light and clever. Her smile was charming and she treated him as an old friend met again in a good hour. She touched his sleeve and tapped him with her fan, and folded her eyelashes down like a fan over whatever truths lay at the bottom of her soft blue eyes. She was clad all in buttery amber velvets and satins, her skin was pure and white, her hair glowed like candlelight, her scent was that of freesias and springtime in that crowded, hot, and cluttered room, and Gideon wanted her with an intensity that surprised even himself.

It was one thing to want her there in the garden at Ivyclose, where, he supposed, she personified all that he'd lost, and he'd known that to take her in his arms was to embrace his lost home again. But even here, and even now, she was again the very spirit of Ivyclose, of every fragile and beautiful thing he'd given up, or seen ruined. He'd fought and killed for money and advancement until his soul had sickened; he'd traveled and hung his hat on so many pegs that he no longer knew or cared where he rested his head; he'd made love to too many faceless women to recall one of them, and she—ah, she made him feel like one of Charles's youngest and most foolish poets.

The need to have her was unsettling him, because for all she was, she was also cool and distant and obviously playing with him. And so he burned with the desire for possession as well as the chill fear of loss.

It wasn't until he'd gotten permission to see her to her rooms in the rambling complex that was Whitehall that he got her to himself at last. He paused outside her room, dawdling in the hall, holding on to her hand until the maid that stayed by her side ventured a peep up to his face, and then, giggling nervously, ducked a curtsy and slid into the room, glad to escape with her life, sad at having nothing else to offer him, after she'd seen the look in his blazingly hot ice-blue eyes.

Celeste remained and stayed still, not knowing what to do now that she was alone with him. She knew very well what lay between them, and that proposed marriage was like a gulf she no longer knew how to bridge with humor or design. She sensed his need, and that was a chasm she had no idea of how to cope with, either with avoidance or withdrawal, or even acceptance.

He made it simpler, and more difficult.

"Well, then, lady," he said softly, moving in close to her . . . waiting . . . moving closer, close enough at last to feel the increase in the light breaths that fluttered against his cheek. "Well, then, love," he whispered, and bent his head and waited for her protest, and, hearing none, satisfied at least that he might try to be satisfied, put his mouth on hers. Her mouth was cool and surprised and his was warm and searching, and he sighed and drew her nearer, and brought one hand to her silken hair, and the other to rest on one small breast.

"No, no, no," she said against his mouth, and he released her, as filled with puzzlement as he was with desire.

"Why, why, why?" he murmured, mocking, teasing her shyness, as he ended each little question with a kiss against her neck.

"I cannot," she said, the harsh note of real fear in her voice stopping him as she drew back.

He closed his eyes, and she was freed at last from

that penetrating look, although his words pinioned her well enough.

"Lady," he sighed, "but I asked you once before, when we began, in a warm garden, not a cold stone hall. If you can't bring yourself to a little thing like this light lovemaking, ah, lady, how can you think to bring yourself to our wedding bed? And if you can't," he said then, opening his eyes to challenge her with their grave and crystalline purity, "then, lady, tell me, or your brother, or the king, and I, and he, and we, will understand, or try."

His home meant everything to him; she knew that. She accepted that she might mean something to him too. And she'd her own dream of him to think about. The problem was exactly that. In thinking about him, she could accept him, but in touching him, in his nearness, she couldn't yet, not with any ease. He was too entirely masculine, too forceful, although too polite to fault for it, because it wasn't a matter of forwardness as much as the force of his very presence. He breathed, he spoke, he felt like nothing she'd ever known and everything she'd been taught to shun.

To say she couldn't love him freely wouldn't be just to lose him forever, it would be to lose both Gideon and Philip's dreams too. And she'd her own. To deny Gideon Hawkes in the flesh what she so eagerly tendered up to him in her dreams would be to lose her vision of herself as a complete woman forever too.

But, she reasoned, recovering herself as she stood apart from him, surely it wasn't too much to ask that she know and trust him first? They weren't actually promised to each other yet. He was too bold, too soon. The theater, the court, all the men she'd seen tonight, on- and offstage, had reminded her of their differences, she decided, relaxing as she found surety and self-control again. There were, after all, years of revulsion at the antics of lesser men to overcome.

Gideon was different. But he must prove it. It would take time, but she could and would have him.

"Gideon," she said, drawing near again and resting her forehead against his chest, because she sensed that her touch affected him as profoundly as any of her words could do, "it takes time. Remember, I came to London to see you and to come to know you. I wouldn't have done that if I hadn't wanted to begin to take the time, would I? Please, you go too fast. Wait for me, will you?"

"Lady," he said, looking down at the light silken curls, and after hesitating, daring to hold her lightly in his clasp, before he realized how she affected his body no matter how lightly he held her, and so put her an arm's length away as he looked down at her. "Lady," he sighed, caught, and accepting it, "I'll wait, but," he said, laughing at himself, and only partly in jest, "please remember, it pains me to."

It was almost as dark within as it was without when he got back to his lodgings; only one candle lit the outer room, and none were burning in the bedchamber. But Gideon didn't need light or help to find his fastenings or tug off his boots, just as he'd told Rountree when he'd come, sleepily, to greet him in the outer hall. Nor did he need more than the vague light from the lesser dark outside, once his eyes had adjusted, to find his way unerringly to his bed. Nor did he need, or want, light when he took her warm and unprotesting form in his arms, and then under his hands and lips.

Mary hadn't been sleeping, nor had she been awake; she'd been lying in some netherworldly limbo waiting so long that that suspended state had become as natural to her as sleep or wakefulness. Jamie had worried, and Jamie had taken her home, hours before, after she'd refused to keep him company at dinner, after she'd refused his stammering foolishness meant as comfort. All she'd asked of him was something he couldn't give her, but still, by not doing so, he had. Because Tristram's companion had prattled every time he'd lifted his mouth from hers after silencing her, and so soon she'd heard all. All she'd needed was verification.

"Tell me, is it true?" she'd asked Jamie at the last. She knew she should never have asked him because it wasn't her place to inquire, nor was it kind to ask it of him. But the question wasn't a thing she could hold back, like her tears. By looking everywhere but at her, by the rise in his color, by chattering immediately about something else, he'd answered her. By not replying, he'd given his reply.

Now Gideon came to her; suddenly he was there, sleek and naked and urgent. He came to her in bed and without speaking, he closed his hands over her breasts and stroked her body and held her back to him as he'd found her, only to turn her and hold her otherwise, his need making him hurried, his need as apparent as it was strong. In his hair he bore the scent of the first cool night of autumn, of fresh wood fires and late mists, and though his hands and body were cool at first, she soon felt them begin to burn as though with fever.

And then, as though the heat had released it, she scented the soft breath of freesias on his skin, of some sweet and lingering springtime perfume there. She knew then, as she'd imagined all the while she'd been waiting, who it was he was still seeing in his inner eye in this darkness, and why he didn't speak, and who it was that had set him afire before he'd ever come to her bed. His bed, she corrected herself as he groaned with impatience and brought himself into her.

But he never forced her, nor was there anything but willingness shown to him, or in her. She welcomed him for her own reasons. One was that he was Gideon Hawkes. Another was that she'd been with him perhaps a day too long, and so could not now ignore the sweetness of his lips, or fail to appreciate his gentleness even in urgency, and the clean, hard body he brought to her. So as he moved with her and then stopped and gasped, "Ah, sweeting!" in gratitude, she felt more than the trembling of his body deep within hers; she knew the beginnings of a strange and terrible new pleasure of her own.

Because the other reason, which she thought of as he lay back with her, catching his breath, was the bittersweet knowledge that she'd gained a hard-won truth. And it filled all the numbed and empty places in her more than even he'd done. Because now she was pierced by a sickening shock of self-awareness, the fearful triumph of knowing she'd been right from the first, and wrong all along. She'd one enormous unalterable fact to bear, to replace the loss of all her flimsy, silly illusions.

Because now she understood just what it was that she'd done, what she'd given up, what she'd lost as well as what she'd never really had, or would ever have. Now, at last, of course, she knew just what it was to be a whore.

# 11

She'd leave, she'd go, she'd close the door and never look back, she'd go home. . . . But where was that? Mary thought, even as she wondered how to pack her things, since she didn't own so much as a traveling bag. Then, stopping still in the midst of struggling to button her old "best" gown, which no longer fit at all, whether she was corseted or not, since she'd gotten into the habit of eating regularly, she thought seriously about what she could do once she left these rooms and Gideon's employ.

She'd ripped her old gown out of her old bundle of clothes and had started to dress in order to keep from weeping as soon as Gideon had left, only moments before. Not that he'd been unkind to her, or cross, or anything but tender. But maybe just because he'd been that, and happy besides, kissing the tip of her nose in a farewell salute before he strode out the door, leaving her without a word as to when he'd be back, or where he was going, because the one was something he didn't have to tell her, and the other was something she already knew.

There'd been two notes awaiting him on the table; she hadn't remembered them until morning, when he'd asked if any had been left for him. He'd ambled from the bedchamber to scan them. One, which was written in lacy lines, as decorative as any pattern on any fabric she'd ever seen, he'd smiled over and then tucked into a pocket of his long coat that he lifted from the floor where he'd cast it the night before. The other, which Mary shuddered at, since the hard black lines of writing seemed familiar to her, made Gideon pause. And as he read it, his brows swooped down until when he was done the face he turned to her frightened her.

"What do you make of this?" he asked.

"Nothing," she said in a small voice. "I can't read. But I can remember very well. The hand is very like one I saw on a note Sir Roger Mobely gave me for you once before, and Tristram . . . Master Jones said to send it to you at . . . Ivyclose." She faltered then; that word was enough to overturn her resolve.

"Ah, well, I see, and sweet meddling Tris likely sent it to Perdition," he murmured, and his brow cleared, but she saw it was for her sake, since she always watched him very closely, and there was still a tightness to his jaw—she saw the muscles in it flutter once—and a coldness at the back of his eyes that didn't deceive her. "Well, it's as well," he said, "because it's nothing.

"Come, pretty Mistress Monk," he said. "Why are you scowling? You didn't frown so last night." He grinned, coming to her and capturing her in his arms, only to tease her out of her worried expression, only to reassure her. But the fact that he was still undressed and soon discovered she was only holding her gown in front of her changed his mind as to why he'd embraced her, and he soon went on to other embraces.

She didn't have to act, as she'd thought she would. That was one of the reasons she was determined to run away now that he was gone. Because she hadn't been able to run away from him in his arms. She'd thought to appease herself by giving him falseness to

equal his own. She'd planned to lie back to watch how
well she'd gulled him, and feel superior as he struggled, searching for his fleshly pleasures, straining gro-
tesquely for release as she watched, pure and uninvolved
and hating him with all her heart. But she hadn't
because she hadn't remained observant and detached.
Not after he'd touched her.

It was clear to her that she hadn't the temperament
for her job. It wasn't that she felt too much pleasure,
it was that she cared too much for him to care for
pleasure. There was none of the ecstasy he always
promised her, but she'd never known that at his coupling. Still, there was the enormous pleasure at being
with him, at seeming to be so important to him. It was
so much that it was almost as profound as the pain of
knowing that such pleasures were different for him,
and she was really nothing at all to him.

A whore shouldn't feel more than the pleasure of
knowing she practiced her trade well, just as any craftsman ought to feel pleasure at a job well done. She'd
be a fool to expect any more love or devotion than any
other tradesman could expect from a satisfied customer; she knew that. So she couldn't blame Gideon,
not really, for in truth, she knew he'd never really
been false with her, because there was no reason on
earth for him to be faithful or honest with a whore.

But whatever she was now, she also knew she'd be
better off hating him as much as her situation, and she
couldn't.

No, it was never the sort of occupation for her. So
she had to go, of course. But where?

Generations of practicality bred into her bones made
it impossible for her to go plunging into the world
unprepared. She'd be an easy mark for thieves if she
wandered the city in her finery. But now she saw that
her old gowns no longer fit, in any way. Vandals and
cutthroats roamed the ruins of all the city of her childhood, there were more deaths and injuries dealt in her

old neighborhood now than had come from the fire—
Gideon had cautioned her on that. Yet, if she wore
her good new clothes, and walked these new streets
alone, what then? Should she go into a tavern to meet
a charming Cavalier, and sell herself to him? Again?
And what then? Again? She'd still nothing to offer
that a man couldn't expect from a good wife, and no
reputation left to be that anymore. It wasn't as though
she were a lady, like those at court, like those at the
theater, like those who sent men beautifully written
messages. . . .

She had to put away the thought when she heard a
rapping on her door. She struggled with her gown,
using the superhuman strength that need gives to the
necessary moment, and succeeding in buttoning it closed,
raced to the door, putting on her shoes on a hop and a
skip as she did so. She knew she was both badly
dressed and disheveled when she opened the door,
and that, she thought, embarrassed, must have been
why both Tristram and Jamie seemed so displeased
when they saw her.

But they saw a monstrously pretty wench, made
prettier because of the hot flush from exertion on her
cheeks, made more wantonly attractive by the way the
outgrown frock fitted so closely to her body, and enhanced further by her flyaway black curls being in
such disorder that any court hairdresser would have
gladly claimed their creation as his own hard labor.
But they frowned for different reasons. One because
he knew it wasn't right for him to feel such surging
desire for his good friend's lover. The other because
he knew it wasn't right for any wench in a city such as
London to open a door without first asking who was
behind it. So they both scowled at Mary, each for his
own reason, and looked over her shoulder for Gideon.

When she told them Gideon wasn't in, they both
flew into a rage, this time for the same reason.

"God's teeth, wench!" Tristram roared, stepping in

and slamming the door behind him and shaking a gloved finger at her. "The first time you did it I thought it might be a forgetful folly. Twice is idiocy! Have you learned nothing? Bad enough if you fling the door open without a by-your-leave when Gideon's in, without knowing if it's friend or foe come to see him or slay him—but to do so when you're alone? Where are your wits? Where were you raised—with the sheep? No, I doubt it—even in the countryside they know better: there are rogues and wandering mischief-makers enough everywhere in these troubled times."

She knew he was right, which made her angrier at herself and so, then, naturally, at him, for reminding her of it. But for all he awed her, being a born gentleman and far above her, and being Gideon's good friend besides, he was not, after all, Gideon. And she was a girl of some spirit and a quick tongue and had been brought up to fight for herself.

"I grew up among friends, Master Jones," she said tartly, sweeping her unruly hair back from her eyes in order to stare him down properly, "in a neighborhood full of good and decent people who cared about each other and me. I can't be expected to know how a *gentleman* and a Cavalier lives, can I?"

"Ho, Tris, take that!" Jamie chuckled, gazing at Mary with purest admiration now.

"I do, and shall. Beg your pardon, Mistress Monk," Tristram said, smiling as he swept into a low bow. "I see now that no number of bad men could be your match. I only ask that you spare me, because I've got a dinner engagement tonight." As she blushed for her sauciness and tried to hide her amusement at his jest, he added, "That's why I've come, to see if you and your red rogue care to join us."

"Ah, well, and . . . but," she said, lowering her head and plucking at her skirt, "but I don't know

when he'll be back, or where he's gone. But I'll tell
him you came and asked," she added quietly, as both
men assumed expressions of unconcern and each for
his own reasons thought that it was damned thought-
less of Gideon to get himself such an uncommonly
vulnerable and adorable little bedmate.

"Then we'll be off," Tristram said, turning to go,
with one hand on Jamie's back, to get him to stop
staring at Mary.

"But wait!" Mary cried as they got to the door.

She'd rather have spoken to Jamie alone. She knew
the meaning of that look in his mild blue eyes, and
though she didn't want him as anything but a friend,
she knew he'd help her if he could. Tristram frightened as much as he amused her; he'd a cool wit and a
quick mind, and she never knew what he was really
thinking and always feared it was the worse of her.
But they were, as Gideon had once said, almost always as if they were joined at the hip, and so she knew
she'd have to ask both of them, and rely on Tristram's
courtliness as well as Jamie's kindness. She'd an idea,
but needed help with it, and knew no one else in the
world who'd give it to her.

"I need," she said as they turned around to stare at
her, "some advice. I . . . ah . . . would rather that
Gideon didn't know it. It's to be a surprise," she said
in a rush of invention, to dispel Jamie's look of sudden
hope and to lower Tristram's significantly raised eyebrow. "For him," she lied, and they knew it, since
they'd neither of them ever seen a worse liar. "I want
to know . . . I'd like to find a . . . tutor," she said.

They stared.

"I want to learn to read. And write," she declared.
"Letters and such, in English," she added helpfully,
when they both only stood looking at her.

"I've a very good reason for it," she said defensively, as she tried to explain her heart's desire, as

much to herself as to them. Because she knew she could never be a lady, but still reasoned that she might take on a lady's trappings, because in her new world that was her only hope of betterment. Or so she told herself, while all the time she knew in some corner of her mind that she was determined to prove, if only to herself, that she could be as clever as the coolly beautiful lady who kept sending Gideon such lovely notes. Or at least, she admitted, in that dark corner that she immediately darkened further, so she wouldn't have to look at it closely again, so she'd be able to read and see for herself what it was that the beautiful lady was sharing with Gideon.

She was as shamed as she was hurt to know that she couldn't do what Gideon's beautiful lady could. She felt as though she were living in a country where people would speak to each other from time to time in a language she could hear but not understand. No one in her family could read more than his name, or needed to, but she did now. Now that she was among them, she hungered to know what the world was like for educated people.

"When I lived at home with people who dealt with money all day, in sales and trades, I did sums, and did them well," she said, raising her chin as she looked up at the two Cavaliers. "Now I live with people who deal with written words all the time, in plays and poems and . . . such, and so I want to understand them," she said, daring them to disagree, knowing they would, and bracing herself for scornful laughter. She gazed at them defiantly, inwardly shocked at her own bravery, wondering how she, a common whore, had the gall to ask such fine gentlemen to notice anything but her body.

It was Tristram who spoke first, kindly and gravely.

"I know several fine tutors who'd be glad of the chance to work," he said seriously.

"I'll pay well," she said at once, horrified at her

stupidity in forgetting that she'd need to do so, resolving at once to sell her gowns to pay if she had to. Gideon gave her pocket money, but she was sure it wouldn't be enough. He'd give her more if she asked, he'd said he would, but she wasn't a good-enough liar to tell him what she needed it for. And it would be cheating to take his coin for a cause that was supposed to enable her to leave him. Because if she could learn, and if she could pass herself off as a lady, she reasoned she might be able to win a better life for herself somewhere. It wasn't much of a hope, but it would do, since it was the only one she had.

"No, you won't," Jamie said, and as Tristram looked at him with surprise, he smiled and said, "Mistress Monk, may I present your tutor? The Baron Claverly, at your service. Please call me 'Jamie' and not 'Doctor,' because although I got passing grades in my own language, mistress, I was lucky to get them. So I can hardly claim a fee. But I can read and write and can teach you to in a twinkling. And will," he said defiantly, glaring at Tristram.

"Oh, doubtless," Tristram said easily, "but I only wonder if you'll get carried away, my dear, and try to teach more?"

"I'm a gentleman, if not a scholar," Jamie said on a shrug, "but a good friend first, Tris, don't forget that."

"I only hope Gideon doesn't," the tall Cavalier sighed.

"But . . . you'll know it's true," Mary said nervously, now that she was nearing her goal suddenly afraid of what she was doing. "I only want to learn to be better than I am. And I only don't want Gideon to know—until I am."

Both men looked hard at her then. It might have been that they both knew why she was wearing her old gown, she thought, since neither of them mentioned it but both had stared at it. Certainly they knew more about Gideon's promised wife, and perhaps even knew all about her own future far better than she herself did. But she never knew why they then both bowed again, Tristram saying, "Lady, I can't see how you *could* better yourself, 'best' having no superior that I know of. But if you'd like to try, why, I'll add my own humble services, if you'll have them. And be sure, your secret's safe with me," as Jamie added, "As safe as you're with me, lady, I give you my word on it."

Then they set to making arrangements for her lessons, refusing to listen to her as she insisted she wasn't a lady.

They walked through St. James Park, alongside the canal, watching the wood ducks, or rather, as Gideon bent to whisper to Celeste, watching the king feeding the wood ducks and trying to keep his beloved dogs from feeding on them, while a crowd of courtiers and Londoners looked on at the spectacle. But it was growing too chilly to stay outdoors longer. Even though Celeste had a fur muff and a warm cloak and claimed she was a country girl, Gideon insisted on seeing her back to Whitehall when he felt her hand tremble with the cold, even within its soft kid glove as he took it in his own gloved hand to help her across a rough patch of the path they followed.

He was being considerate of his needs as well as her own. Because, as he told her as he walked her back to the palace at Whitehall, seeing her in public was just and only that—seeing her. There was such a constant crowd of people around them that they seldom had time to talk, or if they did, it was and would have to be only that—talk. Sound and words and quips and pleasantries, common court chatter and light flirtation, with nothing of the heart or soul in it. And it was important that they at least talk, if they planned ever to do anything more together.

Of course, she agreed with him. The only thing wrong with his plan, she thought as she strolled back with him, was that everyone else at court seemed to agree as well. Because when they saw the two of them breaking off from the group to wander away, her brother smiled, his widow-lady showed every little white tooth as well, and every courtier who noticed, as well as the king, seemed pleased at their desertion. It was, Celeste said in a soft aside to Gideon, like courting on a stage.

"All the world *is* a stage, as Shakespeare said," Gideon agreed, "but you're right, the curtain never goes down on Charles's theater of life. And may it never do so," he added sincerely in an undervoice.

Celeste grew thoughtful. "I don't know," she said quietly. "I think it could certainly be drawn now and again, don't you?"

"Lady," he said fervently, looking down into the pale face that surveyed him so steadily, seeing how it was so deliciously framed by the silver fur on her ermine hood, "if I were behind the curtain with you, they could leave it down forever."

She lowered her head against the cool breeze that had sprung up, so he'd no idea of how she'd taken his compliment, but she seemed inclined to walk on in silence for a while, and so, then, did he.

"It's only high afternoon," Gideon commented as they approached her quarters, "too early to dine, too late to breakfast. The court is out sporting with the king, your brother's trying to do so with the widow, the sun's out full, there's not a shadow to do wickedness in, and I've everyone but the King of Spain's approval and leave to court you," he said, grinning slightly as Celeste hesitated with him at her doorstep. "Will you give me leave to come in and talk with you? Without your maid all ears and eyes? After all," he said reasonably, "you were the one who complained about being onstage, were you not?"

There was everything calm and sensible in his words, and nothing but danger in his posture and his voice. He stood poised, his lean body as languid as any courtier's, but as tensed as any hunter's, his blue eyes brilliant with mockery and interest, and though it was broad and blatant daylight, as he'd said, his tone was smooth and silken as a midnight seducer's. For a man who claimed to be sparse with words, she'd discovered that he could be fluent enough when he wished to be. But he was right: she'd said what she'd said, and they were supposed to be learning about each other. And she knew that, day or night, he'd never force her to anything she didn't want to do. It was what he might compel her to want to do that worried her. But she couldn't acknowledge that.

"Come in, Gideon Hawkes," she said politely, "and, Anne, you may go," she told her maidservant.

He took the chair she offered him, and she one opposite, and they sat and looked at each other, but all the while he smiled and looked at her as though he knew some vast, amusing secret.

"It will be an early winter, I think," she said, searching for some conversation now that she was so acutely aware that they were alone.

"Oh, yes," he said, nodding, never taking his crystal gaze from her, studying her every feature and nuance of expression, "and it will probably have a Christmas in it too. But then, after the New Year, I'll wager they'll be a spring. Then we'll have a deal of rain, and lambs, and flowers. Celeste, if you don't come here to me, I'll have to go there to you, you know," he said in the same light conversational tones.

"No," she said at once, all pretense of easy sociability gone from her, "no, Gideon. I want to know you, and though I understand you believe I can do that in your arms, I must know your heart first."

He sighed. "What's there to know? Ask me anything—I'll have no secrets from you. I've ranged far,

I've traveled by land and sea, I've been a sailor and a soldier and a trader, but you know all that. You know *of* me already. If you want to know me, you must come to me. But if you're afraid to come to me before we're wed," he said, holding up one hand as she was about to protest, "I can understand that. So only say you'll have me, and you will, and there'll be no more problem."

It sounded so reasonable, it seemed to be so clear, and yet she couldn't accept it. All she had to do was to follow her impulse and her wildest dreams and say yes, and consign her life, her future, her soul, and her body to the care of this man forever. But reason forbade what her heart demanded. How could she be sure she could trust him with such valuable gifts? How could she be certain he was any better than a dozen other courtiers in this immoral court? He'd admitted she'd been mistaken and he was no Puritan; how could she be sure he wasn't an utter hedonist who'd tread on her spirit as well as her soul? She was a cautious woman as well as a pure one; if she admitted to any sin, it was for pride in herself for both virtues.

There were a hundred reasons against accepting him at his word. No, more, a hundred she'd been trained to see since childhood, and a hundred more that she could see all around her now at this corrupt and godless court. But while he sat and looked at her with a slight smile on his lips as he stared at her own, she couldn't think of one to mention. So she rose and went to the window and stared out at the autumn afternoon and tried to collect her thoughts and shape them into words he'd understand, she'd understand.

"Celeste," he said suddenly from just behind her, "Celeste," he said, and his breath moved the hair at her ear, "say yes. 'Come live with me and be my love, and we will all the pleasures prove—' "

"Prettily said," she interrupted breathlessly, not turning around to face him. "Are you as full of pretty words as all of the Cavaliers here then, Gideon Hawkes?"

He heard the bitterness in her voice, and shook his head.

"Not my words," he said ruefully. "Sir Christopher Marlowe's, almost a century ago. You prefer something more modern? Well, then, Herrick says to 'Gather ye rosebuds while ye may, Old Time is still a-flying, And this same flower that smiles today, tomorrow may be dying. . . . Then be not coy, but use your time, and while ye may, go marry, For having lost but once your prime, you may forever tarry' . . . with me, please," he breathed.

"I'm not coy," she said repressively, holding herself erect. "I only don't leap to marry you immediately. And I don't read such poetry—you forget my religion, you forget my principles."

"I forget nothing," he said. "It's not a filthy poem. Some of you more vigorous Puritans threw out too many babies with their bathwater. But I'm not here to teach you poetry. Let's talk plainly, then, and of hard things, without the gloss of poetry. Things you may think you can't say while you look at me. So look out the window and listen.

"I've your king's and your brother's permission to marry you. You know about me, but you don't, as well. I understand. We'll have some plain speaking, if you don't care for poetry. Perhaps you feel I don't bring you enough? I haven't a home, although I could buy any other for you."

"Oh, no, I love Ivyclose, I want no other home," she said immediately, turning to stare at him in horror, before she dropped her gaze and spun back again.

"So then you may do well to ask what I do bring you. What can I offer you that you haven't already got? Or that no other man can give you? Those are sensible questions. I've money and health. But what else? Celeste, I tell you that my embrace can tell you more than my words can, and I mean it. And not only because I'm not a man of great eloquence."

She shivered, whether from the tickle of his breath on her ear, the soft touch of his long hair brushing against her cheek, or the meaning of his words as well as his nearness, she couldn't say. He sighed again.

She wore the unlucky color of green, but looked so lovely in it that no superstition would stop him from trying his luck again now. The fresh color gave light to her honey hair and the gown itself suited her. She looked slender and fragile as a frond of new spring fern; she looked like all the promise of renewal to him in the light of the autumn afternoon. He stood beside her and yearned to touch her, but didn't dare to try to with anything but his words yet.

"Celeste," he said softly after a long moment of thoughtful silence, "let me tell you something. A thing you don't know. A secret. About Ivyclose," he said, and saw her interest sharpen, her eyes opening wider until he could see the blue autumn sky clearly reflected in the sides of them, and, nodding to himself, he went on. "Yes, we both love Ivyclose, don't we? But I know something about it that you don't. Because it's a thing only the family that built it can know.

"There is a room, Celeste," he said, drawing closer, pleased that her very name held another key to his manner of wooing her, since the soft sigh of saying it was in itself a feathery caress on her skin that made her shiver, "a hidden room, buried within the innermost heart of it. Yes," he said as she swung about to face him, so rapt in what he was saying that she watched his lips to see the words beginning there, as though to draw them out the faster.

"It's a beautiful room at the very heart of the house. But it's been walled over and sealed up and secret for years upon years," he said, his voice growing softer as he watched her face, and he ached to reach out to her. "It's wonderful in there, Celeste," he promised. "You can't imagine the delight of being there, but I've been, and I know. It's small, private as it is secluded, but like the human heart, it contains everything within it. Its riches are beyond your imagination. The pleasures to be found there are exquisite, beyond compare. Trust me, I know," he went on, whispering now, his gaze locked on hers, "because the thrill of discovering it was beyond my comprehension too. Until I was old enough. And then I went there, and understood. But it's opened only to those who have the courage to seek it, or who dare to ask entry of the true heir. I've the key to that wonderful room, Celeste. Marry me, and I'll take you there with me."

He was smiling, brimming with mirth. She knew there couldn't be such a room, for she'd lived at Ivyclose and knew every inch of it. But he said there was, and she knew from his voice and his eyes that in some way, what he said was true. She was about to say yes, as helpless in the hold of those brilliant eyes as she was lulled by the sweet suggestiveness in his deep voice. But then he left off looking into her eyes and looked to her lips before he kissed her.

She didn't wait to be caught by his kiss. She stepped back at once—the secret, the room, the key to it forgotten, banished by the shock of his lips on hers.

He moved away when he felt her reaction. His smile twisted.

" 'If we had world enough, and time, this coyness, lady, were no crime,' " he quoted softly, " '. . . But at my back I always hear Time's winged chariot hurrying near, and yonder all before us lie, deserts of vast eternity. Thy beauty shall no more be found, nor, in thy marble vault, shall sound my echoing song; then worms shall try that long-preserved virginity . . .' "

He paused to see her wince, and went on tonelessly, " 'And your quaint honor into dust, and into ashes all my lust. The grave's a fine and private place, but none I think do there embrace . . .'

"You don't recognize him when he's not writing of love for anyone but Cromwell? But Mr. Marvell's one of your own, you know. He has heart as well as wit, and friends of every sort, royalist and Puritan. I met him in Holland. We'd some days together, some work for our country—never mind our politics, we've only one country—to do together. I've never forgotten a poem he showed me once," he said as she remained silent, "because for all I don't share his politics, I do his mind on this matter, and so committed it to heart. It's my favorite. Because he also urges: 'Let us roll all our strength and all our sweetness up into one ball, and tear our pleasures with rough strife through the iron gates of life.' Ah, Celeste," he said, grasping her by the shoulders, but only that, only holding her securely at arm's length as he looked down to her, his stern face entirely sincere, "I haven't such words, I can only echo them, not to seduce you, but to ask you to marry me. Why wait, why tarry, if there's no reason to deny me, why not accept me now?"

She'd put her hands on his shoulders and it was as though she were holding on to a rock, a boulder. He was larger than that, larger than life to her with his wild enticing words, his size, his strength; even the color of him was shockingly blatant. Again she felt as much threatened as drawn, and had to close her eyes and collect herself and remember herself and all she stood for. She believed, because of the sudden rush of fear as well as desire that she felt, that if she didn't hold now, pause now, and wait now, she'd be pulled away from herself and would never be able to live at peace with herself when alone behind her own closed eyes again.

She pushed him gently, yet he dropped his hands from her and stepped back as though she'd used the force of three strong men.

"I know of you, Gideon Hawkes," she said, "but I have to know more. I have a favorite poet too," she said.

"Oh, good," he said a little angrily, "I haven't heard a Bible read to me in a long while."

"No," she said serenely, although it took all her effort, "he is good John Milton, and he's of my church too. And I recollect that he says, in part, in answer to just such urgings as your Herrick and Mr. Marvell write about: 'I can fly, or I can run quickly to the earth's green end . . . and from thence can soar as soon to the corners of the moon. Mortals that would follow me, love *Virtue—she alone* is free. She can teach you how to climb higher than the sphery chime . . .' "

She finished speaking and looked at him, so composed and yet triumphant that he couldn't find the heart to dispute her. He didn't think it would do any good for his cause anyway.

All Puritans ought to look like their great poet if they were going to think like him, he thought glumly as he stared hungrily at her. But he didn't say that or another word about her beauty and his desires. She wanted time; he'd have to mark it as she took it. He'd ways of delaying and deflecting his ardor. But he'd seen the way she'd trembled at his touch and at his words, and knew he'd not left her completely untouched. The night, the dark, her imagination, and, yes, the very time she asked for itself—they were his allies. He could wait. Soon, he believed, she couldn't any longer. She'd no male counterpart of his own obliging, pretty little Mary to exorcise the devils he was planting in her virtuous mind and body. She'd no way to buy peace and forgetfulness of temptation, even for an hour, as he had.

"Ah, yes," he said, relaxing, smiling again, "John Milton. He wrote psalms to the Protector, didn't he? To do with 'Cromwell, our chief of men,' wasn't it?"

"Even Charles has forgiven him everything for his genius!" she declared.

"Has he?" he asked lazily, although he knew the answer. He stood back and listened to her defend her fellow Puritan, and smiled as she did. She knew her poetry as other ladies knew their embroidery or cosmetics. He was enchanted by the thought of such a lot of wisdom held in such a lovely container; it was like plucking a fragrant rose, only to find that it had a heart of precious gold at its center as well as color and scent. Now she blazed, now she was having no trouble communicating with him. It was an odd sort of use for poetry in lovemaking, he thought, grinning to himself, and he doubted any man had ever thus gotten any lady into his bed. But if discussing poets led him to the same end with his own learned lady, why, then, he blessed all poets and all their works.

There was a picture of a foolish boy staring at a pie. It gave her no clue. She bit her lip.

"Time's up," Jamie said gently.

Mary frowned. Her black hair was a tangle of curls from the way she'd clutched at it, as though she'd tried to drag her answers out by the roots. She'd a smear of black ink along her determined little chin, where she'd let her quill drip as she'd chewed over the problems of the last hour. Tristram glanced over from the window seat where he'd been reading and watching over his impressionable friend's tutoring, and was glad he'd come. Jamie looked as though he were under strong restraint. His wondering blue eyes were full of a child-like sympathy, but even more than seeming near to tears of pity, he looked as though he were melting with love as he waited for Mary to answer.

"I!" she announced defiantly, because she knew she was wrong.

"L," he said. " 'L longed for it,' remember?"

"I remembered the large L. The little one looks like an I," she complained, embarrassed at her mistake. "It does! What a foolishness. Why didn't they make it look different, like a serpent, or give it a turn or a crook here or there? It's very confusing," she muttered, staring at the letter as though to brand it into her mind by main force.

"Would you like to stop now?" Jamie asked softly.

"No!" she shouted, and then, when she saw Jamie's reproachful look and Tristram turning a cold face to her, she lowered her head as well as her voice. "No, I mean, please, no, Jamie. Unless you're tired of it. But I'm not. And aside from just now, I've done well, haven't I?"

"You've done wonderfully well," Jamie declared. "but you've only begun. You have to be more patient with yourself."

"I'll do better," she said grimly, staring at the chapbook as though it were the incarnation of all her enemies. "I will, just you see. L, and then M and then N," she chanted in a rush. "M mourned for it, N nodded at it, and O—which is very easy to remember because it looks like what it is, nothing," she confided, as both men grinned despite themselves at her gravity, "O opened it! Am I right?"

"More than right," Jamie said, leaning forward, about to say, 'More than adorable,' forgetting himself so much as almost to do more than that, before he heard Tristram clear his throat. "You'll soon be reciting the whole of it," he said instead, leaning back again.

"I will," she promised, thinking: All of it, without a fault. They'd see. He'd soon see. She'd prevail and would know what was in all those books and pamphlets Jamie had brought and laid out on the table, without anyone having to read them to her. There was the Bible and books of letters and a heap of almanacs to read besides, and she would. A world would open to her when all the neat marching lines of symbols and scribbles became true words in her eyes. But that was one day.

Sooner than that, she vowed to herself, she'd impress them, she'd show him, she'd surprise him, she'd be able to recite all of the alphabet entirely, straight through and without stumbling once. Just like a lady might, she thought proudly, just exactly like a lady would.

# 12

---

Half the court was at a masque at Whitehall, most of
the others were at a musical evening given by the Earl
of Whorley and his countess, and the remainder were
at the home of John Stanley. That wasn't to say John
Stanley's assembly wasn't an elegant affair, well-stocked
with Cavaliers and their ladies all clad in their finest,
for they were there in plenty. Their host was an old
friend to Gideon Hawkes and a truthful man besides.
He'd said he'd never met Sir Philip Southern. That
being the case, and there was no reason to doubt him,
Gideon decided there was no reason not to take little
Mary out for an evening of pleasure instead of keeping
her in for one as usual.

The room his host had set aside for dancing was
crowded full, there was much drinking, laughter, and
chatter, and the music played on over it even when
there wasn't dancing. There was plenty of food for
everyone, and too many people for the size of the
room, and so it was a successful affair.

Gideon was in his favorite new clothes, comfortable
in his billowing shirt and soft slouching collar, loose
coat, and full, wide satin petticoat breeches. His high-
heeled shoes were of a soft and supple leather, and his

valet had tied so many ribbons about his sleeves and
legs that he complained that he looked a right may-
pole, but couldn't deny the comfort of such easy dress.
His hat was soft as well, and the draped feather atop it
sloped backward. He was as elegantly got up as any
gentleman there, but twice as comfortable, because,
he decided, looking down at Mary where she stood at
his side awaiting his word as to their next move, he
was three times as contented with his world. At last
he'd pleasure in the present, and every expectation of
a future even more wonderful.

The treat of being taken out had done wonders for
Mary's spirits as well as her looks. She was merrier
than she'd been in a while, and even prettier than
usual too. She'd gained just enough weight to make
her form more girlish than boyish, and, dressed all in a
rich warm crimson velvet gown, its folds gathered up
over a petticoat of deepest plum, she looked, he told
her sincerely, just like a damask rose. And if he thought
she looked at him a little oddly then, it may have been
so, because he'd had little occasion to compliment her
of late. Or it may have been that he only felt it was so,
because until now he'd deliberately avoided noticing
her reactions of late.

Because for all he knew that it was folly, he couldn't
help feeling faithless each time he'd left her alone
these last days and nights, and that had been often,
and he'd avoided her eye each time. Even more foolishly, he'd felt just as false when he'd returned to her
bed even later—although then it was always too dark
to note the expression in her eyes, if he'd thought to
look there at all when he was so otherwise occupied
with other aspects of her.

But she never complained and he never made excuses; she never asked questions and he never offered
answers. Which was exactly as it should be between a
man and his mistress. When things got out of hand
and a wench forgot her place, it became rancorous and

unpleasant for everyone, as witness the hard time Lady
Castlemaine was giving the king these days. So much
so that the jest was that he had to slip away from her
as well as the queen for his pleasures. The talk was
that Charles kept her on now mainly from habit and a
misplaced sense of duty, just because she'd given him
more children than any of his other mistresses. Although everyone could see that Charles obviously didn't
love any of them half so well as he did some of his
other bastards, or dote on any as much as he did on
his eldest: that young, handsome rogue, James, Duke
of Monmouth, got by the doomed Lucy Walter. But
the gossip also had it that Castlemaine's days were
numbered, and rightly so, the way she took liberties,
trying the limits—by scheming, making scenes, and
scolding—of even Charles's famous excessive toler-
ance with his women.

No, Mary, thank God, was no shrew, or he'd not
have kept her, Gideon thought. And he kept her very
well, at that. So for the life of him he couldn't understand why he should be feeling so uneasy about his
actions. Because he wasn't unkind to her. He'd grown
to like her very well, and let her know it too. She was
a charming wench, well-brought-up, and if unlettered,
quick enough. Company to a man in several ways he
wouldn't have thought to ask of a mistress, she was
unlike any he'd had before. She entertained him as
well as his body, because she'd grown to be as good a
companion out of his bed as she'd become in it.

Tonight, then, he was pleased to take her out again.
He'd neglected to lately. It wasn't precisely because
he'd been afraid to have Celeste see her; she surely
must know of Mary, court gossip being what it was. If
she did, Puritan or not, she knew he wasn't one, and
certainly would understand the reason for Mary, a
man's nature being what it was. But for the same
reasons he disliked challenging men to duel, although
he was a superb swordsman, he thought it wiser to

avoid flaunting his mistress before the world while the lady he hoped to marry was in London.

He wasn't wed to Celeste yet, but he'd seen Queen Catherine's face when she watched Charles, her husband, at play with his women or his bastards. Indeed, he couldn't forget it. Although few people noted or cared for what that dull, foreign tongue-tied lady thought, Gideon couldn't forget the sick looks of incomprehension and unconcealed envy and sorrow on her poor plain face. No, when he'd decided to keep Mary close while Celeste and he ranged far, he'd reasoned that if he'd trouble with womenkind, it was that he liked them too well, in too many ways, to deliberately give any of them insult or pain.

Or so he reasoned. But still, he couldn't like the vagrant feeling that stole over him from time to time. He didn't like or comprehend the notion that he was cheating—not when he'd never given his word, or oath of fidelity, to anyone, save for his king.

"Not only can you dance," he said now, distracted from his uneasy musings by his pretty partner's unexpected grace, as he stepped past her in the figure of the dance they were doing, "but you can do it wondrous well, Mistress Monk."

She shot him a saucy look of pride, mixed in with some secret amusement. "I can do a great many things well, Master Hawkes," she said as she moved away lightly.

I can say the alphabet whole, she thought as she danced on to the internal rhythm of the chant of it that she'd practiced all these past days with Jamie, and all these past nights lying alone waiting for Gideon's pleasure. And I can write down each letter in it too, she thought proudly. But I'll spare you the knowing of that just now, Master Hawkes, she told herself smugly, for it's true that education makes one even smarter, and already I'm wiser now than ever before. Now I know I must learn to put the letters together to form words, and know them too. And then, words to form sentences to make sense of, before I'm through. Ah, but when I am—she smiled to herself so charmingly that Gideon cocked his head to the side to watch her as she pranced by him—why, then I'll show you! she thought as she came stepping back to his side as the dance was done.

Mary gazed up at him just in time to see his approving and tender glance, and she smiled back with that new and maddeningly secretive smile she'd grown. That she'd some delicious secret she'd been harboring lately was plain enough for him to see. The only reason he didn't try too hard to pry it from her was that it pleased him to see her so gay, especially these days. He'd wondered how she might react when she heard of his daily courting of Celeste, and never doubted she'd hear of it, even isolated as she was. Not only was London, for all its size, too small to keep such secrets in, he hadn't tried to keep it close. Let her have her secret, then, he thought. It couldn't be a large one, or he'd have heard of it, and however small, if it contented her, well enough.

For a wonder, Tristram and Jamie weren't here tonight, so Gideon would have every dance with Mary, every bit of dinner alone with her, and pass the entire night solely in her company. And for another wonder, he thought, still gazing down fondly at her, it wasn't a daunting thought to take so much time up with this mistress. There'd been a woman in France who had lived six months with him who'd made him pause a day before he'd decided to move out and along again; once there'd been a girl in the Indies who'd lived three months with him whom he'd remembered fondly even six months after. And there'd been one woman in Amsterdam that had almost borne him a child, and he'd honestly grieved when she'd lost it before its time, although he'd not been sorry to leave her a few months later, when he'd got to know her better.

But after all these long weeks in Mary Monk's company, whether in her arms or looking forward to being there after an absence from them for days while she entertained Mother Nature instead, as had recently been the case, he still found himself pleased to be with her. But when he married . . .

And yet, after all, he wasn't married yet, was he? he reminded himself testily, to close the subject and banish the nagging thought. Instead, he bent down to ask Mary if she were hungry again.

"I always am," she answered, grinning at him, "but with all my eating I haven't got much bigger—at least in height," she laughed, "and because of that I wouldn't have a hope of getting my dinner right now—there's such a crowd around the food, I'll wait until I have a chance at it."

"Mistress Monk," he said grandly, "my sword is at your service. Wait here. I'll bring you a plate so full even you'll have trouble finishing it."

And as her eyes widened and she thrilled to hear him promise to do such a flattering, courtly service for her, he bowed before he made a mocking show of swaggering off to where the clamorous company was gorging themselves at a table full of meats put out for their pleasure. He was only half-joking, because he was determined to bring her back a heaping plate, just to see another look of childishly pure delight flashing in her dark eyes.

"I have never forgot a face, and so I know yours, but I disremember where we met," a loud voice said at Mary's side, and she looked away from Gideon to see a tall dark-haired voluptuous woman standing there.

She was dressed both so brilliantly and so scantily that Mary couldn't concentrate on her face at first. The dark-haired woman's gown was so low that her beauty marks vied with the tops of her nipples for attention, and there was a great deal of both to see. But after a moment's thought, as the other woman studied her and frowned in concentration, Mary remembered her.

"Jamie's girl!" she said, and then, seeing the look of incomprehension, added, more properly, "I mean, you were Lord Claverly's escort one night, James Beauchamp —we went out and ate at . . ."

"The Devil! I remember," the other woman said, her face clearing. "I knew 'twas so, I never forget. You were with Gideon Hawkes then. And whom are you with now?"

"Gideon Hawkes," Mary said with shy pride, gesturing to the table where he'd gone, for though there were still so many people surrounding him, his wide shoulders could be seen to rise above the crowd of them.

"Still? Well done," the tall woman said, before she said more quickly, with equal pride in her own trumpeting voice, "Well, and I'm out of Mother Bennet's house now, and have got myself a snug bit of work, I can tell you. I'm with Lord Quentin now— there he is, see?" she asked, pointing a ringed finger at a fattish older man with an enormous black wig, who was wolfing down his dinner while standing at the table, and getting a great deal of it onto his finery in the process.

"It's the best thing, I can tell you. I disremember ever being so well-set. He's rich as anything, and he don't care how it's spent, and I've got money in my pockets, and lodgings with four rooms all to myself, and a maidservant and a footman and a coach to use too, whenever I want it. And a pearl and a ruby out of him already, and he don't come to bother me more than once a week, and even though it's odd, it's over before you can spit, so even my sister, the one what has married a bargeman and lives in her own house, is burning up with jealousy, I can tell you. What does he give you?" she asked curiously, her eyes narrowing as she wondered if there was something lacking or something she'd forgotten to brag about in her bargain,

when Mary couldn't think of how to congratulate her
fast enough.

"How much money do you get?" she asked as well,
as Mary's silence bothered her, and she began to suspect her lord might be behind the times in his payments.

Mary bit her lip. It was none of this creature's
business, but she saw that if she didn't answer, the
questions would be getting even louder than they already were, since each one had risen in tone so far.

"I get what I ask for," she said honestly in a small
voice, because she'd never asked for any.

"Oh?" the dark-haired woman asked, suspicious of
being cheated by her master as well as of being misled
by Mary now. "And so what, pray, does it add up to?
And where does he lodge you? And do you have a
maid then too?"

In her time Mary had wrangled with butchers and
alewives, bakers and fishwives, and if she had to she
wouldn't hesitate to quarrel with a king. But she realized that to insult this overbearing woman would be to
cause a scene, and knew that Gideon would dislike
that above all things, however well she could handle
it. Yet not to answer her would be to insult her. Mary
glanced over to where Gideon was jesting with a friend,
and knew the only way to end this would be to answer
at once, and hope this creature would be satisfied and
let her be.

"I share my lodgings with Gideon Hawkes," Mary
said quietly, "and I haven't got a set wage, and no
maid or footman or coach either. But I'm satisfied."

As she'd said it in a hurried voice, with her head
down and her cheek flushed, the dark-haired woman
thought she understood.

"Ah, I see," she said with a richly tolerant note of
gloating in her voice, as well as one of true pity. "So
the gossip was true. Well, listen, dear, it won't do. I
expect you're new at the game, or deep in love with
the gentleman, and I hope it's that you're new, be-

cause love for them never works out, anyone can tell you that. I know he's seemly, he is, indeed. And probably a pleasure to service if you go in for that sort of thing, each to his own taste, I say. But it doesn't do to love them. I could tell you about my littlest sister, the one what worked the street for this rogue for years . . . but there isn't time. Hist! Listen to me," she said, as if Mary had a choice, as she bent to whisper in a harsh voice.

"Get your wages regular, and get them agreed on early, because generosity don't last once they've got their breeches on again," she cautioned, as Mary winced. "Sharing a bed's cozy, but get separate lodgings so you don't get treated like a wife, because they'll leave you faster if they get to thinking of you as suchlike. Get a maid and a footman or anything you can before it runs out, because what you manage to get, you can sometimes get to keep when they go. And they do," she said more loudly.

Mary wondered how to escape, and not only because she was listening to a whore's advice. But because she understood that it was very good advice.

"Sooth, Mary, grow up," the dark-haired woman said impatiently. "Think to the future. He is. Why, just look. There's his lady. That's her, everyone's talking about her. The lady from Ivyclose. I never forget a name, no matter how odd . . . yes, Celeste Southern, the one the king picked for him, my gentleman says. Beautiful too, isn't she?"

It took a second for Mary to look up out of her well of misery at this, because it had been said in the same harsh, flat tones the woman had used all through her advice. But then she heard the meaning of the words, and then she looked up and heard nothing else but her own thoughts as she stared straight at Celeste Southern, only two bodies' lengths away from her, as Celeste Southern stared straight back at her, directly into her own astonished eyes.

*    *    *

"Yes, there, now she sees you," the Earl of Rochester said excitedly as Lord Mobely interrupted him to say more smoothly, "Yes. The little dark one. Mary Monk. Gideon's mistress. Pretty little thing, isn't she?"

It was wrong to stare. She should have turned on her heel to go. But still Celeste could only stand and look at the small, slightly curved young woman with the wealth of dark curls—the one who stood at the side of the spectacularly painted harlot that she'd thought they meant when they'd suddenly pointed out Gideon Hawkes's whore to her. She stood as though rooted, to stare at the small dark young woman named Mary Monk, who was gazing back at her with no expression but that of wonder in her huge dark eyes.

She recognized her. It was the same girl she'd thought Gideon had been with at the theater that night when they'd met there. The one she'd seen him look down to with that oddly bemused look, the one she'd discounted as being a mere scrap of a girl, the Gypsy-dark girl that she'd overlooked in the pleasure of seeing him unexpectedly—until she'd seen him bend down and graze that dark cheek with his lips. And then the girl had turned such a prettily confused and charming, blushing face to his that Celeste had more than noticed her: she'd never forgot her or that one fleeting moment. Seeing him capable of such gentle warmth had heartened her and softened her own heart toward him. But then she'd thought the girl some daughter of a friend, some young creature with a hidden passion for an older man, perhaps. She'd never guessed that was Gideon's mistress.

She'd known he had one, of course, but she'd discounted it. He hadn't known her when he'd taken one, after all; every man at court had one, and she'd known he'd fallen into wicked ways. That was part of her reason for accepting the notion of his suit; that was part of her crusade. She never doubted she could mend that when she cured him of all his vices. But now, remembering that moment, that rare and loving look that had passed across his own stern face, transforming it, she knew the girl was a formidable barrier to her own hopes, if not the death of them.

But then, she thought desperately, would she want a man who took his fleshly pleasures lightly? Wasn't it a better thing that he cared where he laid his body; wasn't that a sign of a more moral man than the usual run of men in Charles's depraved court? Far better, for example, than these two mischief-makers who'd accosted her the moment Philip's back was turned? The two, she realized now, who'd suggested they come here this very night, and had actually brought them here from Charles's own masque with the promise of more gaiety.

It wasn't the sudden look of anger she turned on first the slight earl, giggling in his excitement as he stood attentive at her side, or the equally furious one she shot at his friend Sir Mobely, before she looked back at Mary, that made them both grow rigid before they slid away into the crowd. It was the fact that Gideon Hawkes had seen them. And then he'd seen Celeste, and then looked back for Mary, before he froze, ablaze with an even greater, though impotent fury, as he saw the two women standing stock-still, assessing each other as the crowd grew still around them.

But she's only a girl, thought Celeste, and not at all beautiful or immodest-looking, or, in any other way I can tell, a whore.

Ah, but she's beautiful, Mary thought, every inch a lady. It isn't just her clothes or her face, it's in the way she holds herself. She's so very beautiful.

The two women eyed each other expressionlessly. But Gideon had seen cats sit and stare at each other, unblinking, for hours, until they erupted in rage and tried to tear each other apart. There was too much pride in both women for that, but Gideon had the strange fear that it would be himself that would be torn to pieces if they ever gave in to their anger. And there was too much theater in the moment. He had to end it as gracefully as he could.

Whatever happened, Gideon thought rapidly, Mary would stay with him, for now. Indeed, she'd nowhere else to go. But Celeste was free to turn and walk out of his life. Mary was, for all her charms, only his mistress, and if she went home in chagrin, it would be his own bed she'd lie across to weep. Celeste was his longed-for bride; her home had once been his own, yet if she left him he'd never see it again. He owed Mary nothing. He wanted everything that Celeste was.

Gideon broke from his inaction and went to Celeste.

As Mary saw him approach the lovely lady, she wasn't surprised. It seemed, after all, entirely natural. Nor was she angry at Celeste then. In fact, when Celeste left off looking at her, she was relieved; she'd felt small and cheapened in the face of the beautiful lady's plain astonishment and hurt surprise. Instead of feeling resentment or anger, she found herself unexpectedly wanting desperately to explain everything to the lady, to beg her pardon, to try to make her see how she couldn't have helped what she'd done or what Gideon had done to her. And when she looked to him, to see him looming taller and more vivid than any other man in the room, with his face set in grim lines again, his tensed cheek flickering even though nothing else in his cold face moved, she shocked herself. Because instead of feeling a rush of yearning, she found she hated him then—for what he'd made of her, mind and body. And mostly for what she'd made of him in her own mind and body.

When he came to Celeste, she was glad to leave off staring at Mary. She'd never doubted he'd abandon the girl when he saw her. But when he did, she felt a twinge of sympathy and a surge of feeling for the little dark girl he'd left standing alone that shocked her to the core. That she could feel a bond with an unrepentant whore? And yet, the girl had seemed so vulnerable, so small and unprotected, so plain when she ought to have been blatant, so timid when she ought to have been bold. And in that first moment when Gideon came to stand next to her, and Celeste felt the thrill of being so close to him again despite herself, and felt another small mean thrill of triumph because he'd chosen her, as she'd known he must do, after all, she shocked herself even further. Because in that moment she found that she almost hated him—precisely for what he made her feel, as well as for what he'd obviously made his little mistress feel. And only part of it was for herself for not having the courage to turn from him forever.

"Lady," he said, taking her hand and stepping in front of her so as to block her line of vision, "I hadn't looked to see you here."

"So I see," she said.

"I am a man, my lady," he said in a low, cool voice. "I can't and won't apologize for it. But I'll beg your pardon if I've hurt you in any way, because I never meant to, nor would I ever if I could help it. Please believe that."

She gazed into his brilliant ice-clear eyes and gave him her hand at last, and nodded as she felt the warmth of his large hand thaw her chilled one and then communicate itself to her numbed heart. Then she was glad she couldn't see beyond him, to where his filthy little whore awaited him. For a moment she was staggered at the sudden virulence of her dislike for the wench, but then she welcomed the flow of anger that she could direct without a qualm of doubt. It wasn't wrong to hate vice incarnate.

"I understand," she said quietly.

"I'll take you home," he said.

"No, no," she answered as she saw Philip making

his way through the crowd toward them, "here is my brother instead."

He couldn't argue now; he was too relieved that she didn't wish to. "I'll see you tomorrow," he said instead, and though his voice was just as toneless and cold, he didn't breathe until she answered.

"Yes," she said.

And Mary stood at the side of the spectacular dark-haired whore and didn't move. She was very glad when Gideon blocked her view of the lady of Ivyclose. She'd never doubted he'd go to her and stay with her. But as he stood and talked with the lady, she found herself wondering how she'd get home. It seemed that was the only thought she'd room for in her head now. She'd never called a hackney cab by herself. She worried as she remembered it was too far to walk, and too late to walk alone, and yet she knew she couldn't stay here. She stood fretting over it absently, not allowing herself to think or feel another thing. So when Gideon appeared in front of her again, and dismissed the dark-haired woman with a few words, and then said something to her, she was so relieved and grateful to see him there that she didn't at once hear what he'd said.

"Mary," he said coolly, "come, I'll take you home."

She was so glad to have him take her hand and wrap her in her cloak and bundle her into a carriage that she could only sit next to him in silence, numbed, but grieving, thinking of the cruel and haughty beauty who'd steal him away, and how much she resented her, and God, and the world, for making things fall out that way.

When they'd got up to their lodgings, and were alone again, he spoke at last.

"I'm sorry," he said, and paused and added with difficulty, "that it happened tonight."

She didn't know what to answer and so didn't, and only folded her cloak over and over in her arms.

"Aren't you going to say something, Mary?" he asked.

"She's the lady you're going to marry," she said, foolishly, she knew, since she hadn't even asked it as a question, because there wasn't a hope he'd say no. And she knew she shouldn't have said it, any more than she should have asked it.

He might have remained still because he knew that. But he did finally speak, after his silence became almost a threat rather than a rebuke for her insolence.

"She's the lady the king proposes I wed," he said. "She's the mistress of Ivyclose."

After she nodded, he said only, "I'm going for a walk, Mary, I'll be back," and he left her.

But he'd never before told her where he was bound when he'd left her, and he'd never reassured her as to his return, and his manner of explaining his lady had never been what she'd expected either. She hugged his few words to herself for hours. When she went to bed at last, she left off her plain shift to show him that her courses were done, and she put on only his perfume, to show him more.

When he returned, exhausted and chilled, near to dawn, he gathered her close in his arms, only to go to sleep almost as soon as he did. Yet she was as glad of it as if he'd made passionate love to her and named her all manner of beautiful names, because he was close to her again and so then she could finally sleep again as well.

"She's packing," the maidservant said as he stood outside her door, "but she'll see you in a moment, sir. If you'd please to wait."

He'd please himself more if he pushed her aside and rushed into the room to plead his case with Celeste, but Gideon had got over acting on his impulses years before, or he'd not have survived very long. So he nodded and stood aside and waited, pretending to

lounge against a wall, for all the world like a bored
Cavalier with nothing on his mind but the feather on
his hat.

He'd roamed the city last night, through ashes and
over cobbles, never noting where he was going, but his
size had been such and his face had been such that no
man or band of men had dared approach him. He
might have welcomed even some savage intrusion into
his dark thoughts; perhaps they saw that too. Women
approached him, often. A legion of London's whores
sought to solace him and earn their bread thereby, but
none were little shy dark-haired ones who were selling
themselves for the first time in order to eat, because
he looked kind, and so he ignored them all. He thought
of Mary, and of Celeste, and the reek of the city
brought him Mary's past. But the first dawn breezes
brought nothing but memories of the sweet country
scents of Ivyclose to him, of roses and freesias and a
past that miraculously drew closer even as it grew
more distant.

He'd slept and then walked to Whitehall this morning, and sworn to himself that he felt Mary's eyes on
his back all the way. But now Celeste was packing her
things, and he wondered if all his hopes were in her
bags as well.

"You may go in, sir," the maidservant said, and
after a sketch of a curtsy she vanished down the hall,
so there was that much hope left, after all, he thought.

She wore a simple gown and a hood over her honey
hair, and he saw that her good wool traveling cloak
hung over a chair. He stood in her parlor and waited
for her to speak, for in truth he didn't know how to
begin this ending.

"I'm going home to Ivyclose," she said composedly
as she came to greet him, noting how his eyes flick-
ered at the words. "I can't bear it here any longer.
But," she said as he was about to speak, to say anything to stay her final words, "I'd be pleased if you'd
come to visit me there, Gideon.

"This court," she sighed as he stayed silent so as to understand her every word, her every nuance of speech, "I can't disguise my disgust for it any longer. Not that they'd care; it would amuse them. They've no shame. there is nothing here but lewdness and mirth at the thought of anything spiritual. There is *such* wickedness here, Gideon," she said, gazing at him with deep sincerity. "I don't believe you can see it, standing so close to it as you are. You don't have to be a godly person," she insisted, "to see the rot in it. Men make mockery of their marriage vows in open spite of their wives and in sight of God. But they're only copying their sovereign king as they forget their heavenly one. Their wives do the same with other men, and then they openly compare each man's skills at what should be unsaid even between husband and wife. And when they aren't doing that," she said heatedly, losing her pretense at calm in her unhappiness, "they go to plays to see the same things—adultery, fornication, and every kind of sin—celebrated."

"You sound like a sermon," he said, and she averted her eyes, because it was true she'd thought up her speech in the night and rehearsed it all through the morning for him.

"It's more than religion," she said angrily. "It affects each moment of my life here. A gentleman speaks to me—of poetry or flowers or his wife's health—and the moment I smile or show sympathy, he asks me to his bed. A kindly older woman sees my distress and offers me her company, and treats me well. I take to her—only to have Philip tell me to stay far from her, since she's known for her love of women's flesh. Two courtiers, both nobly born and friends to the king, befriend us and then deliberately take us to where I can find you shaming me."

He clenched his teeth and she mistook him, and went on before he could defend himself.

"Even that is nothing. If I were to tell you or Philip

of every insult I received, your swords would be busy
from day to night. So I forget most. Or try. But
worse," she said, turning away now and looking aside,
"I found that a man I had begun to learn to trust, who
offered me his heart and hand, made sport of me by
how, all the while, he publicly exhibited his bond with
his mistress."

"I explained that it was without intention," he said
grimly, but she stopped him by shaking her head and
interrupting. "No, you don't understand," she said.
"As I told you, if you're steeped in ungodliness, deep
in Satan's coils, you can't see the difference anymore.
Gideon, it's never that you . . . took her. I can understand, if not . . . if *never*," she said with more force,
"condone such use of God's gifts."

He frowned then, not because of what she'd said,
but because her words happened to stir up a bitter
memory. They sounded very much like the mocking
ones his father had used whenever he drunkenly regaled the family by mimicking the Sunday sermon he'd
sit so nicely through every week, after it was over—
and after he'd locked the doors, of course.

She noticed his reaction and hurried on, softening
her voice as well as her words.

"And I know you've no reason to remain faithful to
me—as yet. But to mock me so, Gideon!"

He looked at her, still frowning, as she said, "To
live with her, Gideon! To actually bide in the same
house, in the same bed," she whispered, hot color
rising to her pale face, "and then to come from her
. . . lodgings to court me. Fie, Gideon, it will not do!

"If you want to wed me, if you sincerely want to
court me, you must move away from her before you
see me again," she said stiffly.

He laughed. "This is a nice turn," he said bitterly,
scornfully, his anger overriding his caution, because
whatever he'd been in his life, he'd never been able to
bear hypocrisy, and whatever he wanted, he never

wanted it if it were tainted with that. "You don't ask me to leave her—just her rooms? What, is your God so purblind he can't follow me down the street when I leave my own pure bed in my own safe empty lodgings?"

"It's not for God, it's for me," she said, and his twisted smile vanished.

"I know I have no right to ask you to leave her, save the right of a good friend giving wise counsel, have I? . . . As yet," she added softly, and he fell silent.

"And if you bide with her, Gideon, I tell you I will always see you with her in my mind's eye," she said with passion. "I'll always wonder how much she knows of me, and worry that as she lives in your home she lives also in your heart, and imagine you telling her everything about me, about us, when you get home to her—like all the other deceivers in this depraved court. Because I don't know you that well yet, Gideon," she cried, "so how shall I not think that?"

He forgot caution entirely and took her in his arms. He held her and stroked her silken hair and murmured consolation. And when she'd done weeping, and looked up to him, red-eyed, he sighed so that she could feel his great chest heave against her heart.

"No," he said quietly, "you're right. How should you know the truth of me, after all? Very well, then. If I come to you at Ivyclose, lady, be sure I'll not come from her bed—in my rooms. If I come, know, without asking, that I'll come from my own most private lodgings. I swear to it now."

She laid her head down against his shoulder, overcome with emotion after her difficult speech and harder request. He soothed her, and buried his face in her sweet-scented hair, and so never saw her smile of triumph. Although she rued it even as she exulted in it, because vanity was unseemly, she couldn't repress it, and so silently promised to do penance for it when she got home. But it was a great victory. He'd never said he'd come to her at Ivyclose, but she was certain he would. He'd never promised to give up his harlot, but she knew he would—first in his lodgings, and then in his bed. Because every great journey began with a step, and she knew she'd begun him on the road to his salvation.

Her pleasure was spoiled only for a second, and only by a curious pang of sorrow for his little whore. She must have stiffened at the thought of it, because Gideon murmured something to her and touched her cheek with his fingertips, and she relaxed. He looked down at her and smiled at how peaceful his small gesture had made her. But then, as she laid her head on Gideon's chest again and felt his hand stroking her hair, she felt even better in reminding herself that she'd done a virtuous, godly thing.

Some devout men of her order believed that fire was the only sure way to cleanse sin from evildoers. Although committing a sinner to the flames to sear his mortal flesh from his bones seemed harsh, it was really a kindness, because it was the only way to purify such souls. Or so she'd been taught, and so she agreed it must be. And so she knew that it was far better for Mary Monk to burn only from the sting of Gideon's rejection now, after all, than for her to continue to earn her way to the flames of eternal damnation later. Celeste sighed at the comforting thought, and then lay at peace on Gideon's breast, genuinely content.

# 13

It was the kindest gift, the most wonderful offering he could have made to her, and Mary tried hard not to cry, not from gratitude, but because of her horror at it. It would have pleased her a week before—no, it would've overjoyed her then. Today it froze her blood. But there was no way she could tell him, so she only ducked her head and forced back her tears, and quickly seized on the next-to-best reason to refuse it.

"Ah, but . . . I couldn't," she said to Gideon, turning her back on the woman who waited before them in their front room, and, whispering so low he had to incline his head to hear the stumbling words, she mumbled, "I could . . . never live with her, Gideon."

He took her by the elbow and led her to their bedchamber, where Rountree and the waiting woman couldn't hear them.

"But she was maidservant to no less than Lady Amhurst before she died," Gideon said then, his annoyance at Mary's ungrateful reaction to his gift showing in his voice as she averted her head from his searching eyes, "and before that," he argued, wondering whether the maidservant's age and sour expression had misled Mary, "she waited on Walter Jervis' wife, and would be there still, her husband says in his recommendation, if his poor lady hadn't died of plague. She can sew, do hair, all else required of her—she has the best credentials, Rountree made sure of that . . . why, she's been in the employ of some of the finest ladies."

"Oh, yes," Mary said in low tones that sounded like a frightened moan, despite herself, "but I am only Mary Monk, don't you see?"

"Ah," he said, and fell still, because he did.

Trust Mary, he thought wryly, she never made a misjudgment in such matters; he ought to have understood from the first moment she'd paled at seeing the woman. Now he saw that the maidservant's sneer might not have been an accident of birth; now he realized that he and Rountree had looked too high. Mary had the right of it. It might've been a clever idea to secure her a maidservant from a fine and worthy home far from Charles's wild court—but such a woman would come to think of herself as equally fine. And although she might tolerate much from an employer close to the king, even stooping to serve a mistress of low birth and lower profession in order to work in these hard times, she'd never let her mistress forget it. And Gideon never doubted that she could do just that. He'd lived and traveled enough to know that there were a hundred small ways a clever servant could master a weak or inexperienced master.

"Out upon her then!" he said immediately. "We'll pay her for time wasted, and waste not a second more finding some younger, jollier creature to serve you, you'll see," he said, pretending he thought Mary unhappy with the woman's age. But as she began to speak again, he remembered her relentless practicality and truthfulness, and so, not wishing to shame her further, spoke before she could, saying softly, "And one young enough to think you a fine mistress simply for not beating her when she makes mistakes . . . you won't beat her *too* often, will you?" he asked, to make her laugh, to make her forget the contemptuous smirk the sour-faced woman in the next room had greeted her with.

"But you must have a maidservant—a woman can't be alone, and I can't always be here," he said, and strode from the room to dismiss the waiting servants.

He wore a thunderous expression that had nothing to do with his task. He hadn't told Mary he was leaving—well, he hadn't decided to leave yet, he was getting her a maid in case he did, he told himself, and frowned. Because he knew all of the things he told himself were sham and prevarication, and was roundly disgusted with himself for it.

Celeste had been gone from London for over a week. He'd done little but merrymaking and sport in that time, but whenever he was idle, however much he tried not to be, he'd thought of little else but her and Ivyclose. The days were drawing in, the winds grew sharper, and soon the Thames would wear an icy skin. He realized his time was running out and yet he remained indecisive. That was a rare and unhappy state for him.

He didn't like to be pushed into action by any woman, or any man, for that matter, nor did he like to be threatened. But for all that Celeste had been fair in her demands, they'd been demands. Yet if he didn't comply, his suddenly revived dreams for his future were threatened. And yet, he argued with himself, as he'd done whenever he'd been alone for a second since that day Celeste had left, for all that her demands were entirely reasonable, he'd this unreasonable reluctance to leave Mary, even to move out to his own lodgings, even if they were to be in the next house from here. When he did, the thin fiction of his having taken her in to care for her, which he knew she

cherished, would be stripped away. She'd be exactly
and only his mistress then, and though that was the
case, and they both knew it, he didn't want to see the
knowledge of it in her eyes.

But winter was coming; time passed, and his opportunities might as well. He'd never been a coward, and
wouldn't be one now. After Rountree and the disgruntled maidservant left, he stood in the center of the
room and gazed down at the fine rug he'd put here,
counting the number of bars in its pattern. Then he
raised his head. It was time. He cleared his throat and
called out to Mary.

"Dress yourself, wench," he shouted. "We're promised to court tonight."

Then he scowled, and then he spoke agan, with no
gentleness or joy, "But first come in here, Mary, I've
a thing to tell you."

She eased out of the bedchamber, and seeing no
one in the room with him, looked at him with a smile
that transformed her worried face into something very
near to beauty. Plain, small, and neat, she delighted
him. She bent into a curtsy fit for her king. Her grace,
he thought again, was uncommonly good to see.

"I await your command," she said with great pom-
posity and rising laughter.

"Wear your red gown," he said abruptly. "It looks
very well on you," he explained in answer to her
confusion and her unspoken questioning of his author-
itative tone. Although he'd never mentioned the matter again, he'd been nothing but gentle to her this past
week since she'd met Celeste Southern by accident.
He'd been full of fun and jest in her company, and
constantly in her company, and full of tenderness and
passionate care in her arms, and in her arms every
night, remaining there, well-occupied, through most of
the night.

Then he turned from her and dug into his pocket
and turned once again to put out his hand to her. A

small wrapped object lay in it, and he thrust it toward Mary.

"For your gown, for tonight," he said.

She took the small packet from his palm wonderingly. And unwrapped it carefully. A smooth round and red pendant set in dull embrossed gold lay there, trailing a golden chain made of tiny interlocking knots. She gazed at it as if it were a wasp.

"It's a ruby," he said carelessly, facing away again, and so not seeing the way she winced and shied at the thing she held, as if it would sink teeth into her own trembling palm. "It will be well with the red, so wear it," he said.

He wished he could turn away from his own damned folly and cowardice as easily, he thought, in a rage with himself, for he'd meant to give it to her as a consolation after he told her he must go, before they parted, so she'd have rich compensation. Instead, he turned in actuality and left the room. And so never saw her weep at the way he'd made her officially his whore now. Just exactly like any other, she thought, remembering the benefits she was supposed to reap from her position—at least, as told to her by the woman at the dancing party that night she'd met the lady of Gideon's heart.

But if she were to be the woman of Gideon's bed, she'd do it right, she thought, endlessly practical, hopelessly loyal, as always. And so she was all smiles and grace and compliance, just exactly like any other whore should be, she thought, when he came to ask if she were ready to go to Whitehall with him.

"Majesty," Gideon said, bowing.

"Gideon," the king said, and his curling smile grew.

"I see he's not here," Gideon remarked conversationally, looking over the crowded room.

"I sent him away for now," the king replied, never

asking whom they spoke of, "so that I could have him
to speak with later. You may not skewer him, Gideon.
'Ods fish, sir, but I won't have it! You came in tonight
with your sword half-drawn, or so't looked to be."

"Ah," Gideon said, nodding, "so that was the reason for your summons. To order me to let Rochester
live."

The two tall men stood side by side, and for all his
easy friendliness, no other courtier approached the
king just then. He'd asked for privacy with Gideon
Hawkes, and even if he hadn't, the look in the red-
headed Cavalier's glittering blue eyes would've discouraged all but those who might've feared he'd do his
sovereign a mischief, if they hadn't been told otherwise. As it was, now that cold bright gaze stabbed the
king.

"You told him to hide, did you, sire?" Gideon
asked. "I've looked for him everyplace he's known to
frequent in London, except for behind one of his
mistress's skirts or under his bed."

"Sooth, you've named it, haven't you?" Charles
said, smiling and shaking his head so that his long
black curls swayed. "Of course he's hidden. He's never
a fool, though he plays at being one. Nor very brave,
either. But I like him, Gideon, I do, and I won't have
him extinguished. At least, not by you. He amuses
me. But I love you, my testy red Hawke, we go back,
we two, don't we? You were fifteen . . . Zounds!
Think on it. Fifteen, and your voice changing—I remember how it cracked so after we'd asked, 'Are you
a friend to Caesar?' that night."

"No, sire," Gideon laughed, "it had changed years
back. That was fear you heard, and nothing more."

"No, a great deal more," Charles said. " 'Aye, friend
and more,' you said then. And so you proved to
be—scouting for the Roundhead troops that were hunting us, alone before us on that dark road, ready to lay

down the sum of those fifteen years for the sake of your king. I don't forget, Gideon."

"Then why not let me hunt one little fool now, Majesty?" Gideon asked.

They stopped strolling and Charles gazed hard at his companion, his dark face unsmiling. Those watching held their breath until they heard their king's rich laughter ring out and saw him clap the Cavalier upon the back.

" 'Od's teeth, but I love you," he laughed. "Always the courtier, always so nice in your manners—'Majesty' and 'sire' and never ask for more intimacy where a hundred lesser men assume it, but never afraid to speak your mind, and never compromising. I'd give much to have more such men about me, I swear it!"

"You could," Gideon said.

"Oh, aye," Charles said, smiling more sardonically now, "you're right again, Gideon Hawkes, damn you. But I seek merriment. I've my thoughtful friends to run institutes of philosophy and science, and my clever friends to entertain me, and I make sure they outnumber the rest. Too many years without laughter, Gideon. The ones we shared were full of danger, but I loved them, and unless I mistake me, so did you. Now I have peace and must keep it, and so find I need merriment instead."

"And you find you need the Earl of Rochester: a little manikin of malice and with a heart as small as his charity?" Gideon asked.

"And the Earl of Rochester: a young man of possibilities and with a wit as large as his list of crimes," Charles rebuked him.

Gideon's face became cold and still, but his left cheek twitched as he set his jaw hard.

"What has he done?" Charles asked lightly.

"Mischief, Majesty," Gideon replied on a sigh, "cruel mischief. Sent notes to my mistress that I thank God she couldn't read, and I'm not a Puritan . . . and," he said, frowning now, remembering, "he made sure the lady you picked for my wife came to meet my mistress too."

"That's all?" Charles laughed. "Then be sure he's frightened of you. Still, I'll put a stop to it. I don't want him ended on your weapon."

"As you will, sire," Gideon said, "but never think to save his life. No one can. If he doesn't end on my weapon, be sure he'll finish himself with his own fleshly one. He'll not make old bones, whether it's me or his own folly that brings him down. Pox and wine level a man as well as cold steel can."

The king nodded as Gideon went on to ask coldly, "And Mobely? Does your hand stretch over him too, sire?"

"Ah, Mobely," Charles said, thinking. "Is he in it too? Sooth"—he shrugged elaborately—"Roger Mobely's a grown man with little to recommend him but young Rochester's friendship. He's yours, if you wish. But, tell me, is this why I've not been asked to your wedding yet? And I was so looking forward to the bedding ceremony. Is the lady of Ivyclose so pure? Most maids would take note of your mistress and copy what they could, so as to please you better. Is she a Puritan maid, then? Is Southern's sister a Roundhead?" he asked, laughing heartily, as if at the nonsense of that thought. "Or what's the delay?"

"Of my own making," Gideon said rapidly. "Misunderstandings, coils, lovers' quarrels. I'm not the most adept gallant, sire."

"You're the worst liar if you claim that," the king said thoughtfully. "It's rare to give a woman a voice in the matter of her marriage, but I did because I think as highly of their wits, in the general run of things, as I do of your wiles in such affairs. Or did I mistake the matter, Gideon?" he asked seriously. "Should I look

into it and smooth, or command, where I may to resolve
all? 'Twas all for your gain, believe me, my friend.''

"And so it will be," Gideon assured him. "No need
to do more, sire. It's only that I'm an odd fellow—I
want a woman's full heart. I'd no more wed a reluctant bride than bed an unwilling wench."

"Then," the king said softly, "be glad you're no
king, my Gideon." They both fell silent then, rueful
and remembering.

Mary had been unwilling when Gideon bedded her;
the king was famous for being disappointed in his
politically expedient bride.

"But I can see why your Mistress Monk would trouble the lady," Charles said on a growing smile. "She's
charming, charming," he repeated slowly. "Very unlike the others here. I envy you your little maid, but
so, it seems, do others. She's new, she's different,"
the king said musingly, "so she's gained a certain
amount of fame."

Gideon looked across the room to where Mary stood
in a crowd of ladies of the court. She'd passed all her
time with them since he'd left her to await his informal
audience with the king. Now several Cavaliers were
beginning conversations with the women, circling round
the knot of them, very like sharks Gideon had once
seen revolving around a fisherman's broken boat, waiting to move in, wondering if their prey was tasty.

There were women of all sizes and shapes in the
group, of all ages and distinctions. The one thing that
united them was the extravagance of their dress, their
hair, the number of their beauty marks, the amount of
paint adorning their faces and the expanses of exposed
skin above their waists. Yet at a glance, Mary, one of
the smaller of their number, and not half so gotten-up,
still stood out from the mass of them. It might have
been just because she was so dark and seemingly plain
that she was noticeable, like a thin brown sparrow in

the midst of a flock of fluffy white-feathered pouter pigeons. Or it might have been that she was the only one not smiling, flirting, or posing. Or even because she was so obviously the one several of the men were staring at. She looked wary and unhappy to Gideon. Unknowingly, his face reflected her feelings.

"Oho!" the king said, mistaking his mood for jealousy. "Now I know who the Puritan is!"

"Exactly so," Gideon said, recovering his poise. "And so, if you'll permit, Majesty, I think I'll take the little sinner home to make her see the error of her ways—and mine," he added, as his sovereign laughingly and heartily made much of approving this new sort of religious practice.

But she didn't whisper "Thank you" or "Oh, yes, please, I'm ready to go," as he had expected her to when he detached her from the group and walked her off to gather up her cloak; nor did she sigh with relief when he'd got her into their carriage; and not once on the ride back to their rooms did she confide her pleasure at being able to leave court. And that was odd, for she never liked to go, and always spoke of how glad she was to leave any such courtly affair.

Gideon didn't react to her unfriendliness. He couldn't. He felt uncomfortably like a thief who suspects all eyes are on his hands in a crowd before he so much as moves them toward another man's purse, because he knew what he intended to do. And so although he'd said nothing as yet, he brooded about her reaction. And because he knew that what he'd soon say would make her angry or worse, it seemed natural to him that she should sulk, even though, if he were to think about it, he'd have realized it was before the case.

But once they'd got to their lodgings, she left off brooding. In fact, she seemed to cheer up enormously. So much so that he found it difficult to interrupt her to speak his mind. Because she began to tell him tales about the ladies she'd met, and regaled him with stories they'd told her—prattling bits of court gossip and snippets of tattle, all told in a bright, high voice that made him look at her sharply.

He pulled off his shirt. "Mary," he said, and only that, and she left off talking abruptly.

"I've a thing to tell you," he said.

He busied himself in folding his shirt, but then after he'd laid it down, he took a deep breath and faced her. His face was gentled by the dim rushlight.

"I'll be leaving tomorrow," he said, and as her eyes widened, he added hastily, "I'm off to Ivyclose again. I'll be back, but," he said, glancing away from her, "not here. That is to say," he went on, not looking toward her, "I'll still see you. But I won't be living here with you anymore. Rountree will be getting me new lodgings, for myself. Of course, I'll still pay your way. And as Rountree will be joining me after he moves my things, I'll have that new maidservant for you, as well as a footman—you'll need a man about for safety's sake. I'll let you know where I'll live, but ask that you not visit me. I'll come to visit you here instead, and often."

"Oh," she said.

"Yes, well, that's the way of it," he said as he removed his breeches.

There was a long silence in the room. He was wondering what else he could say to reassure her as to his keeping her on, when he heard her say softly, as though to herself, "Oh, well, then, I see. Ah. Well, it's very like they said, isn't it? Well, then. Yes. Never mind. Where was I? Ah, yes," she said more loudly, "and then Lord Adair said to the lady, 'Mistress, I believe your husband is nearer than that.' "

She continued her story that he'd interrupted in the same high, bright voice she'd used before.

He frowned and looked to where she sat on the bed,

one shapely leg raised as she peeled her stocking off. "And she looked back at him and laughed," she went on, holding her leg in the air, absently inspecting one high-arched little foot, "but then there was a rattling at the wardrobe, and a man came tumbling out," she said, lowering her leg, and while rising again to turn around, as she unbuttoned her gown, she added, "and it was none other than the tinker!"

She peered at him, looking back over one naked shoulder as she let her gown slip slowly down.

He looked very grim.

"You didn't like the tale?" she asked, her eyes very wide and unnaturally bright. "Then, as they say, I'll use my lips to better purpose," she said, and with her gown still slipped down to her waist, her high breasts above her corset almost entirely exposed to his view, her deep dark eyes altogether hidden from him by her downcast lashes, she came to him and rested her small hands high on his shoulders. He stood silent. She looked up and then down, but not before he saw her bite her lip. Then she whispered, "Ah, well," and lowered her head further to bring her lips lightly to his chest to give him a quick, tentative peck, a scant pursing of the lips, as she kissed him on the corded muscles there. When he still didn't move, she bent her knees and balanced herself by putting her cold hands lightly on his waist, and lowered her head further— until he gripped her shoulders hard and pulled her up to stare into her great dark frightened eyes.

"What are you doing?" he roared at her.

"What they told me I should!" she cried, the tears finally spilling over from her eyes. "That's all they talked about, what they do and how they do it, unless they were telling me how I should do it. I see that I'm not very good at what I do, indeed, I'm not. Ah, Gideon, I didn't know people did half the things they told me I must do to please you! So I tried . . . but how should I know?" and then she didn't speak anymore, she was so busily trying to stop crying against his heart.

"No, no, and no," he murmured as he held her and stroked her slight back. "Old tricks and cheap games. That's never what I want from you. It's your freely given affection I want, nothing more. And if there's to be more to our play one day, it must come from your desire, not your obligation. It will come from sweet experience, and I'll give you that, in time," he said.

"What time?" she asked. "They said you were going to leave me, they said I'd have to look sharp for another protector too," she managed to say into the soft furze of hair on his chest. "You owe me nothing," she said distinctly then, trying to step away, letting him go even as she let him grip her more tightly as he heard her words. "I hold you to nothing you don't want to do. I swear to it. I only wish you'd tell me the whole of it at once, so I know how to go on. Because you're leaving," she said numbly. "So they were right."

"Only leaving these rooms, not leaving you," he insisted.

"But the ruby, the maid, the footman, separate rooms . . ." She spoke the words as though they were unclean ones. "Jamie's girl, the one he took to dine with us, the one I met again at John Stanley's dancing party, she said that was what . . . whores like her—like us—must expect to get before you leave us. . . ."

She fell still. However softly she'd spoken, her words seemed to ring out in the silent room.

"I leave only to return again and again. You must live with someone," he said patiently. "You have nightmares, Mary," he explained, forgetting all the maid's other duties and remembering what had worried him the most in the night since he'd made up his mind. "I want someone with you. No woman lives safe without a man, so the footman will protect you. And the ruby suits you," he said, feeling her tremble, but not with passion for him, and he wished he were already gone from here, or not leaving.

She stayed still. And then, because she couldn't say what she wanted to, she only added, to explain her poor embarrassing charade at being a temptress, her frantic act of fear that she was deeply shamed at now, "They said I didn't know much, and so you'd grow bored with me."

"They've never known what they're talking about. That's why I never chose one of them," he said. "I want none of their tired tricks. It's what they've lost or never had that draws me, it's your very innocence that captures me, Mary," he whispered to her.

"Innocence?" she asked, her head shooting up, tears forgotten in her surprise.

"Yes, innocence," he echoed, thinking, yes, it was a foolish thing to say, but true. And since he couldn't explain it any more than he could deny it, he couldn't say more. He'd let her know in other ways.

He took her into their bed and passed the hours making slow and deliberate love to her, and after she'd got over her anger with herself and him, she responded to him. They clung to each other as though the thought of their good-bye were the strongest aphrodisiac known, and in their parting found a closeness they'd never known before. He was more than kind and more than impassioned, and for the first time he could remember at such sweet work, found himself regretting the end he'd striven to attain as it neared.

She knew it. Not from his hands or lips or his constant praise or whispered endearments of "sweet" and "sweeting," but from what he said when he least knew what he said. For when his great winged shoulders finally folded over her, as his frame convulsed, he cried a broken "Mary!" before he sighed and grew still before he grew frenzied again, and then collapsed, still as death even as he gave her new life. Because the greatest joy she'd ever felt flooded through her then, and whether it was his body or his word that had summoned it, she didn't know or care. But long after her trembling in aftermath had ceased and she lay sated and newly hungry in his arms, the word beat on in her mind, and glowed in her heart like a steady flame, and never had she so loved her own name.

And in the morning, as he'd promised, he was gone to Ivyclose again.

# 14

"Yes, up the stairs," Gideon insisted. "Downstairs rooms have no real histories—only public ones. It's abovestairs where the memories lie."

He led Celeste up the stairs by the hand, restrained from bounding up them only by the tenuous grip he had on her slim fingers as she followed hesitantly behind him. He was like a kite held to the earth by a thin thread in the wind, he thought, his emotions ran so high and so far ahead of hers. He thought she lagged because she was afraid of what he might be seeking in the more intimate rooms they were going to. In any other house, or at any other time in this house, she'd have been right. But he hurried her to the bedchambers only to experience the bittersweet joys of his childhood again, and not the wilder pleasures of his manhood.

But what he found most of, again, was the same stale regret and sense of outrage at what he'd lost, even before he'd lost Ivyclose.

They'd passed the last few days talking and riding out over the estate; they'd spent the nights together the three of them—Gideon, Celeste, and her brother, Philip—dining and playing at cards, and then Celeste might sing to them, or they to her, and then Philip, feigning extravagant weariness, would take himself off to bed and leave them alone. But it was never long before Celeste did the same. And Gideon would go to bed alone, in a room that had been one of his older brothers', without even his indifferent ghost to keep him company, since every stick of furniture in it had been changed and the walls washed to a different color.

Philip must have been as disappointed as Gideon was at the snail's pace of his courtship, because this morning he had gone out, after loudly announcing that it was for the day, to visit with a neighbor. Gideon was elated; he was on fire to seize this first opportunity to pass an entire day alone with his love, just as he'd dreamed of doing all these past days—and years. Like any man returned to his one love, he longed to run his hands and eyes over all of it, to assure himself of the reality of the wonder of it, to reaffirm his presence and lay claim to it again. And the miracle was that he could. Now he had an opportunity to roam, unrestricted and welcomed, throughout the whole of Ivyclose again.

But he still had to wait for an invitation, and bided his time until it came. When it didn't come soon enough, he hinted at it. He and Celeste had spent the early morning walking through the rooms below; she'd taken him around after they'd breakfasted. It had been too cold to stroll through her gardens in comfort, and his every word and sidewise glance showed his interest in the house. The last time he'd been here he'd been too taken with her to do more than note the more drastic changes in his home. Now he greeted every detail of each room with sharp interest, and Celeste trailed after him, hearing the stories of this chair, and that table, finally understanding this odd corner as a grandfather's whim and that extra fireplace built for an ancient ailing grandmother. Then he suggested, in a tone that was too pointed to refuse, that they see the other part of the house: the bedchambers and infant quarters abovestairs.

He craved more intimacy. Seeing only what any guest could, belowstairs, was to him like only being able to hold his lover's hand and gaze into her eyes. He didn't put it quite that way to Celeste. But he made himself clear enough. And so now he wandered in the heart of his heart's home, trying doors and throwing them wide as if in so doing he could finally find the past revealed clear.

But those rooms that were unchanged breathed sorrow at him when their doors were opened, and those that had been transformed were as those in a stranger's house. Even after he'd journeyed so far to return to see Ivyclose real and whole, he found himself visiting the home of his memory again instead. He stared sightlessly at what was actually before him.

"She loved this room," he said softly, looking around the small, spare chamber where lesser lady guests were now housed when they visited Ivyclose.

"Maybe because he never came here, maybe because it was the only place she was free," he said. "But she'd come to sew, she said, and yet I never saw her actually ply a needle here. Instead, she'd sit by the window and look out, as a prisoner might, with just such a hopeless look on her face. Or else she'd sit and stare into the wall as though she saw something wonderful there. That's always how I remember her," he said, staring at what had been so intensely that Celeste could almost see it, "and that's how she'll have to be remembered, since he never had her portrait done. She wasn't beautiful, I suppose. Red-haired like me, and that's a misfortune for a woman. And tall, taller than my father by a head, which I know he never liked, any more than he liked my looking down at him when I'd grown. Maybe," he said bitterly, back from his mother's arms to the real world of 1666 again, turning and shutting the door behind him, "that's why he always kept her on her knees, or on her back, or in her childbed.

"She died young, although I was so young I never knew it. And weary—I always saw that. But never too tired to be loving," he said, and smiled at her; such a world-weary warm smile lit his harsh face that she almost put out her hand to him. But she remembered herself in time, and nodded.

"Be sure she's gone to her just reward," she said confidently, "and it'll be the greater because of the hardships she endured, uncomplaining, as was her duty."

He looked at her sidewise.

"She was no more pious than I, Celeste," he said dryly, "and twice as practical. She knew complaining to be a waste of breath, and she never wasted anything, even words. She'd disapprove of what a parrot I've become," he said, surprising her, for Gideon was more spare with words than any courtier she'd ever met; flowery speeches were their hallmark. Although he spoke more easily when alone with her, he was never as glib at foolish prattle as the men of Louis's and Charles's glittering courts had been. His sensible economy of speech was what made him seem most like one of her own people to her.

"Here—the cover on this chair," he said as he roamed around the next room they came to. "See the threads in it? She salvaged them from a chair we had in the music room. Unwound and worked again—oh, clever Mama, for all she was no seamstress. Don't say it," he said with a bright sparkle in his eyes, laughing. "It's terrible work, you've never seen such a lopsided lion, and the only reason this chair hasn't graced the fire is because this room's so seldom used."

"No, no," she protested, "it's charming, and very old. And we waste nothing here."

"She'd approve that," he said absently. "Harold

wouldn't have. This was his room. He wanted it all gilt and new tapestries from Bruges—he'd expensive tastes. But Father wouldn't allow it, no more than George, the true heir, would. They fought constantly about it," he mused. "Harold never thought his lack of ten months in age a fair enough reason for his not having Ivyclose. He must have raised a toast the night of George's death—it saved him the trouble of continuing to plot it, I'd think," he said, smiling slightly, shocking Celeste to the point that her hand went to her throat to quell the pulse fast rising there.

"You don't mean he'd have killed his brother!" she gasped.

"Oh, no," Gideon said airly, fingering a tassel on the bed hanging. "He was too clever. He'd have hired someone else to do it. My brothers didn't love each other, Celeste," he said, glancing back to her, recalled from memory by her shocked inhalation, "or me. They weren't trained to. They were three born on each other's heels, and they remained there for all their lives, snapping and snarling. It amused my father—he brought them up so. If I thank God for anything now, though I confess I didn't then, it's that he'd no time left for me."

Celeste couldn't speak. Squire Hawkes had been a Puritan, a man of her church, and professed to be of the highest ideals. Everything she heard about him from servants and neighbors bore that out. And here was his son, a self-confessed unbeliever, a Cavalier, a royalist, denying all that. No, for all she might have wanted to, she couldn't believe him. But if she couldn't, how could she even contemplate marrying him?

He wandered the room, inspecting every little article in it, now shaking his head over a pen he found on a desk, now running his hand over a chair back and smiling to himself, gone from her, although very much before her in body. He filled the room just as he occupied even the largest rooms in this house—he

blotted out all other sight. It wasn't just his wide
shoulders and towering height, the well-made width of
him—it was his deep voice and piercing gaze and very
living presence that commanded attention. She studied
the long, lean grace of him as he moved restlessly
through the room, and composed herself again. Of
course, he spoke evil, he was strayed. And must be
saved. It would be a worthy mission.

She'd bring him back to God. She'd reconcile him
with his godly father, and his mortal one too, if only in
death; she'd unite them in spirit as they'd never been
in life. But she'd do it her way, even if it meant the
pretense of bowing to his. Yes, it would be a sin, but a
greater one to let him go on unsaved.

But she didn't have to listen to his wickedness. She
heard it, of course, but she refused to listen as he
ranged through the rooms of his youth, his red-gold
head bobbing along the dim corridors like a living
flame lighting their way, as he went seeking the darkest corners of his past, telling her things she shouldn't
hear and couldn't believe.

"Francis was the best of them, poor fellow," he said
in the next bedchamber, "which isn't saying much. He
seldom struck me, even when he was displeased; he
did a kind thing now and then, and carried fewer tales
to Father about his other brothers. He was happiest
when in town with his wenches and his bottles. The
army was a strange career for him. But then," he
mused, putting down the looking glass he'd stared
into, as though he'd seen his brother's face and not his
own in it, "he never chose it. It may have been another of Father's jests. Still, the army's a strange career for any man."

She heard that. Her head shot up. She'd teethed on
tales of Cromwell's glorious army, her grandmother
often said that the Protector at the head of his troops—
the shining warrior against sin driving the devils out of
England—was the worthiest sight she'd ever witnessed,

and Celeste had always regretted that she'd never seen it.

"You can't mean that," she answered him now. "You were a soldier! You must know that a nation needs an army to protect and deliver it from . . . enemies," she said, remembering how to couch her words, just in time.

"Oh, yes," Gideon said with a chill smile, "I was. A soldier for hire in any army that could afford me. And so I know that in time an army thinks anything opposing it is an enemy. I remember the farmer who didn't want to give up his livestock and cattle to us. It was in a little town on the outskirts of Flanders. He gave up far more. The troops found his wife and two daughters and maidservants far more tender flesh, before they killed them. He ended up surrendering all his stock, his family, and his servants too—before he gave up his own life, watching his women despoiled as he was spitted on the fire like the fowls he wouldn't offer us. I remember," he said bitterly, "although I wish I'd forget. . . . Sooth, where are my wits? Celeste, forgive me. My life's been too harsh to even mention to a woman like you. Forgive me," he asked her, coming to her side and taking her hand, regret and worry in his voice and eyes, because she'd grown white at his words.

"You did such things?" she asked falteringly.

"I changed careers soon after," he said, "because I wouldn't. Someone must kill in battle. That's the reason for soldiers. But they tend to make their own battles if they grow bored. But, come, now look here," he said, leading her away from the room and the painful conversation as quickly as he could. "Here's my own old room, right next door. You must have thought it too small to offer me now. But I liked it well . . . and ah, you'll like this. Do you see that floorboard? Yes, this one.

"Here," he said, raising a corner of the thin carpet

that covered half of it, "step on it. Yes," he said as she obeyed and then started, for the sound the board made was shockingly loud in the small chamber. "It still works. This was the trap I set, so that no one could enter without my knowing. I had to pry that board out and replace it a dozen times until it yelped like a dog with its tail caught in the floor."

She laughed with him, so he took her around the room, showing her all the tiny things she'd missed in it, she, who'd thought she'd known it all, who'd spent so much time alone in this room conjuring up his ghost before she'd ever met him. But now she learned the lesson all historians must, because she found that only the living creator of the past she'd studied knew the whole truth of it.

He moved the bed away from the wall to show her that when a piece of plaster was pried away from the wainscoting, the mouse hole, discovered and then expanded so many years before, could still echo the voices from the kitchens below—so that if the cook were talking to the housekeeper near to the fireplace, every word could be heard. "Which is how I learned the breeding habits of humans, long before I discovered it from the kitchen maid at closer quarters," he added with a straight-face, just to see her look away, unwilling to laugh, too amused to scold.

He showed her all his hidey-holes and secret stores. And then he convinced her that not even a living inhabitant of the past could understand the whole of it. Because then he showed her the scratches he'd made on the wall near the window, where he'd measured himself monthly, waiting to leave his home on the day his head reached to the top of the sill. He showed her the space behind the wardrobe where a thin boy could wedge himself in so that anyone looking into the room would never guess he hid there. Then he opened the window and showed her the slight handholds in the brick that a boy could use to free himself in the night, to scramble down the side of the house like a spider, to reach the lawns, and then the wood, and then the fields below, and then the wide free world outside.

"But you've leveled the wood, and so I'd be scratched to ribbons if I tried it now," he said, "but now I'd never try to leave. Now," he said gently, as he pulled his head in from the window and looked at her where she stood by his side, the past forgotten and nothing but obvious interest in the present in his eyes, "I find I'd like to stay here forever."

She let him place his lips on hers, but when he drew her closer, when he began that which she knew would frighten her, because she knew it would make him forget himself, she pulled away from his warm body and strong hands.

"No," she said softly, "not here, not now."

"Then when?" he asked seriously, standing with his hands at his sides.

"When . . . when we've decided what we shall do," she said.

"I've decided," he said simply.

"I need more time," she insisted.

"Ah, then," he said, "your answer is to be a Christmas gift?"

She began to smile. Christmas was two months away. But before she could decide if that, indeed, would be the case, he left her again—she could see it in the sudden inward look to his eyes, and in that moment surprised herself by wanting to step back into his arms, if only to bring him back to the present, and to her.

"Christmas? Sooth, I have missed Christmas," he mused, "almost as much as Ivyclose. Whenever I thought of it while I was gone from here, whenever I raised a toast to it in some foreign land, I remembered that it wasn't even Christmas at Ivyclose then. Only England holds to the old calendar," he explained. "And so I drank to Christmas in the New Year each year I was away. It wasn't the 'when' so much as the way of it I missed the most. The holly, the mistletoe, the music, the wassail, and oh," he groaned, "the roasts, the goose, the turkey, the plums and minces— s'truth, we English hold Christmas more dear in our bellies than in our churches. . . . At least, we did until your good people came along. I suppose you don't hold Christmas," he asked then, his mood sobering, looking years younger in his disappointment at that thought, "just as my father didn't after he observed his 'reformation'?"

"In truth, I don't hold with it," she admitted, "since I was taught to mark the day by prayer and fasting. But," she added, upset to see how he frowned at that, surprised to see how she needed to reassure him and win back his teasing smile, "I've been holding it any-way, for years. For Philip, and the look of it, you see. So if I must, I can bear to celebrate it," she explained, as though the feasting and merrymaking were a burden—which they were, if only because the silent penance she paid for enjoying it was always equal to the pleasure she couldn't help but feel when she experienced it.

"Then when we're wed I'll make sure you're served ashes and never offer you a bite from my plate . . . although I'll insist on the rights of the mistletoe," he added, so her embarrassment would silence her expected denial of the inevitability of their coming marriage, as he led her from the room.

They had a brief look in at Philip's room, and he never wanted more, since as it was the largest, it had been his father's. Then they'd an even briefer look at her own room, and she didn't allow more, since she found his presence a threat in her own and personal chamber, and thought his eyes held more than fond memory when they gazed on her bed, although it had been his mother's.

But, "Imagine, I was born there," was all he said,

and at that, not for the first time in his company, but for the first time for herself in his company, she was shamed.

She offered to take him into more rooms higher above, where the nursery and servants' quarters were, as well as to where the storage was: where all the bits and unconnected pieces of the past of Ivyclose lay. But he declined the offer, saying he'd enough of the past for now, suggesting they go riding instead.

"But . . . the secret room, the room you said you'd show me, the one with everything so wondrous in it," she protested, to call him back to his study of Ivyclose, as though she felt slighted for his abandoning it, as though she felt it a rejection of herself.

"Ah, well, ah, that," he said, pausing, smiling. He stood against a wall, looking down at her, bemused. Then, reaching into the neck of his doublet, he withdrew a fine gold chain, holding it out to let it swing slightly before her.

"At last you remembered to ask," he said. "I've worn this since I came here, waiting for your question."

She gazed raptly at the gilded key at the end of the chain he held before her until he opened the neck of his shirt, exposing a glimpse of his chest, and then dropped the key back to rest upon his skin again, and she looked away at once, her longing to follow it with more than her eyes astonishing her.

"I waited for your question, but you haven't given me the right answer yet. In fact, you've given me no answer yet. Your lips told me even more," he said, sighing. "You've no longing for me yet. Which is your right. I can do nothing about it but hope. But for all you own this house, that room, Celeste, is mine. It's only for those who are born or wed to Ivyclose. When you say you'll have me, then you'll have the secret of the room." He grinned at her expression.

"For, sooth, lady," he said innocently, "can you blame me? It's a family secret. You want the secret to the room, lady? You must have me with it."

And laughing at her consternation, he led her down again.

The days shortened, the nights lengthened, the cold set in, and one morning they awoke to the first snow. Gideon tore out-of-doors at sunup, just like the boy that he'd been here would have done. His host joined him, and so when Celeste threw open her bedchamber window she laughed until they stopped to stare at her. But she was enchanted to see the way her brother and her suitor warred with each other—to see the way two great grown men, elegantly got-up Cavaliers, all shod in fine leather and silken hose, sank up to their ankles in snow without a care because they were so involved with bombarding each other with snowballs, and flinging fistfuls of snow over each other's fine velvet hats and cloaks.

"Oh, fie, now you'll catch cold," Celeste cried when Philip sneezed. "In—into the house at once. He's got a weak chest," she explained to Gideon, who'd paused beneath her window with a great ball of snow in his hand, ". . . and take off those clothes, and wrap yourself warmly . . . do you hear?" she commanded as her brother dropped his snow with a murmured apology to his opponent and guiltily hurried into the house.

"Shall I take off mine?" Gideon asked innocently enough, though his blue eyes glittered like the sun's reflection on the iced edges of the dunes of snow around him.

"You, sir, may do as you will," she said, retreating indoors again.

She was standing facing the fire in the great room they used in the mornings, when she felt him enter the room as much as she heard his soft footfalls on the carpet behind her. He came in on a rush of icy air, and radiated both cold and heat at her back, and she shivered.

"You tremble? But you never so much as stepped

into the snow," he said as he ran his hand down her arm. "Celeste," he said. "Celeste . . ." He paused. He sighed before he spoke.

"I've stayed here for weeks," he said softly. "I came when the leaves were turning; now the snow's come. I came as a guest, hoping to be more. I still hope, but only a prisoner lives on hope. A free man can't. Still, I don't want to be free, or I'd have gone long since. Celeste, I've given you time. It's time for an answer."

She knew it. Had known it for days. But she'd thought he'd ask at night, some quiet evening after Philip had gone to bed. She'd braced herself for it each night, but all he'd done was to take her hand, or her lips, in a brief kiss. She'd never expected him to ask her to marry him again in a morning room, with the bright daylight all around them, with nothing to hide her blushes in except for his wide velvet-clad shoulder.

"We can be wed in no time if you don't want a great ceremony in London, with our king looking on. It would be a pity to disappoint him, though," he added with only a hint of laughter. "I know he's longing to leer when you're in your bridal bed, and nothing else, at the bedding ceremony," he said, to urge her to take him now instead of tarrying. It was true enough, and he knew from the way her back stiffened that it also might be enough to hasten the moment. But mention of her bridal bed only reaffirmed her doubts.

"I don't know yet," she said truthfully, never turning to face him.

"No," he said with a shade of impatience in his voice, "no, past time for that. You must know."

"But—" she began, but he cut her off harshly, not at all as she'd thought he'd ask again.

"I've stayed here long enough for you to know me. I've told you my past and my hopes for my future. Where is the objection?"

There was no reasonable answer and they both knew

it. How could she explain her deepest fears? She liked him more than enough, but liking wasn't enough, and she'd been taught that loving wasn't important for marriage. Trust was. But every time she grew to trust him, he'd frighten her badly. Because no matter how many times she decided to have him, he'd hold her, and then she'd worry again.

It was one thing to decide to endure his lustfulness in order to save him. But who would save her from him? She grieved because each time it came to the point, she found her faith wasn't strong enough yet. Rational resolve always crumbled at his touch; faith in her religion failed her at his kiss. She'd wed the Gideon Hawkes of her dreams in a second, had done a dozen times, in fact. But the real Gideon Hawkes still terrified her every time he came to her with that look in his eyes, with lust so obviously upon him. She couldn't yet face that. For all he tried to understand her religion, he never understood her upbringing, or knew how great a sin she considered lust: in wedlock, as much as without. So she decided to put him off just once more—just until she could face how great a sacrifice hers must be in order to save him, and turned from the fire at last, to face him.

But found she could say nothing. He stared down into her eyes and took her shoulders in his hands and kissed her before she could do more than part her lips to speak. His hand came up behind her head to hold her still, and his mouth was like the flaming cold kiss of sheerest ice. One moment she flinched from the chill still on his lips, and the next she shuddered at the heat rising there. It was when his tongue, like one wet stab of flame escaped from the warm cavern of his mouth, snaked out to touch her own, that she started, and pushed at him, revulsed and frightened beyond the reach of the pull of his attraction. He didn't release her. She moaned, and, frantic, tried to drag herself away. And almost fell against a table in reaction when he released her abruptly.

He gazed at her with what seemed like dispassion, while all the time he raged inwardly as she collected herself again. He'd been more than patient, he'd been careful and kind and had treated her with all the passion he might show a younger sister. But he knew he couldn't wed her as such, and, his patience growing thinner as the days had grown shorter, had decided to act to settle matters now. How long, after all, could he delay matters? How long could he hold back expressing his manhood before he lost her respect, or his own, for that matter? How much longer could he contain his ever-present appetites? As for hungers— how long could he continue to roam the halls of Ivyclose as a guest, when he passed every moment aching to possess it again, worrying that someone else might snatch it away from him, wondering if his damnable luck would fail him again?

Yet all his care had gone for nothing. She was cool and clear as spring water, he thought, until he touched her. And then she flared for a moment, only to grow cold again. Slight and slender, aloof and self-possessed, it seemed he couldn't hold her, even in his arms; she was as elusive as his dream of peace.

"I can't very well take you by rape, fully clothed and in your own parlor, Celeste," he said coldly. "There was no reason for such extravagant terror. Just as there's no reason to say more. I understand. I'll go. Thank you for your hospitality."

"No, wait!" she cried as his hand touched the door. "I . . . need more time. Once I answer, it will be forever," she said, her light blue eyes wild and wide, as full of real panic at the thought of his leaving her as they'd been at the thought of his making love to her. "You must understand, I'm not like the other women you know. . . . surely you can wait a few weeks for the promise of me as your wife forever—of Ivyclose as yours forever again?"

"Lady," he said quietly, "I don't think I can. I don't

think I will. I'm to London today, and I'll think on it more then. But since being with you day after day is not bringing the answer closer, perhaps leaving will. Or," he said, cocking his head sidewise and smiling a smile she didn't like at all, it was so full of mockery, "Perhaps there'll be no reason for your answer by then. I offered you all my heart, Celeste," he said coolly. "I've no more to give even if you don't want to take it. I wish you well, my lady, and I wish you joy . . . whomever you decide to take to husband in your slow time."

He bowed and left. The gardeners scarcely had time to clear the whole of the long drive to the road before he was upon it, his horse and his valet's leaving hoofprints behind that wouldn't be swept clean until midday.

Philip went wild. He paced the downstairs rooms and shouted at the walls, stopping every so often to glare at his sister, before he took to pacing again. He'd never been so enraged at Celeste since they'd been reunited. But she didn't fear him. She sat with her Bible and pretended to read it as she watched him. She knew him very well. Anger would leave regret in its wake, as always. He was cursed with a soft disposition that could never sustain fury long before it broke free and frightened him as much as it did his intended victim.

"Gone," he raged. "Gone," he moaned again, "along with all my hopes. The widow wanted me," he groaned, his white-hot rage of only moments before—when he'd emerged from his rooms after a day of napping to find Gideon gone, leaving only a note of thanks behind him—already subsiding into self-pity. "I know she did. And now she'll have to take Rigby, or Fowler, or old Lord Eckels, instead."

"Why?" Celeste asked complacently.

"Why? Fool! Silly slut! Because the bargain was

that I'd get her when Gideon took you to wive," he answered, throwing her a lowering look as he sank at last into a chair to grieve more comfortably.

"And has she no say in the matter? If she's half so cunning and winning as you say, I'd think she could convince the king to let you wed. He's said to have a soft spot for all women. And likes you very well."

"Yes," Philip said, brightening a little, "but there's not much I can do here, so far from my widow and London and Charles," he added, looking to her with hope.

"As soon as your head clears, and the road does too, you should go to London, of course. But I shall not," she said flatly as he sank back in despair. "Don't worry," she said calmly, "it's better that I stay here. I might get the king vexed with me. I haven't the winsome ways of your widow. I need the time, anyway. Gideon needs the time to think it over, as well. Never worry that he'll change his mind; the furthest dream is always sweetest. No, you go, explain, and make amends. You're not, after all, responsible for me . . . and as to that, I haven't said I won't have Gideon. I've only delayed my answering him."

"But he's gone," Philip said in almost the same low long tones of the wind that was moaning about the house now that evening had fallen.

"He'll be back," she said, smiling to herself.

"How can you be so sure?" he asked, irritated enough to dare say things he wouldn't if she didn't think him so wildly angry. "He's got a whore in London to keep him comfortable enough—all you've ever given him is the cold side of your shoulder."

"And all she can do is slake his lust. A man needs more," she said comfortably, thinking of his immortal soul.

"Maybe," he admitted, thinking of Ivyclose.

The snow ended, the freeze began, but the roads

were passable, or so Philip insisted. Within a day he was on the road to London, with enough blankets and medicines to ward off any chill, and enough footmen riding alongside him to ward off any other dangers. For the first time in weeks, Celeste had her home to herself again. Yet for the first time, it wasn't enough.

She wandered the halls and roamed the midnight corridors, haunted by a living ghost and possessed with new longings that her old Bible didn't solace. Alone, she thought, again and again—grandmother dead, brother apart, her prospective husband a man composed of elements that both drew and repulsed her. But for now alone, and for the first time, deeply aware and unhappy with her condition.

She lost sleep, she gained doubts, she started at small sounds and hoped for larger ones. So it was that she gave a little leap as she sat in her chair in the morning parlor three days after Philip had left her, when the butler came to tell her she had a visitor.

She had never doubted he'd return. She might have questioned herself, but never him. She knew he'd come back to her, swallowing some of the pride that would be his downfall unless he curbed it. And she'd teach him how to, with the true word to guide them. He'd come back to her again and again until he was fit for her. He'd come back each time with less arrogance, tamer, diminished in pride, lust, and vanity— she'd see to it—until he came to her at last, humble and mild, in the shape of the husband she'd take, and the man her God would approve.

The only surprise in it was how soon he'd come this time. She'd prayed he'd hasten the process of becoming worthy, and sought humility to repress the sudden surge of triumph she felt. She put down her Bible and put a trembling smile upon her lips for him. She stood and looked to the door as she awaited him. And when he entered the room, hat in hand, her smile fled and she gasped aloud.

It wasn't Gideon. It was a tall man, to be sure, but a thin man, narrow of bone and gaunt-cheeked, with dark straight brown hair cropped close to his head. He'd the brown skin of a man who labored in the sun, a straight thin nose, and a pair of expressive dark eyes to keep his face from severity. But no lines of laughter bracketed his thin lips; instead, downturned lines of pain and anger were there. They'd been wrought since she'd last seen him. He'd worn fine but plain dark clothes then; he wore simple countryman's garb now. But she knew him at once, because she'd never forgotten him.

He gazed at her and nodded with grim approval as a light of sudden hope flashed and died in those deep eyes.

"Celeste," John Wentworth said, as though he named her for the first time.

"John?" she asked. "John . . ." she said. "But you were gone to America. Have you come back then?" she asked, and realizing how foolish her question was, since he stood before her, didn't blame him for not answering. She drew in a breath and calmed herself, and then spoke again.

"But how good. To return to England so soon, when we never looked to see you again. Where is your wife?" she asked with admirable calm, "and how many children have you now?" she asked, "and, my heavens, John, all my chatter—why have you come?"

"I return to England because there was no life for me in America," he said plainly. "My wife's dead, and I've one dead child. And I've come to save you, Celeste—that's why I've come here today."

" 'If all the world was . . . ap-ple . . . apple' " she said triumphantly, " '. . . apple pie, and all the sea was ink' "— she grinned like a gargoyle—" 'and all the trees were bread and cheese,' " she read in a rush, " 'what co . . . what cu . . .' "—Mary frowned—" 'what could we have to drink!" she shouted. "I read it all through this time, Jamie, every word of it. And all of it right, didn't I?"

"Yes," he said, looking at her exultant face. "Yes," he sighed.

"Indeed, you have," Tristram said, rising from where he'd been sitting in his usual seat by the window. "Every word. We've a woman of some erudition here, James, we do."

"No," Mary said, deflated, her face growing as woeful as it had been merry seconds before. "No. I read a little rhyme. But it wasn't poetry. It was a little foolishness. I want to read poetry, Jamie. Teach me that!"

"One world at a time, child," Tristram said.

"Nothing gets done by dreaming, or so my father always said. I wish to read real poetry," Mary said stubbornly.

"Here," Tristram said, handing her the little book he'd been reading. "Read here, then," he said as Jamie frowned at him and started to speak.

"Thank you," Mary said, contented, and looked to where his long finger pointed.

"Ah," she said, staring, " '. . . In name of gr . . . great Oc . . . Och . . .' ah, O-something . . ." She paused and looked pointedly at Tristram, who helpfully supplied the word, "Oceanus," to which she exclaimed with relief, "Oh, a name. Well, how was I to know? Now, then . . . 'By the . . .' Ear-teeth? Ear-th, yes, earth . . . shak, shak . . . Oh," she said, as Tristram picked the book from her hand and read quickly and fluently, " 'By the earth-shaking Neptune's mace and Tethy's grave majestic pace, by hoary Nereus' wrinkled look, And the Carpathian wizard's hook, By scaly Triton's winding shell—' "

"Enough," she said on a sigh, "Is't English, truly?" she asked Jamie, who left off glowering at Tristram to answer sadly, "Yes."

"It doesn't make any sense," she said.

"Less than your rhyme," Tristram agreed. "That's the nature of poetry. But it is poetry, by John Milton, and if you want to read it one day, you must begin by mastering the books Jamie gives you, of smaller foolishnesses. Of course, you can always leave off. What does it matter anyway?"

"It matters to me," Mary said, picking up her own book again, to read aloud, " 'What care I how black I be? Twenty pounds will marry me. If Twenty won't, Forty shall, I am my Mother's bouncing girl.' "

"But that's perfect," Jamie cried. "Wonderful, not a stumble or a hitch in it."

"That's cheating," Mary said sadly. "I knew the poem—it's my favorite."

Jamie smiled at her and Tristram couldn't repress his grins either.

"But you read enough to know you knew it," Jamie pointed out gently.

"That's true," Mary said. "Why, that's true!" she cried, "and I never saw it before either!" She stood up and gave Jamie a spontaneous hug, as she would any of her brothers who had pleased her. She never saw Jamie's hands go up to hold her, and then down before they did, nor saw the look of frustration and dismay on his face in the brief moment that she touched him. But Tristram did.

"Won't Gideon be pleased when he returns?" he said silkily, as much to Jamie as to Mary.

"Do you know," Mary said with wonder, "that doesn't matter so much anymore. *I* am pleased," she said defiantly, for Gideon had been gone for almost a month, and she was rebelling against the hurt of it as well as the memories that plagued her. "And Jamie is pleased. So that's all I care," she lied.

Jamie smiled so beatifically that Tristram sighed again.

" 'Sing jig my jole, the pudding bowl, The table and the Frame, My master he did cudgel me, For kissing of my dame . . .' " Tristram quoted. "That's Gideon's favorite," he added when Mary looked to him curiously.

"We haven't come to it yet," Jamie said in a tight, flat voice.

"Yes, well, I hope you won't," Tristram answered, as Mary made a note to look for the rhyme and went on to mull over a new word she'd found in her almanac, convinced that every one led her onward to a new freedom. Because for a certainty, she thought, wrinkling her brow, she'd none now—since whether alone or together with him, she couldn't rid herself of Gideon Hawkes. But she would, she soon would, she vowed.

And then she read the next lines she gazed at without pause, and stopped only to contemplate them after, they made such excellent good sense, unlike all the poetry she'd sounded out today: " 'He that will not when he may, When he would he shall have nay.' "

That, Mary thought, was sensible and true. And she reflected on it while the two gentlemen in the room with her stared at each other, honestly at odds for the first time in their long friendship.

Gideon rode down icy roads and felt no chill, he was so angry with the world, and so on fire to return to London and his home there, and the warm welcome that he knew awaited him in the bed that he'd left behind there. Then he slowed, remembering that he didn't live there anymore.

# 15

"You've come to save me?" Celeste asked her visitor.

"I heard that you were promised to marry the Cavalier Gideon Hawkes," the tall man said. "I think I would have come from across the oceans to make you see the folly of that . . . No," he said bitterly, "I would not have. That's a lie. I've had too much of lies," he said in a hollow voice, passing a shaking hand over his eyes before he spoke again.

"I've returned to England, and I've begun to farm again," he said. "Another man's land, here in Kent, not far from here, because I gave up what little was my own to go to America. I wouldn't have troubled you—you're wealthily dowered, and I've nothing now. But then I heard about your new suitor. How could I not? It's all the talk—how the new owner of Ivyclose will be the old owner of Ivyclose again. How Good King Charles restores all," he said on a cough of a laugh. "All—except for virtue, decency, and godliness. But that's all England wants these days. I thought you were different. I remembered you as different, Celeste Southern."

She was a pious woman, she thought of herself as a godly woman, but she was, withal, a human woman.

She remembered too much to be as calm as she wanted or as cool as she pretended, as she answered him.

"How good that you remembered, John," she said. "I'd thought that you vowed to forget all other women when you took a wife and left me."

"I took the wife the elders gave me," he said wearily. "I wanted you, but your brother forbade it, denied me even seeing you again. I was obedient to that wish, as a good man should be," he said, never meeting her eyes.

"I don't doubt that he forbids it still," she said, "as you say, with more cause than your religion now. But you're here. What, are you less obedient now too?"

"I am wiser, Celeste," he said, looking at her directly, and she was shocked at the bitterness in those dark eyes that had once been so mild. "I've not forgotten or given up the teachings, but I've learned that God doesn't always speak directly to all elders, and he does, indeed, help those who help themselves. Innocence may always be godly, but it is not necessarily always wise. But," he added, staring at her pointedly, "I'm sure you've discovered that already."

"How dare you!" she cried, forgetting her cool confidence entirely.

"I dare," he said angrily, "because I've heard nothing but stories of you cavorting at court, of your new gowns and jewels, and of your new suitor. Of you preparing to marry Gideon Hawkes: a man who renounced his father's deliverance into God's hands, a man of violent nature and a bloody history, a friend to Charles Stuart, and of like nature, a worldly man of lustful pursuits and easy mockery of all that's holy—that's why I dare."

"I can understand that's what you hear, but you don't see," Celeste said with a thin smile, "because, being closer than you are to him, I see the possibility of redemption for Gideon Hawkes, as for any man, and see myself as the medium for it. But you haven't

bothered to see. You were content to only hear, and
judge. You have the vanity to come out of the wilder-
ness to shame me?" she asked. "You? Who went to
America to build a new and holy land, and obviously
failed, and come back instead to accuse me of wrong-
doing?"

She looked away from him when he winced. For all
that she hadn't laid eyes on him for years, for all that
he was changed from the slender, graceful, and comely
Puritan youth burning with zeal that she'd known, to
become this hard, brown, and bitter man she scarcely
recognized, once she had admired him above all
men. She still couldn't like hurting him—for all he had
nearly killed her when he had left off courting her and
taken another to wive and then gone away for what
he'd said was to be forever.

"I tried to do the right thing," he said quietly. "I
left you because your brother wouldn't allow our marriage, and you know that was the right thing. I married Ann Clayton because she was going to America
too, and had no family and needed a husband. She was
a plain, thin girl, Celeste, she'd none of your intelli-
gence or grace, and none of your beauty," he said in a
quieter voice, "and may God forgive me for it, but for
all I knew I should have, because there was no reason
not to, she being a good and decent girl, I didn't love
her, not at all, and never did. In time I might even
have divorced her," he said, as Celeste held her breath
at his words. "No elders would have denied me that,
since no man is expected to stay in a marriage where
love doesn't grow. But she'd no time. She begot a
child."

He saw her startled, then offended expression, and
as she began to look at him with contempt, he said
harshly, "You know better, Celeste, you know the
way of our people. I was married in the eyes of God
and so was bound to try to make it a real marriage.

Unlike your courtiers, I didn't obey my lustful nature so much as God's laws."

She lowered her gaze as he went on. "Ah, but she was a weak woman, and a fearful one, and her term might even have been as hard for her as she complained. We'd settled in a small community in Massachusetts—a hard land filled with terrors for her, from a strangely brief, blazing hot summer with insects, poisoned plants, and wild creatures to contend with, to a long and incredibly bitter winter. We lived among our own kind, and they were a strict order. It was what I had thought I wanted. But you see," he said, as though he were continuing an argument he had with himself, "communities that let in outsiders begin to take on their ways and to lose the ones that they came to America to practice. In New York, Virginia, even Massachusetts, nearby to us, there were Puritan communities as lax and sinful as any others. Ours was pure," he said, and hesitated, as though the taste of that word were too bitter to follow with another immediately.

"She began to birth on a Sunday," he finally said, and fell silent.

He looked at her and then shrugged. "It's taught that a babe born on a Sunday was conceived on a Sunday, which is a sin, of course. So I always believed too. But I knew that she hadn't got the child on the Lord's day, it wasn't possible, and yet still it was coming into the world on one. We'd have been shamed and punished for it, had it lived. That, however unfair, I could have borne as God's judgment for some other sin I did commit. But Ann began to bleed. I went to summon help. Of course," he said quickly, his face working, "no doctor would help a sinner, and of course, to tend the sick on God's day is a sin too. So though I went from house to house, and back again, no one came. Until sundown, when she was dead, with the babe, and my faith in all those we lived among.

"I've not lost my Christian faith, or my belief in our ways, but I'll never follow so strictly in the church again. That's why I'm here without your brother's permission today," he said defiantly.

Gideon Hawkes, she thought, would defy God and king and all men for something he wanted. John Wentworth's defiance was a meager, tame thing by comparison. But still, it took courage, and she always respected that.

"I understand," she said. "But exactly why have you come?"

"To ask you to marry me, of course," he said. "I would not trifle."

She stared at him.

"I know I've not got anything. But I'll work to earn my way. If you defy your brother and the king, I expect you'll have to leave here forever. I'll protect you. I said it was to save your soul," he said, standing before her, turning his plain wide-brimmed hat in his hands, "but that, too, was a half-lie, and I won't lie again," he stressed, as though angry with himself, "but I think if you leave here it will save your soul just the same, because I think you'll never change a man like Gideon Hawkes—for all I've never met him, I know his kind. You'll only either pass a life of misery trying to, or bend to his ways and despise yourself for it. But the reason I ask to marry you is that although I know it's wrong to love first and marry later, I want you for my wife. . . . I have loved you," he said quietly. "I've followed the teachings and wed first and found no love. This time I'd do it differently. Will you have me?"

She paused, and gave him a few minutes of silence so that he understood his words weren't wasted and that she was considering his offer. Then she spoke, and spoke the truth as she knew it; he deserved no less.

"I respect your courage, John. I admire your honesty, and share your beliefs. But I feel nothing for you as I do for Gideon Hawkes. You don't know him. As you felt the challenge of creating a new world in a new land, so I feel the challenge of converting Gideon to our way and bringing him to the light. The danger I face will be solely from my pleasure in my pride when I have done it. And I shall. There's no use arguing about it," she said as he began to speak. "For all your virtues, John, you did fail at your mission." She said the hard thing as gently as she could. "You should see I must try at mine."

He nodded, but then his eyes narrowed as she added, "And one more thing. My brother may not be of the faith, but he does care for me. If I won't have Gideon, I still will keep Ivyclose. So, you see, I have entirely free choice."

He laughed then. And she saw the new John Wentworth whole, and admired him even more.

"No man has free choice, Celeste," he said sternly. "You'd do well to remember that. I'll abide by your wishes. But I'll be available if you need me. I'll come again, if I may, to speak with you. I don't give up hope so easily."

"Understand I don't encourage you," she said, "and I will always welcome you."

The tall brown-skinned, harsh-featured man and the slight, unbending honey-haired young woman stood and stared at each other, understanding each other very well, as they always had.

He wasn't admitted. He stood outside the door to what had been his own home, to what were the lodgings he still paid for, and realized that unless he went around to his new rooms and got Rountree to vouch for him, he'd not be let in. He supposed he should be pleased that Mary's new footman was so careful, but he wasn't. Gideon was cold, and angry, and lonelier than he'd care to admit, and the fool of a footman wouldn't let him inside to wait for Mary.

But he'd be damned if he'd sit on the landing like a schoolboy who'd forgot his key, nor would he linger like a lover in the cold, pacing for her return. He'd go to court instead, where it was warm and where he could find out more about that damned note that had sent him flying from his comfortable new rooms moments after he'd got there to seek out Mary and have the truth from her.

It was better to believe that was why he'd appeared on her doorstep so late at night, so soon after he'd come to London, than admit it was because his comfortable new lodgings were so lonely he couldn't bear them a moment more. But his solitude and yearning had met his anger after he'd read the note that had been waiting all these days for him, and the volatile combination had been just what he needed to fuel him for the ride out into the frozen night to seek Mary. What he'd originally sought had been her usual delight at seeing him home again, her laughter, her easy entertaining conversation, her welcoming arms, and then some even warmer, sweeter ultimate welcome.

But she wasn't home at an ungodly hour, and so his thoughts had also turned in that direction. He was, under the best of circumstances, an impatient man. And he soon found himself in the worst of circumstances. He was embarrassed by his being turned away at what had been his own door, and as frustrated as disquieted by all the unfulfilled needs he had for her. Now the note he'd originally marked down to nonsense, simple vengeance penned for convoluted reasons by his enemies, took on darker meanings.

He took the stairs by threes as he went down them, and swung up on his horse again when he reached the street. The piece of paper near his breast where he'd thrust it after reading it rustled like a serpent stirring there, the words on it whispering in his thoughts as he turned his horse to Whitehall Palace. It was late and getting later, but there was always something merry in progress there. And if Mary were there, and Jamie too, and the note held more than a line of truth, it wouldn't be merry for very long, he vowed.

It wasn't a good rhyme. If it were from Rochester's hand again, his muse had been as drunk as he'd been when he wrote it. "Venus" and "Penis" had been rhymed too often before for merit; "Mary" and "tarry" were trite easy rhymes, "Claverly" and "bravely" were poor ones. But it wasn't the meter or rhyme scheme that had sent him clattering through the frozen streets at this mad hour, nor was it literary appreciation of the one clever phrasing: ". . . the shoemaker's girl and her lord make more than talk, they make merry to music from the horns of the Hawke."

He'd find Mary, and he'd corner Jamie, and he'd have it out with them tonight. If she wanted a new protector, so be it. A woman was entitled to change her mind. If Jamie fancied her, he could certainly understand that. And then he'd certainly kill Jamie Beauchamp, because he'd been his friend. If he himself thought this reasoning was a little askew—and he did, after a moment—he soon lost the thought in the sheer flaming gust of anger he felt envisioning Jamie and Mary locked together in love and deceit.

There was gambling going on at several tables at Whitehall in the groom porter's apartments, as usual. But Gideon only looked in to see if Jamie or Mary were there, and then went on, roaming through the many buildings of the palace, searching. He'd never had much taste for gaming: piquet, whist, or basset didn't lure him. Unlike the king, an indifferent gambler who nevertheless often started the play at Whitehall, although he always stopped when he'd lost one hundred pounds, Gideon never started at all. He wouldn't hesitate to stake his life on the strength of his wit or the skill of his hand, he'd gamble his worldly goods on the constant wheeling turn of world events, and risk his heart on his luck, but never trusted the turn of a card.

In another part of the palace they were playing at blindman's buff, and from the way the ladies and gentlemen were laughing as the blindfolded ladies blundered and groped among the gentlemen, it was clearly just another preamble to the court's favorite game of the night. Gideon deftly sidestepped a young woman who'd peeked from under her blindfold before she stumbled toward him, but none of the other daringly dressed women there were Mary, and neither Jamie nor Tristram was anywhere to be found. But for that matter, neither were the Earl of Rochester or Sir Roger Mobely in sight.

Which wasn't to say, Gideon thought as he paused to decide where to go next, that they weren't present somewhere in Whitehall tonight. There were couples locked in embraces in every dark corner, he'd spied the king himself wrapped in the arms of some dark-haired wench in a dim recess, but he could scarcely challenge strangers on the strength of a glance at a familiar-looking foot or a pair of possibly known shoulders. Then too, there were private rooms everywhere, in which the more discreet could sport. Of course, they'd have been seen going in or out—but Gideon would sooner ask a courtier to slit his throat than to ask after his mistress's and his best friend's whereabouts.

Instead, he stood indecisive. The only way he could accomplish what he wanted was to wait until later in the night or earlier in the morning, and go again to Mary's rooms again and discover all. But he hated inaction as much as he hated that thought, and so when he looked up from his brooding to see a beautiful lady all in crimson and gold smiling at him, he found himself staring back at her. It was all the encouragement she needed.

"Good sir," she said when she came up to him and

looked up into his face as she laid her hand on his sleeve, "I think I've seen your face before. Do you come here often?"

The only reason he didn't laugh aloud was that she looked so very well even as she spoke so very foolishly. She'd a quantity of light brown hair, all in masses of curls, a halo of them fluffed around her head, with extra bunches of ringlets suspended to either side of her face, as was the highest style. The face that aura of hair enhanced was a pretty one; great gray eyes beneath thin plucked brows regarded him with interest, and many small beauty marks of several sizes placed on the artificially blushing countenance called attention to a curving lip here, a straight nose there, and everywhere, to smooth, clear skin. The low-necked gown showed the rise of plump full breasts above a bodice flaunting a long slender waist. Attractive, he thought, his eyes narrowing as he evaluated her as candidly as she did him. No beauty like Celeste, of course, and not half as enticing as Mary, but attractive enough for the vile mood he was in, attractive enough to interest him in the diversion she offered. And certainly more attractive than was necessary to help him to exact a small part of the revenge he felt himself yearning for far more than he did for the lure of this comely, bold creature herself.

"I've been here, but it seems I never knew why until just now," he said, slipping into the teasing tones of a gentleman of the court, even as he spoke the same sort of insincere, extravagant foolishness they did.

She liked it well enough, and showed him a dimple near to a beauty mark above her pomaded lips.

"Oh, marvelous flattery, but do you mean it, sir?" she asked for the sake of the requisite moments of conversation, since she'd already decided she'd have him. He was tall and well-made, and exciting in a rough-cut way, and new to her, and that was above all else exciting.

It was late, and he was as angry at the world as he was frustrated with it; neither his primary nor his secondary desire would be met by this unknown lady, and he knew it. But having her would even the score with Mary. It would teach her not to trifle with him. It would illustrate, and beautifully, how simply he could replace her even before he cast her out, as he intended to do. Of course, it really wouldn't do any of these things for Mary, and he knew it, since he didn't even know where she was right now. But there were times when he refused to know what he did, and this was one of them. So he smiled down at the unknown lady and flirted automatically with her as he wondered in one part of his mind where they'd go to do the thing, and in another, tried to stoke up his desire to do it, so as to take his longing beyond revenge to a healthier lust.

They moved closer together as they moved beyond the wider cast of light of the chandeliers to the half-dusk of true night and fitful candlelight. In the dim glow her eyes became mysterious instead of calculating, her skin became flushed with youthful color instead of rouge, and he could imagine that her need for him was for more than the moment. Her breasts were almost entirely exposed by the cut of her gown; he saw that as she let her soft scarf slip down. When she bent toward him he could also see that they were long and blunt-nosed, tending downward, not firm sweet swelling breasts, tilted up at their tips, such as Mary had. But they were full, heavy, and alluring in their own fashion. And as he passed his fingers over the top of one in a light caress, as he bent to brush his lips against her cheek, he felt her draw in her breath. He allowed himself to believe it was involuntary, before he heard her slight catch of low laughter and knew it was only and merely excitement of a familiar kind for her. But still, her lips against his were warm and searching, just as her hands on his shoulders . . . at his neck . . . in his hair, were, and if they weren't hesitant or gentle as Mary's were, still they were small and a woman's and busy.

Her scent was of heated musks and flowers, and not the soft springtime one he favored and had Mary wear. But she was strongly scented and it wasn't unpleasant to breathe in the essence of her as he moved in still closer and took her in a closer embrace, this unknown yielding woman who solaced his hurt pride and quieted his deepest doubts for a moment, just as her scent and her kiss quelled his lightest fears.

Because if he found her embrace was too practiced, and given too suddenly, still she was safe enough for his health's sake: she was a woman of the court, not a dirty wench of the streets. And if her kiss was too impassioned for no reason that he'd given her, and her hands too eager for nothing he'd offered her either in coin or words, still she was safe enough for his heart's sake too: she was a woman of experience, and none of this had anything to do with him.

He relaxed as he enfolded her in his arms. She was safe enough in every particular. He wasn't careful of his health in the general way, but oddly cautious in intimate ones. He'd a friend who'd once lain with a wench in some dockside tavern, and in short order had his youth cut short by the French pox. It was no easy thing to watch vigorous youth eaten away from within, as swiftly and virulently as if it had been plague. It was even less kind than plague. Because it had taken teeth and nose and bladder, but not life. Since then, he'd always had a care. But never for more than his body, before.

Because something lacked. For all that her motions were as bold as any dockside wench's, as befit any lady from this court, as he took her in his arms while his hands took her breast, hip, and thigh—as her mouth met his wide and her hands touched him more intimately, he felt little stirring but his body. And even that failed him when he realized it wasn't enough. So he took her in a deeper kiss to banish the thought.

He thought of the poem at his breast when her hand reached into his doublet and caused the paper to crinkle, as though it were chuckling about its presence there. Then the rhyming words crossed his mind again, even as his hand closed hard over the breasts close to him. The sniggering words about Mary and Jamie and what they'd done repeatedly, every day in her rooms since he'd gone—"fawning in the morning, granting a boon each afternoon, sharing delight in every night . . ."—ran through his mind as his hands ranged over this stranger's soft body, and his impotent rage turned to good use and actually helped him now.

As she began to twist feverishly against him, he laughed, satisfied that he'd be able to complete what he'd begun, if not in joy then at least in actuality. Still, he put her off for a moment to catch his breath and gather his wits, and look around the room, at least once more, for Mary, before he went farther with his oblique revenge on her and Jamie.

"Why do you stop?" she asked breathlessly.

"Why, where would it end?" he answered lightly, in possession of himself again, remotely pleased at having successfully transmuted bitter anger into a simpler passion.

"Wherever you liked," she said, leaning toward him.

"Not here in public view, lady," he said, idly tracing intimate boundaries she'd exposed to his view with one finger, his coldly amused and unapproachable expression inflaming her further. She was a woman who needed novelty and found his self-possession in passion as thrilling as she'd found true passion years before.

"My rooms then, if you're nice," she said, drawing back, patting at her hair, trying to contain her impatience. If that was his game, she'd play at it too; she loved new games.

"Ah, if you want a nice gentleman, you'll have to

look elsewhere," he answered, looking above her head, scanning the room, absently playing with her body as he'd toy with a bit of candlewax, as he searched for a familiar face.

"I want you," she said, too impatient to merely play now, aroused by this hard-faced Cavalier as she'd not been in months by any man.

"Well, then," he said, gazing down into her glittering gray eyes, weary with looking for the pair of dark ones he sought, more sick at heart than he'd have guessed he could be at the thought of what they might themselves be looking at now, weary of abstinence and the conflicted longings that had racked him mind and body for the past weeks, more than willing to bury his newfound sorrow in this unknown and willing body.

She led him down long halls, pausing only to throw herself into his arms, drag his mouth down to hers, before she'd shudder and hurry him on again, round corners and up stairs, until they got to her rooms. She ordered an alarmed whey-faced maidservant out and closed the door, triumphant, behind them. But now his need, as capricious as his emotions tonight, turned again, and even as he saw her fumbling with her fastenings, he found himself desiring to know at least something of who this was that he'd soon be holding in a counterfeit of love. So he sat himself at a table and poured himself a glass of wine.

"Slowly, my lady," he said mockingly as she looked up, amazed, to see him watching her with a cold smile. "The pot that heats slowest boils best."

His manner thrilled as much as irritated her. She nodded, swallowed down her impatience, and sauntered to the table. She sat opposite him, poured herself a glass of the ruby wine, and took it to her lips. He'd be as much of a pleasure to tell about later as he'd be in moments, she decided, her hands shaking as she placed the glass on the tabletop again. This indifference, this delay, was maddeningly delicious; her friends would be wildly envious, her lovers challenged to try it. If he could withhold, so, then, should she. She raised her head and lowered her lashes over her eyes, going back a hundred steps to earliest flirtation to please herself as well as him, testing the limits of this new method of prolonging pleasure.

"Your name?" he asked.

"Henrietta," she said.

"Your husband?"

"Otherwhere, somewhere, nowhere." She shrugged, causing her uncovered breasts to sway.

It was quiet in the room. She was obviously wife to someone of importance; the room was richly furnished, the bed wide and well-covered with silken hangings. Her eyes held challenge as well as desire; he began to note the fine-grained texture of her skin, he began to forget himself in remembering the pleasures of passion, in thinking of the otherness of her flesh, the alienness of this other body that would so soon be linked so intimately to his. The familiar excitement began to build in him without his fanning it to life now. But the unfamiliar new awareness of the need for something else remained. And caught in the cross purposes of the old demands of his body and the new ones of his heart, he began to let his gaze search her face, looking desperately for whatever else she was besides new flesh, even as he was moved inexorably toward attaining complete knowledge of it.

That wasn't all that moved. At first, as he gazed, unblinking, trying to sink into a haze of desire, noting her moist, slightly open lips and flushed face, he thought it a trick of the candlelight. Or one of his own exhaustion's creation, his eyes playing tricks on him—he was really very tired. He'd stood on lonely decks at sea in the night, and seen mermaids and mountains rising out of quiet waters when the weariness of prolonged wakefulness had been on him. And so he blinked once, quickly, to clear his eyes. But still, the beauty mark moved.

As she gazed back at him, rapt, enchanted with his new game, he stared as the small brown beauty patch near to the corner of her left eye hesitated, paused, then moved again, crawling across her alabaster cheek . . . stopped . . . and then began to make its way across her high coral cheekbone, back toward the curly jungle of her high-dressed hair.

Some men, he thought as he watched, as revulsed as he was fascinated—as the thing froze, as if it could feel his gaze hot on its back—would have plucked the tiny creature up in their fingers and deftly cracked its back, before placing it tenderly in a patch box, to keep as a memento of their love. It was the fashion in some circles, he'd heard. After all, that which had feasted in the recesses of a loved one's flesh was held the most personal souvenir of all—far more intimate, and certainly less incriminating, than having a lover's glove, or garter, or even child, to keep.

She smiled at him, all unaware, thrilled at how he was transfixed by her. He continued to stare, his hand arrested on his wineglass, as the thing took fright and scurried back into the thickets of curls, probably, he thought, shaken into swallowing the last of his wine, to join all its family and friends there.

"And now?" she asked in a low growl of suppressed passion, rising from her chair even as he did.

"And now," he said, "good night, my lady!" and moved so quickly her door had opened and closed again before her gown had slipped to the floor, leaving her standing entirely naked. But not, he thought as he went down the halls faster than a moving shadow—no, obviously—not entirely alone.

It was colder than it had been an hour before, colder than it had been on the long road back to London for all those frozen days before. But he felt nothing now, and so it hardly mattered. He'd seen the light flickering in her window as he'd ridden up the street, and the shifting silhouettes of the two figures outlined there caused a cold fire to burn in his breast.

He unsheathed his sword as he stalked up the stair, and felt numbed to his toes when he saw what he'd expected but never wanted to, when he flung the door wide to see Jamie's wide, astonished blue stare locked onto his. He decided on giving him the clemency of allowing him to draw his blade too, and thereby the grace of dying honorably. But only after he'd seen, out of the corner of his eye, Mary's dark face register joy, and then shock, as she saw his own face, and then his naked sword.

"Dawn or now, it doesn't matter to me, whoreson, sneaking dog," Gideon said through clenched teeth, though it did matter; he wanted it over with now before he could think of the pain of doing it, and so he advanced into the room, never taking his eyes from Jamie. "How many insults do you need? Draw your sword, damn you," he snarled.

Jamie's eyes were still wide with dismay as he reached for his weapon.

# 16

Candlelight shone on the steel blade Gideon held in his hand, and that was all Mary could see reflected in his eyes as he moved into the room toward Jamie.

"Gideon!" she cried. "Why?"

"You dare ask?" he replied, though he never took his gaze from Jamie as he approached him. "Don't you know it's famous news by now?" he asked as he took the note from where it had lain like a canker in his breast and flung it to the floor before her. "My joy's capped only by being the last to know, as is typical in such matters. He's been here every day, I'm told. He's here late into the night, as now. Do you deny it?" he demanded of Jamie as he continued to stare at him.

"No," Jamie said.

Gideon raised his sword and stepped forward.

"Shall I get into line behind him?" Tristram asked, uncoiling from the shadows to reach Jamie's side with astonishing speed. He put his long hand down hard over Jamie's as he raised his sword. "I was here too, every time, you see."

Gideon stood still.

"And was similarly occupied with Mary each time

317

too," Tristram said languidly. "She asked for it. And I assure you it was my pleasure," he added, smiling to Mary. "Will you tell him?" he asked her, before he answered himself, ". . . no, I think instead you should *show* him what we do," he said as Gideon's eyes grew wide.

Mary let out her breath. She'd been thrilled at Gideon's arrival. Seconds later she'd been shocked by his actions, then terrified for Jamie's sake, and now her knotted muscles relaxed as she saw that Tristram had ended the danger. Now, at last she was angry at Gideon's estimate of her. So she lifted her head and went to the table and picked up the first book her hand touched. It was an almanac, and it lay open to the page they'd been working on today before Jamie and Tristram had taken her out for a long and pleasant dinner that had lasted into the night.

" 'Thirteenth of October, ' " she read aloud. " 'St. Edward the Confessor's Day. For those who seek to cure the King's Evil: To know whether a malady be the King's Evil, take a ground worm alive and lay him upon the swelling or sore and cover him with a leaf. If it be disease, the worm will turn to earth, but if it be not the Evil, he will remain whole and sound.' "

She'd not stumbled over one word. She closed the book and stood as tall as she could, triumphant.

But Gideon only frowned, completely confused.

Tristram spoke, softly, tactfully, as careful to let Gideon know the truth as he was to let him know how much the truth meant to Mary.

"It wouldn't be very kind to put Jamie beneath the earth simply because he helped Mary to learn to read about it, would it, my friend?"

"Oh, gods," Gideon said after a moment's pause, lowering his sword at last, "I ought to have known. Skewer me, Jamie, here's my heart," he said, sheathing his blade and stepping forward unarmed. "Or my

hand, take whichever you will, I'll not defend the one
or withdraw the other until you've decided."

Jamie took neither; he only put his hands on Gideon's arms, as Gideon gripped his, and the two men
stood grinning at each other. Until Tristram said pet-
tishly, "I suppose I'm to be the odd-man-out? You
don't greet those you don't threaten with death? Or is
it just that you're one of those men who believe that
their women should be kept ignorant as geese outside
of their kitchens and beds? Some do hold to that, I
know," he said, looking much offended until Gideon
laughed and took his hand.

And then they heard Mary gasp. She stood, holding
the note she'd picked up from the floor where Gideon
had cast it, her eyes wide, and one hand rose to her
trembling mouth as she scanned it.

"And now I know why," Tristram sighed.

Mary didn't weep until the other two men had left.
She only wept then because she couldn't hold back the
combined pressure of both her tears of relief and hurt
pride a moment longer. She only cried against Gideon's hard shoulder because she couldn't find a place
for privacy soon enough. And she remained there,
letting him try to comfort her only because these days
it seemed she no longer knew what could bring her
peace.

"I never meant to hurt you," he murmured into her
sweet-smelling hair, burying his face in it for the pleasure of feeling its cleanliness and texture as much as
for gladness that he hadn't wasted his time doing the
same thing with that infested creature he'd tried to
want hours before. Because even as he sought to mend
matters with Mary, and felt his heart lurch in pity for
her, his desire for her was rising.

"It wasn't that I didn't believe in you," he said at
last, so softly she had to strain to hear it, "so much as
I think I didn't believe you could really want me.

Jamie's pleasant-looking. Very kind. And gentle. I'm not," he said. And then he said no more, but she understood, and for all that his words brought her joy, she almost hated him for binding her even closer with his confession. His fear of his unattractiveness won her over as bragging about his desirability would never have done. This was partly because she knew he thought it was true, mostly because he'd admitted it to her. She held him close and couldn't answer him, and so didn't—with words.

He was moved by how suddenly her sorrow turned to desire, her small shudders of grief turning to long shivers of longing, her soft sobs becoming softer sighs of surprised pleasure, her tears on his lips forgotten in the heat of his mouth. Still, he reluctantly took his lips from hers at last, and spoke again to turn the subject.

"Almanacs?" he asked tenderly. "You study almanacs. Now you can read me good advice for each day. I'truth, I need it."

Her eyes, which had been half-closed, opened to look at him curiously.

"You want to talk about almanacs?" she murmured through lips swollen with his kisses.

"Ah, well," he said gently, deciding it never really mattered if she wanted him or only wanted to assure him of her fidelity. He took her back into his arms, thinking of a dozen ways to love her without discomfiting her tonight, "but you reminded me of the date," he explained. "Still, if you'd rather, we'll think of something," he laughed as his lips found hers again.

She wondered what had brought about his odd hesitation, and then lost the thought in the marvel of his mouth and hands, all thought gone as he bore her back to their bed. All apprehension, all anger, and all reasonable fury were soon subdued as well, by the feel of his familiar body, too long gone from hers, united with hers again.

He left the candles burning, and gazed at her all the

while. He touched her with the gentle care of a physician, and held her tenderly as a friend, and loved her with the slow, deliberate single-minded passion of a torturer, before he fell victim to his own art, and, aching, succumbed to her. They didn't speak when they were done, nor yet again when they began anew, nor after that. There was too much for them to say, and in their separate wisdoms they tried to say as much as they could with their bodies before morning brought colder realities to their lips with the dawning light.

She curled beside him to sleep at last, content, for the time being, not only because she'd never known such feelings of pleasure and completeness, but also because he was there beside her now. Still, as exhausted with his day and his night as he was, he lay awake for a long while after. He considered numbers and counted days, and tried to remember things as they'd been before, as well as those he'd been able to note before he'd been lost in the wonder of her body. And then, only half-convinced of his conclusions, weary as he was, he still found it difficult to sleep.

She rose long after her usual hour, and was glad that her maid had obviously had the wisdom not to disturb them. That gave her pause, as she wondered guiltily what her good little maid Betty would think of her now. Betty hadn't been her servant when Gideon had last been in these rooms. It was foolishness, of course—Betty was an orphan, glad of the work and of a kind mistress, and her opinion meant nothing. Mary wondered what she'd think anyway, now that she'd opened her mistress's door and seen a naked red-headed giant sprawled out in her bed. But then Mary glanced back at the bed, and what she saw chased all thoughts of shame away, as always when she looked at him.

He lay sleeping. His long straight fiery hair covered over his face, but his rawboned lean form lay still, smooth and powerful and yet still oddly vulnerable. Because he lay exposed, and there was something trusting, she thought, in the way that he relaxed so utterly in her bed as he had in her arms. But only a fool who needed such foolish fancies would ever imagine even for a moment that such a man was ever vulnerable, she thought a second later, when he moved his head and his eyes opened to expose her to that keen ice-blue regard.

"Gone from me so soon?" he asked lazily, opening his arms to her. And she came back, shy now in the daylight, to be enfolded there, as he kissed her good morning.

"How do you feel?" he asked as his lips left hers.

"Wonderfully well," she said, although she couldn't meet his eyes, not so soon in the day, not so soon after all she'd done in the night.

"Indeed?" he asked, as if he didn't believe her.

"And why should I not?" she asked, before he took her closer, and his movements made her close her eyes again, because for all she loved what they did, she still could not bring herself to see it. That seemed to amuse him, even as it made him more tender. And so the next time they spoke, long after, when he again asked her how she felt, with more than a smile in his voice, and she answered, "Wonderfully well," there was nothing but belief along with the pleasure to be seen in his eyes.

"What," he asked, after he'd risen and washed and seated himself at the table with breads and cheese and ale set out for him, and saw that she'd seated herself opposite, to only toy with a bit of bread as she watched his every mouthful, "not hungry after all our exercise?"

"No, not really. I'm growing less greedy these days," she said absently.

He paused to look at her, and it seemed he sighed, but then he smiled again. "But not for knowledge," he said, and added, "I'm sorry, I shouldn't have mistrusted you. And I'm pleased. You read well, and learned fast . . . as you do in all things," he added, to see her duck her head and smile in secret pleasure at both compliments.

"I can write too," she said, looking up at him with pride. "More than my mark, and more than my name, and soon I'll be able to read more as well—real poetry instead of just children's poems and almanacs . . ."

Her voice faded as she remembered everything his lovemaking had caused her to forget.

"That wasn't poetry," he said at once, "it was vileness. Verse for pigs, written by a swine. And now I'm going to let the author know my opinion," he said as he arose, "so please stay here until I return. I'll return," he added, as he saw her face.

She nodded, and looked away. After all, she'd no right to ask just where he was going, although she knew. Just as she'd no right to ask when or if he'd ever return, although she feared he might not now, and for more than just the usual worry about whether he'd go to another woman or tire of her. Because she knew he might be going to his death. There'd been a promise of death in his eyes when he'd spoken about the cruel poem, and she, of all people, knew death was an unpredictable guest to offer any invitation to.

"I will be back," he said again later, when he'd dressed and was about to leave, as he looked back from the door to her.

"I promise, I'll be back," he said as she came into his arms and laid her head against his shoulder in silent sorrow and entreaty, knowing she couldn't ask him more.

"I will not leave you," he said gently before he left her, and she knew she couldn't ask for more.

They were in the Old Swan. They, and a dozen of their cronies. If it weren't for that vanity, the inability to hide alone, any more than they could enjoy themselves alone, he'd never have found them. As it was, he'd wasted hours searching their more familiar haunts, but now the courtiers stood out at once from the mass of other men in the tavern. Their bright clothing as well as their loud voices proclaimed them men of note, of money, of leisure and power. And their sudden silence when they saw Gideon Hawkes as he prowled into the common taproom showed their fear of losing it all—to him. For the tall, lean man had murder on his mind and in his eyes, clear for anyone to see, even in the candlelit dark. His voice held even more threat than that, and so when he spoke, no few of them were glad of that darkness to hide their sudden terror in. Even more were relieved when he didn't call their names.

"John Wilmot!" he said in his deep, dark voice. "Sir! Here, to me!" he ordered, as he'd order a dog to heel, a dog he didn't like. "Roger Mobely! Now, sir, to me!" he commanded, his hand resting lightly over his sword's hilt, his booted feet apart as he braced against the darkness and the unknown in the coming fight.

The slender young man came, or was rudely pushed, from the back of the crowd of courtiers. Because he soon was seen standing alone before them, whether because he'd stepped forward or because they'd all, save him, shrunk back, no one could know. Nor did Gideon care.

John Wilmot, Earl of Rochester, was young enough to be son to many of the men there, a stripling youth, a pretty little boyish man, thin and narrow and all aflutter now in his dismay. But no one mocked him for it. No more than they'd ever twitted him for his bragging about his many mistresses or sexual vigor or any of his equally inflated stories about his courage and manhood and daring. Because he'd a tongue that was like a lash, and a considerable wit made up all of malice, and a store of evil tales to carry about every

man there, and no conscience to hold him back from
doing it. And even more, and most of all, he'd a king
he called his friend.

Royal pet and jester, coward and cheat, and clever
foe to anyone who tried to take his place in any place
he coveted, he had enough bravery now to draw in his
breath and face Gideon Hawke's burning eye. Or at
least enough wit not to try to run, Gideon thought
sardonically, as the Earl of Rochester drew himself up
and answered his challenger.

"I am here." He spoke clearly enough, but his voice
cracked on the last word.

"Not for long, I swear it," Gideon said in cold low
carrying tones like the tolling of the dead bell, "if
you're the dog who wrote that charming verse to me."

"How shall I know what verse you speak about?"
Rochester answered in his more usual high and nervous accents, appealing to the onlookers as much as
he spoke to Gideon. "I write dozens of verses—I'm a
poet, you know."

"It's seen the fire, as you soon shall," Gideon said,
taking a step forward, avoiding his opponent's trap,
for no power on earth could have made him make that
vile poem claiming Mary had bedded Jamie public
knowledge.

"And I'm convinced it was from your hand. It wasn't
the first time I've found your verses on my doorstep,
celebrating lies about my life," he added, "although
I'll wager it's the last. Draw your weapon, sir," he said
implacably.

"It was not!" Rochester squealed, turning to the
onlookers for agreement. "It wouldn't be the first time
I was blamed for mischief. I would not—ever—anger
*you*, Hawkes," he said with emphasis, turning to Gideon so that he could see the slow and dawning smile
appear on his full lips, "since I'm wise enough to
know you're a friend of Charles's . . . as you know I
am too," he said, sneering as he emphasized his using

the king's Christian name, sinking in his point as though he'd cast a spear. After incanting that name, he visibly relaxed, clearly feeling safe again at last.

His smile faded as Gideon spoke again.

"Well and good," he said quietly, his face impassive except for a brief tic that flashed along his hard-clenched jaw. "Then one of us can expect to have at least one mourner at his funeral. Whichever of us loses in this fair fight. Draw your sword, sir. You have offended me, and I will have justice done. Here and now."

At that, as the young man's face grew gray, Gideon unsheathed his sword, drew a swift salute with it, and settling on the balls of his feet, waited.

The young earl fumbled for his own sword. It was a handsome one, hanging from an impressive sheath, but Gideon doubted it was a fighting man's weapon. It hardly mattered; he wasn't fighting a man anyway, he thought. But he felt little guilt, and less pity. For all his relative youth, Rochester had already destroyed many other men, and women, if not with his steel, then just as surely with his vicious cutting wit and eternal scheming. It was said he'd a network of spies in Charles's court, reporting to him on every slip and foible so he could turn them to his profit, either in favors granted or by deftly turning them into malicious gossip that would entertain his king as well as his own cruel court. His only excuse was that it could have been true, as was said, that he hadn't been entirely sober in three years. That hardly mattered either, Gideon thought; he'd be explaining all to the highest judge soon enough.

Gideon watched his opponent narrowly, awaiting the first move. He'd saluted, he'd poised himself, and was ready, but wouldn't begin until Rochester did. He wanted Charles to know this had been both fairly fought and won. He'd not like censure, he didn't know if he could bear exile, and had reconciled himself to death years before. If any of that were to be his king's

judgment of these next moments, he accepted that
he'd have to face it. But whatever punishment it earned
him, he'd not allow an enemy to flourish and flaunt
him, since there was no sense living if it was to be in
a state of constant aggravation and despair. Rochester
had angered him and disturbed Celeste, but harmed
neither of them so much as he'd hurt Mary, and he
was sworn to protect her, and he would. It was a
matter of honor, he thought, banishing the image of
her swollen eyes, lest it confuse his own vision now.

"And Sir Roger?" Rochester asked in a shaking
voice as he finally raised his sword.

"I'll meet him when I find him," Gideon said calmly,
watching the wavering sword tip to see where attack
would come and in what style and form.

But when it came, he'd no way of preparing for it.

The sense of the shouted words, the gasps of the
onlookers, and the pain all came in one movement,
and by the time Gideon had wheeled around, the
damage had been done.

Because, "Then prepare yourself, for here I am!"
Roger Mobely cried out gladly from behind him, and
thrust and struck to the bone as he spoke, his sword
grazing the rib on Gideon's side instead of striking to
his heart only because of how swiftly Gideon had
whirled to face him.

Only then did the dark-haired man's face grow whiter,
only then did the onlookers fall deathly still. Sir Roger,
backing up, hesitated—because he saw that against all
expectation, his prey was still very much alive and on
his feet. The crowd around them was silent as they
realized how unthinkably craven a deed they'd witnessed.

Sir Roger's hand grew damp on his sword's hilt as
he looked into Gideon's brilliant eyes. If Hawkes had
died, at once, on the end of his blade, Mobely thought,
there'd have been a dozen eyewitness explanations
given, he'd have paid for a dozen more, and no man
would ever have got to the bottom of the truth, not

even the king. Favored as Gideon Hawkes was, so too was Rochester loved, and since the one would've been silent in his grave and the other had a persuasive tongue, Mobely had been sure he would've been pardoned in time. He reasoned the time wasted waiting safely away from court would've been worth it for Rochester's gratitude for ridding him of this rude redheaded competitor for the king's regard. Not to mention what his relief would've been at not having to fight, however much he'd never have admitted that.

Roger Mobely was a practiced swordsman, but knew Gideon was a famous one, and never was a man to play against such odds. But although he'd attacked without warning and felt his sword pass through flesh, yet still Gideon Hawkes walked light-footed as he came toward him. There was no grimace of pain either; nothing in that frozen mask of living death moved, except for a shiver in his knotted cheek, which sent a thrill of fear up Roger Mobely's spine.

And now, too, a high excited voice rang out. "Dog!" it called, in real fury. "Mobely, you villain," the Earl of Rochester cried, and from the sound of it, it might very well have been as honest an exclamation as it was a spontaneous one. But his onetime companion couldn't listen, not when death walked toward him with such easy grace. He struck out. Only to feel his blade fly up and out, away, as Gideon moved his wrist in a light shrug, deflecting his wild thrust. Again he swept his sword back and aimed for the unprotected heart of his implacable partner in this grim dance he'd begun, and again a languid turn of the wrist prevented him from scoring anything but the curse he let fly with his lunge.

He saw Gideon Hawkes come on, smiling now, moving forward with hell gleaming in his eyes, and Sir Roger thrust again, backed again, stabbed out again, before he staggered back once more and then yet again, his arm aching with the pain of trying to hold on to his weapon.

The clashing steel rang, making the tavern sound like a blacksmith's foundry as the dark-haired courtier retreated, and struck out, only to retreat again, until he was sweating like a smithy as he scrabbled back, all art and style forgotten, swinging wildly with his sword. And the red-headed Cavalier moved forward relentlessly. Until, at last, something like disgust showed in that grim face, and he lightly, almost casually sent the other sword spinning into the air, and placed his own, carefully as a surgeon might, deep into his opponent's shoulder.

He withdrew his blade before Sir Roger hit the floor. And seemed more concerned with wiping it clean than he did with the man he'd just defeated.

"He lives," he said without looking to the floor, where a knot of men had gone to see to his opponent. "I decided it's a worse fate than oblivion for him now. But he'll never fight again—with that arm."

"I never meant it, I never wanted it . . . it was cowardly, unmanly . . . unfitting . . . believe me, Hawkes," the Earl of Rochester babbled, so white-faced he well might have been sobered by what he'd seen, so shaken he might have actually meant it, Gideon thought.

Gideon only nodded, and put away his sword, and bowing, left the earl protesting his innocence in the matter. Rochester had to be content to take the tall Cavalier's nod as an apology noted, and took his withdrawn air and sudden departure as a measure of how the incident had disgusted him. He didn't know, because Gideon took care that he should not, that it was, instead, a measure of how much it had wounded him.

Mary didn't know either, and when he appeared in her doorway, her only thought was such enormous relief that he was there, returned, and returned to her the same day, that she clapped her hands together and rushed to him. And was hurt and wounded herself

when he withdrew his hand from his doublet and held
it up to stop her, warding her away.

"No, no, Mary," he said wearily, leaning back against
the doorframe, "your gown will be smeared."

And then she saw that the hand he'd held up was
red with blood, and then she knew a miracle—that it
was possible to live even though her heart had stopped
beating.

She led him to a chair, above his protests; she sent
Betty for clean linen to bind his wound; she sent her
footman to fetch Rountree from Gideon's new lodgings to tend to him. All of this was done with cold
authority. She began shaking only when she lifted his
shirt away and saw that the wound was on the outer
ribs, not between them, and that for all the gore, it
welled slowly, and so knew that she could afford to be
weak then, since with nursing he'd be strong again.

Rountree came with all speed, and before long had
inspected the wound, agreed with his master that he'd
seen and survived worse, and dressed it. Then he
helped settle Gideon for the night, and left again, but
only after being reassured that he'd be sent for if there
were any unexpected difficulties. Mary thought he was
as cautious as an old mother hen, and since Gideon
was so alert and mocking, believed he thought so too.
But he agreed with Rountree as readily as he laughed
at him. Because as both men knew and neither said in
front of Mary, there was often no way of knowing at
once what damage an injection of thin steel might
have done to something unseen, interior, and vital.

Gideon thought about that briefly after Rountree
had left. He patted the bed at his side, and smiled as
Mary hesitated to come to him.

"What?" he teased her. "Shy of me again? Sooth,
mistress, how many nights must we share before you
come willing to my bed?"

But she'd wanted to obey him at once, and had
hesitated only because she'd not forgotten—in truth,

she had a hard time not remembering—that he'd said it really wasn't to be his bed anymore, for all he paid for it, since he'd got himself another. Yet he'd stayed with her last night, and now this night too? It was almost as if he'd come back to her entirely again. She didn't know how to ask him that without seeming presumptuous, and dared not endanger this new fragile hope in any way. So she said only, to cover her confusion, "Ah, but your side . . ."

"And that's all you'll have of me tonight, I promise," he said as she came to him.

She stretched out beside him, burying her face in his neck as he put one arm around her, and since he couldn't see her eyes, she whispered, "Will you stay tonight, then?"

Then he understood what had made her hesitate, and he grew still himself. She'd reminded him of his promise. And he remembered it before he could think of why he'd made it. For a moment he wondered if he were breaking his word. But then he relaxed, and hugged Mary close.

"If you'll have me, Mary," he said softly, "I'll stay the night."

He'd promised Celeste he wouldn't come to her until he'd left Mary's lodgings and taken up living in his own rooms. This he'd done. Visiting with Mary in her rooms was never living in them; he'd been wounded and needed to rest, recuperation wasn't a permanent thing, and anyway, he wasn't planning on returning to Celeste so soon again. That was a great many reasons given, in light of the fact that no one had accused him of breaking his word but himself, he thought on a sigh.

"Gideon," Mary said as she curled closer, taking care not to touch his bandaged side, "why did you fight tonight?"

"I love poetry," he said easily, "and didn't care for the fellow's composition. Ah, don't tense so, I didn't kill him. A man can't go around killing all the bad poets, you know," he added, grinning. "More's the pity."

"But he almost killed you," she said, drawing away and sitting up so she could look at him.

"This?" He laughed. "This scratch is not almost killing."

She swept some of her tumbled hair from her face and regarded him with wide, sad eyes.

"He never wrote anything bad about you, Gideon. Only me. And Jamie, I suppose. If you'd showed Jamie the poem, I suppose he could have challenged him."

"It wasn't Jamie's task," Gideon answered. "It was mine. He hurt you," he explained, and closed his eyes to rest. Even with his side burning, he was still content and comfortable with Mary at his other side. Her outcry made his eyes snap open again.

"Oh, not for me!" she cried. "You didn't fight for me? But that would be foolishness. Even if what he said wasn't true, I'm just a whore—there was no need to die for me! No," she said, quieting, and staring at him solemnly, "it was for your pride, Gideon, not for me."

He rose to his elbow and took her shoulder in one hand.

"You see too much and too little, little Mary," he said gruffly. "Sooth, you're right, there was too much of my pride in it. But there was an insult to you to be avenged. And I did not die. And you are no whore."

"I sold myself to you," she said.

"You had to survive."

"You once said if it wasn't you, it would've been another," she argued, her eyes searching his face. She hoped he'd argue with her. She prayed he'd say something to lift that terrible name from her, or at least to make it easier to bear, for it weighed heavier on her heart every day he'd been gone from her, and heavier still now that he'd returned.

"I said that?" he asked, sinking back to his pillow. "For a man who says as little as he can," he muttered, "I've managed to say a great many silly things. You're no whore, Mary Monk. I'll kill anyone who denies that—even you," he threatened as he pulled her down to him again and put both hands lightly around her neck and closed them in a mock attack to emphasize what he said, before he put his lips on hers with real tenderness to convince her of what he couldn't say.

"Your wound!" she cried a few moments later, pulling away. Her hand had touched his bandage and she'd felt the wetness there. Now she sat up and stared at it in horror, so distressed that he took the little hand with the slight stain of his blood on it that she held out for evidence in his own before he kissed it.

"Sooth, it's nothing," he said. "It's from before, and only to be expected. I've had worse, I know, believe me. Now, come back here to me."

She resisted his arms and his words, guilty because his hands and his mouth had made her forget his condition.

"I will not have you opening it again," she said defiantly.

"Beware! That's the first time you've ever refused me" he laughed, continuing to drag her down to him.

She worried for her heart even as she did for his health as she answered, "But you said I wasn't a whore. And so I can refuse if I want, can't I?"

He let go of her hand and regarded her silently. She gazed back, fearful as she was determined, and all of it showed in her earnest dark eyes.

"Ah," he sighed, closing his eyes and sinking back again, alone, "it's a terrible thing to be at a woman's mercy."

He hadn't really answered her, but he had, she thought, as she inspected his bandages to assure herself he was right before she lay down again. And nothing would be the same again.

He only kissed her brow, and kept only his arm around her until she slept. But he couldn't sleep just yet. His unresolved yearning kept him awake as much as his side did. He raised his head enough to inspect his bandaging and then lay back again. What he'd told her, inventing the truth because his desire had been driving him so hard, turned out to be true enough. There was only oozing now, time enough for Rountree to change the dressing in the morning. But the sight of his blood reminded him of something to keep him from sleep a little longer.

Facing death had made him think of life. He gazed at Mary sleeping at his side and tightened his arm around her. He'd been a sailor once, and he'd grown accustomed to studying the heavens to find his direction; he'd been a lover before, and he knew the importance of the phases of the moon. He hadn't told the truth when he'd said she never refused him her bed. She had, and prettily, whenever her time of the month was first upon her, because she suffered more than most women at those times. He'd gazed at the moon as he'd ridden down the long road to London, and, remembering, had been disappointed as he'd passed beneath the eastern gate. He'd expected to have to settle for a different sort of welcome from her than the one he'd actually received.

She ate little now, she slept more, and even so soon, her shapely little body showed the slight changes that he recognized when he'd looked for them. And he had, and carefully. This was more than delay, he'd swear it.

He'd had a mistress once who'd almost had a babe; he knew the signs far better than Mary could be expected to. And so he believed he knew, with an admixture of worry and pride, what his Mary didn't as yet—that she was carrying what he found he wanted very much now: their child. But then, he thought, drawing her closer, so that she sighed and murmured in her sleep, what else should he expect of her? He was a man of experience, and she was, after all, still only a child herself.

She muttered a jumble of something and he stroked her hair lightly, so as to let her know even in the depths of her sleep that he was there to chase away all her enemies—from her mythical Death Bird who still visited her in her dreams, to the human foes ringed all around her in actuality. Then he closed his too-observant eyes and lay down to join her in sleep; his side's aching easing even as his worries were, his heart very full, his mistress and her secret treasure secure within his clasp, he was at peace.

Had he thought on it, he mightn't have slept at all that night. Because it was very odd that he fell asleep without once thinking of Ivyclose . . . and truer still that in all his travels across the wide world, never had Ivyclose been so far from him.

# 17

"If he wanted my head, he wouldn't permit your eyes on the meeting," Gideon explained calmly. "He's not a man to enjoy suffering. No, our king's after my explanations, not my blood."

"So you think!" Mary uttered nervously.

"And if I didn't, be sure you'd be halfway to France by now, Mary Monk," he assured her.

She didn't answer. He glanced down and saw her gnawing at her lip as they walked down the long corridor together, on their way to another evening's festivities at Whitehall Palace, on his way to another audience with their king. He stopped her by stepping in front of her, and put his hands on her shoulders as he looked at her, his voice when he spoke as serious as his face was.

"Don't you trust me?" he asked.

"Oh, I do. Yes, I do," she sighed, and gave him a brief shrug before she showed him a brave smile to relieve him of worry. Because she did trust him, and entirely—but she didn't trust in the friendship of kings.

"And when you meet with him, you're going to leave me with the ladies of the court again?" she asked in mock horror, to distract him.

"Better than with the gentlemen of the court," he said as they began walking again. "Be sure to take notes," he cautioned her before the great doors swung open to admit them, "so you'll know exactly what not to be when we get home again."

She laughed, and tried to be as confident as he was as they came into the roomful of milling courtiers and ladies of the court. He'd been summoned to meet with Charles. His wound hadn't healed over yet, but he'd got up from bed when he'd got the king's note, and never hesitated in a step forward since. Mary felt she could be no less brave—at least outwardly. But even as he greeted acquaintances, and she nodded absently to those of the assembled court who seemed to recognize her, she positioned herself so that her eyes could always rest on Gideon. He was her rock, her comforter, and her friend, and even now, after all this time, when she saw him with his equals it was hard for her to believe he was also her lover. Not that he had any equals, she decided, since he was easily the most outstanding, best-looking man in the room.

There were dashing young men in exquisitely ruffled and brocaded garments, festooned with lace. There were glittering smooth-skinned fair men and swaggering mustached, bearded dark ones; lean and trim young gentlemen that looked as if they'd stepped from out of portraits on the walls, except that they were dressed finer, in the latest styles and colors, and substantial-looking older men who looked born to command and determined to continue to. But even though Gideon was all in black, even to his lace-edged appointments, and was without a full wig or a curl on his head, or so much as one patch on his face, he wasn't diminished. No, just the opposite, Mary thought with the combination of smugness and astonishment she always felt when she gazed at him in public. Gideon's unadorned presence seemed to belittle them. He stood taller and looked smarter, stronger, and more distinctive than any of the men surrounding him. And yet for all that, he was with her, and she with him. She couldn't get used to the wonder of that.

So although she wore a fine gown of black to match him, with gold trim to spark and liven her dark looks, still she believed every glance she got was because she was with him. This never made her downcast, but proud instead, and pride was the best cosmetic she could have worn. It caused her to walk head high, while her delight in Gideon made her dark eyes soft and dazzling, so the fierce and arrogant joy she felt made her seem far lovelier than she could have guessed.

But although Gideon noted her good looks tonight, he didn't reflect on them. He was neither so calm nor so assured as he'd pretended to Mary and the world.

So far as he knew, Sir Roger Mobely lived, so whatever lies Rochester had hissed into the royal ear, he couldn't be wanted for murder. Still, he was wanted for something, or he wouldn't have received a royal summons. Whatever he'd told Mary, such a summons was never to be confused with an invitation, and even a man on his deathbed would be well advised to crawl to such a meeting. Charles wasn't a cruel man, he didn't delight in revenge or in bloodletting, that much was true. But severed heads were still decorating London, and would, Gideon expected, so long as kings did. To be sure, he didn't expect that Mary would soon have to gaze up at his head and wonder if he were comfortable on his pike, but there were other, less spectacular, but equally permanent ways in which a king might show his displeasure. He'd been Charles's friend. But since his last public act had been one of hostility to one of Charles's most beloved friends, he wondered if he were still of that number.

It was never his way to cringe or cower, and so when he spied the tall, lean, dark figure of the king threading his way toward him through the great room, Gideon unconsciously put his feet apart as if to center himself before he took a hard blow, and consciously kept his face to its usual inexpressive calm. It might be that Rochester had thought better of mentioning the matter at all. Whatever it was, he would take it as it came. He permitted himself a smile when he rose from the graceful bow he made to his sovereign king.

"Gideon," Charles said with delight in his deep voice, his black eyes sparkling in the candlelight, "I see you've recovered from your injuries."

So much for the hope that the summons might have been for something entirely different.

"Ah, but with such a pretty wench playing nurse, no wonder you look fitter than you did before you went about crippling the gentlemen of London," the king said sweetly.

Mary had smiled up into the dark face above her at the first words the king had spoken, but now she grew pale, and faltered as she arose from her curtsy.

"No, child," the king said softly, to her ear alone, "don't fret. I have as much care for my red-headed Hawke as you do. Come, Gideon," he said heartily, placing his arm around Gideon's shoulder, "let the girl see if she can do better for herself. I've need of a private word with you."

They went to sit in the king's private rooms, where Gideon had been given his first audience when he'd returned to London. But this time neither Tristram nor Jamie was there, and this time Gideon knew the king had more on his mind than an apology. The long, dark face before him was shadowed by more than the half-cast of light from the chandeliers; the half-open slumberous eyes hid more than his thoughts. Not for the first time Gideon was reminded of the immense power this one mortal man could wield, if he wished. The power that he himself had offered his life once, and his fortunes, many times, in order to restore to him. Because he'd felt that if any man deserved such power and could use it wisely, it was this man.

But that had been years before. He'd met this man, his king, when Charles had been little more than the boy he himself had been. He'd joined to help his young king in his desperate escape from England then. They'd met again and again as their paths crossed and recrossed as they, both exiles, sought to escape despair as they roamed across the world. Time had changed many things in Britain, as well as in himself, since then, Gideon realized. He valued life more now than he had as a boy, when he'd believed himself immortal. He'd more to live for, and much more to protect than himself now, and now he understood the limits of his own power to endure despair. He loved this man very well, but was never fool enough to forget this man was his king, with all of a king's rights and privileges.

He thought all this, and knew the closest thing he'd ever felt to real fear of another man as he found himself being studied by those hooded eyes. Yet, as always, he faced fear head-on in order to live with it. Cold blue eyes locked glances with those hidden, knowing ebony ones.

But then the voice, when it came, was troubled, not angry, and though only scant years separated them, the words were as puzzled and solicitous as a loving father's, and not at all as his own father's would have been.

"Where's the difficulty, Gideon?" the king asked slowly. "I'd thought to have mended all with you, and not it appears that I haven't. Was the fault in my command? Or in your desire to obey it?"

"I didn't so much as touch Rochester," Gideon replied.

"Rochester? . . . Oh. No, no," the king said, waving one long-fingered, ring-covered hand dismissively. "You only terrified him, which is a favor to him, and made him see what bad company he kept, which is more than I could do. Mobely's out of it, neatly put

away, though he still breathes. That was well-done of
you. But I expected no less. No," he said impatiently,
"forget that nonsense. I want to know why we've not
celebrated your wedding yet."

It was as well that Gideon seldom showed emotion,
because his mind was blank in that moment, and he'd
not have liked to be seen gaping like a fool at his king.
But not only was his relief immense, the question was
unexpected, and for that one second of time he wondered what wedding the king was talking about.

"Philip Southern's been to see me. 'Od's fish, but
I've just done with wringing out my sleeve from his
tears," the king complained moodily, toying with the
stem of his wineglass as he watched Gideon closely.
"He goes on about his impatient widow and his beautiful sister, and between his sister and his widow he's
his hands full of beautiful women, and yet nothing in
them but thin air, he complains. Not a happy state for
a lusty man. He says you came to Ivyclose, you saw
his sister, and yet left a bachelor still. You saw her in
London, and again at Ivyclose, and yet she's still unwed. And here are you, free, or at least fettered only
by your pretty mistress. The lady awaits, your land lies
fallow. So where does the problem lie? Do you find
her unwholesome? Unseemly? Say it outright, I'll
listen."

"I find her as lovely as he says she is," Gideon said,
choosing his words carefully for Celeste's sake and not
his own now. "Wholesome, seemly, altogether virtuous. But if you recall, sire, it's not only my consent
that's needed. The lady must want me. And she does—
and she doesn't—and so I've decided I can only hope
to win her by waiting her out now."

"Virtuous indeed," Charles said, smiling now, "to
make Gideon Hawkes wait. Is the lady such a Puritan?"

Gideon didn't so much as blink an eye as he raised
his wide shoulders in an elaborate shrug, and answered only, "Sooth, I'm not such a cock of the walk

as to think a lady who mislikes me likes her Bible more."

"But she may," the king said seriously, and as Gideon grew still at his words, he added, "Don't worry, my red rogue, it's only common gossip. But I've found it pays to pay uncommon attention to such. I'd rather have a good tale-bearer in my train than the greatest balladeer. If a king keeps his ear to the ground, he's more likely to keep his head on his shoulders," he said softly, before he looked at the tall impassive man at his table and continued on a sigh, "I'd trust a man like you with my life, Gideon Hawkes, and have done, but I find it valuable to keep dozens of lesser men at my side. Their prattle may keep me from needing such as you, you see."

It was an indication of how much Gideon did see that kept him still as he listened to his king speaking, musingly and at length, in the quiet of the room, as though he spoke to himself as well as to his guest.

"Ah, don't worry for her, Gideon," the king said. "If I'd wanted vengeance on every Puritan in England, I'd be ankle-deep in blood now. No, it's healing I'm after. Revenge is a cheap slut, nothing a clever man should lust after. It has no heart, you see. It grows cold as fast as the desire for it grows hot. Healing's a true and tender love, it takes time, but makes a man whole again. No, it's their own guilt makes them shy of me—Puritans are safe enough beneath my wing, as are men of any faith, so long as they mean me no hurt. Do you doubt me too, Gideon Hawkes?"

It was a measure of Charles's respect for him, Gideon thought, that he asked. It was a measure of his respect for his sovereign that he took time to frame his answer, knowing he could give an honest one and that it would be listened to. Time hadn't changed this man that much, after all, he thought with a surge of pleasure, except for enabling him to hide his aims more completely and cover over his emotions enough to deceive even those who thought they knew him very well. This he approved, since he himself had learned in a hard world that a man who could conceal his emotions could always confound his enemies. He rejoiced even more when he realized with quiet pride that Charles could bare his soul when he wished, and that he wished to now.

"I ought to have known," Gideon said. "Your pardon for thinking otherwise for a moment. She'd fears, you see. So I kept my knowledge of her church to myself. But I should've known. You've deprived your people only of all the executions they longed to see. Sooth, you even let the Jews back in."

"Not hard," Charles said on a smile, "considering they were already here. It doesn't take a wise man to admit he sees what his eyes behold. And why not? They never did me harm. There's been enough blood let within our gates. I want to make amends to all Englishmen. But you—above all others, I sought to do well by you. I wanted to restore your home, and put a rich and pretty poppet in it for your pleasure while I was at it. It seemed a perfect match. I'd seen her in France, in passing, or, believe me," he said with his twisting sensuous smile, "I'd have seen to it that I'd have seen far more of her. Even then I wondered why such a beauty had no affairs to her name by her age, and so I listened to common gossip. It hardly mattered if it was true—I thought you could win her to your bed without trouble, especially since it was a marriage bed. Even Puritans approve of busyness there."

"Do they?" Gideon asked with a wry grin. "But if she's typical, and telling me the truth, you'll never have to worry about them outnumbering the rest of us. It seems to take them forever to make up their minds to get there. Of course," he said thoughtfully, "it could be because of another matter. It could be because of me."

"You?" Charles said. He looked shrewdly at the

man seated opposite him. Then he shook his head, and his heavily curled glossy black hair swung about his long face as he did. "Never," he said, "and you know it. Do you court flattery from your king, Gideon?" he teased. "Your problems may be many, but your appeal to her sex is never one of them. I've observed you here and abroad, remember?

"Oh," he added lightly, offhandedly, in a manner which would have lulled any man who didn't know him, "on that head, I understand you left Lady Henrietta Greene all on a sudden, and all in a heat—both yours and hers—the other night. Can it be the problem has to do with your lack of interest in Celeste Southern, and not the other way round? Could it be that your new little dark mistress has worn you out? Or warned you off other sport?"

Any other man would have had to reach for his sword for saying it. Blue fire flared in Gideon's eyes, as it was. He dissipated his anger by a sharp bark of laughter before answering.

"I doubt I left Lady Henrietta lonely, Majesty. In fact, that's why I left her. I don't please to share my pleasures with anyone, and the discovery that I'd be sharing her pretty body with several dozen other little scurrying ones dampened my interest."

Gideon seldom shared tales of his experiences with women either, and Charles's eyes lit with delight at hearing of this one. He laughed as he stored up the story to use where it might do the most good, or make the most mischief.

"As for Celeste Southern, she's as clean in body as she is in spirit. I find no fault in her except in her hesitation to have me. On my word, Majesty, she hesitates, not I," Gideon said, before he fell silent.

Charles's dark face grew still and grave, and only then could the harsh lines about his nose and mouth be seen plain, even in the ruddy firelight. He sighed, and nodded.

"I do love women," he said. "Too well, in all ways. So much that sometimes I forget they're as bad as men. Too much power is too heady for some. She has more to give you than her hand; in a hasty moment I gave her your home as well. No woman should have such say in her marriage. But I gave my word, and it's my bond. So it's as I thought it might be—and so it's as well that I've been busy in your behalf again since I saw her brother.

"You can't court her if you're her pensioner," the king said harshly as he arose and went to stare into the fire. "The world has no respect for petitioners. I know how hard it is to be a man without a home, I know what it feels like to yearn for that which is yours when others possess it. It's very like a man in love forced to watch as others take pleasure in his lover's arms. No, for the world I'd not have done that to you, my friend. I can't change it, but I can better it.

"You're a man of property again," he said, and held up one hand to stop Gideon's response before he could speak it. "No, not your Ivyclose. For all my powers, I've bound my hands there. But there's a fine estate in the West that's fallen to the crown. It's by the Severn, set in green hills, acres of good land and a handsome manor with it—more beautiful perhaps than Ivyclose—though I know, I know, never to you. I don't expect you to think so. They could have offered me all the Americas and it wouldn't have been England.

"But the manor has no master," he said after a moment. "The heirs are dead or banished or died out, it matters not. It needs a good landlord and a wise lord over it. It reverted to me. I give it to you. There's a title with it—it will be yours. Will you, nil you," he said testily, "I'll not have you deny me that as your mad friend Tristram Jones keeps refusing my honors. It comes with the land."

"And so I'm to give up Ivyclose, and the lady in it,

in exchange for it?" Gideon asked from between his clenched teeth.

"No!" Charles answered harshly. "Do I give up my bits of France now that I have England? Take the estate I give you. I can't think of a better landlord. But now you can go to her as a landed man of great property as well as fortune. I've found that the less you need, the more you receive: if she knows you no longer need her so, she may need you the more. Although," he said more softly, still staring into the murmuring fire in the grate, "I, of all men, know you'll always need your own home."

He looked up after a moment, and then straightened and came strolling back to where Gideon stood, as he'd done since he'd seen his king arise.

"Oh, be damned to you," Charles said. "Unworthier than you sit in my presence. Why is it that the best are relentless in their respect when I want only their friendship, and the worst need only the slightest laxity on my part to make the most of it?"

But Gideon said nothing. He suspected he pleased his king very well by the way he honored him. Charles was as wise as he was cautious. A man who'd seen his father dragged from off his throne to the headsman's block would never stand on ceremony, knowing it was far too uneasy a place to take a stand, for all he might want his due tribute. Now they stood toe to toe, two tall men, their eyes meeting on a level.

"Now you've a fine manor to go with your fine face and fortune. Go try your luck, man. I wish it for more than just your pleasure. It's not only that I think you'll suit; we're both grown men and know that love in marriage isn't necessary—certainly not for men of vision and duty."

His lips may have curled more in bitterness than in his usual humor as he went on in a hard voice, "Kings and common men—we all of us must have a vision of advancement, and pay our dues to homeland and destiny."

He paused, and then, his sardonic smile back in place, he said more gently, "If brave men, both family and friend to us, didn't stick at going to the block for duty's sake, how can any of us hesitate at the altar?"

As Gideon smiled, Charles went on in livelier fashion, "I've given it thought. I particularly wish to see my finest Cavalier mate with a Puritan lass. Only by just such unions, I think, will this poor distracted land be entirely healed at last. Your sons will be the first of a new England. Two such passionate opposites will produce a fine generation—how could they not, coming from out of one split apart by fire and then forged in another one? Now, I believe that such a generation would be my best legacy, don't you? So go to her, and claim her, and know you go with my blessings."

When Gideon didn't answer at once, Charles lifted one dark brow. "Or is there something else you haven't said?"

"There may be," Gideon said quietly, as though the words were forced from him. And they were. Not by fear, but by the fact that he counted this man his friend, and as he was sorely troubled now, he gave him the rare commodity he'd just been given himself—truth for truth. "I can't be sure, as yet. She doesn't even suspect, I think. But I do. There may soon be . . . ah . . . issue from a present alliance, sire."

"Wonderful!" the king crowed. "So the little darkling may be carrying another Hawke for us? By all that's holy, man, where's the problem in that? Your Puritan? She doesn't have to know yet. Send Mistress Mary to your new home in the West until she foals. Or face facts, as your Puritan must. A man gets children by way of his pleasure—there's no preventing it . . . if he's fortunate. Why, 'Od's fish, man, I've dozens. And they're the delights of my life. Look at Monmouth. Is there a better, bonnier lad in all the land?"

But then Charles grew grave again, thinking, perhaps, of all his bonny illegitimate sons and daughters —or perhaps of the fact that he'd no legitimate heirs at all, for all of them. There was nothing of humor, but only a sad and steady knowledge in his dark eyes as he clapped Gideon on the shoulder and held him still and spoke to him.

"If your king can have some dozen bastards, you are allowed your share. And you can own to them in a court of law, as well as in your heart, my fortunate Gideon. You can own them legally if it's your wish, in time, without starting a civil war. Your illegitimate son can be an addition to your life—not a worry to the kingdom."

Then he paused, and gave Gideon's shoulder a shake. "But if that's to be, it will be in the fullness of time. The most you can do now is to send the little brown maid to my own Sir Scarborough—as good a physicker as Dr. Harvey ever was, I promise you—and have him see to her. If you've sown the seed, he'll ensure its being a good harvest, never fear. But that's the far future. Go now and secure the immediate one," he said. "A king must claim his throne. A man should reclaim his home. So go at once to Ivyclose and take the lady to wive."

"A command?" Gideon asked thoughtfully. "It's a pleasant one, but is it a royal command, Majesty?"

"An' if it is?" Charles said with some annoyance. "Pestilent rogue! Take it in the same spirit as I command you to breathe—because I love you well."

"Sire," Gideon said, sweeping into a bow so profound, so mocking, so overdrawn, that Charles was still laughing as he led him out and into the court again.

Tristram Jones and Jamie had arrived to keep Mary company when Gideon had gone off with the king. One look to her worried face and they'd begun jesting and teasing to distract her. She'd smiled, but paid scant attention. But when she saw Gideon leaving the king's apartments, and saw that he and the king were laughing together, her heart lifted.

"Just nothing," Gideon said for her ear as soon as he'd got to her side again. "Rest easy."

And then they'd joined the laughter and merriment at court, and she'd not minded any of it this time. The music was too loud for her, and her head hurt from it; the food was too rich for her, and she felt queasy from the little bit of it she took. The ladies were just as spiteful and lascivious as ever, the gentlemen just as lewd and forward. But all of it was perfect, and Mary was at peace in the center of all of the chaos of it, because Gideon was at her side.

Only once he strayed from her, and only then at the king's command, as he was ordered to partner the king's latest favorite in a dance. Mary planned to refuse all other offers to dance, as she'd denied both Tristram and Jamie. She was content to wait for Gideon and watch him move through the steps of the dance with the simpering lady, but she never had a chance to turn down even one more courtier. Because she looked up to find the king at her side, and a circle cleared around them, because the king wished to speak to her alone.

Then it was as if they stood alone in the room. The music continued to play, the dancers moved to it, but all the onlookers about them fell silent. The courtiers and ladies stared and goggled, expectant—when the king signed for a quiet word alone with any woman, it might be the beginning of something new and note-worthy—for more than mere gossip. A king's whore was a matter of amusement, but any whore could become his mistress. A king's mistress had money and power and might even bring forth another king one day.

This woman Charles drew apart with was Hawkes's

current mistress; engaging enough, with lustrous eyes and hair and a roguish smile. Still, compared to the great beauties at court, only an ordinary little thing, but there must have been something to her—Hawkes's —after all. Tristram grew solemn as he gazed at them, and Jamie, even whiter-faced, pulled at his lip distractedly as he stood apart and watched. Gideon kept his feet to the music and his clear unblinking stare on the meeting between his king and his mistress.

And the king stood looking down at her, studying her with that teasing, tempting smile of appraisal that so many of the ladies were familiar with, and the others longed for. Too far from the others to be heard, too close for the others to overhear, the king had a private word with Mistress Mary Monk.

It might have been that he wondered if she had some sort of hold over his good friend Gideon. It could have been that he saw something in Gideon's eyes that intrigued him when he spoke of the girl, or had heard something Gideon did not say. He was definitely curious about this small, lively woman. He might be seeking to help Gideon; he was undoubtedly Gideon's friend. He might be testing to see if this woman was worthy of his friend. It might simply have been that he wished to know more about Gideon's mistress, firsthand. But he was also obsessed by women, a famous collector of them, a man who found his greatest pleasures in their company, both social and intimate. He was Gideon's friend, but he was also a man, and his king.

"Mistress Monk," he said, his slow and charming smile growing, his dark eyes so boldly appreciative of her that she felt as though he'd touched more than her hand when she rose from her low curtsy, "I'm mighty glad to see you again. Is that rogue Hawkes being kind to you? Or shall I take him to task for neglect? We've not seen you often enough here, you know."

"I'm happy to be here, sire," Mary said softly,

lowering her lashes over her eyes, not in flirtation, but in defense, because she felt invaded—this man, her king, saw too much and tried to see more—"whenever Gideon thinks to bring me here."

"Ah," Charles replied, "but that might be a problem in the near future, I fear. I'm sending him on an errand. To Kent, to a place called Ivyclose."

He saw her grow rigid, he saw her smooth complexion, as softly dark as the blush on a russet apple, blanch and grow green; he actually saw her waver as she stood before him. And because he was a man of complicated desires, it might have been either pity or desire she heard in his deep voice when he spoke again.

"But that needn't stop you, Mistress Mary. I'd be happy to have you come to our festivities as my guest, in his absence."

He might have been attempting to free Gideon to pursue his appointed course without difficulties. He might have thought to set a trap for her, or he might have sincerely felt pity for her loneliness; he might, incredibly enough, actually mean to seduce her. It didn't matter to Mary. She neither knew nor cared, after the king's first pronouncement. Gideon was going away again; perhaps this time he wouldn't return. She needed time to think.

But her king, the king of all England, was waiting for her answer. She was as amused by that as she was pained by any of the reasons for it that she could think of at that moment. And as she was no fool, even then, even when she was so distracted, she could think of several.

"Thank you, sire," she said, and then daring to look up, looked at him directly, as few women, even those he spoke to at close quarters, ever did. She let him see her rueful knowledge, and then said quietly, "But I think I'll wait for Gideon's return."

"So faithful?" he asked, continuing to play at his

own game, and it might even have been that he no longer knew just what it was, he was so diverted by this odd, plain, and plainly appealing little woman with her great dark, hurt eyes. "Is there no inducement I can offer you, then?"

"Sire," she said, and paused only a heartbeat as she decided what she must say. She was a cobbler's daughter, and knew very well what haggling was, and knew that in such transactions only plain dealing would serve a potential customer, king or not. She smiled with obvious regret, and dared to speak, only because she knew she must.

"You can offer any woman in the land anything she'd want, your Majesty," she said sincerely. "You're both kind and handsome, clever and good. You yourself are all any woman could want—except only for one thing: Gideon Hawkes. And that's all I want. It's my misfortune, I know," she added, looking down at last, as she saw the sense of what she said reach him, and startlement and something else spring to his eyes.

He sighed, then laughed, then took her hand in his and brought it to his lips while all the court stared in curiosity and envy.

"No," Charles said, smiling, truly, at last, "it is my misfortune, Mistress Mary."

He stood and spoke with her a few more minutes, until the dance was done and Gideon returned swiftly to her side. The two men looked over Mary's head at each other for a moment. But there was nothing to be seen in the king's face but his usual calm, sardonic amusement, and Gideon's countenance was as cold and implacable as ever—although his jaw was set and his cheek did tense and shiver once.

The king moved on, Jamie and Tristram relaxed, the court found or invented other scandals to amuse them. The night at court wore on as nights there always did, and after another hour had passed, Gideon Hawkes bid his friends and his king a farewell. He took his mistress, whom he'd never let leave his side, and they left Whitehall Palace for the night.

"I had only a moment alone with him. But I understand you did him the favor you discussed with us, Majesty?" Tristram Jones asked as Charles watched the red-haired Cavalier and his petite dark-haired mistress leave the room.

"Oh. My scheme about the manor? To reward him, and to make him more acceptable to the lady at Ivyclose? Yes, I did," Charles said absently, before he turned to smile sadly at Tristram. "But 'favor'?" he added thoughtfully. "I wonder. . . ."

# 18

That night marked the second time she refused him intimacies. Mary pleaded weariness because she couldn't plead confusion, for it was a combination of fear and anger she felt. And yet, again, Gideon didn't seem to mind. Instead, he seemed amused, and appeared pleased to only lie beside her in the dark and chuckle over her account of her meeting with the king. It was as well that they couldn't see each others' faces. He'd not have been able to pretend to such amusement. She'd never have been able to play at being so unconcerned.

"He's said to be a gentle, expert lover. As generous with his favors as he is with his favor. And well-endowed for both. Foolish maid," he said fondly.

"You wanted me to go with him?" she asked, sounding lighthearted enough.

"I'd have killed you," he answered in such a toneless voice she didn't know if he joked or not. Nor did she want to.

"Not him?" she asked instead.

"I'm not treasonous. Only possessive. And he's stronger. Or at least he's got an army at his side. I've only you. Although, at that," Gideon said with unmistakable laughter in his voice, "that might be enough, my fierce Mary."

"But you're going away tomorrow," she said in as uninflected a voice as he'd used before. She learned very quickly.

"As I said, I'm not treasonous," he answered quietly, sobered again.

They each waited for the other to speak. When the silence had gone on so long he wondered if she'd stopped breathing, he added reluctantly, because he'd the oddest fear that if he spoke too much, he'd say far too much that he didn't want to hear, "You will go see Doctor Scarborough? This nibbling at this and picking at that is unlike you. I don't care how amusing Dr. Russell's zany is, or how good your maid says 'Effectual Pills' are, stay away from physick peddlers. It's no small thing to be seen by the king's physician. Do you hear? I told Charles you'd go to Scarborough."

"I will," she said softly, "and if I've something catching, I'll be gone from here before you come back, don't worry."

Her simple statement shattered the calm. He sat up in one swift movement and swung toward her, and, stiff-armed, held himself up over her, his face near to hers, his wings of hair a curtain over them, so she couldn't look or move away from him. She felt his bottled rage in his harsh tones, as well as in the tension in his body.

"That is *not* why. You know that," he said in a voice like a snarl.

But total despair gave her courage.

"Do I?" she asked.

"I'm going on the king's command," he said. "I'll be back."

"And forth," she said in a sad little singsong. "And back, and forth."

He lowered himself to his elbows so that his body grazed against hers; he loosed his hard grip on the

sheets and held her face gently in his hands instead.
Such a little, delicate skull to hold such cleverness, he
thought as he let his lips only lightly touch hers.

"Mary," he whispered, "ah, Mary. What are we
doing to each other?"

But then her arms went around his back so that she
wouldn't have to answer, and then soon enough an
answer was unnecessary. Because what they were doing
with each other was plain, and easy enough to see—if
they had dared to open their eyes, instead of only
feeling all they dared not say.

Gideon left in the late morning, after lingering a
long while with Mary, and it seemed to her—it could
have been, she thought, from the way he kissed her
and then kissed her yet again—it just might have been
that he regretted leaving. Yes, just like a man regrets
gaining a fortune . . . just like any man would hate to
leave a poor plain London whore in order to court a
fine lady in the fine house he dreams of every night—
just so, she reminded herself with disgust when she
realized what she was imagining. Because pleasant as
dreaming was, she had to deal in facts. She always had
done so, and had to even more now. Indeed, that was
the only reason why she was going to see the physician
Gideon had ordered her to on the very day that he'd
left her. The fact was that she was ill, and frightened
because of it.

She took Betty with her, and her footman to guide
them, and dressed as respectably as she knew how.
Because if her employment didn't shame her enough,
her illness did. The sick died, or at least, usually did,
and her health was the one thing she'd managed to
save from the ashes of her former life. Yet it seemed
that now that her life was easier, her health failed her.

She'd wonderful foods to eat whenever she chose
now, but she chose not to, because even her favorite
dishes tasted odd, and off, these days. She'd a fine bed

to sleep on, but found herself drowsing as she sat on hard chairs, even after hours of sleep. And for all the tonics she took, she couldn't rid herself of her omnipresent queasiness, and the merest bite of dinner she took gave her heartburnings for hours after.

It wasn't plague; she knew that sickness all too well. And it wasn't the smallpox, nor any fatal disease to do with running bowels or festering sores, or she'd not have let Gidcon near her—she hadn't been joking about that. But something was sapping her strength and she was very much afraid as she approached the doctors' residence at Whitchall. In truth, she'd have preferred visiting one of the doctors who gave out handbills or free shows in the streets near to home. She'd have been content to buy the pills and elixirs they claimed cured everything. If she had something bad, no doctor could cure her; she knew that. But it was good to believe, if only for a little while, otherwise.

Still, it was an honor to go to the king's own doctor, and more important, Gideon had insisted. So even though she doubted he could heal her, she knew fear couldn't, and so she took a deep breath and went to consult with the learned physician.

It didn't take long at all.

He listened to her words, and then her heart. He looked into her eyes and at her body. He wasn't unkind or abrupt, but even so, it took no time at all to tell her about her complaint. He gave her some powders, and advice, along with his opinion, and told her not to hesitate to return to him again. She thanked him, and the more prettily when he refused payment, and walked home with her maid and her footman, her face entirely calm, and her heart entirely numbed.

And only when she got home again, and was alone again, did she weep.

No, she thought, and "No, no," she sobbed aloud as she lay upon her bed and grieved. But after a time she recalled herself, remembering that weeping did nothing but drain her and was a luxury she could never afford. Then she got up, washed her face, and sat at the window in the last of the light, to think. She'd learned to read, she'd learned to write, she'd learned to act a lady. She'd come a long way, and refused to give up now, just because her body played her false—or at least, just like her heart, had been truer to Gideon than to her own self.

She bore a child within her. She ought to have known; maybe she had, but denied it because she couldn't face it. It was no disease, but just as inevitable to her total ruin. For it was Gideon's child that robbed her of her appetite and her vigor and would in time steal away her hope for the future as well as all her delusions about herself. And Gideon was gone to Ivyclose, on the king's orders as well as on the prodding of his own will, so as to court and wed the lady of his dreams.

As the light died, Mary sat up straight, and thought long and hard. She let her mind stray down along dangerous paths as it explored complex schemes. She'd never drifted with fate, but always struggled against it, and would until she'd no strength left. So she'd been trained to do, and so she was resolved to go on.

No, and no again, she thought, shaking her head in stubborn denial of destiny. It was time to be even braver than she'd been the night she'd first sold herself to Gideon. She had to be. Fate had dealt cruelly with her again. And she would not have it.

There were no leaves on the trees, no beautiful prospects before him; for all the bracing air, it was bleak winter and there was no reason to linger to survey the countryside. But it wasn't the landscape that made Gideon ride so slowly as he made his way back to Ivyclose on this last and most important trip back home again. His pace might be slow, but his mind was so active he'd not have noticed if the land were draped in blossoms and filled with springtime.

Kings, however kind or thoughtful, could be as irrational as they were powerful, but it wasn't Charles's fury Gideon dreaded as he thought of what he had to achieve in the time before him. He had to achieve it, not for the whim of a king, but for his own sake. It would be an embarrassment to admit defeat to Charles, and unpleasant to lose his respect, to be sure. But it would be tragedy for himself if he lost Ivyclose when it was so nearly in his grasp again. Charles decreed this courtship now, and Gideon's own heart yearned for its resolution. And yet he traveled on at a snails' pace, lost in thought.

This time his offer must be made cleverly. This time he must gauge the moment and seize it when it came. This wasn't the time to let his love for Ivyclose close his eyes to the lady of Ivyclose's needs and expectations. He'd told her he'd never return, but neither of them had believed it then. It would be true this time. He'd never beg or plead for her favor or her hand, no more than he'd ever grovel in order to save his own life, if it came to that. If she refused him, he'd leave, and forever. He'd left Rountree at the inn in the village; he'd not even taken a change of clothes with him. He wasn't leaving himself any exit from his own decision.

This time he'd try to win her with all his resources. He'd use guile and cunning. He'd watch and wait and be alive to her every mood and utterance, not attending to her as a beautiful woman he desired, but approaching her with all the care and caution he'd pay to a dangerous enemy. It was as though he were on the eve of battle again; he planned and plotted all the way down the long road east, and lay abed in the silent nights shaping his schemes.

Never once did he permit himself to think of what he'd left behind him. No man could advance while looking backward. So he often told himself, angry at himself, in those long nights as the days grew shorter and his goal grew nearer.

So he was as weary as if he'd ridden at breakneck speed when he finally turned onto the familiar road again. And although it was only late afternoon as he gazed down at the home he'd traveled so far to see, and he'd a fine speech prepared for Celeste, he found he longed for nothing so much as his bed now. His own bed at Ivyclose.

It wasn't really so strange, he thought, as a small irrepressible smile, the first he'd worn since he'd left London, crossed over his face. In the years of his wanderings, he'd slept at inns, and in rented rooms, in castles and sties and barns. He'd had almost as many beds as days passed in his exile. He'd rocked to sleep on ships at sea, and laid himself down to rest on the bare hard bones of the earth. Sometimes, after hard days, if sleep hadn't overtaken him where he stood—or leaned, or sat—he'd stumbled to his makeshift beds, lying down to sleep as though death had overtaken him. Other times, after arduous nights, he'd slept in beds made of down, made up with silk, next to silken ladies in their foreign palaces. Wherever he'd taken his rest, he'd slept as hard as he'd lived. But never so soft, so easy, and so dreamlessly as he did each time he'd returned to Ivyclose—no, not since he'd been a small boy.

Yet each time he'd visited, he left his bed early; he'd bounded up in the mornings, eager to live out his sweetest dreams. Now he sat his horse on a rise over Ivyclose and wondered what sort of man he'd have been if he'd never had to leave it. And began to wonder what sort he'd be if he had to leave it forever now. But this was no time for wondering.

The tall, hard-faced man that sat so silently looking over the rambling old manor beneath him let his smile fade and kneed his horse forward. He'd work to do. No matter how weary, he was determined. He'd promised himself that he'd never pass a night beneath the roof of Ivyclose again until he had his answer of his lady. He was compelled by more than the command of his king and far more than his own desire to regain his home. From the moment he'd left London he'd been in a fever to get the thing settled, over and done with. And at last the time was now.

Her brother was still in London, deliberately so, he'd told Gideon, on a desperately coy wink, so as not to impede this courtship. But when Gideon was shown into Ivyclose, and into the main salon, he found she was not alone.

The solemn, dark-haired, and plainly dressed man stared as hard at Gideon as Gideon stared back at him, as Celeste introduced them to each other.

"My near neighbor and old friend, John Wentworth," she said merrily, "I'm pleased to present to you my far neighbor, and new friend Gideon Hawkes," she said on a radiant smile.

But it was wonderful; she couldn't help thinking that. Gideon was back, returned, as she'd thought he'd be, despite what he'd said. And here was John staring at him as though he really was the devil incarnate. Celeste had never been a flirt at court, here or in France. She'd never played one gallant against another as the coquettes at court delighted to do. But she was, for all her piety, a human female, and couldn't help but be thrilled that these two strong young males obviously distrusted each other because they both wanted her. She might regret her pride later, and worry if there'd been lust and greed in it as well. But now, looking from one stern masculine face to the other, as the two men stared hard at each other, she exulted. It was as simple as that.

The two men nodded gravely, and continued to take each other's measure: John noting Gideon's aloofness and the elegance of his clothes with distaste, as he confirmed his estimate of the royalist before him; Gideon noting how at ease this strange man had been in this house until he'd entered it, wondering if he'd plans for winning it out from under him. They looked at each other in silence, until John Wentworth remembered the time and his place and bowed to Gideon and Celeste.

"I'll take my leave now," he said, "and return when I've further news of the parish . . . if I may?" he asked Celeste.

"You're always welcome here, John," she answered calmly, and he nodded once, and gave Gideon Hawkes one more comprehensive glance before he left them alone.

She lowered her gaze and walked to the window after John Wentworth left, and waited for Gideon to ask what her visitor's purpose had been. There'd been such tension in the air, she doubted he'd take John's visit as a commonplace. But the moments dragged on, and Gideon said nothing. Celeste surprised herself when she began to speak.

"He's a very old friend, indeed. I knew him before I left for France. He's of my church. He went to America and lost his wife and their babe there, and has returned to build himself a new life. . . . I . . . I'm pleased to see you again, Gideon," she said when she realized that she'd been speaking into a long silence.

"I'm pleased to be here, lady," he said.

She didn't mention his lapse—his promise not to return; she was a lady, as well as a woman who knew the grace of forgiveness. And as a lady, she knew how to say the right thing, in the proper tone of voice.

"And why have you come here now, Gideon," she asked, and turned to him and raised her eyes at last, as she added in the lilting, teasing tones she'd learned at court, the ones she'd never used with John, "when all the sport and play is in London?"

He knew this game as well as she did, and if it was what she required, he'd no objection.

"Prodigies have been seen in the sky, lady," he said, "There were gusts, and storms, and hail the size of hens' eggs this autumn. There was even a comet, I hear, though the smoke of London hid it from me—and this after plague and fire. Something rare and wondrous surely comes, lady. The wedding of a Puritan and a royalist, do you think?"

She stared at him. This was more than she'd expected, and came sooner than she'd thought. It was court speech—teasing wordplay with the truth embedded deep in it. He stood before her, as tall and real and vital as she'd remembered him, back beneath her roof again, as she'd dreamed of him, and with the words upon his lips she'd prayed to hear from him. But there was only watchfulness in his ice-bright eyes, and nothing of the abject lover in his tones, and no emotion but keen interest on that hard face. It was very well done, and pleased her. It was as straightforward and honest a proposal as she'd expect from a Puritan like John, all couched in the language she'd expect from a courtier like Gideon. But still, something lacked. He'd said no word of repentance. He'd promised no future virtue. There was no dedication, no humility, in either his words or tone.

" 'This is amazingly sudden, good sir?' " he said in a lightly mocking voice when she didn't answer.

"No," she said slowly, "it isn't—only I don't know yet. Wedlock is forever, Gideon."

"But I haven't got forever to wait for your answer," he said. "Only today. If you don't know now, Celeste, you never will."

"I need time," she said, glancing away from him again.

She didn't. She wanted him now. Every instinct she possessed clamored for her to nod her head, or smile, or step forward into his arms. But her conscience insisted on a sign from him, some gesture to show that it was he who had bent to her will—not because of her pride, she reminded herself, but for the sake of his redemption. Because she knew he could only begin to walk the road to salvation if he first admitted error. She waited.

He gazed at her without speaking. She was all in blue today, blue touched with simple white. Her gown was cut low for the lady of Ivyclose, high for a lady at court, but still it showed the pale skin at her breast, and the long bodice showed her grace and slimness. Her gleaming honeyed hair was not so bright as it had seemed in the summer sun, but it glowed even in the weak winter light. Her eyes were transparently blue, her white brow smooth and clear; there were no beauty marks to distract from her purity. She stood poised and inviolate and lovely—the living spirit of Ivyclose—in her person almost as appealing to him, and just as remote and elusive to him now. A wrong word and all would be lost, a right one and all he'd ever wanted to have would be his.

He walked to her side and took her hand in his.

"What is it that you need time for, Celeste?"

She couldn't answer, and so didn't. Then he thought he knew what she waited for. And he was right, and only wrong because she hadn't known it as well as he did. He took her lightly in his arms, and lightly, gently placed his lips on hers. Although she didn't respond, she didn't struggle or move away, and so he gathered her closer and took her mouth in a deeper kiss, thinking all the while of what this was that he held so close, close enough to almost possess. And then she pulled away.

"Gideon, please," she said.

He stepped back, cool and unruffled, not surprised, or even outwardly distressed.

"Please what?" he asked.

"Lady . . ." he said when she only averted her head. "Lady," he said on an exasperated sigh, "Charles wants this union, and he wants it now. He sees in it—in us—a mating of all opposing elements, a healing. He sent me here."

He frowned. He wasn't so annoyed with her as he was with himself. Because for all his plotting, he was being uncommonly iron-tongued and stilted, and though he knew it, couldn't seem to help it. In the weeks they'd been apart, it seemed he'd lost his easy sense of communion with her. He was brusque where he should have been teasing, and mocking instead of cajoling. It might have been the importance of his mission that made him inept, but he'd never been so clumsy in any emergency before. He swore at himself. But this time it was he who was wrong, for she liked his plain speaking very much and knew how to deal with it far better than his lovemaking.

"I see," she said, and gazed at him consideringly, while all the time her mind worked feverishly and her heart rejoiced. She'd missed his forceful spirit in all these weeks, wondering if he'd ever return; she'd missed that unusual, stern face, and now rediscovered how much she appreciated the tensile strength and control in those arms that had just held her. Still, she needed him to repent his ways, or at least to say he did, and it seemed he might never do so. If he couldn't bring her the words, she couldn't bring herself to accept him. But she could force them to the front—she had to try.

"The whims of kings have never moved my people," she said slowly, before she turned her mild blue eyes to him and asked, with the first sign of conscious desire he'd ever had from her, "There's a more important matter to me. Can I trust you, Gideon Hawkes? Oh, not in managing my estate, not in caring for Ivyclose, but in your managing of my future, and my heart. I'm no longer so religious, but I have my religion, and it means much to me."

But she'd forgotten that he'd never thought of Ivyclose as really hers, and those were the words he answered first, for they'd stung the most.

"Charles has given me another estate," he said coolly, "in recompense. In the West Country. A title comes with it," he added dismissively. "He wanted me to come to you on equal terms, I think. But I think he overdid it," he said on a gruff laugh, before he went on, "I'll never harm you, Celeste. No man can do more than promise that. Trust is as much a part of wedlock as the wedding service, but I'll try to do more than promise."

It was a strange, cold proposal, and it bothered him, but she nodded, and her heart rose.

"I believe you will," she said. "I do believe you will."

He took her back in his arms then, because it seemed the only thing to do; he was generally a quick-thinking man, but now he was at a loss. He was momentarily numbed, astonished; he'd come prepared for all things but this. He hadn't thought it would be so simple, he hadn't really believed it could happen, he couldn't believe it was done. Musing, amazed, he put his lips on hers again, but then only held her close against his heart. Something pinched there, and he put her aside for a moment so that he could reach into his shirt. He pulled up a fine gold chain that he'd forgotten he'd hung about his neck that morning before coming here, and grew a crooked smile when he remembered what ploy it was to fit. He no longer needed it. It was the ornate key to what he'd told her was the hidden room at Ivyclose. Then he took her back into his embrace, and, feeling the curved length of her against him, he remembered her, and bent his head to whisper in her ear, "Now name the day, Celeste, and then, together, we can search out what I promised you."

The vibrations of his deep voice in her inmost ear disturbed her as much as the strong body pressed so close to her own did. That unease gave her a second's respite from the frighteningly strong lure of him, and reminded her of a promise he could make and keep, before they were wed.

"There's one thing more," she said into his blazing

hair, her lips near to his ear. "I can't know what you do when you go to London, Gideon. When we're wed, I must trust you, as you say. But you said you'd no longer live with that . . . harlot . . . in London. And so, my brother says, you do not. But you're still seen with her everywhere, he says. It can't go on. You can't live with her, or amuse yourself with her anymore, it's all the same. I'm wise enough to know you don't have to sleep all night in her bed to please yourself there. You must give her up entirely before you walk to the altar with me—as a boy puts away his toys when he comes to manhood, as a minister must put all sin away from his mind before he speaks before the congregation. Put her aside for all time, Gideon, and I'll be yours whenever you say.

"That's not unreasonable," she said as she felt his long frame tense and grow still.

"No," he said, "no, it's not. But I won't."

She backed a pace away from him as he dropped his arms from her, and for once, all his cold watchfulness fell away as well. Now he wasn't the proud Cavalier, the forceful self-assured man that had beguiled and terrified her. Now he was showing her what she'd always wanted to see, the real man she'd known was there. His face became pale and strained, there was grief and confusion as well as anger there. But the anger was at himself, because he knew his words had been as graceless as they'd been unavoidable, and he knew to the finest detail just how much he was giving away as he spoke them.

"I won't put her aside. I can't. And I don't wish to. I believe she carries my child, Celeste. And I'd never forsake her. I might be able to promise you that I'd never take up with another woman, and might well keep to that. I've no more wish to give you an excuse to cuckold me, in time, than I've any wish to hurt you. But I won't abandon Mary Monk. I couldn't, and won't."

He waited, feet braced apart, for her to dismiss him. Yet his only thought just then was a wildly irrational one: he looked over her shoulder and thought that now he'd never be able to remove the green covers from the two old chairs by the fireside, so as to restore them to the gold embroidery they'd worn before he'd left them, years before. So he was as unready for her answer as he was unprepared for his reaction to it.

"Oh, Gideon," Celeste said, with every evidence of love and warmth that he'd never seen in her before, as she stepped back close to him and smiled. "How good," she said, her eyes alight. "How kind and fine. I understand. I do. How could I not, given my upbringing? Don't worry," she laughed up into his astonished eyes, "don't despair, I understand, and know that a man who admits his mistakes and is willing to live with them is a virtuous man. To see to your bastard child is honorable, to right a wrong you'd done to a poor wretched girl in the days of your heedlessness is more than charitable, it is just!" she said with a thrill in her voice as she rested one cool hand lightly against his cheek where she'd seen it quiver, though all his face remained still. "I knew you were capable of such. You're no common courtier, Gideon Hawkes, I always knew it," she exulted. "I will marry you now."

She wasn't mocking him. And he was as staggered by this as he was by the way his heart grew cold even as he sought the warm lips she offered him.

# 19

Gideon stood in the center of his lost home, in the heart of Ivyclose itself, and held the mistress of it to his breast, and kissed her lips, and knew that he'd never have to leave again. Her mouth was willing, if untutored, her body relaxed against his, everything in her aspect and response welcomed him. And he believed none of it.

He'd never been so distant from his own body, even with the lowest whore he'd bought in drunken desperation, as he was with this woman who'd just promised to be his wife. Because he felt nothing that his body was automatically doing, he was so busily wondering what he'd done right to make everything turn out the way he'd always dreamed and never expected that it would. He hadn't even time yet to be surprised at his lack of passion, or rather, at his passion's lack of conviction.

It was Celeste who stopped the moment by simply placing one hand over his mouth after she drew her own away from it. She smiled up at him dreamily, all her potential for sensuality realized in that one lazy moment when she was supremely in charge of herself and him. Her eyes were half-shuttered over her inner pleasure, her mouth was parted to speak, she'd shed

369

every constraint—she was in that rare moment the woman she might have been had fate not uprooted her, changed her life, and brought her to Ivyclose.

She loved him entirely then. With his guilt acknowledged, confessed, and so obviously bitterly regretted, he became a man of a manageable shape she could fit into her heart. His admitted crime of unbridled passion redeemed him even as it marred him. No longer the perfect Cavalier or the abused boy whose past and future had been ruined by his father and her people, now he was a man grown, a man who'd sinned. By forgiving him that, by being virtuous enough to accept him in the full flower of his sin, she could make him see the extent of it, she could steer him to salvation. Such a passionate spirit could be turned to the service of the Lord; his humility was the key. In offering to redeem himself, in acknowledging and taking responsibility for the poor lost little soul he'd engendered in his whore, he'd already set his foot on that long road.

Now, with the full knowledge of his guilt hanging heavy over their union to outweigh the prideful, blatantly sexual side of him, there was balance. She could allow herself to have him, at last.

Now his embrace didn't suffocate her, trap her, or frighten her. Now his mouth and hands and body were things she could deal with, and, laughing low in her throat, she offered up her mouth to him again in the kiss of peace and gave herself to the embrace of those promised to each other for eternity. She didn't know, she had no way to know, that it wasn't his contrition, but his distraction and confusion that lessened the impact of his lovemaking now.

But her mouth was warm and her soft arms held him to her. And the scent of her hair was of soap, and the texture of her skin was satin. The breasts so close against his chest were aroused, and the curving waist and bottom his hands roved over were the shape and texture of the source of all his anonymous comforts for all those lost years. His body recognized this long before he did, for he was still wandering somewhere far from her, trying to understand what he'd done, what this meant they must do, and why he was loath to do it. But he'd never needed his mind to fulfill the demands of his body.

He kissed her and held her and began to uncover her body, still dazed by his turn of fortunes, all the while telling himself that it was Ivyclose he was being permitted entry to, at last. He was enough of a skilled lover to do all he did deftly, without thinking. So it was never his roughness, or haste, or selfishness that frightened her. He eased her gown down, and nibbled at the corners of her lips before he opened them with his mouth. He was all grace and style, if not heart, as his hands learned her. He was entirely gentle and restrained as he carried their embrace beyond her promise, beyond what she'd been willing to give, beyond what she'd ever guessed she might have to give to him.

Still, it was only her breasts bared to him, and only her mouth invaded by his tongue, and merely his hands roving over her naked skin, only a few moments passed absently, unthinkingly, for him. But the moment she felt herself slipping away from thought in his clasp, easing away from what she'd envisioned, going beyond herself, despite herself, it was too far and too much. And not simply too soon, because it would always be too much for her.

The rapture of her spiritual surrender was doomed to ruin by her physical one. Three things happening all at once called her back from the abyss she'd drifted toward in his arms, unknowing—and in that moment, the first such moment of her life—uncaring. The rough hot surface of his tongue against her own surprised her. The key that hung from his neck stabbed into her tender breast and pained her. And these small discomforts made her aware of what the sudden growing

bulky pressure that rose and strove against her stomach
was. And that terrified her.

"No, no!" she cried, alarmed, awakened, pulling
away, sobbing with the effort and the realization of
her great shame.

"Gideon! No," she pleaded, cringing away from
him as he released her and stared down at her as
though he'd just seen her. And with her hair disor-
dered, her clothes awry, her lips red from his kisses,
the perfection of the smooth skin of one white breast
accentuated by the imprint of his chain and key that
had been pressed into it—he did see her as if for the
first time. And knew his first real surge of pure lust for
her in that second, even as he stepped away.

Her hand went up over her breast as she saw him
looking at it, her eyes averted as she saw the cold fire
glowing in his. They neither of them spoke as she
turned aside and righted her gown, nor did they speak
at once when she faced him again, her gown, her hair,
and all but her smile in place again.

"You go too fast, Gideon," she said in a quavering
voice. "We're not wed yet."

"No," he said sadly, a world of sorrow in his voice,
"we're not."

"You must give me time," she said with more of her
usual reason in her tones. She breathed deeply, and
drew herself up and together again, before she laughed.
"Indeed, Gideon, you go fast enough to please Charles
Stuart, but not me. Still, in time, when we know each
other better, we'll match in our passions as well as our
thoughts," she went on, trying to reassure him, to
tease him out of the great weariness and disappointment she saw on his face. "My religion allows love—it
just doesn't allow it outside of marriage. It will be
better in time, you'll see."

"No," he said quietly, looking down at her as if
from a great distance, shaking his head so that the soft
straight bright strands of hair that she'd dared to touch

swung gently around his face, "no, Celeste, my lady, no, I won't. We've no more time. It's all run out while we stood still."

He smiled and shrugged.

"You, in your wisdom," he said softly, "knew it all the while. 'No,' you said, and 'no' again. Yes, you were right. I withdraw my proposal, I never heard your answer—consider it unsaid, as it would've been if you'd understood. I do now. We won't suit, you and I. Had we all the time in creation, I don't think we could. And now we've none left in which to try."

"It's more than your being a Puritan, less than my being a Cavalier," he said sadly. "It's beyond that. I'm too in love with fire, lady, you're too pleased by ice. We wouldn't heal the rift. No, we'd nullify each other in time. If I melted you, you'd feel weak as water; if you froze me, I'd as surely die too. We'd be less than we are, and we both of us are right—for ourselves— as we are. The ancients said the universe consists of four elements, which cannot mix, but must exist. So it is with us. I respect and appreciate you . . . it well may be that I love you," he said, gazing at her with his sad smile in place, "but for all the love I bear my king and country, still I shouldn't wed you. And for the love of your soul and mine, lady, I'll not."

"Because of a kiss?" she asked, amazed, too astonished to be hurt or shy.

"Because of all of them I'd need, in part, yes," he said.

"Say rather, Gideon Hawkes," she said, understanding coming to her like a slap, along with the sting of his rejection, " 'because of how I need my whores in London'!"

Then she paused, and stared at him, aghast. Her hand flew to her lips, because just as she couldn't yet conceive of how she'd let him use them, she couldn't believe how she'd just abused them herself by allowing such a terrible thing to escape them.

"Because of how I need my . . ." He paused, and this time she clearly saw how his jaw clenched and his left cheek convulsed with a tremor, before he closed his eyes as if at prayer, and then opened them to show her the pain within them as he admitted, ". . . my whore—it's singular, as she is—in London, yes, lady."

"I'm sorry," Celeste said, but he took her hand in his and held it as he interrupted, "No, I am."

"Hard words have been spoken, Gideon," she said after a moment. "Sometimes they're needed to clear the air. Sit with me, dine with me, stay the evening, and rest after your hard journey. It will all come clear then. I'm willing to forget all that's been said," she told him.

He shook his head.

"Thank you," he said, "but it's all that's been unsaid that I wouldn't hear before, that I'd remember now. I'll go now, before dark, I've a long journey before me."

"You'll give up your right to Ivyclose?" she asked.

"So I do," he said softly, wonderingly, gazing around the room as if he could see it clear in the softened early winter's night that was falling over them.

"And go against Charles Stuart's expressed wishes?" she asked.

"If a Puritan can think to thwart a king, his friend can surely do the same," he answered, his teeth showing in a white smile in the dim light.

"And what of the secret room here at Ivyclose? The one you were going to show me? With the key you always wear about your neck? What of all the glittering treasures that lie within, known only to the owner of Ivyclose? I'm the owner of Ivyclose. Aren't you going to stay and show me?" she asked, putting her head to the side, smiling quizzically now, almost amused by whatever game he was playing, now that she'd realized that he was. But she could play at games too.

"Celeste," he said seriously, "that was the only

untruth I ever told you. And at that," he said sadly, thoughtfully, "it wasn't."

She looked up at him, uncomprehending. The tall red-haired Cavalier and the slender honey-haired lady stood, linked by one hand, facing each other in a rapidly darkening room. Their eyes adjusted to the shadows just enough to permit them to read each other's most marked expressions. Hers was one of puzzlement and dawning unease. And his was one of deep regret.

"Celeste," he said softly, "the hidden room, the heart to Ivyclose—it lies within your keeping, not mine. It always has and will. I opened the door to it for you just now, just before. I showed you a hint of what could be found there for us, with me as your guide. You slammed the door shut fast. Now you'll have to discover it with another. The key to it is where I left it with you—imprinted on your heart," he said, and reached out one long finger to touch her breast. She shrank back before she could stop herself.

His hand dropped to his side immediately.

"I wish you joy. I wish you every happiness I couldn't bring to you. Cherish Ivyclose and bring it the laughter it always lacked. Good-bye, my lady," Gideon said as he took her hand and brushed it with his lips. "At least, remember me with kindness. I'll never forget you, you know."

And then he bowed. And then he was gone.

She sat by the window late into the night, waiting for his return. And watched the road the next day and the day after too. She never lost her smile. Not even when her brother arrived to celebrate, and hearing of Gideon's defection, paced the room instead, and stormed and shouted and cried out in rage at her, and Gideon Hawkes, and all the fates.

"He'll be back," she said, smiling.

"No, no," he said, grieving.

"That's what you said last time. And I was right,"

she said, all her faith in her prayers clear to see in her calm and confident face, in her small and secret smile.

"Not this time," he cried.

"He'll be back," she said.


He carried a book of poetry, but put it down unopened when she told him what she was doing.

"No, we won't need that today, Jamie," Mary said, "and not because I'm so learned—at least in my letters—that I don't need more help," she said ruefully, before she smiled again. But I'm going away," she told him. "I'm packing my things, and so right now I haven't any time for my lessons."

"Oh," Jamie said.

She saw how crestfallen he was, and quickly added, "But if I may borrow it? To study on my own? If it isn't an expensive volume—or your favorite, or anything?"

"Oh, yes. Oh, no," Jamie said, reddening in his confusion as he thrust the leather volume to her. "It isn't. Please take it and keep it, please do," he said, although it was both expensive and his favorite, which was why he'd brought it with him today.

"Then thank you," she said, holding the book to her breast, as he sighed and thought that it was true after all, a man could envy a book, just as a man had envied his beloved's gloves in a wonderful play he'd seen.

She missed his expression, because she was looking past him toward the door, and he'd righted it by the time she turned a questioning face to him.

"Tristram's not here?" she asked, puzzled, and then a little alarmed, because Tristram was always there when Jamie was.

"No, no, sick uncle, nothing terrible, just sick to his stomach," Jamie said, giving Tristram's invented uncle his own complaint. Because his stomach knotted up at the thought of her leaving just when he'd gotten up the courage to speak to her for himself, just after he'd been able to convince Tris to stay away so that he could. Tris hadn't liked it, but finally admitted his need to do it, and now that need would go unmet. There'd have been nothing sneaking or ugly about it; it was a fair and honest offer he'd have made, and if Gideon skewered him for it, there'd have been no help for it. A man had to do what he could. Now she was leaving, and now he knew he'd left it for too late, and now he wished someone would end his misery, after all.

But she was looking at him with such concern, he gave Tris's imaginary uncle a reprieve so as to erase that expression on her face, and said, "Ah, well, but he's old. And he may not die. Even if he does, Tris stands to inherit."

She giggled. He'd loved it when she did that. He'd his choice of court ladies and his pick of all the expensive whores in London, and yet he wanted none of them so much as he wanted Mary Monk. He'd been drawn to her from the moment he'd met her. But he'd always lived on the edge of infatuation; it was as normal a state to him as fulfillment was to other men. Because so soon as he had fulfillment, he found another woman to adore. This was different, he'd swear it. For one thing, it hadn't diminished, it had grown to an obsession. Everything he'd learned about her drew him more, until he felt they'd be removing a limb when she was gone from him, although he'd never had her, or dared touch even her sleeve. Not because he feared Gideon's slaying him half so much as he was afraid of angering her.

James Beauchamp, Lord Claverly, stood and gazed sadly at the woman before him. She was small, but then, he wasn't of any great height himself. She wasn't a beauty, but then, he knew his clothes were the first thing anyone ever saw of him when he walked into a room. He was titled and wealthy, but he always thought of his father as being the one with the title, and the money was so much a part of him and his life that he couldn't rejoice in it any more than he could imagine living without it. She was Gideon Hawkes's mistress, but she'd been a good and decent girl before that, and still was, despite it. She was strong, stronger than he was, he sensed. But then, most women were, and she, above all of them, never made him feel less than powerful and wise. She was perfect for him in everything, except that she belonged to another man.

He'd been about to try to change that today.

"When will Gideon be back? When are you leaving?" he asked, so as to have a nice hurt to nourish while she was gone. "When will you be back?" he added glumly, so that he knew the terms of his sentence.

"I don't know when Gideon's coming back," she said, turning aside as though she were looking for a place to put the book. "I'm leaving tomorrow morning, early. And I'm not coming back, Jamie. Not ever."

He heard the words but was so astonished he took a few seconds to review them before he dared speak again. And then, as usual, he thought with dismay, he said something wholly inadequate to express what he wanted to say.

"Why?" he asked.

"Because it's time," she said, "because Gideon's gone to Ivyclose and may even be marrying Celeste Southern right now—"

"Oh, no," Jamie interrupted her to say. "Charles wants to make a grand occasion of it, wedding in the church, bedding at Whitehall. He has great plans for the day."

He fell silent, realizing he'd said the wrong thing again, but for both their purposes this time.

"It doesn't matter," she said. "Maybe that makes it even better. I'd have to go sooner or later. It will be easier before he comes back. . . . And I know," she said quickly, turning to him before he spoke, so that he could see the tears in her great dark eyes, "that he might keep me on anyway, but I don't want to be kept on anyway. Do you see? So I'm going," she said briskly, sniffling and holding her head back up, as though she were trying to look down her short nose at him. "I have to say good-bye, Jamie. And thank you. Because it was your teaching that made it possible for me to go, and I'll never forget you for it."

"But where are you going?" he asked, because he knew he had to think slowly and carefully before he acted, and wanted all his facts together before he did.

"I can't tell you," she said. "You'd tell Gideon," she explained when he didn't speak. "You know you would, Jamie."

"Once," he said slowly, carefully, but distinctly, "once, I would've, you're right. Now, I won't. Because what I feel for you, Mary, is different from and even more important to me than what I feel for Gideon. I love you, Mary," he said, before he could make himself stop and think of a way to put it more prettily, "and I don't want you to go away, and I came here today to tell you that. Only I didn't know you were going away then, of course," he added.

But she found nothing silly in his speech, just as she never laughed at him, and that made him love her all the more as he waited for her answer. And she couldn't laugh at him, because he looked so very sincere, and was, she knew. Now she saw that he'd dressed with extraordinary care today; he wore his new wig, the one he usually wore to evenings at Whitehall, the one that was such a mass of curls that it did make him look as innocent and sweet as a spring lamb, as Tristram had once said. He wore his finest cape and waistcoat too, and his breeches fluttered with ribbons, as did his sleeves. His face was not the face of a boy he seemed when seen from up close, but he was an amiable-looking man, and a gentle one. And for all she'd seen him in the embrace of numerous women, she'd never thought of him as a man at all before this moment. It might have been that he suspected that, because he added, "I want to marry you, Mary Monk," after he saw her expression.

"I mean," he said, "what would be the point of my offering you a place as my mistress, when you've got a place as Gideon's? I have to offer you more. Something he can't. I don't care what you've been half so much as you seem to. I don't know any women who weren't something or other before I met them, and most of them will continue to be. But even if you don't love me, and I don't expect that you do, you'd never hurt me, I know that.

"I need a wife. My father's been after me for years. I'm much older than I look, you know. And we need an heir. My father will like you," he added quickly, "if that's what's bothering you. He'll like anyone who doesn't take advantage of me and who cares for me. Of course, you'd never cheat me, and I can make you care for me, in time, I think, because I'll be very good to you. I'd want you to live at our country seat, with our children and my father, and I thought you wouldn't mind, since you don't like court much anyway. I'll confess, I'd like to spend some time at court now and then. But you don't have to come with me. I . . . I won't promise to be faithful," he said quietly, "because I don't know if I can be. But I'll try—if you like."

She simply stood and stared at him.

"Ah!" he said, hitting the side of his fleecy wig with the palm of his hand. "I forgot. I want you because you're very sweet, and clever, and kind. And good to look at, and I'd like to make love to you too, and always have. Very much. Will you have me? Don't worry," he said as he saw her about to laugh, or cry, "Gideon won't kill either of us. You kill a man for trifling with your mistress—but I've never heard of a man killed for marrying her."

"Jamie," she said, shaking her head. "Jamie," she said again, drawing herself up straight. She wore a simple gown of a creamy color; it wasn't the best thing for her dark looks, because she seemed pale and uninteresting today. But that didn't change the fact that he wanted her; he knew she could look better. Still, for all it was drab, he admired the way the long tight bodice showed her neat little figure to good advantage, and pleased himself by studying her without concealment for once, as he waited for her answer.

"Jamie," she said, "I was going away to live in the countryside. I've saved up my money, and I've earned my clothes. That's all I'm taking with me. That, and my good little maid, Betty. She knows of a village—not far, not near—where I can live with economy. I'll make myself known as the Widow Mudge—well, it sounds like 'Monk,' so I won't have trouble answering to it. And I will. I can read, and I can write now. And I can act the lady. So when I have my baby, no one will talk. And so someday, maybe I can marry someone too. Well, even the king wanted me, once, if not to marry. Yes, I'm going to have a baby," she said, and turned her head then, and caught a broken breath.

He stared at that neat bodice that was turned to him in profile and stayed very still.

"Oh. Well, even better," he said.

She wheeled around to stare at him as though he'd run mad.

"We'll say it's mine," he said. "My father will be beside himself with happiness. We need an heir, you know. And I've never even spawned a bastard one that I know of. So it might be the best thing, after all, at that."

"Oh, Jamie," she said, and then she began crying, which made him feel much better. He knew what to do when women cried. He walked to her and then he took her in his arms and held her as she wept. He reveled in the feel of her little body next to his, even though he was completely like a brother to her then, even though she shook with sobs, not pleasure, against him. Too soon, she pulled away.

She ran her hand beneath her nose and sniffled and looked up to him with reddened eyes. She looked terrible, and then she looked up at him and giggled, and pleased him very much again.

"Oh, Jamie," she said, shaking her head, "your wig makes my nose itch," she laughed. But then she grew sober.

"Won't it be lovely for you?" she asked, holding her head to the side, "when you and I—a little dark woman and a medium blond man—produce a great big gangly red-headed baby? Well, not at once, but in time," she added, when she saw his expression. "Your father would have to be as blind as he's kind, to be delighted about that. No, thank you, Jamie, you're very good. But I'd never do that to you. Or to the baby. That's the only reason why I'm leaving, you know. I think Gideon would pay for the babe, and maybe even keep me on, but I won't make the babe pay for Gideon and me all his life. My baby won't ever be called a bastard," she said fiercely, as her hands curled into little fists, until she recovered herself and added on a smile, "unless he gets someone very angry."

Then she grew solemn as she said, "I wasn't brought up to live the way I live, but I couldn't help it. But neither will he be, and I can help that. Because he'll be the Widow Mudge's child, and not Hawkes's bastard—do you see?"

He did. He was not as witty as Tristram, or half so quick as Gideon. But in time, he did see, he always did, and sometimes saw even more. Or else they'd not have befriended him or valued him in the first place. They were too clever to need him as a fool; they were too wise to need a jester. She understood that when he spoke again.

"Then I'll take you to a smaller village—not near at all, and even further from here, but near to my estates. Because I want you safe. And where I can look after you. You'll have your baby, Mrs. Mudge. And then you'll marry me. I'll be the babe's adopted father, so he can be as red-headed and gangly as he pleases. I only hope that 'she' isn't, if it comes to that," he said on a small smile.

"And by then," he said very quietly, "you may be able to want me. I don't know if you'll ever love me as you do Gideon. But I don't expect it. I think I can bring you to love me as Jamie, and that will be all right with me."

This time she stayed in his arms until she was entirely done with crying.

"I'll make all the arrangements," he said before he left her. This time he was able to take leave of her without Tristram at his side urging him to go before he did something foolish. Because for all he still wanted her, and maybe wanted her even more now that he'd actually held her close, he knew he'd have her one day, and was willing to wait for that day. He was a man who cherished longing, after all, and unfulfilled longing for a woman was the hardest thing to find at Charles Stuart's pleasure-loving court. This was a new and wonderfully extended course of unfulfilled yearning he was embarked upon, and he was already savoring it.

"Pack your things, and prepare your maid," he said after he'd given her a brief, brotherly kiss upon the most innocent part of her anatomy he could think of—her forehead. But because he'd never kissed any woman there before, it thrilled him, and it took him a moment to recover before he added, "I'll send our instructions, and prepare for our trip. We can't leave tomorrow, but we will as soon as all's readied for you."

"I have to leave a note for Gideon," she said. "I won't tell him where I'm going. Or about the baby. Please don't tell him either. I know what I have to do. He's been kind to me—it's not his fault any more than it's mine. So I'll tell him why I'm leaving, aside from the baby, and tell him I've got a friend to look after me, to relieve his mind. It's only fair. Someday, if we have to, we may tell him the friend was you, but not now, please."

He paused with his hand on the door. He nodded.

"He'll understand," he said, then checked. "Don't forget to lean into your Y's" he cautioned her. "Sometimes they look too much like P's, you know."

"Oh, Jamie," she said, and she smiled as she wept when he left.

# 20

The traffic into London was congested, and every coach, cart, horseman, and person on foot going there seemed to be in the road in front of Gideon. There was a popular execution to be held today, no fewer than six villains to be topped, and everyone wanted to be there first in order to have the best view of the spectacle. Gideon only wanted to get to the palace in order to see if he'd be included in the show next week. Never a patient man, and aware that he was a formidable-looking one, he used that fact to his advantage now. His face clearly showed his willingness to hasten anyone in his way along the same road that the unfortunates they were going to see would be taking later. Crowded as it was, a path was cleared for him.

He might be hurrying to his own funeral, he thought wryly, although he really doubted Charles would send him to the block for disobeying an order to march to the altar. Charles disliked murdering to an almost unkingly degree. Even on his return, years before, he'd selfishly allowed the public only the pleasure of watching his chiefest enemies being publicly hanged, drawn and quartered, and treated to the joys of watching their own entrails burned before their dying eyes.

Because he'd pardoned, exiled, or ignored the rest. That wasn't to say that royally sanctioned death was a stranger to London Town.

Many heads still watched over London with sightless eyes. Cromwell himself, or that mummified skull that had once held Cromwell's clever brain in it, dug up and detached, still perched on the highest rafter of Westminster Hall—to warn, without words, of what came of disobedience to the crown, and show how even the mightiest were common flesh in death. But still the disappointed public noted, and loudly grieved, that there were fewer each year on display everywhere. True enough, Gideon thought; apart from his compassion, Charles Stuart, after all, was the very man to realize that dead men left live enemies to contend with. And he was, above all, in love with the pleasures to be had exploiting quick and lively bodies, and not interested in turning them, however entertainingly, into dead flesh.

But Gideon knew there were many ways a man could live and wish that he'd been cleanly killed instead. And knew one of the best ways to discover them was to defy a king, however congenial he was.

Making a good marriage wasn't much to ask of a loyal subject. Except, Gideon thought as he pointed Rountree toward his lodgings and told him to go on alone—deciding the situation called for him to ride straight to Whitehall instead of going home to change his travel-stained clothes first—except, of course, when that subject was a damnable fool. Fool enough, at least, to differ on the subject of what a good marriage was, and willing to be damned for his foolish convictions. Still, he thought as he rode up toward the jumble of buildings that was Whitehall Palace, he'd had no home to call his own before. If it came to that, he'd roamed the world with nothing in his pockets but his own two empty hands once before too. He could do it again—if they left him his hands, he thought as he gave his mount to an ostler in the courtyard. And if he brought his head back on his shoulders from this interview, he thought as he straightened his shoulders and his coat and strode into the palace to ask for an audience with his king, whom he'd just disobeyed.

He ought to have changed his clothes first, Gideon decided when he saw Charles's face as he entered the room. Nothing escaped those lazy, half-closed heavy-lidded black eyes, and the look of extreme interest that replaced the slightly concerned one that Charles had been wearing when he'd come in told him his king suspected half, if not more, of what he'd come to tell him. Gideon disliked that soured, curling smile that grew on Charles's dark face, and liked it even less, although he'd thought he'd want it more, when Charles waved a languid lace-fringed hand to empty the room of ladies and courtiers so that they could speak alone. His luck was out in all things, Gideon sighed, because this was no intimate room he'd been received in this time, but rather a room of state. He had to look up at his king on his raised chair when he spoke. And when the king spoke, it was down to him.

"Well, Gideon," Charles Stuart said sweetly, "back so soon from my errand, and back in such haste? Shall I send the word for the cages of snow-white doves to be readied? I thought to release them as you and Celeste Southern took your vows—a nice touch, I thought, and a way of giving the rabble dinner even as we at court sit down to ours.

"But where is the beautiful lady?" the king asked with an exaggerated air of mock chagrin. "Changing her clothes, I expect, not like her ardent groom, so impatient to be wed that he forgets all else in order to arrange it faster, and so comes hotfoot to me. Testy, impatient rogue. Sir Philip is already off to Ivyclose with a cargo of champagne in his train, ready to celebrate with you two. How vexed he'll be when he gets

there and finds you two have already come to court.
In such a hurry to marry, then? How pleasant."

Gideon stood, patient as an oak tree, waiting for his
king to stop toying with him. Something in his exhausted and tight face must have reached the king,
because he left off his conversation about wedding
plans and looked wholly and truly sympathetic at last.

"Refused you again, sir? 'Od's body, what a vexatious wench. Beware when her brother claims a girl is
a 'good, obedient one.' I ought to have known. My
own mother claimed a certain French princess was
'douce and docile, kind as she was pretty-mannered.'
She had it from the girl's mother, of course. I'd have
put that princess in a cage against any wild thing in the
land and felt sorry for the beast," he mused.

"It's ever thus," the king said, shaking his head.
"Are you ready to have me step in to prod the lady,
Gideon? Pride's all very well, but the thing ought to
be done before she's too old to bear fruit and you're
too old to bare her, don't you think?"

"Majesty," said Gideon, shifting his feet so that he
stood exactly on balance, his face expressionless, his
voice soft and uninflected, but clear, "the girl was
willing. It was I who backed off. I don't wish to marry
her."

It was a little thing, really. Both men knew it. No
vast territories would change hands. No fabled fortunes would fall to the crown through this proposed
union, no foreign threats would be nullified by it, no
religious leaders pacified, no great houses unified by
achieving it. It was only a union that had originally
been proposed in order to right a wrong done to the
groom, allow the bride's brother to better himself,
and, finally, to satisfy a king's whim. But a king's
whim was any other man's demand. And a loyal subject should know that.

Charles didn't speak at once. His eyes grew wider,
and then concealed themselves again as he sat looking

inward, his long fingers drawn into a steeple he studied as if he'd find what he wished to say inside them. The richly dressed king, with his long curling ink-black hair and dark visage, sat above and in front of his standing subject, and the lean and rangy travel-stained Cavalier didn't so much as lower his eyes, much less his proud and blazing red head. But after a silent moment he spoke again.

"Majesty," he said, "I'm not an eloquent man, at best. Even if I was, I'd be at my worst trying to explain a thing I don't wholly understand myself. But I owe to you more even than to myself—since I'm a plain fellow who doesn't have to know why I do what I do—to try."

When the king said nothing, and did not so much as lift his head to signify that he heard, Gideon took it as leave to go on.

"You sent me to woo and wed the Lady Celeste," he said. "I agreed. You said—and I remember eloquence even if I'm not gifted with it—that a man must look to advance himself in his choice of a bride, and do his duty to his king and country thereby. You said this union was one you particularly wanted to see because it was one that would unite Puritan and Cavalier, heal the land, and in time bring forth the new England. I remember that well—it was well-said. But it was wrong, sire."

At that, the great dark head lifted, and onyx eyes stared at Gideon, surprise and growing anger in their dark depths. Gideon didn't so much as blink his own shockingly blue eyes as he continued.

"Puritan and royalist are not England, sire, and never were. Their coming together in a marriage bed or in a meeting hall wouldn't produce a new England, either. I wouldn't have known that, in the common way. It was a common little woman who taught me it. She's the one I'd wed if I live to wed," he said, on the first smile he'd given his king so far, and when it wasn't returned, it disappeared, and he shrugged and went on.

"You've met her, sire. Mary Monk. A shoemaker's daughter from an alley near to Friday Street. Orphaned by the plague, homeless from the fire, daughter to a man of respectable trade, who, she assures me, had no politics. But, she said," he said on a slight smile, as though he'd forgotten that the King of England stared at him, judging him, "she was sure he preferred the royalists, since they liked a good, ornate shoe that could cost a pretty penny. 'A tradesman's politics are in his purse,' she says her father always said. And there was his strength, and there's the strength of England itself.

"We have but one king," Gideon said thoughtfully. "He has, as we know to our sorrow, only thousands of true supporters. He had his Puritan enemies, and they know, to their regret, that they've only hundreds of friends now. But the rest, the most of the country, survived their argument, as they did plague and fire, and increased despite it. And always will. I've come to believe that my Mary Monk, and men like her father, and all the guildsmen and craftsmen and farmers and freeholders and artisans in this land, far from both court and cathedral, are what is really England. They don't plot to pull down or bring up kings. They've no time for such sports. They go where kings and leaders push them, it's true. But no further, because they are Englishmen. They number above hundreds, and beyond thousands. They survive because they have the capacity to learn.

"It's from them that your new England will come, Majesty," Gideon said with conviction, "not from the mating of passionate Puritans and royalists. Mary Monk taught me that. She sold herself to me in order to survive. I don't think our Puritan lass would've done it. She'd have preferred death before I dishonored her. Mary Monk chose life, with dishonor, and she's turned it to honor. She will survive. Still, that's not my reason. My decision is no political matter."

Gideon met his king's eyes; there was neither pleading nor arrogance in them or in his voice as he spoke.

"I love her, Majesty," he said. "I don't wish to marry my lady Celeste and keep Mary Monk besides, as I suppose I might do, with no shame. Because I am, I discover, a simple man. I've room in my heart for only one woman to love, and I wish to love my wife. I've room in my heart and mind for only one leader— and I love you well, my king. In the old days, that dark night when they asked: 'Are you a friend to Caesar?' in order to find out if I would betray or aid you, I answered yes without hesitation."

And as Charles began to relax, with nevertheless a sad crooked smile on his lips, because he was as used to flattery as he was disappointed to hear it, Gideon went on without pausing for breath.

"But I was not, and am not, a friend to Caesar," he said as Charles's eyes flew wide.

"I am, I hope," Gideon said, "a friend to Charles Stuart, King of England—no royal Caesar who rules over slaves, but king to all the free men, the simple men, the common men who are England.

"I cede my right to Ivyclose. A king must claim his country, sire, else he's no king at all. He's wed to his destiny before he's born. But a man must be more than his house, or else he's no man. I return your estates in the West. I'll give up everything, even my life, if it comes to that, for the right to choose my own future. I'm not thinking entirely with my heart, Majesty—or even with that other organ I so often mistook for my heart when I was young," he said ruefully. "I'm only trying to do as you bade me. I want to take a wife for advancement and because of the debt I owe to king and country. With her, I believe, I'll advance my humanity, and pay my debt to my king by helping him begin what I believe will be the new England, God willing."

Gideon fell silent, and raised his head higher as he waited for the king's pronouncement. Charles looked to see him standing outwardly cold and still, frozen with dignity as he waited, with infinite weary patience, to find out if he would win the petition or lose his worldly goods, or life. But Charles could read men. He'd had to learn how to in order to save his own life in the years of his exile. And so now he could also see all of Gideon's person aflame with conviction, blazing with defiance. He crackled with tension from the top of that fiery red head to his fever-bright eyes, Charles saw, and knew what it was he read in the flash of internal lightning that coursed down one lean cheek to Gideon's hard jaw, despite his holding it tight.

He'd spoken treason, he'd spoken truth, man-to-man, to his anointed king. He was wrong, Charles thought. It wasn't women like Mary Monk who would bring forth the new world he wanted, or at least, not without men like Gideon Hawkes to aid them. Survival alone never made for greatness. It would take men like Gideon Hawkes to teach the survivors how to keep their souls intact. Gideon Hawkes, who would lay down his life for his king's right to rule, but who would be ruled by nothing but his own wild heart.

No, not a bad legacy to leave England. If men like this and women like his little Mary would be his subjects and breed the future, he would be content.

"Sooth!" Charles Stuart said at last, coming down from his lofty chair. "If you are so plainspoken, Gideon, God save me from eloquent men!"

It was odd that there was no footman to answer the door, odder still that the door was open, but not strange at all, Gideon saw, after he entered Mary's rooms. *His* rooms, he corrected himself, and soon to be entirely his alone, he saw. Because there was a traveling case by the door, and Mary's maidservant paused in her bending and packing something into it, a look of guilty shock stealing over her face even as the O of her mouth closed when she saw him. So he wasn't at all surprised, as he heard Mary's query go unanswered, when she came out of the bedroom to find out what had silenced her talkative maid, and froze in her tracks when she saw him.

She didn't fly into his arms, as he'd imagined her doing, all the way here from Ivyclose, all the way to Whitehall Palace, and all the way back from there. She didn't light up with joy at seeing him, as she'd so often done when he'd returned to her. He might've gone once too often, he thought uneasily as he noted that she didn't blush and look away either, as he'd thought she would, at seeing he'd discovered her preparing to leave. She only motioned for her maid to leave, which the poor wench gratefully did, dropping her tasks at once and scurrying out of the room. It was the maid's amazing furtiveness that told him as much about Mary's plans as her own attitude did.

Because she put up her chin, as she did whenever she'd something difficult to do, he remembered, and she stood as tall as she could, and faced him directly. She wore a new gown, red over an underskirt of peach, and it suited her exactly, he thought; she couldn't look prettier. But not beautiful. Small, and as pretty as any of a hundred pretty maids to be found in the streets of London, she wasn't half so lovely as the lady he'd just left behind at Ivyclose. He sighed for the foolishness of the human heart, before he spoke to her.

"Oh," he said, "a trip. Where are we going?"

"I'm . . . I'm leaving, Gideon," she answered.

" 'I'm leaving Gideon,' " he mused, coming into the room. "And going where?"

"Away," she said, and when he didn't answer, but only stood looking at her expressionlessly, she blurted, "I wrote you a note, telling everything."

"Except that, I suspect," he said. "Am I right?"

"Yes," she said, wishing Jamie had got the arrangements made an hour sooner, wishing that she'd already left the note and left this house as cleanly she'd be leaving her life behind her, wishing she could stand here forever, looking at him.

He looked tired and saddened, but, as always, he filled the room and her sight entirely. He swept off his wide, plumed slouch hat, which surprised her, because that was a thing a man did only for royalty, before he deliberately threw it over her traveling bag. She left off wondering then, and straightened her back and her purpose.

"We had an arrangement," he said coolly.

"But with no promises," she reminded him, watching as he paced to the window and looked out, his back to her.

"None," he agreed. "What promises has Jamie made? Oh, come," he said wearily, "I've just left Charles, your other admirer, and he said nothing. It has to be Jamie."

"You think I couldn't manage on my own?" she asked angrily.

"Oh, I know you could," he answered, turning around to her at last, "but I doubt my friends would let you. Tris would've talked you out of going, but Jamie . . . ah well, Jamie's a romantic fellow. Is he giving you a house? Jewels? What was the offer, I wonder?"

She was as angry as she was horrified at his idea of her. But before she could pick from any of the terrible retorts that came to her, he spoke again, softly, sadly.

"No," he said, "I won't play, after all. I do know better, Mary. Your pardon, please. But I've been playing so many games of late . . . But why? Please, why are you leaving just now?"

"Because," she said, looking aside as she spoke, repeating the words she'd written so painstakingly in her note, "I thank you for taking care of me for so long, but it's time for me to move on."

"Are you saying you no longer care for me," he asked quietly, "or are you saying you never cared for me?"

All the color left her already pallid face.

"I sold myself to you, but I'm not a whore," she said in a whisper. "You yourself told me that. Now I've had time to think about it more, and you were right. I'm not. I'd not have stayed on with you after I'd gotten a night of sleep and enough to eat, Gideon, no, not even then, I think, if I hadn't begun to care, even then. I care more now. I care very much," she said, her voice shaking, refusing to say "love" for fear she'd never leave if she did, and, afraid that he knew that, she added quickly, "but I must go now. I have to. That's all," she said, while she still could say it clearly, as her eyes grew red, although she kept her head high.

"And what of our baby?" he asked.

"He told you!" she cried. "The physician swore his silence, but he told you!" She was wildly grieved. That secret had been her crutch, her treasure, the only thing she could call her own in this world where she owned nothing that he hadn't given to her. And though he'd given her the baby too, it was still her secret, her own. It had been, but she ought to have known better than to trust in kings or their servants, she thought, sorrowing at the thought of such treachery. But then, as ever, accepting the worst and trying to get on with it, despite it, she planned an escape. He couldn't keep her here against her will for all those months, she thought; there'd always be a time to steal away . . . Jamie might thelp . . . but her frantic thoughts whirled away when he spoke again.

"No, he didn't," he said softly. "I knew before I left, before I sent you there. Mary," he explained gently, "I almost had a babe born to a lady of mine once before. Your small appetite and listlessness might have been anything. But I can count, you know. And then your breasts changed—they did, I saw it, Mary my love, I watched for it. They changed in size and texture and their tips were redder too, as were those nether lips—oh, don't blush—didn't you know? I know you very well, Mary Monk.

"But not your heart, it seems." He frowned. "I'sooth, of all times, why leave me now? You knew I'd take care of you and welcome the babe. You must know that," he said, coming close enough to take her hand. "Even if you thought me no better than the others at court, you must've known that," he said.

But she tore her hand from his clasp and turned a look of such ferocity upon him that he was amazed. Her fright, her shyness, and her embarrassment evaporated in her fury.

"Because of that, I'm leaving," she cried in a clear, high voice. "Because it's no longer just me. Because I'll not have a child known as 'Hawkes's bastard.' Never! No! I see them everywhere at court—fine, proud, good young men and women never to be known as 'the prince' or even 'Charles's son' or 'the duke's daughter' or 'Lord So-and-So's son' or 'Sir So-and-So's daughter,' but 'Charles's bastard' and 'the duke's bastard'—all of them, and forever. Oh, yes, some of them call it an honor, but I can't! I may not be very much, Gideon Hawkes," she said, too angry for tears, too sad for them as well, "but I am Master Monk's daughter, and my brothers would've been thrashed if they'd not wed the mothers of their children . . ."

She stopped, because she refused to lose the little control she had left, and wouldn't listen to him tell her all the reasons she knew too well why he couldn't help her in this, sorry beyond words that the word "wed" had ever escaped her lips.

"My child will have a name, even if it's a made-up one," she said simply. "I come from a respectable

family. I may have turned whore, but I'll not shame
that family name, or my child. I'truth, it's a thing,"
she said quietly, at last, accepting the inevitable, "I
doubt you'll understand. But it doesn't matter. I'll do
well for myself. And I wish you joy, Gideon, I do."

He looked not half so angry as he did exhausted.
And he didn't argue or threaten her, as she'd feared
he would. She'd prepared for argument at least, because she knew he was a possessive man, and would
want some say in the raising of his child, even if he
was done with its mother. That was how all the men at
court behaved, as did their king. But he was calm and
almost amused, and he looked more relieved than
angry as he gazed at her.

"Joy in what?" he asked.

"In your marriage," she said, looking aside. "I'm
told it's to be soon?" she asked, marveling at the
freedom of speech her leaving him had already given
her with him.

"I'm not going to wed the lady," he said.

She gasped, understanding his sorrow now, and,
oddly, against all her judgment, pitying him for his
failure, for his loss of his lady, for his loss of Ivyclose.

'And if you leave now," he said, "I'll have no wedding at all. I want you to marry me, Mary Monk."

She stepped back a pace, and held her hand over
her heart. She didn't know what manner of game he
played, nor did she want to.

"Because of the baby?" she asked, since that was
the only thing that made sense.

"No," Gideon answered, "I'm not such a fool. Mary,
sweet Mary," he whispered into her hair, because
she'd been so stunned she had come into his arms, or
at least she'd not resisted as he'd pulled her there, and
he reveled at how right she felt there, "I wish this
child to be born and outlive Methuselah, but know too
well how often the seed doesn't bear. Remember, I've
almost sired a baby before. No, Mary, listen, do . . .

no, don't turn away. I want to marry you for your own
sake and mine. I knew your body long before I knew
your heart, or my own. But let's make a bad beginning
into a good ending, can we?"

She drew an arm's length away and looked steadily
into his brilliantly blue eyes.

"I'm a common girl you took from the streets," she
said.

"I'd challenge any man who said that," he answered
gravely.

"She refused you," she said, refusing to accept the
wild joy that had sprung into her heart.

He extinguished his gleaming stare for a moment,
but when he opened his eyes again they were clear and
level.

"No. Although she did—in a way," he said, as her
heart plummeted, before he added, "so I ended it."

"Mary," he said huskily, as she didn't answer and
he saw her confusion and fear, "the tree needed only a
little more shaking, perhaps, but I decided to leave off
shaking it, although the fruit trembled on the bough.
It may never have ripened enough for me, and I think
it was too fragile and would've been bruised had it
fallen to me. Mary," he said, the closest thing to a
plea she'd ever heard from him in his voice, as he
looked down at her, "no more, please. Remember? I
don't talk about women to women. It's not meet. Or
kind. Be satisfied, my love. I left off courting her—to
ask you to be my wife. Will you have me?"

"You want her," she persisted.

"I need you," he said.

She didn't answer, afraid to take him in error, lest
he blame her for it for the rest of his life. She was
more helpless in her fear than she'd ever been in her
longing for him, because fear was always her greatest
enemy. She hesitated to take what she'd feared dreaming of, for the greater fear that it would be better to
leave her dreams intact than to take what wasn't hers.

He sighed. "I defied a king for you. What else would you have of me? I'll speak in the good, plain tongue of a respectable tradesman, then. You're no exotic fruit, Mary Monk, and you know it. But you're my plain and steady diet, without which I cannot live. Don't belittle common things. I don't. You're as near and necessary to me as my own plain, common, steady heartbeat. I would wive you and keep you by me always."

"And the king?" she asked, disbelieving everything she heard.

"Understands. He's generous," he said, smiling as he felt her body relax against his in his embrace, realizing he'd never lost her, "and so," he added more merrily, "he gives Ivyclose to the lady at Ivyclose; a plump widow, well-dowered as she is well-covered, to her brother; and aside from letting me keep my head, he's given me an estate somewhere in the West. It's richer, he says, more beautiful than Ivyclose, and a title goes with it, my duchess—what do you think of that?"

"But Ivyclose?" she cried in sorrow, forgetting herself, remembering what he was leaving, what he even now couldn't keep his desire for from his voice.

He drew her closer, his arms so tight about her it pained her, but his words cured all, ". . . is only a house," he said into her ear, "a thing of stone and brick. We'll make our new home so complete, our children will shudder at the thought they might've been brought up at some other place called Ivyclose instead. That book you've been poring over, learning to read—I'm no expert at it, but I remember it says that the generations of men are as leaves of grass. Seasons turn, Mary. Be sure our children will know Ivyclose only as a place in their father's addled memory. And want it that way. As I do now . . ." He paused, and put his lips to her cheek, his face against her hair.

"When I'm with you, Mary Monk, I'm home," he breathed at last. "I no more understand it than you do. But it's so."

"But Ivyclose . . ." she whispered, and it sounded like a whimper, because for all his beautiful words, she thought she knew his heart.

"Ah, Mary," he said softly, "who in the world gets everything he ever wanted?"

She closed her eyes and lay against his chest. Her lips were closed too, over her answer.

Because she knew such a person, she thought, as she felt his arms close around her, and felt his heart's slow, sure beat against her ear, and breathed in the scent of him. She knew such a person very well, and although she had never thought herself a religious person, she thanked God that she did. And promised silently that she'd thank him all her life for giving him to her.

Then she wept a little, before she looked up at Gideon and dashed her tears away angrily, complaining that only he could make her miserable even as he made her happier than she'd ever been in her life.

"I'll make you happier still," he suggested, lifting her and carrying her toward the bedroom.

"Oh, no!" she protested, struggling until he had to set her down, although he didn't release her. She looked distracted, bleary from weeping, but rosier from some internal struggle. He sighed, wondering if she thought her impending motherhood would have to end their pleasure, prepared to have to lecture long and convincingly before he brought her to bed again.

She cast her glance down to her toes, which curled in their slippers. "Jamie's waiting for me," she said meekly.

"Ah, poor Jamie," he said, so relieved he could have kissed his rival. "I'll tell him. It's best that way. I know him and I don't blame him—i'truth, I pity him. But he's a good man and he'll find a good woman in time—but his own, this time. He's below—in the street?" he asked.

"He should be soon," she admitted.

"Then I'll wait below for him," Gideon said, "and then I'll be back, so please get into bed, Mary, and remember where I left off. Oh . . . But wait!" he said, frowning, and glaring at her. "I didn't have to tell you that. You never answered me. But if you agree to marry me," he said in a wheedling tone, grinning all the while, "you'll always be able to ask where I'm going, or if I'm going to another woman, and when I'll be back. Because I'll never go far, and never to another woman, and always hurry to return to you wherever else I go. Come, Mary. Will you have me?"

For all his jesting, for all she was only a common girl he'd taken from the streets of London, his paid mistress, his act of charity grown into his habit—and she thought they both knew it—there was still doubt and no little apprehension in his eyes as he waited for her answer. His hands on her back were still, his long frame tensed and waiting. She heard his restless anxiety in his words as well as felt it, and was amazed that he—who needed her so little—wanted her so much. There was a stillness in the room.

She could, he thought, get on without him. He could, she thought, do very well without her. But he'd never let her go, he promised himself. But she'd never let him regret it, she vowed silently.

She touched his cheek, and felt it quiver beneath her fingers; she raised herself up on her toes to touch his lips with hers, lightly.

"I'll have no other, Gideon Hawkes," she promised, and paused, her wide dark eyes searching his face, brimming with all she couldn't say. Because for all her new education, she didn't have words big enough and complicated enough for the rest.

She didn't need them.

"Jamie will wait," he muttered as he drew her close again.

But when the maidservant told James Beauchamp, Lord Claverly, that the master had returned, and Jamie noted how the time passed, and the maidservant added, for a coin, that she'd last seen them weeping and kissing together before the master had shut the door on her nose, Jamie sighed and looked up one last time at the empty stair, and left. And, used to longing, knew he'd again lost what he'd never had.

So for once, Lord Claverly had a great deal in common with his king when they stood together and watched the newly wedded couple taking their leave of well- and ill-wishers of the court a few weeks later.

"Rochester says it's a wedding of the sparrow and the hawk," Jamie said glumly, vaguely annoyed with himself because for all it was a timid enough rhyme the earl had composed and secretly circulated for the occasion this time, it was still a mocking one, and yet he didn't feel angry enough to challenge Rochester to the death, for it for his friend's sake. And even though Gideon only chuckled at it, he was himself vaguely and guiltily aware that he secretly enjoyed the rhyme for the way it salved his wounds.

"His poem's a play on 'Cock Robin,' " Jamie said, "but he's substituted "Hawk' for 'robin' and named her a 'sweet street sparrow' and says there's to be no public bedding after the wedding and that it's best, because the sparrow's already got her eggs in the nest, or some such."

"I'truth, Rochester's an ass," Charles commented, his dark eyes never leaving the bride as she stayed by her new husband's side. "There's nothing like a little London street sparrow," he said thoughtfully as he watched how the groom hovered over his bride, and for all that he had and had restored to him, in that moment he envied them with all his heart.

Then he saw them enter the coach, and the dark

curls of the woman came to rest on the wide shoulder next to her in the coach, and he saw the fiery head of his favorite courtier rest against them in turn, and he shrugged and smiled his usual twisting smile.

"They'll have colorful offspring," he mused. "Oh, and on that head, Jamie, my lad, I agree with Tristram Jones," he said, turning to stare at the young man in his splendid new costume as he stood by his side, before he commanded, "My cousin Elizabeth was the last one to wear a red wig and do it at all well, hereabouts. 'Od's fish, fellow, if a wig made the man, I'd have got me a red pelt and won the wench myself. So consign that damnable thing to the fire!"

He laughed until he heard the truth in what he had said. Then he watched the newlywed couple as they rode out into the West Country. And they never looked back.

# 21

She sat, where they'd placed her, in the sun in the garden. Like a favorite plant, she thought. The sun was weak enough because it was only early spring, but it felt good on her face, and she imagined she could feel its warmth down to her bones. But she imagined a great deal these days.

She was wise enough to be still about it. The children were careful enough of her; no need to make them think she'd lost her mind along with her strength and her youth. So Celeste sat in her rose garden and wondered if she'd live to see them bloom again this year, as she'd done for so many decades before, and let her mind drift down along the many paths she'd laid out there in her youth, in her middle age, in her old age, so long ago.

But her ears and eyes were still sharp enough, although the damp had got in her bones and the years had done their damage to her body. She heard the noise of a coach pulling into the drive, and she saw someone alight. And then she thought that perhaps she'd drifted off to another time, or death itself, or life anew, because she saw the tall red-headed wide-shouldered man step down and thought it was Gideon Hawkes come back to her at last.

She was old, but not addled, and in a moment, that moment that her eldest, John, came out himself to greet the man on the steps, she saw that the hair was a tone too dark, and the cut of the clothes too close and modern. And as the young man and John, deep in conversation, came down the paths to approach her, she saw that the familiar-seeming face was craggy enough, but softened by youth and laughter as Gideon's had never been.

"Mother," John said in the usual falsely jovial way that he spoke to her these days, as though she didn't know as well as he did that she'd no purchase on tomorrow morning, "may I present Lord Gareth Hawkes to you? He says he's got a message for you."

"My lady," the young man said, bowing over her hand, and she noted his voice was a true tenor, and felt curiously betrayed at that, although she knew it was foolish.

"I've come to bring you something, lady," Gareth Hawkes said, dropping to his knees, sitting balanced on his haunches there beside her, as though he weren't a grown, elegant young gentleman, as though he were a good and considerate boy.

She felt curiously young again, and felt the need to let him know that a good mind still worked within this cage that had become her body.

"Gareth Hawkes?" she asked. "Gideon's grandson?"

"No, his youngest son, lady," he answered, smiling, a roguish smile very like his father's, as she stared at him, thinking that all of them, the young ones, children and grandchildren, seemed alike to her now. "I've four brothers and two sisters survived till today. And they've young ones too, some almost as old as I am. I was a complete surprise, lady," he said, grinning, now very like Gideon to her eyes.

"And how is your father?" she asked.

"He's gone, lady," Gareth Hawkes said, his face suddenly solemn, now exactly like his father's. "A half-year now—last autumn, it was."

Half of a year? Last autumn? she thought, wondering, and I didn't feel it? And the sun didn't dim?

"But he went easily, and never passed a serious sick day in his life before his end, and knew when it was coming, and never suffered. Ah, don't weep," he said gently. "Sooth, it was a good end to a long and happy life. I never knew or saw a man more pleased with his life either—so when he asked us not to grieve for him, we almost agreed," he said in a sweet, familiar teasing tone. And she was comforted. Until she looked up and saw something that startled her badly.

Strange dark brown eyes looked back at her from Gideon's face. But at her sudden jolt and change of expression, the brown eyes blinked and grew so troubled and concerned that she recalled herself. This was Gareth Hawkes. The dark eyes were worried, warm and caring, and all at once, not so strange to her anymore. She remembered. And smiled at him. Encouraged, he went on.

"I'truth, he was clear to the end. That's why I'm here. Just before he left us, he called me to his side and bade me open his wardrobe and bring him his strongbox. He opened it and gave me this—and said I was to return it to you, since he'd no need for it anymore. This is the first chance we've had to travel, else I would've come sooner. I wanted to give it to you personally, as he asked me," he said.

He held out his hand. And there on his glove was the key. A small tarnished key on a thin gold chain. She opened her hand and he dropped it within. And then she could scarcely see him, her eyes flooded so.

She heard John speaking with the boy, saw the blurred reflection of that somber young face through her wet eyelashes, and then Gareth Hawkes rose to his feet and agreed to take a tour of Ivyclose—to see, as John said, what had been his father's home.

"I'll be back, lady, if I may," he added before he left, concern for her in his voice, because he was a polite youth. And because he was one, he added softly, "Nor can I stay long—my mother awaits me in the carriage."

That shamed her, until she realized, despite Gareth Hawkes's protests to John that his mother was more comfortable within, that if his mother were able to travel down to Kent to visit with grandchildren as he said, she was able to leave the coach to visit with them—if she were any more willing than she herself was for such a meeting. What was the point, after all, now that they'd lost all they'd had in common?

As the two men left her, Celeste opened her hand and gazed down at her palm. The key lay in an ugly, bony, speckled hand, one of the stranger's hands that she found in her lap every so often when she looked at the present. She seldom did anymore. But she looked to the future as much as the past.

It was good that young Gareth was touring Ivyclose now; he'd meet Fanny there. That wicked minx, naughtiest of her granddaughters, such a trial to her good sober father. But then, John was so like his father— Lord receive him in heavenly rest—gone these past ten years: practical and earnest in all things. Not like Fanny, or herself. No, she corrected herself. Not so. Not really. She'd never been like Fanny; perhaps that was why she loved her best. It would be good, it would be ironic, having Gideon's son mate with her granddaughter, like a promise kept, after all these years. More like a wish fulfilled, for she'd never stopped thinking of him for all these years. Never.

She heard of his marriage, she made it a point to hear of his children. After the first was born, she'd married John Wentworth. And borne him as many children, plus two, as Gideon had of Mary. But she never saw Gideon again, because he never came to London, and from what she heard, he never strayed from Mary's side in any other way, either. How odd to think that bold Cavalier had been as constant to Mary as her poor sober John had been to her. How odd, and how hurtful still, even so far into the new century as it was now.

Because she'd betrayed John. Often, if not always. In her thoughts, of course, because she'd been as good a wife as John had been a husband. But she'd wondered, had never stopped wondering, what it would have been like . . . if . . . Not all the time, of course. There'd been the years of hope in the beginning, years of involvement with the babies and the bearing of them, years of trial with the children as they grew. But even then, she'd often wondered. Mostly, in the nights, when John would turn to her and take his husband's kiss, and then raise his nightshirt and take his ease with her. Such a simple, hasty thing it was. So brief, so foolish, really. Although it always left him breathless and grateful. That was when she'd wonder: what had Gideon been talking about? What had she been so afraid of? She always had the uncomfortable feeling they weren't the same things at all.

Once, a hundred years ago, when she was young, between her fourth and fifth children, John had been tired one night. It had taken him a long time. And only then, and only briefly, had she felt something else begin. Insidious, odd, exhilarating too, it had taken up all her attention and taken her breath away in that moment, as well. It discomfited John so when he saw her reaction, he drew away, and only ended it after she'd assured him she was well. But then, and since then, she'd wondered what would have happened if she'd not been the one to draw away, that other time, so long before.

She was able to think of that now, she knew; she was very brave now, of course. She'd dragged herself away from Gideon's lust then, and rightly so. It was only wrongly so now that she'd nothing left to fear losing; she understood that. Age had blunted desire as well as shame for it. It was all one to her now, an interesting problem to consider. Pride, dignity, purity—all that had been so important then, meant little anymore. Perhaps living so long had shown her they were very different from what she'd thought they were. Maybe it was like that poem he'd quoted about the grave being such a fine and private place. It was a bad poem, she thought. She discovered the grave was neither fine nor private, only inevitable and yawning for her. No matter. None of it mattered. Not now, when memory mingled with reality to bring her peace at last.

She was always brave in her fantasies, after all. And only allowed herself her fantasies now, when she was unable to act on them. She doubted God would mind them, if they brought her easy sleep; she wondered if God cared at all, and slept anyway.

Now she wondered if Gideon had thought of her too, all down through these years. He'd kept the key, hadn't he? Until he'd known he'd never be able to use it, until he'd been about to draw his last breath. She'd never know. But at least she knew now that he'd thought of her at the end, as she'd thought of him since the beginning.

She might have dozed then, sitting in the sun as she sank into a golden reverie. But she opened her eyes to the real day when she heard the gravel crunching underfoot as John and Gareth Hawkes strolled back to her. The young man made his bows, and then bent to her ear again,

"A beautiful home. Just as my father said. Thank you, my lady. If I may come back someday?" he asked.

"If I am here, I'll welcome you. If I'm not, my family shall. You're always welcome here, Gareth

Hawkes. Give my greetings to your mama," she said
with dignity, no matter how much it cost her.

She watched as John walked him back to his coach,
and saw, for a moment, as John greeted her, a glimpse
of the wizened white-haired lady who looked from out
a window.

And Mary gazed in astonishment at the thin old
woman who even in the mid-day sun was wrapped in
so many shawls that she looked like a gypsy fortune-
teller and not the respected Lady of Ivyclose. At least,
so she looked at first glance. But then Mary disre-
garded the varicolored wrappings and noticed that the
woman beneath them lacked both color and flesh, and
that only the glitter of the sun glancing off her eyes
showed she didn't lack life.

Mine enemy grows old too, Mary thought, and then
was ashamed of herself for it. Because now that Gideon was gone, they'd no more reason to be enemies
than friends. And most amazingly of all, as she thought
it, she found that all she could feel was sympathy for
the old woman watching her with such stillness and
glittering eyes. Because for all that she herself still
grieved, and listened for the echoes of his voice, and
started whenever she heard a footstep, momentarily
beguiled into hoping it was his—for all she still ached
for the sight of him, she knew Celeste's was the greater
loss. Because she'd never had him, in any way.

Now she no longer begrudged this odd errand, or
fretted over the reason for it, wondering why he'd
kept the key all these years. She chose to believe it
was only Gideon's fastidiousness, so like him to remember all his debts before he left. Very like Plato,
she thought, smiling slightly, the way he'd remembered he owed a cock just before he drained his last
cup. Oh yes, Gideon had taught her far more than her
basic letters over the years. He'd helped her to a
superior education of heart and mind and body. Remembering, she felt the warmth of his love surround

her again, flooding through her as though he were
beside her still, as thrilling, yet constant and comforting, as he'd been for all those years. Some things even
death couldn't end, so she knew what she had to. She
sighed, and let the petty fear go. She could let Celeste
have a thought of his at the end, whatever it was.
She'd so much more of him, and still did.

The carriage swayed as Gareth seated himself beside her. His hand closed over hers, recalling her to
her physical self. She looked down to see that so
familiar, so often replicated hand engulfing hers entirely, and felt the warmth in his voice as well as his
flesh.

"Done," he said softly, "I did the errand he wanted,
Mama, though I still don't know why he wanted it."

He looked his question at her, but she pretended
not to see it.

"You did what he needed," she said firmly, "for
whatever reason."

She watched out the window for as long as she could
before the coach drove away, and then she never
looked back again.

They had stared at each other, or so Celeste fancied
they did, for the distance was too far to be sure, until
the coach pulled off.

"Imagine!" John said when he'd returned to her.
"He's a duke's son! There's money there, and it's a
good family. Hawkes was a Cavalier, true, but is everywhere well spoken of. The boy has great address.
A match mightn't be out of order, do you think?
Elizabeth had her eye on him, you know. And not to
wonder—a well-looking, well-spoken lad," he said.

"Not Elizabeth!" his mother snapped suddenly.
"Fanny. It will be a good match."

"But Elizabeth's the elder," John protested.

"Fanny," she said angrily. "I wish it."

"Fanny, then," he sighed, for he was a good and

decent, obedient man, like his father. "If he comes back," he added.

"Oh, he'll be back," she said.

And hearing herself, grew still.

"He told me about that key," John said, some excitement creeping into his voice. "What a tale! Imagine, a hidden room. One of the oldest at Ivyclose, his father said. Secret, hidden in the very heart of the house. And he said you knew where it was!"

She looked down at the mottled stranger's hand in her lap and uncurled the thin fingers. She saw the key and the imprint it had left incised on the dry palm, as though it were young, firm flesh it had been pressed into when her hand had convulsed so tightly as he'd spoken.

"But where is it, Mama?" he asked, eagerly as a boy.

"I don't know," she said. "I never found it."

# There's an epidemic with 27 million victims. And no visible symptoms.

It's an epidemic of people who can't read.

Believe it or not, 27 million Americans are functionally illiterate, about one adult in five.

The solution to this problem is you... when you join the fight against illiteracy. So call the Coalition for Literacy at toll-free **1-800-228-8813** and volunteer.

## Volunteer Against Illiteracy.
### The only degree you need is a degree of caring.